WINNERS

CW00418345

WINNERS

LOUISE BRODERICK

This novel is entirely a work of fiction. The names, characters and incidents in it are the work of the author's imagination. Any resemblance to actual persons, living or dead, events or localities is entirely coincidental and have no relation to anyone bearing the same name or names. All incidents are pure invention and not even distantly inspired by any individual known or unknown to the author.

Published 2018
By Lavender and White Publishing,
Cornwall,
England.
Email info@lavenderandwhite.co.uk

LOUISE BRODERICK 2018

The moral right of the author has been asserted.
Typesetting, layout and design Lavender and White Publishing.

A huge vote of thanks to superb artist Tony O'Connor of White Tree Studio for allowing me to use some of his amazing paintings for my book covers. More of Tony's equestrian and animal paintings can be found on his website www.whitetreestudio.ie

All rights reserved. No part of the text of this publication may be reproduced or transmitted in any form or by any means, electronically or mechanical, including photocopying, recording, or any information storage or retrieval system without the written permission of the publisher.

The book is sold subject to the condition that it shall not, by way of trade or otherwise, be lent, resold, or otherwise circulated without the publisher's prior consent in any form of binding or cover other than that in which it is published without a similar condition, including this condition being imposed on the subsequent purchaser.

www.lavenderandwhite.co.uk

CONTENTS

WINNERS

CHAPTER ONE

Paris O'Shea couldn't stop smiling. She kept feeling her face splitting involuntarily into a huge grin when she remembered the previous evening.

It had all started normally enough. Her boyfriend, Derry Blake, had asked her out to dinner. Then they had gone back to Westwood Park, his home, for a nightcap. That was when things had become a little unusual. They had been sitting on the opulent velvet sofa in the lounge, watching the flickering embers of the fire cast dancing shadows around the picture-lined walls. Suddenly, as she watched wide-eyed with amazement he had slid off the sofa and knelt on one knee in front of her.

"Paris," Derry had said, quietly, "I love you. I love your strength, your independence." He took her face in his hands. "And I love your beauty."

Paris had felt tears of joy prick her eyes as he reached into the pocket of his jacket and pulled out the most gorgeous ring that she had ever seen and said: "Will you marry me?" And when she nodded, speechless with emotion, he had slid the ring onto her finger.

Derry Blake was all that she had ever wanted.

It had been almost dawn when they finished celebrating their engagement. They had taken a bottle of champagne and two glasses upstairs, making love until they were exhausted. Later they had lain in his enormous four poster bed, drinking and making plans for the future.

As she drove into the stable yard at Redwood Grange, her home, she realised that the grooms had already arrived to start the morning stables.

She dashed into the feed rom to tell Merrianne, her head groom, the wonderful news. "Derry's asked me to marry him!" she breathed excitedly. Then noticing Merrianne's dour expression, added, "oh I know, I know. We are going to be late – I'd better go and get changed!"And then she was gone, dashing across the yard to the house to break the news to Paddy, her father.

Merrianne kicked a plastic bucket across the feed room. Bloody Paris had all the luck! Why couldn't she find someone rich and gorgeous to marry? She sighed bitterly.

Paris came back outside ten minutes later, still grinning. She had changed out of her dress into a smart wool trouser suit, ready to go racing. They were taking two horses: Paris's own horse Destiny and Dark Admiral who belonged to Ollie Molloy. Dark Admiral was the favourite in the race. Ollie owned a chain of bars and restaurants around the Irish midlands, and many of the horses at Redwood Grange stables were his. Many of his family and business acquaintances were coming to the meeting at Limerick today and it was essential the horse went well. Paris had done all that she could. The horse was fitter than he had ever been. And the competition in the race could easily be beaten. But there were a thousand things that could go wrong between the start and finish of a race. And if Dark Admiral were not enough to worry about, it was Destiny's first race and Paris was riding the mare herself.

Merrianne led Destiny into the lorry and rubbed a soothing hand down her glossy neck. The young mare looked fabulous. Fit and ready to show the competition what she was made of. Then Merriane jumped back quickly as the mare laid back her ears and swished her tail angrily. She really was the most bad-tempered creature Merrianne had ever come across! How Paris could possibly love her so much was beyond her!

Paris jogged across the stable yard to fetch Dark Admiral. The gigantic grey horse turned towards her and dropped his head politely into the head-collar that she held up to his nose. She led him across the yard towards the lorry.

Merrianne led the horse up the ramp, tied him in the stall next to Destiny and then ran hastily back down the ramp. Together they lifted the heavy ramp into place.

"Have we got everything?" Paris asked dreamily, still smiling happily.

Merrianne nodded. Paris wouldn't have known if they had gone without the horses. She was a million miles away, dreaming of the new life she was going to have as Derry Blake's wife. Merrianne scrambled up into the passenger seat. "Let's go."

Paris turned on the engine and manoeuvred the big lorry expertly out of the yard.

"Have we got the silks?" she asked.

Merrianne glanced over her shoulder to where two sets of jockey's silks hung, one in the red and purple colours of Ollie Molloy and the other in the blue and yellow that Paris wore when she rode her father's horses, or her own. "Yes," she snapped back, coldly. She was sick of Paris, always on her case, checking and double-checking that things were done. Insisting that they were done again if they didn't meet her exacting standards.

"Saddles? Bridles? The list was endless as Paris reeled off everything that they needed for the day.

Merrianne and Paul one of the other grooms, had loaded up the lorry early that morning and thankfully when Paris reached the end of the list, everything was accounted for.

At the end of the long driveway Paris turned the lorry onto the main road towards Limerick.

"What do you think about cream silk for my wedding dress?" she mused dreamily.

Merrianne began to wish that she had gone to the races in the car with Paddy, Paris's father. She had thought that going with Paris was the lesser of the two evils; now she was not so sure.

To go in the car with Paddy was an experience in itself. The whisky fumes that came from his breath were enough to make the passenger drunk. His driving, if lacking Paris's aggression, was just as erratic and he used any gear-change as an excuse to brush his hand against the leg of any female passenger, especially the young grooms.

Paris heaved a sigh of relief as she turned the lorry into Limerick racecourse. She had managed to make up the time on the road. Fortunately there had been very little traffic around, apart from a small red car driven by an old man. But he had soon pulled over when she had driven the lorry right up behind him. She manoeuvred it into a parking spot between two huge lorries with Kildare number plates and switched off the engine. With relief, Merrianne straightened out fingers that had been clamped on the edge of her seat.

"I'm going to declare the runners," Paris said, climbing out. She set off across the lorry park to tell the officials that Dark Admiral and Destiny would be racing.

Merrianne watched Paris march off on long slender legs, head high, long auburn hair swinging. "Arrogant bitch!" hissed Merrianne.

Just then a loud wolf-whistle rang out from one of the lorries and Paris felt her face split into a broad grin.

"Derry!" she yelled, breaking into a sprint towards a large dark-blue lorry. Derry Blake, her boyfriend, was leaning against the side of his lorry as she ran headlong into his arms.

"I missed you," he said, when they came up for air.

Paris grinned and ran her hand through his gleaming dark hair. "How could you miss me? It must be all of three hours since you saw me last," she smiled, raising her face towards his for another kiss.

"Three minutes is too long," he mumbled beginning to unbutton the top buttons of her shirt. She felt herself turn to liquid as his fingers slowly caressed her skin, teasing one aching nipple until she was weak with the weight of her longing for him.

"Derry" she sighed, regretfully wriggling away from him. "We have races to win."

"Damn, I can think of lots of things I'd like to be doing to you," he breathed, reluctantly releasing her buttons.

Arm in arm they walked across the racecourse, which was deserted apart from other trainers, hurrying about their business. Suddenly Paris felt Derry stiffen with tension and she turned to see what he was looking at.

Walking towards them was Tara, Derry's sister, and her husband Morgan Flynn.

"Tara looks exhausted," snapped Derry bitterly.

Paris looked at his stunningly beautiful sister. She didn't look any different than usual to her.

As their paths met, Morgan nodded curtly at Derry while Tara flung herself at her brother.

"Derry! How lovely to see you!" She smiled happily, standing on tiptoe

4

to kiss his cheek

"Paris," said Morgan, pulling her gently to one side. "Just the person I wanted to see." They walked a little distance away.

Paris glanced back at Derry. He was glaring ferociously at Morgan, as Tara clung to his arm, smiling up at him with obvious delight.

"I need a rider for Sugarloaf," Morgan said, running a work-callused hand through his hair in a distracted gesture. "JJ Kelleher should have been riding him, but apparently he's in hospital, had to have his stomach pumped after drinking too much. Won the big race yesterday for Michael Walsh and they had one hell of a party." Morgan raised his eyes skywards in an expression of despair. "Would you be interested in the ride?"

Paris considered his offer for a split second. "No problem." She grinned holding out her hand for Morgan to shake. Sugarloaf was the hot favourite in the first race of the day. Morgan's bay horse had won all of his last three races and, judging by the competition, looked unbeatable in today's race.

Morgan's handsome face split into a broad grin. "Thanks, Paris." He turned to smile delightedly at Tara and gave her the thumbs-up signal.

Tara grinned back and raised a gloved hand in thanks, while Derry looked furious.

"I'll bring the silks into the weigh room for you," said Morgan as they joined the others.

"What the hell did he want?" growled Derry a few minutes later as he and Paris continued on towards the weigh room.

"I've accepted the ride on Sugarloaf," Paris said sweetly, waiting for the outburst of temper that she knew would accompany this announcement.

"What!" exploded Derry, halting mid-stride as if he had been punched by a heavy weight.

"I'm going to ride Sugarloaf in the 2.30," Paris repeated slowly, as if he were deaf, or mentally deficient.

"Jesus, Paris," Derry grumbled bitterly, "how could you?" He snatched his arm back from where it had been entwined in hers as petulantly as a sulking child.

"Sugarloaf is a brilliant horse," Paris said, gaily, ignoring her sulking fiancée. She knew that he hated Morgan, but their jealous rivalry was nothing to do with her and she would have no part in it.

"He might be a good horse, but Morgan Flynn is a total jerk! You know how I feel about him." He thrust his hands deep into his pockets

5

and hunched his shoulders miserably, taking her acceptance of the ride as a personal affront against him.

Paris shrugged. There was no way that she was going to turn down a ride on one of the best horses running today just because Derry didn't like the trainer.

At the entrance to the weigh room Paris turned to face Derry and seized his face between her hands. She kissed him softly on the mouth, pressing her body against his and sliding her tongue gently between his resisting lips. She felt the tension slide out of him as his mouth opened to kiss her back. It was impossible for him to be angry with her for long. She pulled away abruptly and said, with a laugh of triumph. "Make sure you put some money on Sugarloaf!"

CHAPTER TWO

Paris grimaced in disgust face as Morgan handed her a coat-hanger from which hung the brightly coloured silks that she had to wear in the race. The brightly coloured jacket was covered all over with enormous red hearts. "Thanks," she muttered, wryly, already imagining the comments that she was going to get from the other jockeys.

She pushed open the door to the changing room and went into the steamy atmosphere. Inside the room was filled with benches and hanging-rails, like a school changing room. Steam escaping from the sauna room and from the hot bodies of those who had just ridden in the last race almost hid the array of benches and discarded clothing. Amidst the chaos lounged a dozen or so near-naked jockeys, chattering and gossiping and joking with each other. None of them made any effort to cover themselves up as Paris entered the room. Lady riders did not come in for special treatment. In the corner farthest from the door two jockeys had discovered a scented bar of soap in the bag of one of the young apprentice jockeys, put there by his mother. The lad was being teased mercilessly and the jockeys were tumbling, naked, like fighting puppies for possession of the bar of soap.

"Hi, Paris!"

Paris averted her eyes. Not that there was much to look at. The weedy jockeys were nothing in comparison to the lean, hard, well-muscled body of Derry.

"Riding Sugarloaf, are you?" asked John Moore.

"Morgan Flynn just asked me – seems like JJ got very drunk and had to have his stomach pumped."

"Again!" Came the snort of derision in reply.

Paris changed quickly, feeling the knot of tension gripping her stomach. She was beginning to regret accepting the ride on Sugarloaf. There was enough to do with her own horses, without spending the time racing a horse she didn't know. Merrianne couldn't really be trusted to get the horses ready in time for their races. What if anything went wrong with Dark Admiral? It would all come back on her shoulders, not Merrianne's. Paris could just imagine how Derry would love it if something went wrong.

She trooped out with the other jockeys. There were ten in all. Young lads, having their first season, shivering from nerves and the biting cold that blew in from the open door; others older, experienced - laughing at a joke, jostling with each other with an easy camaraderie born of long experience in the tough world of racing. The security guard held open the door, sharing a joke with a familiar face, as they trooped in a line out into the parade ring. A sea of faces peered at them from around the edge of the ring, spectators leaning against the white fence assessing the horses and their riders.

Paris made her way across the grass towards Morgan. She smiled, trying to appear nonchalant, as Morgan took her arm.

"OK?" he quizzed her. She managed to grin with a confidence that she did not feel. "Grand." She followed his eyes to look at the diminutive bay gelding, Sugarloaf. Kate, Morgan's groom, her long red hair blowing in the wind, was leading him around the parade ring. He looked half asleep, walking quietly beside Kate, with his head down, ears lolling to either side, in sharp contrast to the other horses, who danced beside their grooms, ears sharply pricked, heads high, alert and ready for action.

"Don't let that fool you," Morgan said, reading the concern in her face. "He will perform when the time comes."

"I've got my mortgage on Sugarloaf!" shouted a man in the crowd.

Morgan glanced towards him with a grin. "Just let the horse keep his own pace until two from home, then ride him hard to the finish," he explained to Paris. "He runs like he walks, with his head down, but don't interfere with him, just leave him alone and he will bring you home in the lead."

As he finished speaking the bell rang to signal that it was time for the jockeys to mount, Kate led Sugarloaf towards them and pulled off his rugs. The small horse danced a few steps as if to show that he was awake after all.

Kate held him as Morgan took Paris's knee and flung her into the saddle. She fumbled for her stirrups as Kate led the horse around the ring. He felt tiny and, most disconcerting of all, his head was down between his knees. She should have been looking at the crowds through a pair of sharply pricked ears, but on Sugarloaf there was nothing at all to obstruct her view. A ripple of applause rang out around the ring. Paris suddenly became aware that 'Congratulations' was being played over the loudspeaker system. "This is for Paris O'Shea and Derry Blake who, I have just discovered, got engaged last night," came the distorted voice of the announcer over the tannoy system. A fresh burst of clapping rang out around the ring. Paris grinned, delighted with the goodwill that she could feel.

Kate looked up at her, pulling a stray wisp of unruly red hair off her forehead. "Lucky you," she mouthed.

The horses began to go out onto the course, bucking and plunging in their eagerness to be off. Sugarloaf stood patiently as Kate unclipped the lead-rope and then set off sedately after the others. What the hell had she let herself in for, wondered Paris as Sugarloaf loped along, as quietly as an ancient riding-school cob.

The starter dropped his flag and the horses charged towards the first fence. Paris felt as if she were perched in a very precarious position on the tiny horse. Her every instinct told her that she had to pull the horse's head up until it was in a more normal position. How could it ever run a race with its head down to the ground? She resisted her instinct, conscious of Morgan's words. The first fence loomed up and the horse raised his head momentarily to assess the jump. She felt him gather himself together, then, as if he had springs beneath his hooves, he took off. She had the disconcerting feeling of being in mid-air with nothing beneath her, then they were over the fence and thundering towards the next one with the other horses bunched tightly around them. Paris began to relax. The horse was good. She could feel his power and strength beneath her, packed into his tiny frame. It was easy to see how he had won all of his races.

They passed the packed stands, a momentary hectic mass of colour and roar of noise, and then they were heading back out into the silence of the countryside again with only the thunder of the horse's hooves on the muddy ground in Paris's ears.

Out of the corner of one eye she could see the horses beside her were beginning to tire, exhausted with the long fast race. Beneath her Sugarloaf

9

still felt like a fresh horse, his legs pounding like pistons over the churned grass of the track. With Morgan's words ringing in her ears, Paris brought her whip smartly down Sugarloaf's sweat-dampened shoulder. Far beneath her she saw the tips of his ears flicker backwards in disgust as he redoubled his efforts.

They took the last two jumps alone and galloped towards the finish line, to a deafening roar of delight from the crowds. As they crossed the line Sugarloaf ground to a shambling trot, his job done; he would expand no more energy than was absolutely essential. He shuffled into the Winner's Enclosure as if every stride was an enormous effort. Paris slid from his back and began to unbuckle her saddle. The straps were slippery with sweat and her fingers trembled with the adrenaline that was coursing through her veins. She hauled the saddle off the horse's sweat-drenched back. His sides heaved like a pair of bellows. Kate threw a rug over him to prevent him from getting a chill.

"Brilliant race!" Derry threw an arm around her shoulder and drew her towards him. He wiped a smear of mud tenderly from her face and then bent to kiss her. How quickly his earlier anger had vanished now she had won, Paris mused briefly. She winced as flashlights exploded in her eyes as the cameramen converged like frenzied sharks to take a picture of the golden couple of racing. Top trainer, Derry Blake, and his fiancée, Ireland's top lady jockey, Paris O'Shea.

"Paris, over here!" called one of the cameramen, and she felt herself hauled bodily away from Derry. "I want a shot of you with Morgan and the horse." She stood beside Sugarloaf, who was hamming it up for the camera and pulling faces and tossing his head, delighted to be the centre of attention yet again. Morgan was positioned at the other side of the horse.

"Thanks, Paris, you rode a great race," he said, trying to speak while fixing a broad grin on his face for the benefit of the cameras.

"He was amazing!" Paris had to yell over the noise of the crowds. She was aware of Derry standing to one side of her, furious at being pushed out of the photographs.

Their shots taken, the cameramen dispersed. Paris hurried to the weigh room Derry and Morgan on either side. The race on Sugarloaf over, she focused towards her next ride. She had to get into her own racing silks as soon as possible and back into the parade ring ready to get on her mare. Destiny was a difficult mare to manage at the best of times; only Paris could handle the highly strung and quick-tempered animal in the stables and on the gallops at home. Paris felt the familiar knot of tension twist in her stomach again. She had to get back to her mare. She should never have left Merrianne to get Destiny ready, though all she had to do was to take the tetchy mare out of the lorry, saddle her and bring her to the parade ring. Paddy would have been there to help. Surely the two of them could cope with that? The thousand things that could go wrong flashed before her.

"You rode a great race," Morgan said to Paris as they hurried towards the weigh room.

Derry snorted. "Of course she did." He put his arm possessively around Paris's shoulder. "She isn't Ireland's number one lady jockey for nothing."

Paris cringed inwardly. Why were they always sniping at each other? She didn't have time to be stuck between them while they tried to wind each other up. "And will you want her to ride Sugarloaf for you again?" asked Derry, in a politely sarcastic voice, that implied that Morgan had better not.

"No need," grinned Morgan, triumphantly, brushing an imaginary bit of fluff from the sleeve of his tweed jacket. "One of the biggest racehorse owners in England promised to buy Sugarloaf if he won today. I've just sold the horse for an obscene amount of money. All thanks to your fiancée." With a chuckle of delight he turned on his heel and marched away, leaving Derry glaring after him in disgust.

CHAPTER THREE

Paris once again pushed open the door to the changing room. Two other lady riders were already there.

Tamara Cunningham stood at the mirror, smoothing foundation over her high, aristocratic cheekbones. "We thought that you had chickened out of riding," she sneered, examining her reflection critically.

"No chance," snorted Paris, unbuttoning the mud-splattered silks with one hand and pulling her own silks out of the battered leather overnight bag she had left on the wooden bench at the same time.

The other lady jockey, Millie Walsh, sat at the far end of the bench, ready to go, flicking her short whip nervously at the toes of her leather boots. Millie was short and chunky, the solid muscles of her thighs outlined beneath the thin fabric of her breeches. She looked at Paris and raised her dark eyes skywards in annoyance at Tamara. "Take no notice," she told Paris, pushing an unruly strand of dark wiry hair back beneath her skull cap.

Tamara, undaunted, continued to bait Paris. "Since you are doing so well today, I hope that means that I might have a bit of competition in the next race," she smirked, scraping distractedly at an imaginary speck of mascara from beneath eyelashes so caked that they looked like hairy-legged spiders attached to her eyelids. Tamara's father was a tremendously wealthy pet-food manufacturer. His wealth allowed him to indulge Tamara's every whim. She was a poor rider, but her father's money allowed his trainer to buy her top class horses and that meant she won more races more than she otherwise would.

Paris heaved a sigh of relief as she came out of the weigh room with the other jockeys and into the parade ring. Merrianne was already leading Destiny around there. Destiny looked magnificent. The red wool rug that she wore showed off her muscled quarters, the dark colour of her legs and her black mane. She looked the best of all the horses and, at least for the moment, she walked calmly beside Merrianne, looking regally at her surroundings through bright, intelligent eyes.

Paris walked towards the parade ring, ignoring the looks of amazement from the spectators leaning over the white guard-rail. She had got used to the stares as they spotted that some of the riders were girls, amongst the tough-looking wiry male jockeys.

Derry joined her. "Horse looks well," he said, nodding in Destiny's direction, his eyes darted quickly over the other runners parading around the ring, fixing on his own runner, a tall wiry grey horse. "Not as good as my Kilcolgan though," he joked, turning mid-stride to kiss her.

She pulled away. "She is the best horse here," she said firmly, prickling slightly with annoyance. Derry had always been dismissive of the mare's potential. He did not have the patience to nurture any animal that was highly strung and difficult.

Derry grinned and pulled her to him again. "We'll see. The winner gets to chose the night's entertainment," he murmured wickedly, his teeth nibbling at her earlobe.

They stood in the centre of the parade ring, surrounded by the other trainers who were huddled in little groups with the owners of the horses, all weighing up the competition.

Paris entwined her hand in Derry's and thrust it into the enormous pocket of his camel overcoat. "Then I hope that your horse wins," she murmured huskily into his ear. "You always chose the best entertainment."

He squeezed her fingers as she pulled away. "We'll soon know," he said.

Paris spotted her father and Ollie Molloy standing amongst the other trainers, both red-faced and swaying slightly. She walked across the grass towards them, acknowledging the congratulations that were shouted from all directions.

Paddy grinned benevolently at her; he seemed to be having trouble focusing his eyes. "Great girleen," he nodded to himself as he swayed, tucking his hands in the lapels of his jacket.

A rough hand hit her in the middle of her back. "Hey, Champ," Ollie Molloy's drunken slurring voice assaulted her ears.

"Hello, Mr Molloy," Paris said, through gritted teeth, Destiny was enough for her to worry about without the pair of them making fools of themselves.

"Grand win – I had a good lump of money on you." Ollie said, putting his arm around her shoulder and hugging her roughly towards him.

Paris gasped as she breathed the whiskey fumes on his breath. "Thanks, Ollie," she smiled tightly, pulling herself out of his grip.

Ollie reeled backwards as he released his hold on her. Only colliding with Paddy prevented him from falling over.

Paris scowled: the last thing that she wanted around her now was two drunks to disrupt the horse. Why the hell couldn't they have stayed in the bar? There was enough to do without the two of them getting in the way. One of the other trainers also scowled angrily at them. This was a fraught time for all of the trainers. Trying to get the highly strung, explosive horses safely onto the course was hard enough without drunks reeling around upsetting them.

"Grand girl – grand horse," Ollie grinned benevolently.

The bell rang to signal that it was time to mount. The huddles of jockeys and trainers broke up, surging towards the horses that plunged in anticipation of the race ahead. Destiny's ears twitched in alarm, picking up the sudden tension in the air, and Merrianne's face turned a sickly shade of green as the mare began to prance, terrified that she would lash out with one of her front hooves. She still had a dark purple bruise on one of her thighs from the last time Destiny had got upset about something. A film of sweat had broken out on her forehead in the effort of holding onto the mare who was dancing from one delicate hoof to another as if the tarmac surface was boiling hot.

"Now, this is how I want you to ride the race," Paddy was slurring in a loud voice. Paris clamped her lips together in a tight line. Why the hell hadn't they stayed in the bar, she thought, looking at the disapproving glares they were getting from the other trainers. Merrianne and Paddy were struggling to keep Destiny still while they took her rugs off. Paddy was tugging ineffectively at the straps that held it in place while Merrianne hung grimly onto the mare's head. Finally Paddy succeeded and slid the rug off the mare's quarters.

"Good luck," Merrianne mouthed. Paris stood by Destiny waiting for Paddy to leg her up - but Paddy was so drunk he couldn't co-ordinate his movements and staggered against the mare's flank.

"Allow me!" Derry appeared as if by magic, seized her leg and threw her skywards into the saddle. "Hurry up, I can't wait to get you home," he grinned, giving her calf a playful squeeze as the horse bounded away.

Paddy twisted his lips into a parody of a smile. "Time to place our bets," he said very slowly and deliberately. Ollie nodded his head with equal slowness. "Right." The two men wove their way unsteadily across the grass towards the brightly coloured stands of the bookmakers.

A biting wind was blowing as they rode out of the parade ring onto the course. Paris shivered, the wind cutting straight through the silks she wore, billowing the thin fabric against her skin. Destiny danced beside Merrianne, her teeth champing at the bit, thin flecks of foam splattering into the air as she tossed her head in excitement.

"Your horse is going to wear herself out before she gets down to the start line," hissed Tamara cattily, riding alongside Paris on her big chestnut horse, Highland Fling.

"At least it will give your nag a chance then," Paris shot back.

"Take no notice," smiled Mille, serenely. "With any luck her horse will buck her off on the start line."

Paris rode out onto the track, the mare quivering with excitement beneath her. Her ears sharply pricked as she gazed around her at the strange surroundings. Tamara's Highland Fling kicked out and Tommy McAvery swore furiously at Tamara as the horse's hind legs missed his kneecap by inches.

"Maybe that will put manners on her," commented Mille, gathering up her reins and kicking her horse, Amazon, into a canter alongside Paris.

Paris nodded briefly. She did not want to talk. She just wanted to concentrate on the race.

The ten horses lined up, cavorting and dancing in a frenzy of anticipation. Long seconds trickled by and then finally the flag fluttered down and the race was underway.

Destiny jumped away from the start with the rest of the horses, her dark ears flat against her outstretched neck. Paris crouched low over her mane, the wind loud in her ears above the thunder of hooves. The first fence came up. Paris eased her reins as Destiny took off, clearing the jump easily.

Out of the corner of her eye Paris could see Tamara crouched low over her horse's mane, her lipstick-reddened mouth clamped into a tight line of concentration. They approached the next fence side by side. Then Tamara whipped Highland Fling hard down the shoulder and he took off for the jump too soon and hit the top of it hard, sending him sprawling to the ground. Destiny, jumping immediately afterwards, landed almost on top of the other horse. There was a flurry of tangled legs and bodies as Destiny too was brought to the ground.

As if in slow motion Paris saw hooves and legs all around her, and waited for the pain of a hoof hitting her or a heavy body rolling on her, then the mare was scrambling to her feet. Paris was dimly aware of her foot, high in the air, trapped in the tiny stirrup-iron, then she was bumping along the ground as the mare, terrified by the strange weight flailing beside her, began to gallop, trying to escape the demon she thought was chasing her. There was a searing pain as Paris's leg came free.

She thudded to the ground and slid gratefully into the warm blackness that enfolded her.

CHAPTER FOUR

The ambulance bumped slowly across the race course and began to gather speed as it reached the cinder track that led out to the main road. The sirens began to wail, plaintive above the hum of noise from the stunned crowds. Merrianne leant against the white guard-rail and watched bleakly as the horses walked off the course. She should have been waiting to lead Paris in after her race on Destiny, instead she was paralysed with shock. The accident had been a bad one. Paris had been badly injured. That had been obvious from the way the medical attendants had clustered around her while a stunned silence settled on the crowd.

The horses began to file through the gate off the race track, sides heaving and covered in mud. Their jockeys, red-faced and puffing with the exertion, cast sympathetic glances in Merrianne's direction, all concerned about Paris. Her accident had put a dampener on the celebrations. Millie Walsh's Amazon had won the race. Millie though was in tears as she rode through the gate. "How's Paris?" she shouted over the roar of congratulations from the crowd waiting to welcome her into the Winners Enclosure.

Merrianne shrugged, helplessly. "I don't know!" she called back. "They just took her away in the ambulance."

Millie stifled another sob and wiped her eyes on the back of her sleeve as she rode away. Even Tamara Cunningham was subdued as she rode back. Her horse had been caught quickly after the fall and she had remounted and carried on. "It wasn't my fault," she snapped petulantly.

"No, it never is," sniffed Millie, glaring at Tamara.

Merrianne watched Destiny coming up the track towards her, being led by one of the stewards. "I'll take her off you," said Merrianne, walking out onto the track to take the mare.

"She's got herself worked up pretty badly," the steward said, standing aside to let Merrianne take her reins. They both stood for a moment and looked at the mare. She was wet through with sweat and quivering all over. Blood was pouring from half a dozen nasty-looking wounds on her flanks and shoulders. Her dark eyes rolled with unseen terrors, her nostrils flared red with every rasping breath that she took. The steward touched his hand to his forehead in a brief gesture of farewell and then jogged back down the empty course to take his position before the next race. Merrianne led Destiny slowly through the racecourse towards the lorry park, everyone turned to gaze at them sympathetically.

Merrianne led the mare up the steep lorry ramp. Her mind was in turmoil. Should she call the vet? What would Paris have done? This wasn't fair. She was only the groom, she didn't want to have all of this responsibility. She should have been in the bar now, celebrating the earlier win, not worrying about injured horses. Wearily Merrianne shut the partition that closed Destiny into her travelling stall. The mare became frenzied, plunging, trying to free herself, snapping at Dark Admiral who was peacefully eating his hay in the adjoining stall. Merrianne shot out of the lorry before Destiny tried to sink her snapping yellow teeth into her arm and heaved the heavy ramp up quickly.

There was nothing to do now except go home. Paddy had quickly withdrawn Dark Admiral from his race after the accident. But how would they get home, thought Merrianne, resting her head against the cool side of the lorry. She had never driven the lorry before. Paris always did that. Paddy and Derry had gone to the hospital, Ollie Molloy had disappeared, but he was too drunk anyway to be of any use whatsoever. What on earth did they think she was going to do? They had all been so concerned about Paris, no one had given Merrianne and the horses a thought. Slowly Merrianne straightened up and looked around the lorry park. Surely someone would help her. Drive the lorry home for her. There was no one in sight – they were all still in the racecourse enjoying themselves.

There was no choice. She would have to drive the lorry home. It couldn't be that hard. She could drive a car. So... Merrianne reached up and heaved open the door and then clambered up the steps into the cab and settled herself into the driving seat. The steering wheel was enormous and her face felt as if it was pressed up against the vast expanse of the windscreen. She found the key, hidden in its usual place above the sun visor, and wiped her sweating palms across the legs of her jeans. The engine fired as she turned the key. She put it into gear and let out the clutch. The lorry lurched forwards at a seemingly terrifying speed. Merrianne jammed her foot hard on the brake and the lorry stopped dead and stalled. The sound of horses scrambling to keep their footing in the jolting lorry made Merrianne wince; the valuable horses could easily be injured if they fell in the tight partitions. Merrianne could hear herself breathing rapidly in panic and could feel her heart pounding against her ribcage at an alarming rate. Tears of fear and frustration spilled down her hot cheeks and splashed onto the huge steering wheel.

Then the door was suddenly wrenched open, sending a blast of icy cold air into the cab. Morgan Flynn clambered up. "Move over," he said, taking hold of the steering wheel to haul himself into the seat. Merrianne moved thankfully into the passenger seat. "I think I'd better drive you home," he said with a wry grin.

"I've never driven it before," replied Merrianne, humbly, wiping her tears with her sleeve. "But what about Sugarloaf and your lorry?"

"My head groom is taking care of everything," Morgan started the engine again and reached out to pull the door shut.

"I'll follow you," called a woman's voice from outside.

"OK, Tara, See you in a while!" He slammed the door shut and shoved the lorry into gear. Merrianne caught a glimpse of Morgan's wife as she climbed into their car. Morgan drove slowly across the lorry park. "How's Paris?" he asked, as he halted the lorry at the exit onto the main road. His handsome face was shadowed with concern.

"I don't know. They just took her off to the hospital – Paddy and Derry went with her." Merrianne stifled a sob. She was exhausted. All that she wanted to do was to get home and go to bed. To wipe out this dreadful day. But there was still so much to do. All on her own – the stable lads would be gone home long ago.

Morgan fished in the pocket of his tweed jacket and handed her a crumpled handkerchief. "Here," he said, quietly.

Merrianne wiped her eyes and stole a glance at Morgan. He was staring hard at the road ahead, his face impassive. Then she remembered the accident that had killed a jockey who was riding for him. That had almost ended his career as a trainer. What if Paris died? The fall had been horrendous. Merrianne had seen the two horses rolling to the ground, their legs entangled. Then the awful moment when Paris was dragged along the turf, her body bouncing over the churned grass. Then lying so, so still. How could she survive that?

By the time they arrived back at Redwood Grange stables it was dark. Their headlights swept the stable yard as Morgan steered the lorry in. He turned off the engine. "I have to go," he said, handing her the keys. "Will you be able to manage the horses?"

She nodded slowly, thinking about the nightmare of work she still had to do. Merrianne lived in a small flat at the top of the main house. At first it had seemed a good idea, living on the job as the head groom, rent free, all her bills paid. Now, though, she wasn't so sure. There was no escape from the horses and the interminable work. And of course no escape from the tiring routine of looking after the horses when they came back from racing. And tonight she had to do it all alone.

They got out of the lorry. It was bitterly cold in the yard. Merrianne drooped with weariness, hoping that Morgan would take pity on her and stay to help. Stray wisps of straw blew in frenzied circles as the wind caught it. The horses in the stables began to whinny and bang on their doors in anticipation of their feeds.

"Tara's here." Morgan was looking towards the long driveway from the main road. A pair of headlights were crawling slowly towards them. "Let us know how things are," he said pulling the sides of his jacket around him against the wintery night air. Then he went to meet the car. Tara tooted the horn as they drove away, leaving Merrianne in the dark, deserted yard.

"Fuck," she complained bitterly. There was at least three hours' work ahead of her.

Merrianne stomped into the tack room and turned on the lights, flooding the yard with brightness. The concrete glistened with a sheen of ice that turned to a thousand tiny stars in the glow from the electric light. There was so much to do. The horses had to be taken off the lorry, they all needed to be fed, then she had to take all the droppings out of the stables, top up the water buckets, refill the hay mangers. The list seemed to be endless.

She never had to do as much work in her last job, thought Merrianne, miserably, as she trailed back across the yard to the lorry. If it hadn't been for Jamie Lynch she would have still been at Blackbird Castle stables. He had persuaded her to have an affair with him. And then, when his wife found out, he had to let his wife sack her. The whole sorry business had been his fault.

Merrianne undid the fasteners on the lorry ramp and let it down. She pulled the partition back and stood wide-eyed in shock, looking at Destiny. Paris's much-loved mare was unrecognisable. Even in the dim light cast from the arc lights around the yard it was obvious that the mare had been very badly upset by the accident. She was quivering with fear and wet through with sweat. Merrianne gingerly inched forward, talking gently to the mare whose eyes rolled with terror at her approach. Slowly she undid the rope and pulled the mare towards her. Destiny half stumbled, half fell down the ramp. Merrianne led her slowly along wincing as she brought the mare into the bright lights of her stable. Destiny had looked to have some nasty injuries at the race course, but now she looked awful. Merrianne unclipped the rope from her head-collar and jogged across the yard. She had better bathe those wounds to stop them from becoming infected. She dragged Dark Admiral off the lorry and put him into his stable. Quickly made up the feeds for the other horses and fed them. Then she ran a bucket of warm water, added some antiseptic, pulled off a wad of cotton wool and hurried back to Destiny. The mare cowered at the back of her stable, head down, her sides heaving. Merrianne squeezed out a fistful of cotton wool and went towards her. Suddenly the mare exploded with a flurry of snapping teeth and forelegs that raked the air close to Merrianne's head. Merrianne abandoned the bucket and bolted for the door. Maybe she would be better in the morning.

CHAPTER FIVE

Merrianne had just thrown hay into the last manger when she saw headlights coming slowly up the drive. She slammed the stable door and stood in the yard, shivering with cold and tiredness, as a taxi pulled through the gate. It came to a stop outside the house and Paddy got unsteadily out. Merrianne walked across to him.

"Merrianne. What a great girl," slurred Paddy, trying to shut the taxi door. His co-ordination wasn't good enough for him to shut the door and turn around to speak to her, so he ended up half shutting the door and sprawling across the boot of the car. He held out his hand and she pulled him upright with some difficulty. The taxi driver, obviously glad to be rid of his drunken passenger, seized his moment and roared back down the drive.

"How's Paris?" she asked, steering Paddy towards the house.

"Help me inside." He wobbled precariously towards the rose-beds.

Slowly they inched towards the house. Merrianne propped Paddy up in the porch while she fiddled with the house keys. She opened the door and snapped on the lights. Paddy, as if waking from a deep sleep, suddenly stood upright and lurched inside. Merrianne clenched her fists angrily. If it wasn't enough to have the whole yard to do on her own, now she had to deal with a bloody drunk. She longed for a deep, hot bath, to soak away the grind of the day and relax her aching shoulders. No chance of that now, she fumed silently.

Paddy, holding onto the walls, propelled himself into the sitting-room, where he proceeded to bounce off the furniture as he opened the cupboards and drawers. "We'll just have one for the road," he said, rummaging in the back of a cupboard. After a lot of banging and clattering he finally unearthed a bottle of whiskey. He pulled out two glasses and poured a liberal amount into each. He left one on the table and took his own and slumped down heavily on the sofa.

Merrianne reached for the glass and brought it slowly to her lips. The smell of the whiskey made her gag.

"How's Paris?" she tried again.

Paddy didn't seem to hear her. He swirled the whiskey around in his glass, gazing intently at the amber liquid. Then before her eyes he seemed to crumble. He put the glass down heavily on the arm of the settee beside him, where it wobbled precariously before she grabbed it. When Paddy looked up his eyes were glassy with tears. "She's awful bad," he whispered, hoarsely, then to her utter horror he began to sob - loud, harsh sobs. "She's going to die."

The insistent buzzing of her alarm-clock roused Merrianne from a restless sleep. Every time she had closed her eyes she had seen that terrible fall. Sometimes she really despised Paris, hated her success and that she had everything that she herself wanted. But she would never have wished anything like this to happen to her. Groaning, she switched on the bedside light to make sure that she didn't fall back to sleep. She heaved herself onto her elbow, a blast of icy air billowing around her warm body. "Fuck it," she growled, shoving the sheets viciously out of the way and thrusting her feet out onto the floor. Today was going to be a nightmare, she was convinced of it. She groaned at the thought of trying to get the stable staff to do anything without Paris there to cajole them. Paddy had drunk himself into a stupor the previous night, so she would get no sense out of him, or any help. And there was Eddie Doyle to contend with as well.

She dressed quickly, then as she drew back the curtains and glanced out of the window she growled in temper. "Eddie," she snarled through clenched teeth. The lights were already shining brightly over the darkened stable yard. The horses peered over their stable doors, eager for their breakfast. Eddie Doyle, the old man who came to help with the stables was already in the feed room, where she knew that he would be making a mess, spilling oats

23

everywhere and giving the horse the wrong feeds. "You come early just to spite me, don't you?" she muttered, pulling on her sweatshirt. She stamped downstairs. Loud snores came from the direction of Paddy's room.

It was bitterly cold outside, frost glittering on the frozen puddles in the powerful arc lights. Merrianne walked gingerly across to the feed room.

"Ah," Eddie bellowed, "I've made a start!"

Eddie was as deaf as a post and always spoke at an incredible volume, assuming that no one else could hear either.

"That's great," Merrianne enunciated slowly, gritting her teeth. She found Eddie the most annoying man she had ever met. He was so superior, always assuming that he knew better. He might have spent a lifetime in racing yards, but he had never progressed from shovelling shit. If Eddie was so clever, then why had he never been promoted?

Eddie looked at his watch pointedly. He loved to think that he had been on the yard first. It was his way of getting one over on her. "I've made up the feeds!" he roared, gesturing towards a muddle of buckets and spilled feed.

Merrianne managed a tight-lipped smile. "Great." She felt a knot of tension building in her stomach. There was absolutely no way of telling which feed was for which horse. "You give them out – the lads and lasses will be here soon," she said, staring hopefully through the open door into the darkness beyond, longing to see the other grooms arriving to start the daily routine.

"Paris having a lie-in?" smirked Eddie maliciously.

"Oh Eddie!" Merrianne felt a momentary pang of sympathy. Eddie was devoted to Paris; she was so good with him, having an immense reserve of patience. Gently she explained what had happened to Paris and watched with a guilty feeling of satisfaction as his face crumbled. The other staff began to arrive one by one, all listening wide-eyed as she told what had happened to Paris before blearily beginning the daily routine. Eddie, stunned by her news, was worse than useless.

Merrianne walked slowly across the yard to Destiny's stable, filled with dread. Paris usually looked after the mare herself. Merrianne wondered what kind of a mood she would be in now.

Dawn was beginning to break, the first streaks of red blazing across the black and golden sky. Normally the mare would be leaning eagerly out of her stable, banging the door with a hoof in protest at the slowness with which her breakfast was being delivered. Today, no eager head looked out of the door. Merrianne opened the door. Destiny stood at the back of the stable, her head down, like a bull about to charge. "Hey, girl," said Merrianne nervously, stepping into the stable. Destiny moved with lightning speed, lunging forwards with hooves and teeth. Merrianne darted quickly out of the stable and slammed the door behind her. That was the last time she would try to go in to the mare. Let Paddy sort her out, if he was ever sober enough.

Merrianne fetched hay and forked it over the door into the mare's stable. Destiny raised her head and bared her teeth nastily at Merrianne. "Suit yourself," growled Merrianne. "Mad bitch!" As she turned Eddie was looking at her reprovingly from the doorway of the stable that he was mucking out. He was obviously unimpressed by her treatment of the mare. Let him go in to her, she thought, raising her head haughtily and stalking across the yard to give one of the stable lads a roasting for dropping straw all over the yard.

The lads and lasses began to exercise the horses. The first five horses were brought out and ridden quietly around a rubberised track that circled the yard, then out up the road to the gallops. Paris or Paddy would usually accompany them to assess their fitness and readiness for the next race. Then they were brought back to the yard and the second lot of horses began their daily exercise.

Merrianne walked away towards the house. She would never manage to work with Eddie without Paris to pour oil on the waters that boiled between them. She loathed the cocksure little man.

"Paddy, are you going to the gallops?" she shouted from the house doorway. There was no reply. "Paddy!" she yelled again, kicking off her boots and padding into the house. A silence so thick that she could have cut it reverberated through the house. She went slowly up the stairs. Suddenly the silence was broken by a loud snore. Merrianne puffed out her cheeks in a sigh. She banged loudly on his bedroom door. "Whaaaaa!" roared Paddy, as the loud noise penetrated his fuddled brain, sending spears of pain shooting into the back of his eyes.

There was no time to observe proprieties. Merrianne shoved the door open. "Paddy," she snapped urgently, "the horses are heading off to the gallops. Get up, will you?" On autopilot Paddy flung back the covers and lurched out of bed. Merrianne had time to glimpse with distaste a vast expanse of pudgy white flesh as his pyjama top flapped open, then she slammed the door shut and stamped back downstairs. She had enough to do without having to play alarm-clock to a drunken racehorse trainer.

Paddy emerged from the house a short time later. He looked terrible, his face grey and pinched with worry. "I've just rung the hospital," he said, in a voice that cracked with emotion. "They keep saying that she's going to be all right. I know they aren't telling me the truth. She's going to die, I know she is."

Merrianne looked away, as he wiped his eyes with the back of his hand. She didn't want to start crying too.

"Come on. I'll take you to the hospital," Merrianne said, taking him gently by the arm. The grooms would have to manage the yard themselves for once. If Paris was as bad as Paddy thought, he really should be there with her.

"Thank you for coming with me," whispered Paddy as they walked through the hospital, his breath still stinking of whiskey.

Paris lay, white-faced except for a livid gash across the side of her cheek, in a quiet side room. She looked tiny and frail in the hospital bed. Derry sat in an armchair beside her. The racing newspapers were scattered all over the hospital-green bed cover and a litter of paper cups and plates were discarded on the windowsill behind him. There was also the faint, but distinctive aroma of cigarette smoke lingering in the antiseptic air of the hospital. As they came into the room he yawned and stretched, languid as a giant cat.

"How long has she got to live?" Paddy gulped, wringing his hands together, as he crept across the room and stood over his daughter, looking down at her with a face like a sorrowful bloodhound.

"Oh, about another fifty years, hopefully," grinned Derry. "Concussion is not usually fatal."

CHAPTER SIX

Paris knew what it must feel like to be a very old lady. Every part of her body was agony. Movement was absolutely impossible. She groaned, the harsh noise escaping involuntarily as she tried to lift herself into a sitting position. If only someone would come and help – she just needed pulling upright and then she would be alright. No one was going to come though.

They had said that she must stay in the hospital for at least another few days. But she had told Derry to come for her. She needed to get home. It would be wonderful, she thought, to lie here and rest, but she had to get back to the stables. There would be all sorts of disasters without her supervision. Merrianne was not a great stable manager – her mind was like a sieve and Paris always had to check that she had done the necessary jobs. Especially when she had a date with yet another of the rich men she tried and usually failed to maintain a relationship with.

Paris jerked herself back to wakefulness. She had been drifting off to sleep again. How wonderful it would be, to slip into that comfortable, warm safe place where the pain disappeared and just sleep until she felt well and strong again! But she couldn't. She had to stay awake. Had to get out of here. Gritting her teeth with determination and to stop herself from crying out, she extended an arm across the cool bedclothes and hooked her fingers around the edge of the bed. She rolled over onto her side. Now she could drag herself to the edge of the bed and roll out. Sweating from the exertion, she finally succeeded in hauling herself to her feet.

The room swam before her eyes. Please don't let me be sick, she pleaded silently, clamping her mouth shut. Forcing her legs to move she went to the bag that Paddy had brought in for her the previous evening and pulled out a pair of jeans and a jumper. It took ages to dress, every movement was agony. Only sheer determination to get out of the hospital forced her to keep going. Finally dressed, she lowered herself gingerly onto the edge of the bed to wait. How long would this pain last, she wondered. Every muscle and joint felt as if it had been crushed and pulled out of place, which, as she had contemplated when she regained consciousness, they probably had been.

The accident was a vague memory that she did not probe. She remembered Destiny's pricked ears as she rose to take the jump, then a blur of horses rolling and tumbling. She shuddered at the thought and blanked it out purposefully. She could have been killed, but it did no good to even think about what could have happened.

There was a clock over the door. Derry was already half an hour late. Nothing new there. But she wished that he would hurry up. She needed to get out of here, away from the dry antiseptic atmosphere and the echoing corridors with hushed voices and squeaking shoes hurrying past the door.

Her cheek throbbed. She must be black and blue where a horse's hoof had belted her head. She touched a hand gingerly to her cheek as she had done countless times since she had woken up in the hospital bed. There was a cut; she could feel the knots of the threads where it had been stitched. The hands on the clock shifted again. Where the hell was Derry?

Her eyes roved around the room, bored, trying to curb the temper that was making her want to yell and scream for Derry to get her out of here. There was a mirror on the opposite wall. It drew her, as unerringly as a car's headlights draw a rabbit to its doom. She inched herself upright again and then, holding onto the metal rail at the edge of the bed, shuffled her way relentlessly towards the mirror. Then, there she was, reflected in the mirror, white-faced in the harsh lights of the room, tousled hair slicked greasily to her head and hanging limply to frame her face. Eyes wild with horror at the sight that greeted them. Her cheek. A red, angry-looking gash ran from her cheekbone to a spot level with the end of her nose. The stitches looked clumsy and childlike, puckering the skin, pulling her eye downwards. She looked like Frankenstein's monster. Pain ignored, her hand flew to her mouth as she gave a gasp of horror. Then she burst into floods of tears, sobbing with self-pity.

"Well," exclaimed Derry, coming through the door a second later, "is that any way to greet the winning trainer of the 1.45 at Tramore?" He enfolded her in a cautious hug, careful not to squash her bruised body.

His tweed jacket was coarse against the skin of her cheek. She breathed in the smell of horses overlaid with the faint tang of the aftershave he wore.

"What on earth's the matter?" he said, putting his hands on her shoulders and propelling her gently away from him.

"My face," she wept, spanning the horrendous cut with her outstretched fingers. "Don't be a baby," he said briskly, grasping her wrist and tugging her hand away. He studied her for a moment, turning her face this way and that in the light, then he tutted impatiently. "You'll be fine in a week or two."

Paris noticed that he couldn't quite meet her eyes. She felt her breath catch in her throat and swallowed hard. She mustn't cry again. Derry hated hysterical women. Stepping out from the hot, dry atmosphere of the hospital felt as if she had been given parole from prison.

"You're better off out of there," said Derry, holding Paris's arm as she gingerly manoeuvred herself into his Jeep. He looked back at the bland outline of the hospital with a shudder. "Full of sick people," he said, slamming the door.

They arrived at Redwood Grange an hour later. It was good to be home even though the yard looked a mess, loose strands of straw blowing listlessly across the tarmac and a pile of buckets lay abandoned outside the feed-room door. Things had slid in the few days while she was away. But at least she was home; she would soon have things running efficiently again.

Derry stopped the jeep outside the house and turned off the engine.

"I wonder if Paddy is in," he whispered wickedly, reaching over to kiss her and surreptitiously slide his hand inside the buttons of her shirt. "I have missed you terribly and I need to take you to bed." For once Paris hoped whole-heartedly that Paddy was home. She could barely move her legs let alone open them.

Hurrying to get her inside, Derry grabbed her bag off the back seat and then shot around to open the door for her. He marched up the path to the front door while Paris hobbled stiffly behind him.

The door opened as Derry reached it and Paddy burst out with a roar of delight. He enfolded Paris in a bear hug that made her wince with pain as he gripped her aching ribs too tight. For once he was sober. There was no

29

reek of whiskey on his breath. He had dressed in a smart pair of cords and a checked shirt, instead of the old clothes that he usually forgot to change out of. "I thought that you would never come home," he whispered hoarsely stroking her hair as if he couldn't quite believe that she was real. "Where's Merrianne?" Paris asked, wincing as his fumbling hand caught one of her bruises. "How is Destiny?"

"Merrianne's gone out for the evening with some man," Paddy said.

"How's Destiny?" Paris demanded again.

"Don't worry about the mare!" he said quickly.

"I want to go and check the horses," said Paris as soon as Derry had put her bag down in the hall.

"No chance." Derry shook his head with a good-humoured smile. "Bed rest, the nurse said."

Paddy went into the lounge, and out of the corner of her eye Paris could see him fishing a glass and a bottle of whiskey out of the press. "Take Paris up to bed, Derry, and then join me for a celebration," Paddy mumbled his head half buried in the press as he searched for a second glass.

"Better do as your father says," Derry grinned wickedly, propelling Paris up the stairs. Paris climbed wearily up the stairs. She needed to go and check the horses, not to be put to bed like a child. Then as she entered her bedroom the bed looked so inviting all she wanted to do was to lie down and sleep. To let the pain vanish as she drifted off into oblivion. Before she had a chance to get her breath back after the exertion of climbing the stairs, Derry came to stand behind her. She could feel the warmth of his body, like a radiator against her aching back. His hands slid deliciously over her breasts and then began to undo her shirt buttons, pulling the fabric apart to caress her breasts. "I want you so badly," he murmured, sliding his hand down the front of her jeans and wriggling an expert finger inside her.

"I want something too," Paris whispered sexily, leaning backwards to rub her cheek against his neck.

"Mmmm," he nibbled gently on her earlobe. Then his moans of pleasure turned to one of great displeasure as she pushed herself away from his body.

"I want to sleep," she said, firmly.

Derry pounded down the stairs, whistling good-humouredly in spite of her rejection. Paris slowly undressed and crawled under the covers. What a blissful relief it was not to have to move and fight the constant pain that every movement brought! She closed her eyes and let herself drift away, aware vaguely of the hum of noise from downstairs as Paddy and Derry hit the whiskey bottle. Much, much later the noise of the Jeep driving away woke her and she lay, in the twilight area between sleep and wakefulness, listening to the sound of her father getting steadily drunker, cursing as he crashed into the furniture.

Paddy had found solace at the bottom of a whiskey glass since he found his wife in bed with one of his jockeys. Paris was five years old when her mother left to live with the jockey. For many years her father had managed to merely use the drink as a crutch, but as Paris grew older and she relied less on him, he had no need to remain sober. And his drinking became steadily worse. Somehow he ran a large and successful training stables, where socialising and drinking were part of the scene. But his wife's betrayal had left him a broken man.

The sunlight streaming in through her bedroom windows woke Paris with a jolt. No one had woken her. She should have been in the yard hours previously. There was so much she had to do. Cursing her own stupidity for not setting her alarm-clock, she struggled out of bed with as much speed as was possible with the limited movement that she had. The house was deserted; Merrianne and Paddy were already outside hard at work.

She opened the front door. The yard was a hive of activity. Lads were pushing wheelbarrows loaded with manure, and the first lot of horses were just disappearing out of the drive. Paris walked stiffly across the yard. Merrianne was nowhere to be seen. Eddie sidled out of one of the stables, sly as a rat, and fell into step with Paris. "Thank goodness you are back," he said, bristling with self-importance at being the bearer of bad tidings. "There has been one fuck-up after another!" He rubbed his gnarled hands together with delight at the prospect of all the gloom and doom that he was about to spread.

Paris, in no mood to listen to Eddie's malicious gossip, stopped and turned to face him. "I see that your muck heap looks a bit untidy."

Eddie prided himself on the way that he shovelled the discarded manure into an enormous, but very neat square pile. He glanced in horror at the heap of dung, cut to the quick at being criticised.

"Maybe you could sort it out and then tell me all the problems later," said Paris.

Eddie shuffled off with as much dignity as he could muster, muttering under his breath.

Paris walked towards Destiny's stable. No pretty bay head looked out. Maybe the mare was out in one of the paddocks. She reached the stable and peered inside, and immediately recoiled in horror. Her much-loved horse was unrecognisable. She stood at the back of the stable, head down, hunched against the wall, surrounded by a mess of uneaten hay. Every rib was clearly visible and thick yellow pus oozed from a dozen wounds. Paris felt her breath catch in the back of her throat at the sight of her precious horse. All of the hopes and dreams of the last few years were shattered in an instant. Destiny would never race again.

CHAPTER SEVEN

"He were quick," muttered Eddie morosely, leaning against his fork to watch the tail-lights of the vet's jeep disappear at lightning speed down the drive.

Paris tutted in disgust. "What a bloody waste of time," she moaned, shifting her weight painfully from one leg to the other. Even six weeks after her accident every bone still ached like hell.

Paris had tried everything to make Destiny better, but still she cowered at the back of her stable, barely eating and trying to savage anyone that went in to her.

Eddie heaved himself upright, his wrinkled face alive with mischief. "I never saw anyone jump over a stable door as handy as that lad," he said in a serious tone, thrusting his huge hands into the depths of his trouser pockets and shaking his head sadly. "He'd have managed it too, if his trousers hadn't caught on that loose piece of hinge."

Beside Paris, Merrianne gave a huge snort of amusement and then they were all laughing. Destiny had gone for him so quickly that he had jumped out over the stable door. His baggy trousers had caught on the hinge leaving him hanging in midair, jerking like a frenzied marionette as he tried to free himself.

Paris turned once again to lean on the stable door to look at the mare. "Will you ever be well enough to race again?" she asked Destiny miserably.

The jovial mood evaporated and Eddie and Merrianne slipped away to continue with their work. Destiny raised her head and looked intently at Paris. Then she tossed her head, ears back, nose thrust forwards in an aggressive gesture. Paris felt the familiar lump return to her throat. She had cried so many tears over this mare.

All of her hopes and dreams had been pinned on the young mare since she had been born. Paddy had bred Destiny from one of his favourite mares. Her sire was The Moose, one of Ireland's best National Hunt stallions. Paddy had given the foal to Paris as a birthday present. She had spent hours with her, finally training her to be ridden. She was the fastest, bravest and most contrary horses that Paris had ever ridden. She knew that she was going to be one of the greatest racehorses of all time. Maybe even better than the famous mare, Dawn Run. Now all those dreams lay shattered, because of a stupid fall.

Derry drove into the yard. Paris waited as Derry parked his jeep and walked towards her. She was glad of the distraction – anything to take her mind off the horrific sight in Destiny's stable. She caught her breath as he walked towards her, long legs clad in green corduroy trousers. Even after two years together she still felt a thrill when she saw him, her body craved his, the feeling of his skin, the delicious male smell of him made it impossible to concentrate on anything when he was around. It was hard to believe that he belonged to her. And that later on in the year he would really be hers. Forever.

"Hi, gorgeous," he said, casually, dropping a kiss on her mouth. He tasted of coffee, cigarettes and mints.

She didn't feel very gorgeous. The scar on her cheek still looked as raw and livid as it had the day she came out of hospital. The stitches had been removed but the line, jagged and red, remained, a brutal reminder of the accident.

"How's the mare?" Derry said, feigning an interest Paris knew he did not feel.

Paris felt a surge of gratitude towards him. She knew that to him Destiny was just another horse and she was grateful for the attention he gave her in pretending to be interested in how she progressed. He must by now be truly sick of hearing about Destiny and injuries. He leant against the stable door, looking critically at the mare. Paris watched him surreptitiously, taking in every line of his face. She watched his dark eyebrows draw together in a frown and his mouth disappear into a tight line of concentration. Then slowly he shook his head and turned to face her. "That mare should be shot," he said gently, pulling Paris into his arms. "She isn't going to get better."

"She is. I know she is!" Paris whispered. Tears, already close to the surface, began to spill down her cheeks. "Paris. Look at her," said Derry gently, taking hold of her shoulders and turning her to face the mare. "She's so evil-tempered she's bloody dangerous"

"She's just another horse to you," raged Paris, her fingers gripping the top of the door tightly. "I love her. I can't just give up on her."

Derry shrugged. "I think you are wasting your time." Then turning on his heel he stalked off towards the house, calling back over his shoulder, "The racing's about to start on television. Are you coming in?" Paris glared at the straight, arrogant line of his back as he strode across the yard. How she hated him sometimes! He was halfway across the yard before she began to follow, as fast as her limping strides would carry her. Then as he reached the door Derry turned and hurried back to Paris.

"Oh my poor darling," he said gently, sweeping her off her feet and into his arms, carrying her like a child. "I will never, ever have you put to sleep."

"Damn that man," cursed Derry as he watched Morgan Flynn's horse, Golden Mile, canter sedately over the winning line lengths ahead of the other runners in the first race of the day. His sudden explosion of temper jerked Paris fully awake from her doze. The heat of the fire and the warmth of his body as she lay against it, stretched out on the settee, had lulled her gently to sleep. She was exhausted. Night after night the most terrifying nightmares had been disturbing her sleep, leaving her feeling tired and tetchy. She was afraid to close her eyes in case the nightmares returned, with their horrific images of flailing hooves tangling around her body, trapping her and she would wake with a yelp of horror, arms thrashing to free herself. She sat up, it wasn't very polite to drop off to sleep when Derry had come to see her. Her scared cheek felt strangely numb where it had been resting against the cool cotton of Derry's shirt.

The next race started. Derry leant forward, concentrating hard on the television, studying the runners. "I'm interested in the favourite in this," he commented, reaching for the newspaper to check the horse's form.

At the fourth fence two of the horses fell, sprawling on the ground, sending their jockeys rolling along the turf. Paris gave an involuntary cry of terror, and grabbed Derry's arm. Derry gave a snort of laughter and half turned towards her. "It's only a fall," he grinned, looking at her quizzically as if he couldn't quite believe what she had just done. "See," he gestured towards the screen with his head. The horses had got up and galloped after the others and their jockeys were standing beside the fence staring ruefully after them. "They're OK."

"Sorry," she apologised. "They surprised me, that's all."

Derry raised his eyebrows and shook his head as if questioning her sanity.

Paris chewed her bottom lip fretfully; she felt as if she was guilty of the most enormous faux pas. She could never, ever tell Derry that she was terrified to ride.

Ever since the accident she had made excuses not to ride, saying that she ached too much, anything to keep from facing the dreadful feeling that nagged at the back of her mind, that she was afraid to get on a horse again. That knowledge was too awful to contemplate. Horses and riding were her life. To never ride again was unimaginable, but when she had finally plucked up the courage to try, that morning, the results had been worse than she could have ever dreamed.

The yard had been empty; everyone was out on the gallops. Paris had been waiting for this quiet time to see if she was able to get on a horse again.

The tack room smelt of leather and horsehair. The ancient terrier who slept in a basket in the corner close to the wood-burner raised his head, rheumy old eyes peering blankly, sniffing eagerly to see who it was. He thumped his tail on the edge of his wicker basket when she spoke gently to him. She pulled a bridle down from a hanger and heaved a saddle off the wooden rack. Her ears were filled with the sound of her own breathing, harsh and loud in the silence of the dusty room. She found it hard to swallow the lump that had lodged itself in her throat. Slowly, her muscles aching with the weight of the saddle, Paris walked decisively to a corner stable in the yard. She opened the door and went inside.

Sausage was her father's old hunter. He had a long back and plump belly which gave him the nickname. Years ago he had gone by a far more exotic name, but Sausage was now firmly tagged onto him. He was the oldest horse on the yard and the quietest. He was occasionally used by Paddy to ride to the gallops to watch the other, more frisky thoroughbred horses work. He never paid the blindest bit of attention when they capered and bucked, but could stand for hours, big ears lolling, eyes fixed on the distant horizon as if he was recalling hunts of years gone by. Sausage lifted his great shaggy head from the heap of hay on the floor of his stable and stood while she shoved the bit in his mouth, pulled the bridle over his ears and then buckled his saddle into place. Easy, she thought, fumbling dreadfully with the girth straps, her fingers trembling so much that she could barely pull the leather strap into place. Finally Sausage was ready and she led him out of the stable. He was huge, his head high in the air, feet as big as dinner plates. She led the horse to the mounting block, a tall heap of breezeblocks that were sometimes used to get on the racehorses. Sausage stood patiently as she climbed the mounting block. She was level with his saddle, the stirrup dangling inches away from her foot. All that she had to do was to put her foot in the stirrup and get on. Sausage sighed and shifted, resting a back leg, patiently waiting for her. She couldn't breathe. Her throat was so tight that only short gasps of air went in and out of her lungs. She had to get on the horse. It was so easy, just one quick movement. Sausage was so gentle. He would never do anything to hurt her.

No one would believe the Paris that was standing on the mounting block if they could see her. This was the girl who could leap onto young wild thoroughbreds without a fear in the world. Who would laugh as they bucked and capered, her knees gripping their sides, sitting as if she was glued to the saddle. But this was the girl who was covered in cold sweat, barely able to breathe, her whole body quivering with fear at the thought of getting onto the big, broad back of the quietest horse that was ever bred.

She shoved her foot into the stirrup. And leant forwards ready to get on the horse. Nothing happened. Her muscles simply wouldn't carry her onto the horse. Then taking a deep breath she lunged upwards, heaved her leg painfully over the back of the saddle. She was on. She took hold of the reins with trembling fingers. Her legs quivered so much that she could see the fabric of her jeans twitching in time with the muscles. A black haze swam in front of her eyes, her heart pounded painfully against her ribcage. Gingerly she nudged Sausage's broad belly with her heels and he shambled forward across the yard. There was a rushing noise in her ears, loud over even the harsh sound of her breathing. They went through the gate and into one of the fields that surrounded the stables. Sausage moved as cautiously as if he

37

was carrying a china dinner service.

A dozen young thoroughbreds were grazing in the adjoining field. Seeing Sausage shambling across the grass they lifted their heads and ran to the fence to gaze excitedly at him. Sausage lifted his great shaggy head and let out a loud bellow of a whinny in greeting. His belly vibrated with the effort, and he jogged two strides to impress the youngsters with his massive presence. Paris flung herself off the horse in panic, landing on the rough grass with a thud that knocked the wind out of her, and lay sobbing with anguish as Sausage nonchalantly began to crop the grass beside her. She couldn't ride. Her life was over.

Eventually Derry stood up and stretched pleasurably. "No rest for the wicked," he yawned. "I had better go and kick ass at Westwood Park – the staff get lazy when I'm not there." He dropped a kiss on her unscarred cheek. Paris followed him out and watched as he got lithely into his filthy jeep. Each panel was covered in thick mud from churning around the fields watching the horses work, and inside the floor and seats were covered in abandoned newspapers and cigarette packets.

"See you soon," he said, through the open window. "Don't forget we've got Lady Oakwood's party next week."

Paris nodded in what she hoped was an enthusiastic manner. The last thing that she wanted to do was to go to a huge social gathering, where everyone would stare at her scarred face and ask stupid questions about the accident. She leant on the wall and watched his jeep jolt away, until it was hidden by the tall trees that lined the drive. The yard was deserted, none of the lads or lasses had yet returned from their homes to do the evening stables. Twenty horses watched quizzically over their stable doors, wondering if they were going to be fed early. Paris rubbed the back of her hand over her eyes, miserably dashing away the tears of desperation that were spilling unchecked down her cheeks. What use was a jockey who couldn't ride?

CHAPTER EIGHT

Paris pulled the woolly scarf tighter around her face. The livid scar that raked across her cheekbone ached horribly in the biting April wind that was gusting across the racecourse.

"The Snooty Fox looks uptight," Derry said, his penetrating gaze roving over the jogging bay horse that snatched nervously at his bit and barged constantly into Merrianne who was trying to lead him around the parade ring.

Paris followed his gaze. He was right, of course, but she had been trying to ignore the fact that the horse was so upset by having a different jockey. "He usually settles when he gets out onto the track," she said, quietly, the strong wind taking her words.

Derry thrust his hands deeper into the pockets of his tweed overcoat and pulled a wry face. "That was with you riding him." he said pompously. Paris felt her fingers tighten around the form guide book that she held. The whole day was going horribly wrong. The Snooty Fox was desperately unhappy about being ridden by JJ Kelleher, the jockey she had found for him.

The bay horse was nervous and sensitive at the best of times. It took constant pampering to make him eat the feeds that were given him and Paris would often spend hours sitting with him, persuading him to eat. Today, with JJ riding him, the horse was worried, his tiny ears flickering backwards and forwards, his eyes rolling backwards showing the white corners.

Beside her his owner Ollie Molloy stood, watching, his whole body taut with temper. Out of the corner of her eye Paris could see his lips working as he muttered to himself and occasionally he shook his head as if in disbelief that Paris would not ride the horse, his wild red hair billowing in the wind.

"I thought that you would have been fit enough to ride by now," he snapped petulantly, tugging on her coat sleeve and bellowing into her ear. Paris turned towards him, and his blue eyes bored into hers like a diamond-tipped drill bit.

"Ollie," she said, hoping he wouldn't see the fear in her eyes, "I am still injured – it would be stupid for me to ride the horse. JJ will give him a good ride, you'll see."

She turned away to watch the horse, hoping that he wouldn't be able to see that she was lying. The fact was that she couldn't ride any horse. She had not been on one since the day she had tried to ride the placid old Sausage. Even the thought of getting on a horse made her head reel and her breath grow short. She hadn't told anyone, but sooner or later she was going to have to. Eventually she would run out of the excuses that were sounding more and more feeble.

The Snooty Fox suddenly ran backwards, scattering the trainers and owners that were watching the horses walking around the parade ring. Merrianne was almost dragged off her feet, but just managed to cling onto the leadrope. JJ yanked at the reins in temper as the horse lashed out with his hindlegs, narrowly missing Valerie Johnson, the elegant woman who owned Rochdale, Derry's runner. Valerie stepped back hurriedly, almost overbalancing as her high heels sank into the damp turf. Paris grinned despite herself as Derry deftly stepped forwards and caught Valerie around the waist and pushed her gently upright again. Valerie simpered with delight, fluttering her heavy eyelashes in Derry's direction. Paris glared at the two of them. Women were always flirting with him, and it annoyed her that he played along with them.

The horses went out onto the course.

"This is a fucking waste of time," snapped Ollie petulantly. "That horse only runs well for you." He scowled peevishly and stalked off towards the Owners and Trainers bar to drown his sorrows in a glass or three of whiskey. His head ached and his eyes felt raw from being up all night entertaining a young secretary who worked for him. He had been trying to get her into bed for weeks now and she was still managing to give him the run-around.

"Fucking waste of time," snarled Ollie, again, a short while later. The

Snooty Fox stood in front of them, sides heaving, head lolling as Merrianne sponged his sweat-drenched body with warm water.

JJ shrugged. "He burnt himself out in the parade ring." He slid his tiny saddle off the horse's back and turned abruptly away.

Ollie, his long teeth biting his bottom lip in temper watched the tiny jockey weave his way across the grass. He threw his catalogue down on the crushed grass amongst the discarded betting slips where the pages blew fretfully in the wind, and stalked away, red hair billowing beneath his flat cap.

"Never mind," Valerie squeezed Paris's arm. "At least my horse won." She took Derry's arm with her other hand and gazed up at him in open admiration. Paris felt too numb to care.

"Let's go and celebrate," Derry said happily, leading the way towards Valerie's husband's hospitality box.

Paris slipped her arm out from Valerie's clutches and let them walk on without her. She followed at a slower pace, miserably contemplating how angry Ollie had been.

It was terribly hot in the hospitality box. David Johnson, Valerie's husband, had removed his jacket and sprawled in one of the plastic armchairs that lay strewn around the room, dark circles of sweat staining the armpits of his purple shirt. "Great horse," he bellowed, raising his champagne glass. He breathed out a plume of cigar smoke complacently, and regarded them through half closed eyes.

Paris slowly unwrapped her scarf. She was terribly conscious of her scar.

"Sit with me," bellowed David, banging the seat beside him. Paris sat down. She wanted to go home. She was in no mood for being fawned over by David.

The next race started. Derry turned the sound up on the overhead television and sat down to watch. They were all engrossed in the race, when at the final fence the leading horse took off too early, leaping wildly at the jump. His front legs caught the top of the solid brushwood fence, sending him sprawling. The jockey lurched precariously for slow seconds and then catapulted to the ground.

Paris grabbed David's arm in a reflex gesture of panic. He yelped loudly as her fingers dug into the pudgy flesh and he spilled his drink into his lap.

But Paris held onto his arm, eyes still fixed on the television screen, seemingly oblivious to David's reaction.

"Paris, what the —" Derry grabbed her hand and prised her fingers from David's arm.

Seconds later tears began to pour down her face as David glared at her, rubbing his painful arm petulantly, and staring at the large wet stain on the front of his trousers.

"Sorry, I'm sorry," Paris sobbed, weeping frenziedly into Derry's shoulder.

"For fuck's sake, Paris, get a grip on yourself!" Derry hissed, pulling his phone out of his pocket as the shrill ring-tone sounded above the commotion. "Lady Oakwood," he trilled smoothly into the mouthpiece, his eyes still fixed on Paris in temper. "Of course I haven't forgotten the party..... no.... of course not... yes, see you later." He snapped off the phone and turned to Valerie. "Must go, darling," he said, leaning forward to kiss her affectionately on her wide mouth. "We'll see you at the party." He steered Paris out of the room as if she were a naughty child that needed to be put to bed.

The carpark was already beginning to empty as they drove out. Derry nudged his low-slung sports car out into the stream of traffic, barging his way unashamedly onto the main road. Once away from the racecourse he put his foot down hard on the accelerator and the powerful car surged forward, as he drove silently, anger oozing from every pore. Paris stole a look sideways at him. When he was angry a vein throbbed just beneath the sleek dark hair on his temple. Now she could see the vein pulsing beneath the skin. His long fingers were clenched tightly around the leather-covered steering wheel.

"What the fuck was all that about?" he spat at last, viciously changing down a gear to power around a corner.

Hot tears spilled silently from her eyes, and she bit her lip hard to stop herself from sobbing. "I'm sorry," she whispered, humbly, shrugging helplessly. "I just......" the words trailed away as she tried and failed to explain her reaction.

"I'm sick of this prima-donna behaviour," Derry growled, sulkily. "It's time you got back to normal. When are you going to start racing again? There's nothing wrong with you now."

"My leg still aches like hell," Paris snapped defensively. "Maybe in a week or so."

"It's time you got back to normal." Derry reached for her hand. She heard the change in his voice as he struggled to control his temper, "You were the life and soul of any party, but now...." His voice trailed off miserably.

"Should be a good party," he said, changing the subject.

"Lady Oakwood's parties are always brilliant," replied Paris tentatively, glad that at least for the moment Derry had forgotten about her outburst at the races.

"What are you going to wear?" he asked.

She began to relax; maybe he wouldn't bring it up again.

"The pink silk?" she mused. The hedges at the side of the road were a dark blur as the car cruised along.

"God no, that makes you look like my granny! I don't want anyone saying that Derry Blake's girlfriend looks like a freak. Wear the grey one I brought you in Annabelle Lynch's shop – you've never worn that."

Paris sighed miserably. She didn't even want to go to the party, least of all in the low-cut, clingy creation that Derry so obviously loved. She had hated the dress when he had first brought it for her and had shoved it right to the back of her wardrobe, hoping that he would forget all about it. Unfortunately, he had remembered it.

Later she changed into the grey dress. It fell into place, gliding over her waist and hips like a second skin. She moved towards the mirror and gazed in naked horror at her reflection. She had washed her hair and blow-dried it so that it fell in a sleek waterfall each side of her face. Beneath the glorious mane of hair her scar stood out, a harsh, angry red against her sickly pale complexion. She had lost so much weight since the accident, fretting about Destiny and worrying about the guilty secret that she was concealing from everyone, that now her hip bones jutted out beneath the grey sheen of the fabric.

She turned slowly, grimacing in horror at her reflection. The back of the dress plunged daringly low, thin spaghetti straps criss-crossing the back sexily. Now beneath her jutting shoulder-blades every rib was clearly visible. She couldn't go to the party. It would be unbearable to have everyone staring at her with distaste lingering beneath their glances of sympathy. They would be able to see through her pathetic show of daily bravado, they would be able to see her for the coward that she really was. Derry wouldn't want to be seen with her. He wanted a glamorous girlfriend, who everyone admired, not some feeble creature who would become the object of everyone's pity.

There was no way that she was going to the party. But how on earth was she going to get out of going? Paris bit her lip anxiously, wishing that the Paris that she had been before the accident would come back. She had loved parties, was full of fun and life. Now it was as if she saw everything through a dark veil and moved through life as if every footstep were an immense effort.

Bleakly she shrugged off the grey dress, letting it fall from her shoulders. It slid to the floor and lay like a cast-off snakeskin on the rose-patterned carpet. She wiped away the make-up that she had so carefully applied and, shrugging on her dressing-gown, went wearily downstairs

"I thought you were going to Lady Oakwood's party?" said Merrianne, coming into the hall as Paris walked downstairs. She pulled off her boots and straw spilled all over the carpet.

"I really don't feel up to it," Paris sighed, slumping down on the settee.

Merrianne followed her into the lounge, tutting in disgust. "Not wanting to go to a party," she muttered under her breath. "What I'd give for a decent night out!"

Paris laid her head back on the back of the settee. What heaven it was just to lie back and close her eyes and rest her aching legs. The thought of going to the party and standing all night, aching all over, cringing as everyone averted their eyes from the red scar that crossed her cheek, was horrible. She longed to go to bed and to sink into blessed painless oblivion. Merrianne was welcome to go; she herself certainly didn't want to go.

"Why don't you go instead of me?" she mumbled. Her eyelids felt like lead and it was an effort even to talk. Merrianne didn't need asking twice.

By the time Derry arrived Merrianne was changed and raring to go. "Darling," said Paris sleepily as Derry came into the lounge looking devastatingly handsome in a black tuxedo and white bow tie, "I really don't feel up to this party – I thought Merrianne could go with you instead. She deserves a night out. You won't mind terribly, will you?" Derry looked Merrianne up and down, his eyes widening. Then he shrugged. "Doesn't seem as if I have a choice, does it?" he said frostily. He dropped a polite kiss on Paris's forehead and stalked out. Merrianne tottered after him on impossibly high stiletto heels. Paris closed her eyes. She should go up to bed, but the climb upstairs seemed such a formidable task. Paddy came in from the yard, shrugging off his coat. Icy air clung to him changing the temperature in the room instantly.

"I couldn't face the party," Paris whispered sleepily, prising open her leaden eyelids. "So I sent Merrianne with Derry."

"So I see," snarled Paddy, wrenching the top off the whisky bottle and slopping a generous measure into a glass. "You're a bloody fool."

CHAPTER NINE

At the end of the Redwood Grange drive Derry slowed the car. Merrianne felt as if she could touch the tension and anger that reverberated from his every pore. There was an intense silence, broken only by the crackle of the sports car's wide tyres on the gravel. The car ground to a halt. Merrianne surreptitiously studied Derry's haughty profile. His straight brows were drawn together and his lips were so tightly clamped together that they had almost disappeared. She wished that she had not come. This was all a horrible mistake. Derry was obviously furious.

Suddenly he turned towards her, the leather driver's seat creaking gently. Merrianne turned to face him, half afraid of his famous volcanic temper.

"I shouldn't have come," she said hoarsely, her throat tight, unshed tears close to the surface.

"Nonsense," he said, without any warmth. "It was good of you to come to keep me company."

He was devastatingly handsome. How could Paris want to stay at home rather than be with him? He reached his arm forwards towards her. Merrianne's jaw dropped open like a hinge. He was going to kiss her. She felt his arm brush across her breast and the hot flush that spread across her face as she realised he would have felt her nipples rising in response to his touch.

"You should put your seatbelt on," he said, rapidly withdrawing his hand, which had the seatbelt in it.

Merrianne felt a rush of breath escape from her lips. Thank goodness it was dark, so that he wouldn't be able to see the embarrassed blush that was making her face feel as if it was on fire. He was just getting the seatbelt. How stupid of her to think that he was going to kiss her!

Derry clicked the seatbelt into place. "Now you're safe."

Safe was the last thing that she felt. She was sure he had known what she had thought. How stupid he must think she was!

The car swept silently along the deserted lanes. Merrianne stared at her reflection in the darkened window, lit up by the aeroplane-like lights on the dashboard. Derry's face was reflected beside her own and she studied him covertly as he concentrated on the road. She wanted to squeal with delight. It was hard to believe that she was actually sitting in an expensive car next to Derry Blake. Derry Blake, her employer's fiancée. Nirvana for women everywhere.

Oakwood House lay in a damp hollow of impenetrable forest. A weed-encrusted driveway wound through the undergrowth skirting a murky lake before opening out into a cracked concrete forecourt that was already full of parked cars. Cars spilled out of the forecourt and were abandoned on the side of the driveway, wedged between the trees and rocks.

Derry spotted a parking place and swung the car off the drive. "Here we are," he said, turning off the engine.

Merrianne gazed out of the window with increasing horror. Everyone was so beautifully dressed and looked so elegant. Her outfit was completely wrong. Derry got out of the car, so she had no choice but to follow him. She slammed the door and pulled her long coat tighter around herself. A couple walked past them, feet squelching on the wet leaves.

"Hi, Derry," called the man. "Hi, Pa ..." His voice died away in embarrassment as he realised that she was not Paris.

Derry smiled shortly at her, a taut smile that did not reach his eyes. "This way." He took her arm politely and steered her towards the house. Oakwood House reared up before them as they walked along the rutted drive, a tall square forbidding building. Dark ivy climbed over the house, sprawling over the windows with clawing tentacles. They joined the other couples that were walking towards the heavy wooden arc of the front door, which gaped open, revealing a cavernous hall, brightly lit with banked fires and shimmering candles.

Just inside the entrance hall stood a tall, wiry elderly woman whose wrinkled face had the sly look of a fox. Merrianne recognised Lady Oakwood from the races. Beside Lady Oakwood stood her husband, short, plump and complacent, plying all the women who went in with kisses.

"Lady Oakwood!" exclaimed Derry, taking hold of the woman's bony shoulders and dropping a kiss beside each of her whiskery cheeks.

"Derry, darling, how good to see you!" She gripped his shoulders with a vicelike grip. "And …?" she said, quizzically, arched eyebrows raised skywards as she looked at Merrianne.

"Merrianne," Derry said disdainfully. "She works for Paris as a groom. Paris couldn't come."

"Ah," Lady Oakwood said, looking Merrianne slowly up and down with a barely suppressed shudder of distaste. Her husband, eager to grapple anything remotely feminine, rather than the bony, masculine figure of his wife, seized Merrianne around the waist and dragged her towards him, kissing her full on the mouth with flabby, garlic-tasting lips.

Merrianne fought the urge to wriggle free and punch him on the nose.

Once they were past the host and hostess, Valerie Johnson, who Merrianne recognised immediately, swept across the hall to claim Derry. "There you are at last," she giggled, flirting furiously. She gave Merrianne a cursory glance and dismissed her immediately as of no consequence.

"You look beautiful!" Derry held her at arms' length and looked at her approvingly. Valerie wriggled her shoulders so that the breasts her plastic surgeon had remodelled swung tantalisingly in his direction. Her dark eyes sparkled mischievously beneath a brow frozen with botox injections. Derry turned to Merrianne as if he had suddenly remembered that she was there. He gestured towards a door. "The cloakroom's over there. Please excuse me."

Merrianne opened her mouth to speak, but before she had the chance Valerie had linked her arm through Derry's and had led him away. Merrianne watched open-mouthed with fury. She might have been thrust on Derry by Paris, but it hurt be to abandoned as if she was of no consequence. She clamped her mouth shut tightly to stop herself from weeping bitter tears of rejection.

The cloakroom was crowded. Heavily made-up middle-aged matrons jostled with slender blonde clones to shove their coats in the direction of an ancient crone clad in a black dress and white apron. Her lace cap was askew, perched precariously on top of tight grey curls, her wrinkled face damp with sweat as she battled to contend with the masses of coats and shawls that were being thrust at her to hang up. Gingerly Merrianne removed her coat, looking enviously at the beautiful dresses of the women that surrounded her.

Then as she handed her coat in she noticed one of the women beside her nudge her companion and gesture in her direction. Why had she been so eager to accept the invitation to this party? She was completely out of place amongst all of the expensive and tastefully dressed women. She hovered inside the cloakroom, desperately aware that her skirt was too short and that her top was too clingy. She could see the swell of her breasts escaping from the confines of her bra and pushing against the cheap, glittery fabric of her low-cut top. A woman beside her, dressed in a long velvet dress with a wide silk sash around her waist, looked at her in disdain.

Clutching her handbag in front of her like a shield Merrianne crept into the entrance hall. An impassive man wearing a long black tailcoat was circling the room with a tray of drinks. He thrust the tray in her direction. Merrianne seized a glass of champagne and downed it like lemonade on a baking hot day. She gasped as the bubbles hit the back of her throat. Bolstered by the champagne she wandered through the rooms, looking for someone that might look familiar enough for her to talk to. Tight, impenetrable circles of stiff backs greeted her in every room. Stuck-up bastards, she thought miserably, moving towards the open fire that roared in an enormous fireplace. At least she could stand here and pretend she was warming herself, rather than looking as if she had been abandoned. The stiflingly hot room hummed with the sound of conversation. Merrianne warmed her bottom against the fire, surveying the splendid room. How she would love to live somewhere like this, amidst priceless antiques and paintings with a thick carpet and tall windows concealed by long velvet curtains.

Another man in a tailcoat came into the room. "Supper is served," he announced over the roar of conversation.

Merrianne waited until the room had emptied of all the glamorous people before she joined the queue for supper in the dining-room. Derry was ahead of her in the line, engrossed in conversation with Valerie. When would the party end, she wondered bleakly. How long before she could pull off this wretched cheap-looking outfit and crawl with relief into her bed. The line shuffled forward with aching slowness. As if he could feel her looking at him Derry turned and caught her eye. Merrianne felt herself redden under his gaze. Why did he make her feel like some naïve schoolgirl enmeshed in her first serious crush. She saw him mutter something to Valerie, who looked at Merrianne coldly, then to her surprise and relief he wove his way through the people towards her.

"Enjoying yourself?" he asked, Seeing her empty glass, he made a gesture with his hand and instantly one of the tail-coated men was refilling it with more champagne. "Yes. Thanks," she lied. She was damned if she was going to let Derry see how out of place and miserable she felt. "Are you?" she asked tentatively, but Derry was already on his way back to an indignant-looking Valerie. Merrianne watched as she gave him a tight smile of welcome as he joined her again.

The queue shuffled forwards until gradually Merrianne found herself beside the buffet. The tables creaked and bent with the weight of food. Enormous whole turkeys, hams, sides of beef jostled with dishes of salads. A large pink salmon curled haughtily around a silver platter. A basket of oysters garnished with lemon quarters was almost empty.

A silver-haired man was scooping one out into his mouth, smacking his lips with enjoyment. "Try one," he said, offering one to Merrianne. She shook her head, repulsed by the slimy-looking lump glistening in the oval shell. "Go on," he persisted, holding one out to her. Tentatively Merrianne took the oyster shell and the fork he held out to her. He squeezed lemon juice over it and then waited, smiling with anticipation as she forked the oyster into her mouth. She swallowed, pleasantly surprised by the salty sea tang. "See," said the man, approvingly, showing her how to leave the shell face downwards to signify that it was empty. "Delicious, aren't they?" A moment later the kind man almost choked on an oyster as his wife tapped him on the shoulder. Merrianne took one look at the small, piggy-eyed woman with the tight perm armoured to her head with hairspray and beat a hasty retreat.

Next door the dancing was just beginning. Lady Oakwood was happily flinging her gamekeeper around the floor in time to 'Rock Around the Clock'. Merrianne winced as she saw her ladyship's stiletto heel dig into the man's foot as they jived. Merrianne took up a position leaning against the wall where she could watch the dancing.

"You should be dancing!" yelled a voice in her ear and Merrianne found herself seized by the wrist and dragged onto the dance floor. A tiny and very spotty-faced young jockey who she vaguely recognised enfolded her in a bear hug and proceeded to haul her around the dance floor. He was very drunk, she realised, as they wobbled precariously close to Lady Oakwood and her gamekeeper. Clinging to the jockey's shoulder to stop either of them overbalancing, she saw Derry rapidly bearing down on them, his tuxedo jacket abandoned, his shirt clinging to his sweat dampened body. In a flash he hauled the jockey by the scruff of the neck and tossed him to one side as if he were as light as a feather. Merrianne grinned in relief.

"Dance?" he asked and she stepped happily into his arms.

Derry was the most incredible dancer. Merrianne gripped his shoulders and let him guide her skilfully around the dance floor. His muscles were taut beneath her fingers. She longed to move her hands over the planes of his back and the swell of his arms. She longed to touch his dark hair, move her hands over the taut planes of his face. He was so gorgeous, so terribly desirable. Sex oozed from his every pore. He was so different from the slobbering pricks that she usually ended up with. She stole a glance at his face, only to see that he was looking down on her, a half smile of amusement dancing in the corners of his beautiful mouth, while his eyes danced with wicked good humour. Merrianne felt as if he could see into the depths of her soul. He knew that she wanted him and he was toying with her, like the stable cat toying with a mouse before it kills it. The music ended and Derry gently disentangled himself from her, "I think it's time we headed home," he said, leading the way off the dance floor.

He stopped the car outside Redwood Grange. "Thank you for coming with me," he said, coldly polite again. Then he dropped a sudden kiss on her lips, his mouth cool against hers, tasting faintly of whiskey. And as abruptly he pulled away. "Goodnight." It was a stern dismissal.

"Goodnight and thanks." Merrianne got regretfully out of the car, pulling her long coat around her thighs. And then he was gone and the evening was over. Merrianne touched her fingers to her lips where he had kissed her. Paris was a fool to let him go out alone.

CHAPTER TEN

Paris woke to the sound of rain hammering on the roof above her bedroom. She rolled over and hugged her knees to her chest to warm herself. Rain. That had to be good for the runners today – two horses who loved the deep, muddy going that the rain would produce. If only she could stay in bed forever! The whole day stretched ahead like some enormous mountain that she had to climb. She had no energy to get through the day, no desire to see the horses running, no buzz from the thought of seeing Derry. Nothing. Just a mind-numbing exhaustion and dread of being around people at the races who wanted to stare at her scar and maliciously enquire why she wasn't riding yet. She got slowly out of bed and pulled back the curtains. The yard below was still in darkness, but in the powerful arc lights she could see the rain lashing into the puddles that had formed in the concrete. Shivering she dressed and dragged herself downstairs. Merrianne's coat was draped over a chair in the lounge, the faint smell of stale tobacco and beer emitting from the fabric. Footsteps thundered down the stairs and Merrianne appeared, shoving her tangled blonde hair into a elastic band.

"Sorry," she said, guiltily. "I guess I overslept. I'll give the horses their hay." She grabbed her raincoat and dashed out into the rain, ducking her head against the downpour as she ran.

Usually Merrianne lingered in the kitchen, chatting. Anything to put off the moment when she had to actually go and do some work. Paris scowled, Merrianne obviously had some guilty secret to hide. She wondered bleakly what had happened the night before between Merrianne and Derry and wished that she could dredge up the energy to care. Paris followed Merrianne outside, hunching her shoulders against the rain, but not caring that it was soaking through her jacket. She let herself into the feed room to mix up breakfast for the hungry horses that were eagerly hanging their heads over the half doors, neighing at her to hurry up. Even lifting the tops off the containers that held the feeds seemed an almighty effort. Brightly coloured silks hung in one corner, ready to be taken to the races.

She should have been wearing the red and yellow chequered colours that belonged to Ollie Molloy. The horse, Our Racehorse, was one of the favourites in the race. She had told him that she was still suffering with her painful ribs. If only it was just so simple as a bit of pain. The mental agony of the terror that assailed her was far worse than any pain. The nightmares still had not receded, leaving her feeling tired and tetchy all of the time. She could handle the horses on the ground, but the mere thought of getting on one again brought her out in a cold sweat.

When the feeds were made up Paris looked out of the door for Merrianne to help give them out. There was no sign of her. What the hell was she doing? Paris leant on the frame and bellowed her name so hard that it made her throat prickle. Merrianne sauntered over from one of the stables, her eyes looking anywhere except at Paris. "Feeds ready?" She smiled a bright and false smile.

Paris bit her lip to stop herself yelling at her. "That's right," she snapped tetchily trying hard not to picture Merrianne and Derry together. Merrianne piled the buckets one on top of the other and sauntered back across the yard to give them out.

Paris took a feed into Destiny's stable. The mare stood at the back of the stable tossing her head aggressively. Paris walked forwards and the mare, realising she was unafraid, put her ears forward and plunged her nose eagerly into the bucket of feed. Paris put the bucket of feed down beside her and ran a gentle hand down her glossy neck. She was slowly recovering from the accident. The nasty wounds that had cut deep into her flesh had healed. But Paris was the only one that could go into her stable without being savaged. Paris had wondered whether she really was not afraid of the mare, or whether she really didn't care if she killed her with a savage kick.

53

It was raining when they reached the racecourse. Paris pushed open the lorry door and rain billowed into the cab. "Bloody hell," she snapped turning to grab her coat from behind the driver's seat. "Fuck!" She slammed her hand on the steering wheel. She had come without her raincoat. She finally unearthed a filthy windcheater that belonged to one of the grooms underneath a pile of head-collars behind the seat. That would have to do. Damn Merrianne! Of course she had a raincoat on.

The rain quickly soaked through her jeans and the jacket as she ran across to declare the horses. She was drenched and shivering by the time the first horse was due to run. Merrianne led the tall bay horse, Red Arrow, around the parade ring. He walked proudly, oblivious to the rain.

"This weather should suit him!" Paris yelled into his owner Joe McHugh's, whiskery ear. Joe grinned and gave her the thumbs-up signal. Red Arrow was the oldest horse on the yard. He was also one of the most useless, but Joe loved him passionately. Joe was the oldest owner on the yard and loved nothing more than a day out at the races, regardless of whether the horse did well or not. Just to be there was all that counted. Red Arrow ploughed around the muddy track gamely before he finally fell at the sixth fence. Joe let out a roar of delight as the horse scrambled to his feet and charged after the other runners. "He's getting better," he yelled at Paris over the roar of the crowd as the mud-splattered winner thundered over the line. "He fell at the first fence the last time he raced."

Paris caught the look of contempt on Merrianne's face as she stalked off to catch Red Arrow.

Derry, who had a horse running in a later race, came across the racecourse towards her. He smiled politely, but his eyes were cold in his handsome face. "Well done, Paris, you've worked a miracle on that old horse," he told her pulling him towards him for a chilly kiss. "Fuck off," snapped Paris, pushing him away. She was really in no mood for Derry's sarcastic sense of humour today.

"Suit yourself," said Derry shortly, retreating.

Two races later, Paris waited in horror as the Molloy family of four stocky, loud children strode across the parade ring towards her, led by Ollie, their father, a dark overcoat swinging around his short fat legs, his square jaw thrust resolutely forwards. Trotting at the back of the group was Mary, their mother, who was even shorter than her husband, but even wider, with a purple, boxer-like face. Their horse, the aptly named chestnut gelding,

Our Racehorse, was being led around the ring by Merrianne. Paris shivered. She wished that she were anywhere else except trapped with the dreadful Molloy family.

"He had better win!" snarled Ollie Molloy in greeting as he reached the spot where Paris stood. He blew out a plume of thick smoke from his cigar and threw the butt of it arrogantly across the grass.

"I've put a packet of money on him," said Mary loudly, much to the derision of the other owners standing in the parade ring.

The gaggle of equally loud and obnoxious children surrounded them, pointing at the horses and cat-calling, as the ring steward scowled witheringly at Paris.

The jockeys trooped out into the parade ring, their colours bright against the grey rain that fell thickly from a leaden sky.

"Make sure you ride him properly!" Ollie thumped Walter Bollinger, the jockey, on his shoulder. Walter reeled backwards at the blow. He looked relieved when the bell rang and the horses were led into the centre for the jockeys to mount them.

After the second attempt to give the jockey a leg up onto the horse that was spinning in frenzied circles, Paris barked at Merrianne to keep the horse still. Her nerves were ragged and she knew it. She looked across the parade ring to where Derry was flinging JJ Kelleher up onto the broad black back of his runner, Booty. She should go and apologise for snapping at him earlier, but even walking across the grass to him seemed too much effort.

The horses went out onto the track. The previous races had churned the turf to mud. Our Racehorse sloshed through the mire, head low, ears flattened against the downpour.

"We're off to the owners' and trainers' bar," Ollie said, blowing the smoke from another cigar into her face.

"I'll come with you," said Paris, blinking her eyes as the smoke stung them. Ollie and Mary were dreadful clients. Always moaning about how their horse ran, expecting it to win every time out and complaining bitterly if it didn't. She had better ply Ollie with drink to keep him good-tempered, in case the horse didn't do well.

"You look like a drowned rat," Derry ran up behind her.

"Thanks," she snapped crossly. She didn't need to be reminded of the fact, then immediately regretted snapping at him. So much for apologising.

"We'll get a drink in the bar," he said, coldly, holding the door open for her.

The owners of Derry's runner, Lucy and Vincent Potterhill, had joined the Molloys and were crowded around the overhead television watching the runners as they circled before the race started. The tall, horsy-looking Lucy and her elegantly tweedy husband, Vincent, looked distinctively uncomfortable beside the gangster-like Molloys.

"That's our horse!" yelled one of the children, jumping up to point to the horse with a grubby finger.

Lucy and Vincent looked at one another in horror at the company they had found themselves in.

Derry fetched drinks for everyone. Merrianne trotted after him, to help bring back the drinks. Paris leant against the wall, making sure that her scar was against the wall so that no one could see it. She could feel steam rising from her damp clothes in the hot atmosphere. She watched Merrianne simpering as Derry handed some of the drinks to her to carry, a growing feeling of annoyance prickling somewhere deep inside her. The little tart was coming on to Derry. Derry said something to Merrianne, his mouth pressed close to her ear. Merrianne laughed, tossing back her damp blonde hair and batting her eyelids seductively at him. Paris accepted the drink from Derry with a tight smile. Silently she cursed herself for not going to the party, for letting a slut like Merrianne loose around her boyfriend. Paris stared blankly at the television her head filled with a thousand horrible images of Derry and Merrianne. That little tart couldn't keep her hands off any man for a minute. But she had just been too miserable, too exhausted. Derry would forgive her. They would pick up the pieces of their crumbling relationship when she felt better.

"Hadn't you better wait near the track to lead Our Racehorse in after the race," she sniped at Merrianne, and for a brief second had the satisfaction of seeing the disappointment of being sent away from the fun flash across Merrianne's too pretty face.

"Come on, Booty!" Derry hissed.

Paris focused on the screen. Booty, Derry's runner, and Our Racehorse were neck and neck scrambling up the run in to the finish line. Walter was wielding his whip, urging the horse onwards.

"Yeeeeessss!" screamed Mary Molloy, clanking her glass against her husband's as Our Racehorse just put his nose over the line in front of Booty. Ollie almost flattened Vincent as he shoved his way out of the door to get to the Winners' Enclosure. Mary and the horde of children jostled their way out in his wake.

Derry remained, staring at the television screen, shaking his head in disbelief. "Steward's enquiry," rang out the nasal tones of the announcer over the noise of the race course.

"Fuck," sighed Paris. Ollie would be furious if Our Racehorse was stripped of his win. She hurried out of the bar in Ollie's wake, glancing back at Derry. He remained staring at the rerun of the race on the screen, never once glancing in her direction.

Our Racehorse walked in off the track, his mud-splattered sides heaving like bellows. Booty came in behind him, his head low to the ground, exhausted by the effort. Ollie grabbed his horse's bridle and led it through the crowds.

"We have to wait," Paris said, putting her arm on his to stop him leading the horse into the winner's place. "There's a steward's enquiry. They think that Walter got in the way of Booty on the run up."

"Places reversed," came the bleak announcement over the tannoy.

Ollie went wild, flinging his cigar to the ground in temper and stamping viciously on it.

"You stupid bitch!" he snapped, grabbing Paris by the collar and pulling her forward so that her face was inches from his. She could smell the stale tobacco on his breath. "You should have ridden that horse. That bloody jockey was useless. I pay you to win with my horse. You are going to regret this!" Then releasing her abruptly he stalked away, followed by his brood. One of the children turned as they walked away and gestured back with his middle finger.

It was good to get home. Paris left the grooms under the careless supervision of Merrianne and went into the house. She was soaked to the skin, shivering as she made hot tea and got into a deep bath. Why had she been so nasty to Derry? She had made some caustic comment when he had come to sympathise with her over the race. She had seen the hurt in his eyes. Really she should spend some time with him. They were growing further and further apart, but somehow she couldn't find the energy. Sod Ollie. It was the jockey's fault that the race had been stripped away, not hers.

A car pulled into the yard as she dried herself on a warm towel. "Damn," she hissed pulling the curtain aside to peer into the yard to see who had come. She was looking forward to an evening in front of the fire, not one spent entertaining clients.

Frowning, she saw Ollie's car in the yard. "Oh no," she sighed. He had come to complain again. She dressed and went wearily downstairs.

Ollie sat by the fire, his large hand wrapped around a glass of whiskey, while Mary mooched around the room. Paddy was pouring a whiskey for himself with a hand that trembled; his face looked grey, and he seemed to have suddenly become an old man, bent and weary.

"Ollie," she greeted him, sitting down. Her father was silent, the atmosphere tense. Ollie took a long swig of his whiskey and smacked his lips contentedly. "Paris," he smiled, looking like a cat toying with an exhausted half-dead mouse. "I have come to call in a debt your father owes me."

Paris looked at her father who stood by the fireplace, his face ashen, "I borrowed money from Ollie," he said quietly, "a lot of money. And I can't repay it. Ollie is taking Redwood Grange."

CHAPTER ELEVEN

Paris's heart seemed to stop. "What?" she said, incredulously.

Ollie busied himself with poking the embers to stir the flames back up. Mary lit a cigarette and continued to mooch around the room, fingering the curtains with a look of distaste growing on her boxer's face.

"I think that you heard the first time," Ollie said smugly. "Your father borrowed a lot of money from me to fund his gambling." He poked hard at a log on the fire, splitting it and sending red embers spilling out all over the fireplace. Paris watched bleakly as one landed on the carpet and began to smoulder. The room filled with the smell of burning wool. "An awful lot of money," Ollie continued, the words rolling from his mouth as if he were savouring a delicious vintage wine. "And now I want it back." Mary sniffed. "And Redwood Grange is the only way he can pay." She twisted down her thin lips with an imperceptible shudder as if Paris's home was the most horrendous dump imaginable instead of a beautiful stone house, rambling and ancient, nestling in the heart of parkland that had been planted generations before by Paddy's ancestors.

Paris gripped the back of the chair to prevent herself from fainting. Her head was filled with a rushing sound. Surely Paddy wouldn't be so stupid as to gamble away their home ... their business ... Redwood Grange ... the stables, almost as old as the house, forming a long L-shape to the side of the house, surrounded by barns and sheds that had developed in a dreadfully inconvenient and higgledy-piggledy fashion over the generations, someone adding a building here and there to suit their own requirements. It was all inconvenient, and labour intensive to operate. But home. And beautiful, incredibly beautiful. And she loved every weatherbeaten stone of the place, each of the cracked stone slabs in the yard where the grass determinedly shoved its way back through in spite of the efforts of the grooms and Eddie to keep it in check. And now … Slowly she looked from Ollie's red-veined, round self-satisfied face to her father, standing in the corner like a naughty schoolboy, his aristocratic face pinched and grey.

"Tell me this isn't true," she demanded.

Paddy lowered his eyes and stared at the carpet. "I can't," he whispered.

"Oh Paris!" Ollie stood up abruptly. His red, ugly Rottweiler face was filled with hatred and the satisfaction of winning. "I'll give you a month to get out," he sneered, barging roughly past Paris. Mary trotted after him, a short, tarty skirt revealing a vast expanse of cellulite-pitted legs.

The car drove away, leaving the room filled with a thick, horrified silence. Paris sank slowly onto the settee. Paddy broke the silence with a harsh sob. Numbly Paris held out her hand towards him. Paddy grasped her hand and she pulled him gently onto the settee beside her.

It seemed ages before he was calm enough to talk. "I ran up big gambling debts, Molloy helped me settle them," he said simply. "I used the house as collateral. He said he would never touch the house – it was a joke between us."

"Well, now he has," Paris heard her voice seeming to come from a long way away as if she were shouting down a tunnel. The whole room seemed in sharp focus, the bright fire, the brightly patterned curtains, the carpet, dusty and covered with straw and muck. The home that she loved. Now it belonged to someone else.

"I still own Blackbird Stables," Paddy said quietly. "I didn't give him the deeds for them."

Paris swallowed hard; there was a lump in her throat that felt as if it would choke her. Blackbird Stables. The abandoned stable yard and half-derelict cottage that had been used as isolation boxes and staff cottages in the days before her parent's marriage had broken up.

The stupidity of him overwhelmed her. He had gambled away their home. All that they were left with was a tumbledown ruin, a shattered shell. Suddenly she couldn't remain in the room with him, the urge to beat his pathetic face was too strong. Shaking her head, she leapt to her feet.

"Paris," he pleaded, reaching his hand out towards her.

She brushed his hand roughly away. "Leave me alone!" She stumbled from the room and outside into the cold night air, gasping for breath as if she had been submerged in water.

On impulse she got into her car. She needed Derry. He would make sense of all that was going on around her. He would make it alright. Maybe they could bring the wedding forward. She could leave Paddy to his own stupid mess. Paris shoved her foot hard and aggressively on the accelerator, teeth clenched in anger as she gunned the car hard down the drive, feeling it sliding on the corners, not caring. She shot out onto the road at the bottom, in front of a car which was coming towards her. The driver had to brake hard to avoid colliding with hers, and she shoved her foot down as a loud horn sounded and lights flashed angrily in her mirror. She hurtled down the country lanes, foot hard on the accelerator. She was going so fast that she overshot the turn-off into Westwood Park and had to slam the brakes on hard. The car screeched to a halt, tyres protesting and then she reversed back and swung between the tall stone pillars that marked the entrance. The beech trees that lined the drive made an eerie tunnel above the car, their branches twining together like Paddy's outstretched hands.

Paris stopped on the gravel forecourt, filled with a desperate need to be safe within the confines of Derry's arms. His jeep was abandoned beside the steps that led up to the front door. She stumbled from the car. The night air was scented with the smell of the gardens, the early spring flowers, mixed with the odour of the stables, wafting gently on the night breeze. She ran up the steps and, not bothering to knock, shoved open the huge front door. Voices were coming from the lounge.

She walked swiftly down the corridor, beneath the scowling gaze of half a dozen portraits of Derry's ancestors. The huge chandelier above her swayed gently in the breeze from the open door. Following the sound of voices she went towards the lounge and pushed open the door.

Derry lolled against the fireplace, glass in hand. Behind him roared a huge fire, which cast red lights and flickering shadows into the darkened room. On the squashy leather sofa sat Valerie Johnson and her husband. David was obviously very drunk and lay slumped against the arm of the sofa, his head back. The stunned silence that had accompanied Paris's entrance was broken by a loud and contented snore which reverberated from David Johnson's mouth. Valerie glared open-mouthed at her as if wondering at her audacity in barging into their gathering.

"Hi," Paris smiled weakly, clutching the door handle.

"Paris," said Derry smoothly straightening up and putting his glass down firmly on the fireplace. He looked at her in askance, amusement at her obvious discomfort dancing in his eyes. "How good to see you," he said, his voice icily polite, "but we are just going out to dinner."

"I …" she said hesitantly. "I just needed to see you for a moment." Why on earth had she been so impulsive? She should have stayed and sorted Paddy out, rather than running to Derry like a child with a cut knee. But she was here now; she would tell him the news and go home. They could make plans for their future tomorrow. He came towards her, the same polite smile fixed firmly on his face. "Excuse us, please, Valerie," he said crossing the ancient Persian rug with the grace of a cat as it closes in for the kill. He seized Paris's arm and propelled her into his office.

"I'm sorry," Paris stammered as he closed the door behind them.

Derry shrugged and smiled coldly. "What did you want of me all of a sudden when you couldn't be bothered with me any other time?" Derry drew back the long silk curtains over the tall windows, looking briefly out into the darkness as he did so. Wearily he sat down at the enormous heavy wooden desk that stood in the window alcove.

"Dad's gambled Redwood Grange away. Ollie Molloy has taken it over." The words tumbled from her mouth in an unstoppable torrent. Hot tears spilt down her cheeks and splashed onto the leather top of his desk. The need to be in his arms was unbearable.

Derry came from behind the desk and enfolded her in his embrace. "I heard that was about to happen. Molloy was bragging at the races how much money your father owed him."

"He came tonight and said we had a month to get out," she wailed, burying her face in his shirtfront.

Derry sighed and prised her arms from around his neck. "Paddy has been very stupid." He shook his head wearily. Then he led her gently to the high-winged chair beside his desk. "Paris, sit down, there's something I need to tell you."

She sat down heavily, dabbing her eyes with the large cotton handkerchief that he handed her. Derry was wonderful. He was going to suggest that they brought the marriage forwards, marry quickly, and then she could move into Westwood Park with him. Leave the stupid Paddy to his own fate.

"And so you see I just can't continue. I really, really loved you, but not how you are now. I ..."

"What did you say?" Paris had been so deep in her own thoughts that she hadn't heard a word that he had said.

Derry reached across the desk and picked up a pen, which he twirled absently between his fingers. "I said that I couldn't continue with our relationship. I'm sorry that I'm telling you now, but there's no point in dragging our dead relationship on just because you've had a nasty shock."

Paris felt the world stop. "Why?" Dead? What did he mean? Her mind groped to understand.

"Because," he said, his eyes seeking hers, the corners of his wide mouth pulled down tightly – the mouth that she loved to kiss, the mouth that she could no longer kiss, that was now denied to her, "you have changed .....since the accident. You aren't the girl I loved so much. And I don't want to be with the person that you have let yourself become. My Paris was amazing, brave, carefree ..." His voice trailed away, his eyes roving around the room, not able to look at her.

"Derry," she pleaded, "I need you."

The door opened. Valerie poked her head around the door, "Derry," she smiled. There was lipstick on one of her teeth; Paris was amazed that she could still notice small things like that. "We must go. They won't hold the table all night."

Paris stared at the floor. There was a paperclip beside the table leg. She heard the chair creak as Derry got to his feet. He moved towards her. She looked at his brightly polished brown brogues. There was a smear of mud across one of the toes. She could smell his aftershave. His hand fell onto her shoulder briefly. "I'm sorry, Paris." Then his hand was gone. "Keep the ring. I don't want it. It will only remind me of what we had and lost," he said bitterly. The door closed. He was gone. She could still feel the weight of his hand on her shoulder.

CHAPTER TWELVE

Merrianne heaved her bags out of the taxi and watched it drive away until it was lost from sight, disappearing around a bend in the narrow tree-lined lane. "Brilliant," she muttered wryly. Two years spent working for Paris and now she was back home again. Two years since she had moved back home when Jenny Lynch had thrown her out when she had discovered Merrianne and her husband in a rather embarrassing situation in the stable of the Punchestown favourite. Now she was back again. Back to square one. She was two years older and had progressed absolutely nowhere. No husband, no boyfriend, and now, that Redwood Stables had closed down - not even a job. Thank you Paris.

She opened the wrought-iron gate. It was still as rusty as it had been two years ago. If she had progressed nowhere it was patently obvious that neither had her mother. Picking up her bags, Merrianne marched down the path towards the house. A gambolling pack of diminutive terrier puppies darted out of a shed, yapping furiously. One seized the back of her jeans with tiny needle-like teeth and clung on as if its life depended upon it. "Oh God," Merrianne sighed, "what a dump!"

The house, a tumbledown stone farmhouse lurked in the middle of an apple orchard and what to the uninitiated would appear to be a scrapyard. Tumbledown sheds, covered in ivy and nettles which held them together, housed a veritable zoo of assorted ferrets, puppies, and ducks. An enormous hairy, pink pig was housed in the remains of an old van; her long snout appeared now, peering out of the cracked windscreen, flapping her long ears as she squinted though pink eyes with great interest at Merrianne.

Merrianne shuddered in disgust. Every time she was forced to return to the Hippy Hovel, as she thought of her mother's home, she remembered vividly why she had left it in the first place. At least being here would make her get another job quickly – anything not to have to stay here.

The front door, which had originally been painted green, was covered in scratches where years' worth of dogs had clawed at the woodwork in their attempts to get let in to the warmth of the kitchen. Merrianne fumbled in her bag for her key. Finally she unearthed it and let herself into the house. The door opened straight into the kitchen. The red-tiled floor was filthy and covered in muddy dog paw-prints. Ancient pine furniture creaked beneath the weight of the dust and junk that was piled on it. Merrianne shoved her bags into the lounge. Shula, her mother, obviously was not home. She would take her bags upstairs and then come down to wait for her. She was probably off painting a mural on someone's wall. The lounge assaulted her eyes with the riot of colours that sprang out from every surface. Shula's prized collection of china plates and ornaments crowded on every available surface, hung from the walls and were propped up on the dresser. Shula's taste was exotic, fake leopardskin cushions clashing horrendously with Indian fabric curtains left over from Shula's hippy pot-smoking days when Merrianne was a baby. "Oh mother!" winced Merrianne looking with increasing horror at the room. How could she ever feel relaxed in something like this?

"Whaaa?" yelled a startled male voice from the lounge. A young man scrambled to his feet from the depths of the grimy sofa. "What the fuck do you want?" he exploded, glaring at Merrianne.

"I live here," she snapped glaring at the tousle-haired man who she assumed was her mother's latest live-in lover. The gangly youth in the baggy jumper and ripped jeans was not much older than herself. Shula was getting worse. Her taste in men, always pretty bizarre, was really getting extreme.

"Where's Shula?" Merrianne snapped, tilting her chin and glaring down her nose at the hippy.

"I'm here!" Shula bounced into the room behind her, clutching a frail-looking terrier puppy. She flung herself at Merrianne, planting kisses on both cheeks. Her love for the exotic was painfully apparent in her clothes. She wore leopard-printed leggings and a vast Indian-style top, her long blonde hair wild and tangled. She looked about eighteen. And a cross between a tart and a tinker, thought Merrianne, pursing her lips with disapproval.

"This is Charlie," Shula announced exuberantly, releasing Merrianne and wrapping herself around the toyboy, who grinned smugly back at Merrianne. "You're back then for a while?" She put the puppy to her shoulder as if it were a baby.

Merrianne shrugged. "I guess so. Redwood Grange has closed down."

"I'll make some tea while you get settled in."

Shula turned and walked back into the kitchen, while Merrianne heaved her bags upstairs to her old bedroom. Charlie was engrossed in rolling another wafer-thin cigarette and obviously wasn't going to offer to help.

Merrianne's bedroom was at the front of the house, overlooking the gnarled apple trees and sagging sheds. She always kept the window firmly shut to keep out the eye watering odour that wafted from the pig's shack. The room was as she had left it two years before, but with dust lying thickly on the surfaces. The air smelt musty, unused. Merrianne sat down heavily on the faded pink bedspread with a sigh of utter misery.

She slept badly. All night through the thin walls of the house she could hear her mother and the dreadful Charlie, making love. The noise only highlighted her own loneliness and desperation.

She stamped downstairs in the morning. Shula, her hair tangled around her head in a blonde cloud was eating toast in a ridiculously short nightdress. She leapt to her feet and fussed over Merrianne, pouring her tea from a chipped teapot and arranging toast and a jar of revolting-looking home-made marmalade in front of her. Charlie rolled himself a cigarette and looked disgruntled.

"So?" asked Shula, sitting down and leaning across the table towards Merrianne, her unlined face turned eagerly towards her daughter. "What are your plans?"

Merrianne helped herself to a slice of toast and pulled the butter dish towards herself before the ash off Charlie's cigarette fell into it. "I need to find another job and quickly," she said, smearing butter over the toast having first surreptitiously wiped the dirty-looking knife on the edge of the tablecloth. Neither looked too clean.

Charlie perked up, delighted that he was going to be rid of the cuckoo so quickly. "I'm going to go into town and get the newspaper and have a look at the racing jobs," she said.

"I can give you a lift," Charlie said eagerly, plainly glad to have any chance to get rid of her. He shifted in his seat, looking for somewhere to stub out the thin roll-up cigarette that was now burning dangerously close to his nicotine-stained fingers. Merrianne pushed a saucer towards him before he dropped the disgusting cigarette on the floor. Shula looked lovingly at him, her eyes glazing with the memory of the previous night's cavortings.

"Great." Merrianne twisted her lips into a semblance of a smile. She could imagine nothing that she would want to do less than get into any vehicle with this disgusting creature. But if it got her into town and closer to a job she would do anything. "Haven't you had enough of the horses yet?" Shula asked, rising suddenly and beginning to clear the table ineffectively.

Merrianne glanced at her mother and then looked quickly away. Her body, although still slender, was definitely not suitable to be brandished around especially at breakfast-time in a nightdress more suitable to a toned teenager. "I love the racing scene," she lied. The racing world was a gateway to a better life. She just needed to find a nice rich man …. and there were plenty of them involved in racing.

"How long are you staying?" growled Charlie.

Shula smacked him playfully on his wiry forearm, "Charlie," she scolded, "Merrianne can stay here for as long as she wants. This is her home!"

Merrianne looked away. How could she tell her mother that she had only come here because this was the last resort? She had nowhere else to go. No money saved, of course, that she could have used to rent a flat of her own. She had no choice but to come here.

They left for town an hour later. Charlie owned a large red van. Shula and he sat in the front. Merrianne would have to go in the back. Charlie opened the back door to let Merrianne in. The whole back of the van was covered in dust and rubbish. She clambered in, bending painfully to avoid the low roof and sitting miserably on the spare tyre amidst the remnants of plastic bags, empty feed sacks and tools. He lit another of the awful cigarettes and gunned the engine into life. The back began to smell strongly of diesel, making Merrianne curl her lips up with distaste. She hoped that he drove quickly so that she could get out of here. Unfortunately he did, and she spent the journey cannoning off the sides of the van, trying vainly to keep her seat on the impossibly hard spare tyre.

Finally Charlie jerked the van to a halt in the main street of the town.

"Thanks a million," said Merrianne sarcastically when he opened the van doors to let her out. "I'll make my own way back." She shot off along the main street, quickly, wanting to put as much distance between her and the van, hoping that no one that she knew had seen her getting out of the grotty vehicle.

She bought a copy of the Irish Field and found a table in a café to read it in peace. She opened it at the jobs page and began to scan the adverts. A few moments later she came to the conclusion that there was nothing remotely suitable. Unless she wanted to be the head girl in the yard in some backwater in Scotland. Idly she stirred her cup of coffee and sipped the tepid brew. What the hell was she going to do? Depressed, she finished her coffee and left the café. Maybe she should try to ring some of the equestrian job agencies to see if they had anything on their books. There didn't seem to be any jobs in the newspaper.

She mooched along the street, gazing aimlessly in the shop windows. There was a beautiful dress in one of the clothes-shop windows, a slinky floor-length halterneck in a shocking pink. It would have looked gorgeous against her pale skin and blonde hair. If only she had the money to afford beautiful clothes like that! She wished that she had a wonderful rich boyfriend who would spoil her, so that she would never have to live with her dreadful mother and her stinking boyfriend. Never have to worry about losing her job. Never worry about money. Life was so unfair. All of the fat, ugly, spoilt women that she saw at the races, all married to wealthy, successful men. While Merrianne, gorgeous and nice, was left, poverty-stricken and alone.

Life was so unfair. Paris had Derry and she treated him like dirt and she had lost him. That served her right. Spoilt bitch. She had got her comeuppance in the end. Derry had come to his senses and finished with her, just after Ollie Molloy had taken over Redwood Grange. Merrianne had lost her job soon after, but she had the satisfaction of knowing that if she was badly off then at least Paris had lost everything too. She had been devastated when Derry had ended the relationship, pale and quivering like a leaf as she told all of the staff lined up in the tack room, that the place was closing.

"That would suit you," said a voice at her side, startling Merrianne out of her musings.

"Derry!" she exclaimed, feeling her face darken with surprise. God, she must look a mess! She hadn't even washed her hair that morning.

"Are you going to buy it?" he said, turning to admire the pink dress. "Not really my kind of thing," lied Merrianne. She was damned if she was going to tell Derry that she hadn't a penny to buy the dress even if she wanted it.

"What are you doing with yourself now that Redwood Grange has closed down?" he asked, looking Merrianne slowly up and down.

She had the feeling that she was naked beneath his penetrating gaze. "I guess I'll get another job. Eventually." She shrugged. "I'm going to relax for a while first though." There was no way that she was going to let him think that she was penniless, virtually homeless and desperate for a job. If there was one thing that she had learnt it was to never let anyone see that you were down on your luck.

"Come on. Let me buy you a drink" said Derry, gesturing towards the open doorway of a bar.

"OK," she replied, coolly. They walked across the street. "Really, there's no need you don't have to buy me a drink," she said as he held open the door for her.

"I'd like to anyway," he said, steering her towards a seat. As he walked to the bar both of the girls serving the drinks jostled with each other in the narrow space behind the bar to get to him first. He was so handsome and had such a tremendous presence that he had that effect on people. Merrianne watched him ordering the drinks. The barmaid who had lost out in the rush to be the one to serve him was gazing at him open-mouthed in naked admiration.

"So," he said, sitting down and handing her a glass of Guinness, "tell me what your plans are?"

"Well, none really," she replied, airily. "I'll live at home for a while and see what comes up."

"Uhhuhh," he nodded. "Is that OK with your parents?"

Merrianne laughed, nonchalantly. "Of course. They wouldn't care if I never worked." It wasn't really a lie. Shula wouldn't give a damn if she were begging on the street. And she had never met her father, so presumably he didn't give a damn what she did either.

She took a sip of her drink. Why the hell was she pretending?

"That's great," Derry replied, with a smile and turned the conversation to more general matters. "Ah well," he said when they had finished their drinks, "I must go." He stood up. The girls behind the bar were leaning against it, gazing at him.

"Look," he said, picking up his mobile phone, "if you decide you want a job, come and see me. I always thought what good work you did for Paris. It's a shame you aren't looking for a job."

CHAPTER THIRTEEN

They never slept. She was sure of it now. Shula and her toy-boy lover were still fucking in the room beside her. Merrianne lay awake, staring at the shadows from the apple trees on her ceiling, listening to the frenzied creaking of the bed next door and her mother's moans of pleasure. This was getting ridiculous. Every night since she had been here they had kept her awake listening to their noise. She was exhausted. How could they keep going?

She started as Charlie clattered down the uncarpeted stairs in his boots. Dawn was breaking, thrusting pale light into her room. She must have slept for a few hours when the house finally went silent. Outside the animals began a fierce clamouring as Charlie opened the front door, the warped wood screeching with protest as he dragged it over the stone-flagged doorstep.

Merrianne buried her head under her pillow, longing to go back to sleep.

The puppies began to yap. The ear-piercing din was too much, she would never be able to go back to sleep now. Merrianne scrambled grumpily from her bed; hopefully today would see the end of this hell. She was going to go to the races and talk to Derry about the job that he had mentioned. Why the hell had she pretended that she didn't need a job? Why had she told him that she had only been working for Paris for something to do? As if she was some society heiress? Why had she implied that her parents would love her to be at home as long as she wanted? That she had no need to work? Idiot! She had cursed herself silently for days now, since she had met with

Derry. She should have asked him for a job the day he had bought her a drink. Now, though, she knew that he would be at the races. That would be the ideal opportunity to pretend to bump into him and then manage to manoeuvre the conversation around to his offer of a job. Maybe this time tomorrow she would be on the way to Westwood Park to work for him.

She bathed, washed her hair and dressed carefully in a suit that Paris had once discarded. The beige wool jacket and long wrap-over skirt suited her pale complexion and blonde hair and showed off her figure. When she walked the skirt flapped open to reveal a long expanse of toned leg, which she liked. Merrianne admired her reflection in the mirror. She looked as good as any of the rich bitches that she had to be nice to in the parade ring. She went downstairs to the accompaniment of a loud wolf whistle from her mother.

"Look at you!" said Shula approvingly. "Doesn't she look great?" She nudged Charlie who nodded obediently. He just wanted Merrianne to go away again. His idea of a love nest was not one where he had to share his woman with her daughter, especially one who wasn't much younger than he was.

Unwillingly, Merrianne hitched a ride in the van to the races. Shula and Charlie were off to sell some of his awful pottery at a street market in Galway. She scrambled out of the back of the van, looking around furtively, hoping that no one she knew would see her. She marched away from the van trying to pretend that it was nothing to do with her, until to her enormous annoyance Shula reached across and honked loudly on the horn as they passed her on the lane. An elderly couple were walking into the race in front of her, and they jumped off the road in alarm. The elderly man looked at Merrianne askance. Merrianne raised her eyes skywards and tutted disapprovingly. "No consideration," she snapped, hoping that the couple hadn't seen her getting out of the van.

She bought a race card and made her way into the race course. Although the sun shone, there was a biting wind cutting across the tarmac of the concourse, blowing discarded betting slips like autumn leaves. She found an empty seat beside one of the bars and sat to study the programme. Derry had a horse running in the third race. She decided that she would make herself seen while he was in the parade ring. Hopefully then she would get the chance to talk to him later on.

As the horses came in from the second race, steaming and filthy, veins standing up on their sweat-drenched coats like roads on a map, she wandered nonchalantly across to the parade ring. She must be cool, pretend that she just happened to meet him. Derry was in the parade ring, watching his horse being led around, with the owners, a self-satisfied-looking man with a much, much younger woman on his arm, who periodically looked at him and giggled coyly and then slyly looked back at Derry. Derry glanced in Merrianne's direction and she waved hopefully, but Derry did not respond.

The bell rang and the horses were led into the centre of the ring. Derry legged his jockey deftly up onto the back of the dancing grey horse. The young bimbo giggled in Derry's direction and he looked down at her with an indulgent smile. They were walking in her direction. Merrianne dived away from the rail and barged her way through the crowds until she reached the entrance to the parade ring. Derry and his companions would come through there in a few moments. Merrianne shoved an old lady out of the way.

"Really," the old lady scowled, pursing her mouth into the tight shape of a cat's bottom.

"Hi, Derry," Merrianne grinned as Derry passed her.

"Oh hello," he said, distantly, looking at her uncomprehendingly.

Merrianne felt a hot flush creep over her cheeks. Damn, he hadn't even known who she was! She stood there smarting with shame. She had missed her chance. She should have told him that she wanted a job the other day when he had bought her a drink. The crowds melted away from the white rail. Merrianne felt the old lady dig her maliciously in the ribs with a bony elbow as she turned. She followed the crowd miserably and found a space to watch the races. In the stands she could see Derry gazing through his binoculars, watching the race intently.

Merrianne tore her gaze away from Derry and tried to concentrate on the race. Derry's grey horse, So Soon, was the favourite. Far in the distance she saw the starter's flag flutter downwards and the race began. The grey horse loped along in the middle of the runners. As the race thundered past the stands the roar of encouragement from the crowds rang out. Merrianne felt herself turning to stare at Derry's profile. He really was gorgeous – Paris was a fool to let him go. So Soon came to life as the horses turned towards the stands again. He put in a magnificent jump at the last fence and thundered over the line five lengths ahead of the other horses. When Merrianne turned to the stands Derry had gone. Then she caught a glimpse of his dark hair as he weaved through the crowds to the Winner's Enclosure. Merrianne walked slowly after the crowds that were rushing to catch a glimpse of the victorious horse. What was the use? Derry wasn't going to talk to her. This had been a complete waste of time.

So Soon stood proudly in the winner's spot, his head nodding up and down, pushing with delight at his grinning groom, who kept covering his mud-splattered face with kisses. The photographers lined everyone up for photos and then the horse was led away.

Merrianne froze. Derry was coming towards her.

"Sorry I couldn't talk to you earlier," he grinned, delighted with his victory.

"That's OK," she smiled, trying to be nonchalant beneath the red blush that she was sure must be staining her cheeks. Perhaps he would think the wind had brought out her colour. "Well done!"

"Thanks," he said. "Do you want to join us for a glass of champagne?" Merrianne hesitated. It wouldn't do to appear too eager.

"Lovely," she smiled politely and then let him take her arm as they walked to the owner's and trainer's bar.

The owner's and trainer's bar was crowded and hummed with the noise of drunken revelry.

"This is Merrianne," Derry said, introducing her to the couple whose horse had just won the last race. "Vincent and Lucy Potterhill." He caught the eye of a harassed-looking barman. A large bottle of champagne was produced. Derry popped it open expertly and filled the glasses that the barman had lined up. "To So Soon!" he toasted the horse.

Lucy giggled approvingly and downed most of the glass of her champagne.

Merrianne took a deep gulp of the icy liquid, gasping as the bubbles exploded on her tongue. "Lovely, isn't it," Lucy said, smacking her lips and holding out her glass for Derry to refill.

"Come on, drink up," he said, waving the bottle in Merrianne's direction.

"Congratulations, Lucy!" bellowed a whiskery-faced old lady, shoving through the crowd to enfold Lucy in her arms.

"That was a good win," Merrianne said to Derry as Lucy and Vincent drifted away with the whiskery lady.

"Thanks." He tipped more champagne into his glass and then into hers.

The pale liquid spilled over the rim of the glass and cascaded over her fingers. She put the glass down on the bar and shook her hand.

Derry seized her hand and gently licked her fingers. "Shame to waste it," he said softly, his eyes boring into hers. Merrianne felt her stomach lurch. He was gorgeous. For a long moment she thought that he was going to kiss her, but then the moment passed. "I have another horse running in a while," he said, suddenly, breaking the heady tension that was zinging between them. "Do you want to come and watch it?"

Merrianne followed him out into the stalls where the horses were being saddled. Her head was spinning with the closeness of Derry and the heady champagne. What had happened back there?

Back at work Derry was coldly efficient – admonishing the groom for not being quick enough and then not holding the horse still while he saddled it. Merrianne leant against the wooden side of the stall, enjoying being able to watch rather than having to work on the horse. Normally she would have been the one putting on the saddle under the watchful eye of a tense Paris, who would be firing off a tirade of abuse if anything went wrong.

"I would rather be in bed with you," Derry hissed as they followed the horse into the parade ring.

Merrianne felt her heart begin to pound. She should talk to him about a job. But he was gorgeous. She could imagine how his mouth would feel on hers. It had been the most erotic thing she had ever experienced when he had licked the champagne from her fingers. She could imagine that he would be the most expert lover. Hazy from the champagne she wondered how the muscles of his back would feel, and what it would be like to be entangled within the hard muscles of his thighs.

The horses went onto the race track. "We'll watch from over here," said Derry, strolling towards the white rail that marked the edge of the race track. Spectators crowded around them, jostling forwards for a good spot to see the race.

Merrianne leant against the rail. The horses were cantering down to the start. She felt Derry slide his hand around her front and cup her breast. His lips nibbled deliciously on her neck and ear. The race started. She felt her skirt lifted gently from behind, the cool wind caressing her legs as his hand slid between her legs and inside her knickers. "So wet," he whispered huskily in her ear as his finger slid inside her. Merrianne leant back against his chest. She should move away, tell him to stop, but in the heady haze of the champagne the feeling was too delicious to stop. As his expert fingers moved deliciously over the throbbing bud of her clitoris Merrianne gripped the rail tighter to stop herself falling as the waves of pleasure began to grow somewhere deep within her. As Derry's horse thundered over the finishing line the waves of a delicious climax washed over her. "Yeeeesss!" she shrieked in triumph.

CHAPTER FOURTEEN

Merrianne leapt out of bed like a scalded cat. Derry lay sprawled across the crumpled sheets fast asleep, his face as innocent as a child's. She sat down again abruptly as pain seared through her head. A wave of nausea swept through her from what had to be her worst hangover ever. The bedclothes were rumpled, strewn across the massive four-poster bed. She winced, vaguely recalling the owners' and trainers' bar, emptying as they partied. Then sweeping along the dark lanes in Derry's car. Then an even hazier recollection of firelight and romping bawdily on a carpet. Firelight flickering on bodies, her own loud demanding cries of pleasure. Oh shit. What a tramp she was. Worse than her mother. She had to get out of here. Before Derry woke and found her here.

What a fool she had made of herself! Pretending that her parents were wealthy. Pretending that she had just gone to the races on a whim. Pretending that she didn't need a job. And how easily she had let him have sex with her. What a stupid, cheap tart he must think her. Merrianne ran a distracted hand over her face. Her skin felt as dry and rough as sandpaper; there was an awful taste in her mouth; stars danced lazily in front of her eyes. Derry stirred, stretching in his sleep with the languid grace of an athlete, his long arm reaching across the bed as if seeking her body.

Merrianne froze, not wanting to betray her presence. She had to go before he woke fully and found her there. What on earth would she say to him? Hi, thanks for the sex. Can I have a job, please? I don't usually have sex with my employers. Ha! What a joke! Jamie Lynch and before that … she didn't even want to think about it. She had messed up again.

She heaved herself off the bed, her feet landing on a thick, soft deep burgundy carpet. Two empty cut-glass champagne flutes lay upended beside the bed, leaning drunkenly against a pile of Thoroughbred sales catalogues. A quick glance around the room confirmed her worst fears. Her clothes were nowhere to be seen. A man's blue shirt, the tropical sea colour of Derry's eyes was draped across the dark wood of an elaborately carved dressing-table. She darted across to it and wriggled the still buttoned shirt over her head.

Merrianne darted to the bedroom door and then paused, looking back at Derry regretfully. He was beautiful, his tanned, muscular body outlined beneath the sheets. How many women had cavorted in the bed with him, how many had admired the heavy carved posts that guarded the four corners of the bed, like sentries minding their master? How many had fingered the heavy silk damask drapes and admired the view over the parkland from the tall bedroom window? Before Paris there had been dozens, hundreds maybe, all flocking to be fucked by Ireland's champion jockey. Silently cursing her own stupidity, Merrianne turned, pulling the door gently shut behind her.

She found herself in a long, bright hall. Light flooded in from a tall window that looked out over the parkland. She could see mares and foals grazing in a well-tended timber fenced paddock in front of the house. Two of the foals were play-fighting, rearing up at each other, long spindly legs raking at the air, before racing away, revelling in their speed and power while their mothers watched their offspring anxiously. Oil paintings of racehorses and hunting scenes jostled for space against the white wood panelling of the stairs, hung on long chains from a rail that ran around the ceiling. The stairs curved gently down into a hall, and down there somewhere were her clothes.

Clutching her head in an attempt to lessen the pounding, Merrianne padded softly down the stairs, her feet soundless on the thick blue carpet. She reached the bottom of the stairs and stopped, stunned by the sumptuous beauty of the house. Stern portraits of what she assumed were Derry's ancestors scowled down at her from the walls. "Where are my clothes? And where are the aspirin?" she hissed quietly at the sombre portrait of a dark-haired man, who so closely resembled Derry that it could have been his reflection in a mirror. The portrait regarded her solemnly. Only its eyes twinkled with mischief.

A tiled hallway led into the depths of the house. Merrianne gingerly inched forward, pulling the shirt down further over her bottom. A door stood half open; inside she could see the relics of the previous evening. Her clothes trailed over a deep gold damask sofa and over the Persian rug in front of the grey embers of the fire. Cold like me, she thought, darting thankfully into the room and pulling on her clothes. Gold velvet curtains were still drawn firmly over the windows, casting an eerie pale light into the room. A bottle of wine lay on its side, a stain of spilt liquid spreading over the myriad colours of the ancient rug.

Merrianne scanned the room. She needed a telephone, and quickly. She would telephone for a taxi to meet her at the end of the drive. Go home. Pretend that this had never happened. Find a job far away and never look back. And never, ever get drunk again. Clutching her shoes in her hand, she went back into the hall and began to open doors, searching desperately for a telephone. Yet even with her head pounding and her stomach churning, Merrianne savoured the richness and beauty of the house. What must it be like to live somewhere like this? To wake every morning and know without doubt that all of this belonged to you.

Sighing with relief, she found what must be Derry's office. A telephone sat in the middle of an enormous desk strewn with papers and books. She shut the door behind her and leant on it, weak with relief. Soon she would be out of here, dashing down the drive to the taxi that would take her home.

Merrianne pulled out the enormous leather-backed chair, sat down at Derry's desk and pulled the telephone towards her. The room was lined with dark wood, masculine and expensive-looking, with luxurious leather chairs and heavy wooden furniture laid out beneath paintings and photographs of Derry holding enormous silver cups beside grinning owners and steaming racehorses. Outside through the tall window she could see the gravel forecourt in front of the house. Derry's sports car stood at a rakish angle, abandoned close to the pale cream of the stone steps that led to the front door. As she punched the first number of the taxi firm into the phone, the door swung open. Merrianne started with embarrassment.

She felt a sigh of relief escape from her frozen lips as the wrinkled face of an elderly lady poked around the door. Merrianne paused guiltily as the woman came into the room.

"Good morning," said the crone, with more than a hint of sarcasm in her voice. She padded across the carpet on legs knotted with varicose veins like a gnarled oak-tree, clad in thick flesh-coloured tights that dangled beneath a shapeless black dress. Mrs McDonagh had looked after the house since Derry had been a little boy. She had seen an endless procession of women draped in various stages of undress around the house. But she had loved Paris, who had always fussed over her, thanking her for any kindness, making sure that she felt appreciated. The beautiful, feisty girl had tamed the wildness in Derry, with her love and great courage, and now he had dumped her when she needed him. Mrs McDonagh would never accept anyone else coming in to take her place, especially the endless line of tarts that Derry had always attracted. She reached the edge of the desk and leant down towards Merrianne. There was an unmistakable odour of sherry on her breath as she spoke. "Could I get you some coffee?" she said, her voice thick with sarcasm.

Merrianne opened her mouth to explain what she was doing, but instead could only nod. "Yes, thank you. That would be nice."

The woman nodded her head slowly as if she were going to say something and then decided against it. She backed away, slipper-clad feet shuffling on the carpet.

Merrianne watched as the door closed softly behind her and then grabbed the phone and began to punch in the numbers. The sooner she was out of here the better. And she certainly was not going to wait for the coffee. She drummed her fingers against the tooled leather of the desk as the telephone connected. "Jesus, will you hurry up," she pleaded, listening to the telephone. Suddenly it was answered. "Any Time Taxis?"

"I need a taxi immediately, Westwood Park, the end of the drive," spat Merrianne into the receiver.

The taxi ordered, Merrianne leapt from the seat, wincing as the pain shot through her eyeballs, and dashed out of the house. As the door slammed behind her Mrs McDonagh shuffled up the corridor with the coffee. The gale from the slamming of the door ruffled the lace cloth on the tray that she carried.

"Not staying then?" she muttered, diverting her route from Derry's office to his bedroom. She may as well take him the unwanted coffee, save her a trip later.

Merrianne ran down the steps and marched across the gravel forecourt. The fresh air made her feel better, clearing some of the pain from her head and making her feel less nauseous. Her footsteps crunched loudly on the gravel. She pulled a face in horror – the sound was so loud that surely she would wake Derry. She hurried on, imagining at any second that he would open the window and bellow at her to come back. Once through a set of stone pillars and a low stone wall that marked the forecourt of the house, the gravel gave way to a long tarmac drive. She jogged away, guiltily as a thief stealing away into the night.

The drive turned through a line of tall beech trees bordered by rhododendron bushes. Gasping for breath Merrianne slowed; she was hidden from view now. Safe. Thank goodness that she had got away before Derry had found her. She shuddered at the thought. How embarrassing to wake with him in the morning! How cheap and tarty he must think her! Letting him do whatever he wanted. She felt sick at the thought.

Then she stopped. There was a small gap in the satin sheen of the bushy rhododendrons, through which she could see the house. She froze, stunned to immobility by the beauty of it. The tall, red-brick house was the colour of a damp fox. Ivy, wisteria and winter jasmine draped themselves over the sloping structures of the walls and roof, hiding the house like a shy girl covering herself in a intricate lace shawl.

Tearing herself unwillingly away from drinking in the timeless beauty of the house, Merrianne walked down the grassy verge of the tree-lined drive. The tarmac was marked with countless hoofprints from the horses that were ridden up and down it every day. Sheltered by the tall trees, the drive was so peaceful that she longed to lie down on the springy turf and sleep again. The taxi was waiting at the end of the drive. Merrianne pulled the door open and leapt in. As she gave him her home address she caught sight of herself in his rear-view mirror, her eyes lined with smeared mascara, her hair tousled from being sprawled on the carpet in the fireside romp. How many women had he picked up from Westwood Park in such a dishevelled state, she wondered bleakly, rubbing furtively at her eyes with a spit-dampened tissue. What was she supposed to do now?

CHAPTER FIFTEEN

Charlie was clipping the claws of one of his terriers on the table as she went into the house. "Back then?" he said, screwing up his dark monkey face with the effort as he gripped the wriggling terrier with one hand and the nail-clippers in the other.

"Looks like it," snapped Merrianne, slamming the door shut and leaning against it in relief to have got away from Westwood Park before Derry woke. She would never drink again. Ever. The unbearable pain in her head had subsided to a dull throbbing behind her eyes. How she longed for some quiet where she could get her thoughts back in order and put everything in perspective!

Shula drifted by in paint-stained overalls, holding a painting of a jumble of shapes in hideous shades of orange. "Hi Merrianne, did you have a good time at the races?" she asked absently. When she was working Shula's mind drifted – Merrianne could have been away for a week and she wouldn't have noticed.

"Great," snapped Merrianne, cursing Paris and Paddy for the thousandth time for losing Redwood Grange and putting her out of a job. How the hell was she supposed to cope with living with this pair? Shula propped the picture against the overflowing washing basket that she had abandoned on the kitchen table. "What do you think?" she mused, stepping back to admire her creation.

Charlie released the terrier which leapt exuberantly from the table and disappeared under the china-laden pine dresser, where its growls of annoyance could be heard echoing on the slate floor. "S'nice," he grunted, tilting his head to look critically at the mishmash of colour.

The telephone rang beside Merrianne and she snatched it up.

"Where did you go? I woke up and you had gone." Derry's voice was silky smooth in her ear.

Merrianne threw the receiver down as if it was red hot. She couldn't talk to him now, not after last night. What an awful cheap tart he must think she was, just to go to bed with him on the strength of a few glasses of champagne. She cringed as she remembered scrawling her telephone number on his race card, drunkenly demanding that he should ring her.

"Who was that?" asked Shula, turning the picture so she could admire it from another angle.

"Wrong number," snarled Merrianne, diving upstairs to the sanctuary of the bathroom. She stripped out of her much-loved racing suit. The horrendous memory of her skirt being lifted mingled with the plaintive memory of how gorgeous it was. How could she have let him do *that*? And worse still, how could she have enjoyed it? Oh Christ! She ran the bath and sank into the scalding water, scrubbing her body as if she could purge the memory of the feeling of his hands roving over her body and his lips moving so tenderly against hers.

By the time the water had gone stone cold she felt better. She had made the most dreadful fool of herself, but it was over now. Now she just had to pick herself up and get on with things. Yet again. She let the water out, feeling the icy tendrils of wetness trickle down her shoulders and legs as she lay, still sprawled there as it sucked down the drain. Then heaving herself out, she scrubbed herself dry on one of her mother's rough towels, the fabric scratchy against her damp skin. Finally after rubbing body lotion over herself she dressed. Then froze, still as a fox that hears the hunting horn in the distance, watchful and afraid as the telephone began to ring again.

"Merrianne!" Shula screeched from the bottom of the stairs. "Derry Blake on the phone for you!"

Damn, Merrianne thought, clenching her teeth together in tension. Why hadn't she left the receiver off the hook? Why the hell had he rung her? She never wanted to face him again. She had blown her chance of a job, exposed herself as a cheap bimbo.

Merrianne plodded furiously downstairs. Shula had left the receiver on the table beside the phone.

"Hello," Merrianne snapped crossly into the mouthpiece.

"I woke up and you had gone. I rang you and you slammed the phone down on me," Derry said petulantly.

Merrianne glanced at her reflection in the mirror, eyes flashing with temper, her mouth clamped in a hard, bitter line. "I….. I had things to do," she said, lamely. She just wanted to get rid of him, she couldn't stand it if he assumed that she was just a cheap lay.

"What could have been better than spending the morning in bed with me?" he replied, softly, his voice in her ear was like smooth, warm chocolate sliding across ice cream. For Derry the morning had been a revelation. Used to having to prise stray women out of his bed by force, to find that one had gone before he woke was a new experience. And not one that he had enjoyed. He missed Paris desperately, but he could not cope with her when she became needy and insecure. A replacement was needed urgently to restore the status quo in his life. And Merrianne had been a good-looking, pleasant, obliging candidate for the role. And once Derry had shone his light on a fortunate individual, he did not like the thought that she would not want to bask in its glory.

Merrianne felt her will begin to crumble. "I'm sorry, it was rude of me to clear off like that, but I …" She clamped her hand around the receiver to stop it from trembling so much. Just talking to him was turning her to jelly.

"Look," he said, decisively, "I enjoyed being with you yesterday – have dinner with me tonight."

She sat down heavily on the bottom stair. "OK." The words came out as if they were being wrenched from the depths of her soul. Why was she going out with him again? He was just using her for sex. That was what Derry Blake was all about. He would drop her like a hot brick once he had fucked her enough to get her out of his system and then where would she be? Lovelorn and jobless again.

Six hours later she was sitting at the bottom of the stairs again. This time dressed in a plain black skirt and long-sleeved T-shirt with a silvery grey jacket over the top. In spite of her earlier reactions, she was now utterly exhilarated to be asked out with him again.

An hour later she realised that he wasn't coming. Disappointment sat bitterly on her shoulders. A heavy tear slid down her cheek and splashed on her handbag which she was clutching on her knees. Why the hell had she let herself get so wound up about him? Derry Blake was just an out-and-out bastard! Everyone knew that. Paris had tamed him alright, so they said, but they had all wondered how long she would keep him. He had obviously changed his mind about taking her out again. The telephone rang, loud in the silent house. Merrianne leapt to her feet to answer it and then paused, looking at it, waiting; she wasn't going to give him the satisfaction of knowing that she was waiting for him.

Then she picked it up.

"Merrianne?" It was Derry; he sounded vague and breathless.

"Yes?" she managed to make her voice sound as if she hadn't a clue who he was. "I'm so sorry, problems with a mare," he explained.

She could hear the sounds of the stable yard in the background. He was probably ringing from the tack room. "I'll pick you up in a while – we can have some supper here."

Something snapped inside her. That was his game. He was going to pick her up, take her back to Westwood Park. Sex and then home again. Just to satisfy his needs. "No thanks. I'm doing something else now," she said firmly and slammed the phone down. She leant her forehead against the hall mirror, the glass cool against her burning forehead. How had she let him get under her skin so easily? She had promised herself that it wouldn't happen again. She was not going to be hurt again. Men always wanted to use her for sex. But not any more. Not after Jamie Lynch; she had learnt a hard lesson there.

The telephone shrilled again. Merrianne sat at the bottom of the stairs listening to the insistent noise echoing around the hall. Suddenly the lounge door was flung open and Charlie burst out. "For fuck's sake, answer the bloody thing, can't you! I'm trying to watch bloody football!" He slammed the door so hard that the pile of unopened envelopes piled on the table beside the telephone fluttered to the floor.

"Fuck off, prick," snapped Merrianne leaping to her feet and snatching the receiver. "Hello," she said coldly.

"Please don't put the phone down again," Derry said.

Merrianne felt her knuckles whiten as she clutched the telephone, every instinct wanting to slam it down again to sever the connection, but somehow she knew that Derry wasn't going to be deterred once he had made his mind up about something.

"I won't." He might be making her talk to him, but there was no way that she was going to make it easy for him. "Look, I'm really sorry about earlier on – please come out with me another night, let me make it up to you."

Merrianne shook her head wryly. Derry really didn't like a woman turning him down. This was obviously a new experience to him. How incredible it would be to have Derry really want to be with you! How annoyed that bitch Paris would be if she started a relationship with Derry! And what if Derry fell head over heels in love with her? That would really serve Paris right for being a spoilt madam who always had everything she wanted! What a delicious revenge, thought Merrianne looking at her reflection in the hall mirror. Her eyes shone with mischief.

"OK," she willed herself to say unenthusiastically. "Some other night."

"Tommorrow? I'll book us a table at Ruby's."

Merrianne felt her jaw sag. Ruby's. One of the most exclusive restaurants in the district. "Tomorrow …" she pondered. What on earth was she going to wear to go to Ruby's? "I can't make it tomorrow. How about the next night?"

"Perfect," said Derry. "I'll pick you up."

"I'll meet you there," Merrianne said firmly. There was no way that she was going to let Derry come to her mother's hovel. One look at Shula and he would run a mile. She was better sticking to her story about the rather more glamorous family. "Eight o'clock." She replaced the receiver without waiting for a reply. She ran a shaking hand across her clammy forehead. Derry really was keen.

From his reaction to her rejection of him, he obviously didn't like to be turned down. He wouldn't be used to having to do all the running when trying to get a girl. He was used to the girls falling all over themselves to get to him. Merrianne felt a delicious surge of power. She might have made one mistake, but now she was in control. Derry was going to have to do the running. She was going to drive him mad. He was going to have to work hard to get her this time. The reflection in the mirror tilted its chin proudly. This time she was going to be the winner.

CHAPTER SIXTEEN

"How The Mighty Are Fallen," muttered Paris miserably, reading the headlines of the newspaper. It's All Over was emblazoned in huge letters across the sporting pages. She read on, taking in the lurid details that the press had gleaned: the near-fatal fall which had all been through her bad riding, how she had lost her nerve and would never ride again, how Derry had dumped her, sick of temper tantrums and rows, how Redwood Grange had been lost through bad business and owners not being happy with the yard. She read on. Paddy's own fall from grace was brutally portrayed. They had once portrayed him as an enthusiastic and sociable party animal who was famous for his betting successes. Now he was portrayed as a pathetic drunk whose wife had left him for a jockey. A few short weeks ago they had been writing of her successes, the great, fearless rider that she was, and the wonderful yard that she ran. Now it seemed they couldn't wait to tear down the icon they had created.

There was a photograph with the article. Herself and Derry, laughing gaily in each other's arms, The Rosenberry Cup between them, which she had won on his horse, Hunter's Moon. How distant those days seemed! And how she missed him! If only she could feel his arms around her once more! The pain of her loss was dreadful; sapped of all her strength she drifted from day to day, cast on a surging sea of emotion. Sometimes she woke and it felt as if it was all a dream; that she would find that she was the old Paris, proud and fearless, in love with Derry, successful and happy. Then with a jolt she would remember. Derry had dumped her. He didn't want her any more. She was a coward and he couldn't love her any longer.

Now she could only look on as a stunned spectator, as Redwood Grange and the stables were dismantled around her. The furniture was loaded gradually onto the horse lorry and moved to Blackbird Farm, ready for when they finally moved there. The horses had gone to different trainers, or had been sold, all except Joe McHugh's horses. He had refused to move them and had said firmly that he was sticking with Paris and Paddy and that they must train the horses from Blackbird Stables. Paris had shrugged, beyond caring about anything anymore. There were no facilities to train horses at the farm, just ramshackle stables and a few fields. Joe was being a fool, but she no longer cared.

The staff had gone as the horses were moved. Walking away impassively, already discussing new jobs, new lives. Merrianne had gone too, livid at having to go back to her mother's house. She had barely said goodbye when she had left, scrambling hastily into a taxi and being driven away without even a backwards glance. Only Paris and Paddy remained to supervise the moving and dismantling, with the disgruntled Eddie grumbling all the time about unruly removals men and how untidy the yard was. Eddie had refused to leave them until they were gone from Redwood Grange. Paris felt that in reality Eddie needed the job to get him out of the house and away from Maria his nagging, miserable bitch of a wife with her wild mood swings and horrific temper.

Paris lay down the newspaper. She didn't have the energy to read it any more. She felt beyond pain, beyond the vicious barbs of the journalists. The room was full of packing boxes, all labelled with their contents, their lives packed away neatly. It was hard to imagine that soon she would not be able to sit in the sunlit window seat she loved so much, or to sleep in her bedroom, cosy and safe under the sloping eaves of the roof. Never come home again along the long paddock-lined drive, seeing the stone house, the colour of wet sand beneath a silvery grey slate roof, nestling in the splendour of the gardens, like a jewel lain in a colourful silken cloth.

She had always known that she would leave Redwood Grange one day, when she married, but had thought that it would always be there to come back to. But now, her much-loved home was gone. Lost on some ridiculous gambling spree. Soon to be the home of the Molloy's, the Family From Hell. They would walk and sit in the places that would be out of reach for her.

If it was hard to comprehend a life without Redwood Grange, it was worse to live a life without Derry. It felt as if a part of her had been ripped away, without anaesthetic, leaving a raw, festering wound. Her heart ached with the pain of losing him. Her clothes hung off her body she had lost so much weight. Her eyes, red-rimmed, ached with crying, sobs that seemed to wrench themselves from the depths of her tortured soul. Her hair hung limp and lifeless around her shoulders. A black depression left her lifeless and listless, unable to sit, unable to rest, but when she sought solace in work she was unable to concentrate. How the hell was she supposed to get through the rest of her life without him?

Paris took a cup of coffee and went outside. She sat down wearily on the stone seat in the garden. Here, hidden by its arch of honeysuckle and clematis that entwined above her head, she could sit, sheltered from the breeze, and look out over the almost deserted yard. She leant against the backrest, feeling the curved metal cool through the fabric of her T-shirt. She felt numb, wrung out, as if she had been through the spin cycle of the washing machine. Nothing seemed real any more. It was hard to grasp the reality of what was happening, watching her life being dismantled.

She watched impassively as a lorry made its way slowly up the drive, its aluminium sides glittering almost maliciously in the spring sunlight, flickering as it passed through the trees. She felt like a war victim, who has lived through the most appalling horrors and can feel nothing more. Draining her coffee cup, she stood up and pasting a smile of welcome on her face walked through the garden and out into the yard as the lorry pulled to a halt with an aggressive hiss of its airbrakes. The cab door was flung open and a small man, with a face like a constipated monkey, scrambled out.

"Awight, darlin'," he said in an ear-grating London accent, "I've come for two brood mares, Duchess and Strawberry Shortcake." He fished in the pocket of his baggy jeans and produced a crumpled piece of paper, which he shoved into her unwilling hand. The man barely reached her shoulders. His jeans looked as if they belonged to someone much wider and taller; they fell around his hips and hung in drapes around his dealer-booted ankles.

"They're over here." Paris thrust the crumpled paper into her pocket and stalked across the yard.

"Closin down, are yer?" A young thuggish-looking guy had come out of the other side of the lorry and jogged after them. His eyes darted around the yard, like a hungry rat.

"Yes." She was in no mood for pleasant conversation with these two. The thought of her two beloved brood mares being taken away by these two was killing her. They were destined for the manicured paddocks of a Kildare stud and these two men were from the horse-transport company that had been booked to deliver them to their new home.

The mares were in adjoining stables. They looked out anxiously, unused to the change of routine, seeing their companions going away and not returning.

"I've got head-collars," said the younger of the two men, swinging two grubby-looking pieces of nylon in her direction.

"Thanks." She took the head-collars and went into the first of the stables. Duchess was a tall, dark bay mare, with kind eyes and a soft beige muzzle. She whickered softly as Paris closed the stable door and nudged at her for reassurance. Paris slid the head-collar over her elegant nose and gave her neck a final rub. The old mare had been around since Paris had been a young girl. She remembered, vaguely, her winning at Cheltenham, the loud applause and pushing crowds terrifying. And then more recently, giving birth to Destiny, Paris's own mare. Paris, on her knees, filthy with blood and muck, helping to pull the foal out.

She led Duchess outside and handed her to the monkey-faced man. He looked her up and down critically, seeing only the age-dipped back and distended belly from years of producing winning foals. As she went to fetch Strawberry Shortcake he produced a pack of cigarettes with a defiant gesture. Smoking was never allowed in stables because of the fire risk. Strawberry Shortcake laid back her chestnut ears and thrust her head out in a grumpy gesture. Paris rubbed her neck, crooning softly to her, comforting the mare and telling her not to be afraid. She slipped the head-collar on and led her out.

The younger man grabbed the lead-rope from her. "Come on!" He jerked the rope to make the mare follow. "I want to get home early tonight." He pulled down the lorry ramp and began to lead the old mare up into the lorry. She placed one delicate chestnut leg on the rubber matting and then refused to go any further, a donkey-like stubbornness glinting in her eyes.

" 'old this," said his companion, chucking Duchess's rope at Paris. He fetched a long whip out of the cab of the lorry and raked it across Strawberry's shining chestnut quarters. The mare laid back her ears and lashed out with her back legs, narrowly missing one of his protruding ears. "Fuckin bitch," he roared, leaping out of the way. He slashed viciously at the mare in temper while she reared and plunged in terror at the unfamiliar rough treatment.

"Stop it!" Paris let go of Duchess's lead-rope and flung herself at the man.

"Oyyyy!" he bellowed, thrown off balance by her attack.

"Don't hit her like that!" Paris snarled, grabbing hold of the whip and wrenching it from him. "She'll go in if you just give her a minute." She took Strawberry's lead-rope from him and the mare followed her quietly into the lorry.

Duchess stood in the yard, quivering with fright.

"It's OK, girl," Paris said gently, taking hold of her rope and leading her up the ramp. The shouting and commotion had really upset the old mare. Damp patches of sweat marked the shiny hair on her neck and her flanks quivered. Paris tied the rope and, giving the mares a final pat, walked down the ramp. The two men glared angrily at her as they flung the ramp into place and stalked into the cab.

The lorry pulled away, then there was an almighty bang from the back. The lorry jerked to a halt and the men jumped out.

"One of 'em's fell down," snapped Monkey Face, undoing the ramp again with impatient hands. He wanted to be on the way so that he could be in the pub quicker. Duchess was in a heap on the floor. Paris gave a gasp of horror.

She leapt into the lorry and knelt beside her beloved mare. But Duchess was dead. She must have had a heart attack when the lorry pulled off. The commotion to get them into the lorry had upset her so much that she had literally died of fright.

"Shit!" The young thug slammed back up the ramp. "We'll have to stop at the knacker's on the way back – get them to take that old bitch off."

"Awight, out you get," said Monkey Face to Paris, "we've got to be on our way."

But Paris was not to be rushed as she knelt by her mare, saying a last farewell.

Sometime later, shivering with the emotional turmoil, she watched them drive away. How much more of this could she take?

CHAPTER SEVENTEEN

The house was silent. Empty. Their possessions gone to Blackbird Stables. Yet the silent, nurturing soul of the house remained – peaceful and benign, the warmth oozing from the ancient stonework like a cloak around her shoulders. There was no reason to linger now. No packing to be done. The rooms were empty, silent. Her footsteps echoed as she walked slowly from room to room, drinking in the beauty of the house, trying to absorb every inch of it, because in a moment she would have to walk away and would belong here no longer. She wandered into the lounge, her favourite room. Even stripped and bare the room was beautiful. Light from the French windows flooded in casting shafts of light on the dark wood panelling of the floor. Tiny specks of dust danced in the shadows. And beyond, through the French windows, the sheltered garden where she loved to sit. A flash of colour through towering foliage of the hydrangea bushes caught her eye. The Molloys had arrived. Paris felt the muscles of her jaw tighten. Even her last moments to say goodbye to her home had been denied her. Turning abruptly she walked out of the room, shutting the door. The click of the lock had a sound of finality in it. She walked along the hall, out of the front door and slammed it behind her. Then, tilting her chin high, she walked proudly down the stone-flagged path to meet the Molloys.

The Range Rover crunched to a stop outside the house. Paris stood in the yard and waited. Paddy sat in the passenger seat of their jeep, silently watching, his face a grim picture of misery.

"Ready for off then?" bellowed Ollie Molloy, heaving his bulk out of the driver's seat.

"Looks like it." Paris glared at him.

Ollie, used to riding roughshod over everyone he encountered, was not perturbed by her antagonism. He stood in front of her, chubby legs wide apart, on expensively shod feet that looked too small to support his bulk, and beamed with delight at his new acquisition. He tucked shovel-like hands behind the astrakhan collar of his black wool overcoat and proudly surveyed the house. Paris wanted to punch his square jaw. The rear doors of the Range Rover were flung open and the young Molloys exploded from the vehicle, bounding like irrepressible puppies into the yard. Dermot, a sixteen-year-old clone of his father got out more slowly and came and stood beside him, grinning smugly and looking Paris up and down lecherously. Paris glared back at him. Horrible little maggot! Mary sidled out of the car to join them, her face twisted into a semblance of a smile. Paris held out her hand, dangling the key in her fingers. There was an undignified scuffle as the Molloys surged forwards to grab it. Mary, with all the speed of a pickpocket, won the tussle and grasped the key triumphantly between her nicotine-stained fingers.

"Better be on your way then," smirked Ollie, taking Mary's arm and leading her up the path to the house.

Paris wondered if she could move. Her legs felt like jelly, as if they would crumple if she tried to walk. Leadenly she forced herself to move, and watched herself as if in a dream moving to the car. Paddy stared fixedly out of the windscreen, his fingers frantically twisting a corner of his jacket. She got in and began to drive away. The Molloy family lined up outside the front door, watching, triumphant smirks twisting each of their faces. Dermot Molloy waved cheerfully. Then Paris and Paddy were out of the drive, silent, each trapped in their own separate horror. Leaving forever.

Blackbird Stables slunk in a damp hollow a few miles away from Redwood Grange. Paris drove in silence. She could hardly bear to have Paddy near her, let alone make conversation with him. How could he have been such a fool as to trust scum like Ollie Molloy? How could he be such a fool as to gamble on such a scale in the first place. She turned the car off the main road and bumped slowly along the rough track that led to the farm. Blackbird Stables had once been used as extra stabling for Redwood Grange. If a horse had been suspected of having a virus it had been transported to the other yard to protect the remainder of the precious horses. Stable lads and visiting jockeys had used the house as lodgings. Then when Paris's mother had left, Paddy had lost his way in life, the business had faltered, then struggled on in a smaller, less vibrant version of its original and Blackbird Stables had not been needed. Now it lay disused and unwanted. Until now.

Paris winced as the underside of the car hit a rock that jutted out on the track, grating against the metal.

Blackbird Stables was a sprawling red-brick building. Various owners had extended the original structure, giving it a curiously lopsided appearance. The stables and sheds had been built at the time of the original building, an L-shaped block of red brick, pitted and faded to a thousand shades of red like the fur of a mangy fox.

She stopped the car and laid her head sadly against the steering wheel. Rooks cawed loudly from the surrounding trees, angry at having been disturbed. Paddy put his hand on her head and she shook it off in temper. How could she ever forgive him?

"We had better go in," Paddy said quietly.

Paris sat up slowly and faced him. "I suppose we had." Bitter sarcasm made her voice cold. She got out.

Trees surrounded the house, the woods rising on three sides, making the house dark and damp. On the fourth side paddocks of poor, rushy grass stretched down towards a river, which glittered in the distance. Even in the spring sunlight the place felt damp and cold.

Paddy made his way up the mossy path to the front door and went inside. Paris followed him, depression making her feel exhausted and lifeless. Inside the house was dark and cold, smelling of damp and misery. She slammed the door behind her. This was where she now lived. It would never be home.

From one of the rooms along the dark corridor she could hear Paddy rustling in one of the cardboard boxes that contained their possessions. Then the clinking of glass against glass. Paris went towards the sound. In a room at the end of the corridor the furniture from their lounge had been dumped; it lay abandoned at awkward angles, like cars badly parked by drunken drivers. Surrounding the furniture were the cardboard boxes of china and silver cups, remnants of a past life.

Paddy was on his hands and knees having unearthed a glass and a bottle of whiskey. He had filled half of the glass with the amber liquid. "Slainte," he said, bitterly, raising his glass in her direction.

"I think I'll join you." She rummaged in the box, fingers delving into the newspaper-wrapped objects. She pulled out a cylindrical parcel of newspaper, unwrapped it and held out a cut-glass vase, prize for best-turned-out horse at Galway races. Paddy poured whiskey into the vase with a shaking hand. Paris raised it to her lips, shuddering as the fiery liquid made her splutter. Might as well get drunk – there seemed to be nothing else to do except blot out the horror of life.

"Soon look grand in here," Paddy said, tentatively sinking down on the sofa.

Paris got slowly to her feet and sat down at the opposite end. The huge leather sofa looked out of place in the dark room. "Yes," she said, quietly. She had to try to forgive him for being so fucking stupid. They were in this together.

"We can put all the pictures of the winners up in here," he said, waving his glass towards the wood-panelled wall. "It will make a nice office."

Office. Paris just managed to stop herself snorting in derision. The paperwork that their tiny yard would produce could easily be completed on the kitchen table. The operation was so small that they didn't need an office any more. She stood up suddenly, unable to bear staying in the room with him any longer, listening to his pathetic plans for their bleak future.

"I'm going to go and check the horses."

Outside in the stable yard the appearance of neglect was even stronger. The paint peeled on the sagging stable doors that hung from broken hinges, weeds ran riot in the cobbled stone yard and in the gaps in the concrete paths. A broken plastic bucket rolled mournfully backwards and forwards in the yard, blown by the ever-present breeze. And as she watched an enormous rat strode leisurely from one of the stables, paused to look at her arrogantly before sauntering towards the hay-barn.

"Get away!" yelled Paris, chucking a stone at it. The stone arched through the air and landed ineffectively yards from the rat, who after pausing to glare at her continued on his journey.

Only a few of the horses had come from Redwood Grange. Joe McHugh's horses a few broodmares and young thoroughbreds. And Destiny. Paris walked over to her stable and looked in. Destiny picked listlessly at a small heap of hay. She was still very skinny, but Paris felt that she had truly recovered from the accident. She had clung determinedly to her life. Just like I have to, thought Paris. She went into the stable and stroked the mare's soft coat. Paris sat down in a corner of the stable and watched her mare pick at the hay. Life felt like a nightmare. Soon surely she would wake up and find that all of this had been a mistake. Finally she stood up. She couldn't sit here and mope all night. Straightening the mare's rug she walked out of the stable. She leant against the door. The pain of losing Derry was still raw and unbearable.

She laid her head against the cool brickwork of the stable. How could she live here? How could she lose her home and lose Derry? If only she could get him back. Then, all pride gone, she got into the car. She had to go to him. Had to make him take her back. He would make everything bearable. If only she could feel his arms around her again and his lips against hers. Everything would be alright.

She ran up the steps at Westwood Park and pressed her finger against the doorbell, holding it there. "Hurry, Derry," she whispered, her breath coming in heaving gasps. The door swung open and Derry stood looking at her impassively. He looked gorgeous, tanned, impeccably dressed; she caught a whiff of his masculine aftershave. He raised one eyebrow sardonically. She was suddenly aware of her filthy clothes, her tearstained face and the stench of whiskey on her breath.

"Derry!" Paris looked at him, imploring him with her eyes to melt and take her back.

"Paris," he said, his voice cold, surprise registering in his green eyes.

Paris stumbled forwards, clutching at his shoulders with her trembling fingers. "Derry, I can't stand it anymore," she sobbed. "I need you, please, I beg you, please take me back. I can change, I'm sorry that I was so pathetic. I'll do anything!" the words tumbled out in a torrent of desperation.

Derry was silent, his body rigid against hers. Then slowly he grasped her arms and pushed her gently away. Paris turned her face to look up at his and as she did so a movement behind him caught her eye. She froze in horror, staring wide-eyed past him into the house. Lolling against the bottom of the stairs, blonde hair impeccably cut and streaked, wearing a beautifully cut silk sheath dress that clung to the contours of her body like a second skin and wearing an expression that would have done justice to a cat that had just swallowed a gallon of cream was Merrianne.

CHAPTER EIGHTEEN

Paris tied Destiny in the yard and began to groom her. The simple routine took her mind off the dreadful devastation that was now her life. She did not have the energy to tackle the mountain of jobs that needed doing around the house and the yard, but she found a kind of peace in the rhythm and routine of caring for the few horses that remained in her care. She ran her hand down the mare's elegant body. The vicious cuts that had marked her had healed. Destiny was beginning to get better. Paris wished that her own scars had healed so well.

She looked up in surprise as a car drew into the weed-strewn yard. No one had bothered to visit them since they had moved to Blackbird Stables. Even the feed salesmen, once the bane of her life hadn't been near the place. Then as she watched, speechless with anger, a tall, elegantly dressed woman got out of the car, walked towards the house and then went in without bothering to knock on the door.

Paris flung the brush she had been using down in temper. "What the hell does she think that she is playing at?" she hissed through gritted teeth. Then abandoning her grooming she stalked across the yard and into the house. She slammed the front door shut and strode down the dark corridor to the room that Paddy was calling his office. "Paris," he grinned with delight as she flung open the door.

Paris froze in the doorway. "Well, this is a touching scene," she said sarcastically, leaning against the door frame and surveying her father and the woman coldly. They were sitting at opposite ends of the sofa. Paddy, dressed in his casual cords and a frayed cotton shirt, looked stunned. He was grinning delightedly – twenty years had miraculously vanished from his appearance. The woman, blonde hair fading to a soft shade of grey, looked stunning. Her elegantly checked jacket and skirt looked expensive, cut to show off a figure that would have been the envy of a woman half her age. Only fine lines, creasing the corners of her eyes when, as now, she smiled, gave away her age. "Paris," she smiled, stretching out a hand topped by manicured nails. "Hello, Mother," snapped Paris shortly, pointedly ignoring her outstretched hand. "What the fuck do you want?"

Paris could feel herself trembling with anger. How dare her mother come here? After all that she had put Paddy through. He had fallen to pieces when she had left, gaily leaving without a backwards glance to set up home with Paddy's stable jockey. He had come home from the sales early and found them in the shower together. It had fallen to Paris to pick up the pieces, to drag her father out of bed in the morning to make him get through the days. Then she had watched his slow descent into alcoholism as, unable to face being without her, he had sought solace in the bottom of a glass. It was all her mother's fault and Paris hated her.

"Have you come to gloat at us?" she hissed bitterly.

"Paris!" Paddy silenced her instantly and Paris turned to face him, hot tears of misery prickling the back of her eyes. "Don't speak to your mother like that."

Paris swayed, in shock. How could he want her here? How could he even breathe the same air as her after all that had happened?

Paris turned and stumbled from the room and out into the sunlit yard, gasping for breath like a drowning man. Blinded by tears, she went across the yard and untied Destiny, fumbling clumsily with the knotted rope, tugging at it in frustration until finally it came free. She led the mare into her stable and sank down in the clean straw and laid her head in her hands. Her whole life had gone wrong.

"I thought I would find you in here."

Paris looked up, eyes narrowing with hatred.

"You always went in with the horses when you were miserable when you were a little girl."

"So you found me," she whispered bitterly, between clenched teeth.

Elizabeth walked across the deep straw – with amazing ease for someone dressed in high heels and a tight skirt, Paris thought reluctantly. She stretched out a hand and stoked Destiny's scrawny neck. "You two are lucky to be alive."

Paris wrapped her arms around her legs and laid her head on her knees. "What do you want?" she said quietly.

Elizabeth stopped caressing the mare and moved away from her. She halted by the window, looked out through the dusty glass and put her hands on the iron grille that stopped the mare from breaking the glass. "I heard about what had happened, your accident, losing Redwood Grange. I wanted to come and help." She shrugged her shoulders in a helpless gesture and then slowly turned around and leant against the iron grille. With the sunlight shining behind her she was in shadow, and Paris couldn't see the expression on her face, but her voice was gentle.

Paris glared at her mother. How could she have stayed away and then come back, just to torment them. "We don't want you here. We're doing all right without you. We have managed for the last …" Words failed her as she tried to pluck the amount of years out of the air. How long had she been gone? "God knows how many years," she snapped finally, giving up on her calculations. "So you can just clear off back to where you came from." Her scar began to prickle as the blood flooded into her cheeks.

"I should have come before," Elizabeth murmured quietly, "but I was too afraid of the reception that I would get. Too proud to come and say sorry I made a mistake."

Paris gave a snort of derision. She got to her feet and leant against the wall, hands clenched into fists, only sheer lack of energy preventing her from flying across the room and pummelling the face of the woman who was her mother. "You didn't think about us back then."

Elizabeth gave a hollow laugh. "I've thought about you every day since I left."

"If you cared so much why the hell did you go in the first place?" But why argue? What was the point? She didn't even want to speak to her. She bolted across the stable and struggled to open the door.

Elizabeth shot after her and grabbed her wrist. "I fell in love," she snapped, her fingers clamped tightly around Paris's wrist. "Is that so wrong? Have you never been in love, Paris?"

Paris shook Elizabeth's hand off her wrist. "Loved and lost," she said, wryly. She turned to face her mother.

Elizabeth had tears in her eyes, her lipstick-darkened lips clamped tightly together to stop herself from crying out.

Paris wished that she could feel some pity for her, some emotion, anything other than this bitter hatred. "You left me, and I hate you for it" she said bitterly.

Elizabeth reeled away as if Paris had hit her. "I didn't mean to," she whispered, covering her face with her hands. Paris could see that beneath the long, painted nails her hands were wrinkled and spotted with age. "I fell for Declan. He was our jockey – good-looking, charming." She gave a hollow laugh at the memory. "Paddy was so busy, always working, I felt neglected." She shrugged at her own stupidity. "Then when Paddy found out he gave me an ultimatum. Him or Declan."

"And so you chose Declan and left me," Paris said, forcing the words from a throat that was tight with emotion.

"Paddy said I could have you when Declan and I could provide a home for you." She found a tissue in her jacket pocket and blew her nose loudly. "It didn't last with us. Declan just wanted fun, not a full-time relationship. Especially not with a clinging woman who was missing her child." She turned to face Paris, her eyes pleading, begging forgiveness from her daughter. "Paddy wouldn't let me have you and I was too proud to come back to him."

Paris shook her head slowly. "You should never have left in the first place. You were just a whore who couldn't keep her knickers on. Go away and leave us alone!" She wrenched open the door and dashed across the yard to the safety of the house. Elizabeth watched Paris bolt into the house and slam the door behind her. Sighing, she let herself out of the stable and shut the door carefully behind her. The ramshackle house was closed against her, its sloping red walls forbidding and indifferent to her plight. She got into her car and drove wearily away. Becoming friends with Paris was going to be a long job.

Paddy looked up expectantly as Paris walked into the kitchen. She saw the look of delight die in his eyes when he saw that it was her and not Elizabeth that had walked in.

Paris pulled out a chair, sat down at the table and sullenly rested her chin on her hands.

"Where's Elizabeth?" asked Paddy.

Paris shrugged. How could he even bear to say her name? "Gone," she snapped. She was aware of him glaring at her before he shot from the kitchen, his footsteps clattering on the sagging stone-flagged hall.

Then she heard the scraping of the door as he wrenched it back and bellowed "Elizabeth!" Silence. Then the door scraped back into place and his footsteps came slowly back down the hall.

Paris shook her head in disgust at the disappointment in his voice. "Good," she muttered under her breath, reaching across the table and pulling the racing newspaper towards her.

"Why were you so horrible to her?" Paddy asked, as he pulled a chair out and sat down opposite Paris.

She could hear the undercurrent of temper in his voice. She snorted in derision. "Why!" she raged. "She's just a whore!" She turned the pages of the newspaper, pretending to read, but was painfully aware of him glaring at her from across the table. She hated bad feelings between them.

Finally his silence became unbearable. Paris looked up.

He was still looking at her, an unidentifiable expression in his eyes. "You mustn't say things like that about Elizabeth." He spoke her name reverently.

Paris glared at him sceptically, his green eyes were misty with unshed tears. "How can you want her here after all that happened?" she said quietly, shaking her head in disbelief.

A slow smile spread across his weatherbeaten face, turning up the corners of his eyes, and when he spoke, his words shook her to the core. "Because I love her. I never stopped loving her," he said simply.

CHAPTER NINETEEN

The months trickled by. Life without Derry stretched ahead, empty and without purpose. Paris managed to occupy the days, forcing herself to tidy up the house and the yard, to make them habitable and clean. Now the house gleamed with her obsessive polishing and cleaning. Anything to occupy her hands and still the mind that roved restlessly over her loss. The yard was tidy, not a weed remained. The stable doors, fixed by Paddy on one of his better days, gleamed with new paint, applied frenziedly during one afternoon when the pain of missing Derry had been unbearable.

Life, had assumed an air of normality. Joe McHugh's old horses had been trained. Paul and Sean, two of the lads who had worked for them at Redwood Grange, came during the spare hours between morning and evening stables, to ride out Joe's horses. The old pasture along the riverbank had proved to be perfect for galloping the horses, the springy turf cushioning their delicate legs as they pounded along, swift as the river in full flow. Red Arrow had even managed to complete a race, much to Joe's delight. The horse had never managed to cross the finishing line in all the time that he had owned it. Paris had been worried that Joe was going to have a heart attack, he had danced and leapt around so much in excitement.

But the pain of seeing Derry again had been too much and she knew that she couldn't go to the races again. She would do all of the training at home, and Paddy would have to take the horses to the races.

Memories of her past life tortured her, flashing into her consciousness like darts of pain. Memories of Redwood Grange would come with the way light danced in the yard, reminding her of the light in the garden there. Closing her eyes at night brought no respite; in her tortured imagination she could feel Derry's arms around her, feel his breath on her neck, his lips nibbling her ears sexily. She would wake with a start and lie, tears trickling down her cheeks to soak the pillow, knowing that somewhere close Derry lay with Merrianne.

Merrianne. Paris closed her eyes to blot out the image of her smirking face as she watched Paris crumble. How quickly he had replaced her! Had he secretly always wanted Merrianne? Maybe he had always had her as well.

Paris looked at her watch. Paul and Sean would be here in a few minutes. She had better go and get the horses ready for them. Two o'clock. How many hours before she could go to bed and try to sleep? Try to blot out the misery, hoping there would be no nightmares. Red Arrow and Handy Sandy were in the stables beside Destiny. Paris took off their rugs, ran a brush over their sleek coats and saddled them up ready for the lads to get on them as soon as they arrived. She had just finished when they drove into the yard, horn blasting to announce that they had arrived.

"How's it going?" they chorused, fishing brightly coloured skullcaps and whips out of the car boot and wrapping suede chaps around their legs to protect them as they rode. "Grand," lied Paris. She leant against the warm metal of the car bonnet as they fetched the horses out. The lads vaulted lithely into the saddles, skinny legs dangling as they gathered up the reins and shoved their feet into the stirrups. If only she could join them, thought Paris, but she knew that the very thought of getting onto one of the horses would reduce her to a quivering wreck.

"Just give them a hack on the roads and then we'll give them a work-out by the river," she told the lads as they rode out of the yard. While they were gone she refilled the water buckets and took the droppings out of the stables. If only she was not such a coward! Shovelling horse shit and carting water was all that she was good for any more.

A short while later they returned from giving the horses the essential road work to make their legs tough enough to withstand the rigours of the race track. She opened the gate for them to ride into the fields. Destiny, shading herself under the wide leaves of the oak-tree, watched without interest as the horses jogged across the turf. Handy Sandy stretched his head down, and cantered sideways, eager to be allowed to run. Red Arrow walked calmly beside him – he never wasted any energy unnecessarily, by jogging and cavorting.

"Do a couple of circuits at half speed," Paris told the lads as they reached the springy turf of the riverbank, "and then give them a good pipe-opener."

The gentle gallop would maintain the horse's fitness, while the faster gallop would be good for increasing their stamina. She leant against a tree and watched as they crouched low over the horse's ears, hands low, huge grins on their faces at the sheer exhilaration of galloping against the wind on fit, powerful horses. Paris grinned happily, lost for a moment in the pleasure of watching, as they hurtled over the rickety fences she and Paddy had constructed out of brushwood.

As they thundered past her again she caught Paul's eye and gave him the thumbs-up. "That'll do!" she yelled, her voice lost in the racket the hooves were making on the turf.

The lads slowed the horses and walked them slowly along the riverbank to cool them off, finally bringing them into the water to cool their legs before riding them slowly into the yard.

"We'll just be back at Walsh's in time for evening stables," said Sean, glancing at his watch as he slid off the horse.

They held the horses as Paris ran her hand slowly down each of their delicate legs, carefully checking for any signs of cuts or damage that could cause problems if left unattended. Then, after leading the horses back into the stables, they dashed back to the car, unbuckling helmets as they went. A second later, waving goodbye and promising to be back the following afternoon, they were gone, hurtling up the drive leaving a cloud of dust lingering in the trees. The silence settled again like a dark cloak, the excitement of the day over. Paris untacked the two racehorses, brushing the sweat marks from their coats, and then threw their rugs over them again.

She crossed the yard. She would bring Destiny in from the field, then there would just be time to have a cup of tea before she fed the horses. Then as she watched, wide-eyed with horror, the field gate swung slowly open. It must have been left open when they brought the horses in from their exercise.

The field was empty. Destiny was gone.

She dashed across the yard and into the field in the hope that the mare might be lying down somewhere and be safe after all. She reached a high place in the field and searched around desperately with her eyes. It was obvious that the mare was not there. The empty field mocked her for being so stupid as to leave the gate open. She ran back into the yard as fast as she could, panic making her short of breath. She could hear her breath roaring in her ears as she paced over the rough ground, the uneven surface making her wince as it jolted her still painful body. How long had the gate been open? Had they left it open when they went to gallop the horses, or when they came back? Her mind was a total blank.

"Oh shit," she wailed. A loose horse was a deadly danger to itself and everyone else. If Destiny got out onto the road there could be a terrible accident.

Paris ran to the saddle room and grabbed a rope. Destiny was already wearing a head-collar.

But how long had she been gone? She had to have gone up the lane. Clutching the lead-rope Paris began to jog up the incline through the trees. To her relief, hoof-prints marking the soft earth at the edge of the track told her that Destiny had come this way. She jogged on, hoping at every turn of the lane that she would see the mare grazing, safe from the treacherous traffic that hurtled occasionally down the road. But by the time she reached the end of the lane there was still no sign of Destiny. She stopped. Which bloody way had she gone? Left or right? Then in the distance a movement caught her eye. Destiny was a mere dot on the horizon, trotting rapidly away, obviously delighted with herself to be going on a jaunt. "Bloody hell!" gasped Paris. How on earth was she ever supposed to catch her? Wearily she trudged up the road after the rapidly disappearing dark shape, praying that a car wouldn't come screaming along and plough into her. That scenario didn't even bear thinking about. On and on she trudged. She lost sight of the mare when she disappeared around a bend in the road.

The road stretched ahead, winding through hawthorn hedges and tall stately beech trees. The lacy white heads of the cow parsley reared above cheerful yellow buttercups, all brushing against her as she trudged along the pot-holed tarmac.

Then, her heart lifted as, far ahead, she could see the mare again. But now someone was with her - and was leading her along the road towards her. Destiny was safe. Paris breathed a silent prayer of thanks and began to run. When she was close enough to see that the mare was being led by a tall, blonde-haired man she slowed to a walk. "Thanks for catching her," she panted, as she reached them, weak with relief. She clipped the lead-rope onto Destiny's head-collar and unfastening the tatty bit of nylon rope that he had been leading her with.

"It's lucky for you that I caught her. These roads are dangerous for loose horses. You could have ended up being sued by someone if she had hit a car," said the man.

"Thanks, I know all of that," she said shortly. The last thing she wanted was to be lectured by some know-all, grateful to him though she was.

"You should check your fencing," he started again. "You mightn't be so lucky next time."

Paris clenched her teeth and flushed. How dare he start preaching to her! Did he imagine she was an idiot? She glared at him, looking at him properly for the first time. He was tall, younger than she had thought when she had been walking towards him. He had the ruddy, tanned face of someone who spends their life outside, and his hair was streaked blonde by the sun.

"Thank you. I do understand the risks." She thrust his rope towards him.

He took it, then held out a large work-roughened hand for her to shake. "Kane McCarthy."

She took his hand gingerly. It was warm, the skin surprisingly soft. Paris caught a glimpse of very straight white teeth and was aware of his blue eyes crinkling in amusement. At the fact his words had obviously needled her? At what he perceived as her incompetence?

"Lucky for you I was around, Paris," he said and grinned disarmingly.

And so he knew who she was.

"I have all the luck," she said somewhat sourly.

"Not true! Today was my lucky day too!" he guffawed.

What was so bloody amusing? Paris spun around on her heel and began to walk away. "Thanks again," she called over her shoulder, making an effort to iron the annoyance out of her voice.

"Have a good walk home," he laughed behind her.

God, the man was an idiot!

CHAPTER TWENTY

Paris stopped sweeping the concrete path and looked in amazement as the man that had caught Destiny hurtled into the yard in a rattling, squeaking rust-riddled jeep. "I've brought you a present," he shouted out of the jeep window.

He wondered for the twentieth time that morning if he was doing the right thing. Paris looked a wreck. Her hair flew in a tangled mess above a grey, pinched face. Lifeless blue eyes stared at him impassively. She had the look of a war victim, seen on the newsreels, cowering, shell-shocked in the ruins of a bombed-out house. Her clothes hung off her emaciated body, through her T-shirt he could see the outline of her ribs and prominent collar bones, tiny jutting breasts hardly showing beneath the baggy fabric. She was a mere caricature of the gorgeous woman whose career he had followed from when they were at school. She had been a year below him, unapproachable and untouchable, even then, filled with the unshakable knowledge that she was beautiful and wealthy. And when she had started racing, riding first in point to points and then on the racetrack he had followed her career. He had known about the accident and that Paddy had lost Redwood Grange. He had heard in the pub that they had moved to Blackbird Stables. And then when he met her on the road he had been completely stunned at the change in her from the confident, gorgeous lady jockey to the frail shell she had become.

"You had better behave," he said now, putting his hand down and rubbing the black face of the sheep who was curled in beneath the passenger seat beside him. Daisy chewed her cud, her teeth working mechanically, not at all amused at having been hauled out of her pen and shoved into the noisy, smelly jeep, amongst the junk that Kane had thrown onto the floor. "I'll miss you, Daisy," he said, gently pulling at one of her ears. She was called Daisy because he had found her early one morning, just born, a broken daisy flower stuck to the afterbirth slime on her head. He hadn't been early enough. Her mother had died trying to give birth to Daisy's twin. Without the shepherd's assistance the old ewe had died of exhaustion. Furious at himself for catching an extra half an hour in bed when he should have been out checking the sheep, Kane had tucked the newborn lamb into his jacket and set off for home.

As if to make up for his neglect of her mother he dedicated himself to ensuring that Daisy survived. Every two hours, day and night, he bottle-fed the lamb until she was strong enough to be put out with the others. If she missed having a mother she never showed it, happily playing with the other lambs, bouncing on the broad woolly backs of the staid sheep as they lay down in the fields and playing tag through the grass. But when Kane appeared she had all the peevishness of a neglected wife. Bleating furiously, she would hurtle from the far end of the field when his jeep drew up, to butt delightedly at his legs with a hard little head.

It had been a major decision for him to give up the young sheep, but maybe his gesture would help Paris. The mare that had been running loose on the road was as highly strung and neurotic as a PMT-crazed woman. He could see that she needed something to calm her down, if Paris couldn't.

Paris ran a hand through her tangled hair, annoyed at herself for caring that she must look a sight. She hadn't even had a wash or run a brush through her hair, or put any make-up on. For the last few weeks there hadn't seemed to be any point. Derry wouldn't be calling around and there was no one else she wanted to impress.

Last night she had slept well for the first time in weeks and had come out into the yard straight after getting up. She hadn't been inside since.

The good night's sleep seemed to have refreshed her, giving her a new energy and making her situation look a little less hopeless. Blackbird Stables could be turned into a nice yard, eventually. And well, even though at times she really didn't want to since Derry had dumped her, she had kept breathing. Life was going to go on whether she wanted it to or not.

Kane walked around to the passenger side of the jeep. Paris found herself staring at him. She was disturbed by the way he was getting to her. There was no way that she was interested in him. So why was her heart pounding so hard and why was she so concerned about how she looked? He had long legs, encased in ripped faded jeans through which she could glimpse tanned skin with a smattering of blonde hairs. And the smallest, neatest butt. She averted her eyes. He had annoyed the pants off her, telling her how to care for her horse. She knew that gates should be shut, knew how deadly the roads were. It had been an accident, a slip of her mind. And it was no wonder, after all that she had been through recently. And now, just turning up on the yard without any reason! To check on her fences perhaps?

He wrenched open the passenger door and then leant inside. There was a commotion of banging and noise and then he re-emerged with a wriggling and extremely cross-looking sheep in his arms.

"What's that?" she exclaimed, wide-eyed in astonishment.

"A ewe for you," he panted, as the sheep slithered towards the ground.

"I can see it's a sheep," she said patiently, a faint smile twitching the corner of her mouth.

"You look beautiful when you're angry," he grinned, looking at her through Daisy's furiously twitching black ears.

Oh God, he was going to try to be funny again!

"Open the bloody stable door," he gasped, fighting to hold the squirming animal that was now bleating furiously as if it was being murdered. He gestured towards Destiny's stable. The mare, curious at the commotion, was leaning out over the door, ears sharply pricked.

"What the hell do you think you're doing?" Paris asked, bewildered.

"Open the fucking door," he gasped, hitching the sheep up again as it wriggled downwards.

"That's my mare's stable!"

"Just – open – the – door! Then I'll explain!"

Paris flung open Destiny's stable door. With a snort of alarm Destiny wheeled away and stood quivering at the back of the stable.

Red-faced with the effort, Kane managed to haul the sheep to Destiny's door where he dropped it, gasping with relief. Daisy, relieved at being released from Kane's bear hug shook herself crossly and suspiciously eyed the enormous animal that she was sharing the stable with. Then as her pale amber eyes caught sight of Destiny's pile of sweet-smelling hay, she strolled nonchalantly across the stable and began to tuck in.

Paris slammed the stable door shut. "What are you playing at?" she asked, glaring from him to the woolly beast who was tucking greedily into Destiny's hay while the mare stood wide-eyed at the back of the stable.

"The mare needs a gentle companion to calm her down," Kane grinned, wiping his dirty hands on his jeans. "Any fool can see that." He looked into the stable, relieved to see that the mare had not tried to hurt his beloved Daisy.

"She got hurt in a racing accident," Paris explained, wishing that he would go away and leave her alone.

"I know. I read the newspapers," he said. "You've had a pretty rough time." He stretched out his hand and gently touched her scar.

Paris jumped back as if she had been burnt.

Kane shrugged. "The sheep will help to calm the mare down, you'll see." He gestured into the stable.

Paris followed his gaze. Destiny was sniffing the sheep suspiciously, her elegant neck stretched to its limits, eyes watchful, ears pricked and alert. Then she snatched a mouthful of hay as if she were afraid that the sheep would steal all of it from her. "A lot of racehorses have sheep, or small ponies, even goats to keep them calm," Kane said, leaning against the stable door and looking in at the mare and the diminutive sheep. "They are so highly strung that a companion with them helps them." Daisy regarded him balefully, chewing on the hay feverishly.

"Thank you, Mr Race-Horse-Expert, for your opinion," Paris snapped sarcastically, annoyed that she hadn't thought of getting a quiet companion for Destiny. But she bit her bottom lip to stop herself grinning as Destiny thrust her ears flat against her head and stamped aggressively at the sheep to warn her against eating all of the hay. Daisy raised her head nonchalantly and bleated, her mouth wide open, sharp lower teeth brown below a long pink tongue. The mare jumped to the back of the stable, offended at being spoken to so rudely in her own stable. Then deciding that the sheep was not a threat, she shoved her head into the hay and began to eat hungrily, determined to eat more than the greedy usurper.

"We had a sheep that kept our pony company when I was a kid."

"Should have been a goat when you were a kid," Paris muttered in reply.

He ignored her jibe. "They followed each other everywhere. You can keep Daisy, the sheep, for as long as you want – but take good care of her. She's a special pet of mine. I hand-reared her after her mother died in labour."

Paris was moved by this little story. Mr Know-It-All must have a good heart after all.

Then he added: "And make sure you keep your gates shut."

Oh, for God's sake! She had been rearing horses all her life! What kind of greenhorn did he think she was? What an infuriating man!

Paris wished that he would go. His presence was disturbing in more ways than one. She was put out by his insulting attempts to lecture her and by how much he obviously knew about her, but apart from all that, his touch had stirred something in her. Something that she didn't want. She had loved Derry and look where that had got her. She would never trust another man. And she would never, ever be attracted to anyone else. Ever. Even if he was very good-looking. He was bound to be another heartbreaker, and when her heart eventually healed she was never, ever going to risk it being broken again.

She needed to get rid of Kane McCarthy now. She turned to walk away. "Thanks then," she said by way of brusquely. "It's very kind of you."

"My pleasure," he grinned. "I think that you could do with some company of your own."

The cheek! "I'm fine as I am," she said, flustered that he could see the hurt in her.

"So I see," he said, with a grin. "I'd like to volunteer for the job when you're ready. I farm over at Amis Cross, just up the road, if you ever need a friend."

Her heart began to pound. "I don't need anyone," she said through gritted teeth, taking up her brush and beginning to sweep the yard, making the dust fly.

"Be good," Kane whispered over the door at Daisy.

Kane got into his jeep and started it up. The engine rattled in protest. He wound down the window as he drove slowly away, then he leant out and shouted, "I think you do!"

111

CHAPTER TWENTY-ONE

The blonde woman was terribly glamorous. Her long, impeccably streaked hair fell in a golden waterfall around her shoulders. Ice-blue eyes stared out though long thick eyelashes, in a tanned face, air-brushed to St Tropez gold. Her clothes, especially chosen for a day at the races, were immaculate, made from expensive fabrics, well cut to accentuate the curves of her body, tasteful and elegant in their simplicity of design. She picked up an ivory-handled hairbrush and ran it down the sleek waterfall of hair with a smooth white hand, the white tips of her French polish flashing in the mirror. Finally she laid down the brush and stood up, looking with satisfaction at her reflection in the enormous mirror that filled one wall of the bedroom. The previous night she had watched her reflection, upside down, as she lay being fucked to the point of exhaustion, spread-eagled on the bed, her hands bound with silk ties to the curved posts of the bed. She stood very close to the mirror, so close that her breath misted a circular patch in front of her mouth. "You look a million dollars, Merrianne." she said, smiling with enormous satisfaction at herself. This was her dream come true. A gorgeous home, a luxurious lifestyle, money, prestige and of course Derry, her glamorous, wealthy boyfriend.

Life with Derry wasn't easy, but it certainly had its benefits, she mused. She thought happily about the shopping sprees, hitting the exclusive boutiques with Derry critically discarding or approving outfit after outfit, returning to Westwood Park laden with expensive-looking carrier bags, like a scene from Pretty Woman. He had made a bonfire with the clothes he had looked at in horror when she had pulled them out of her suitcase after she had finally moved in with him. He had made a heap of them in the apple orchard and poured a can of petrol over them. The black smoke had plumed skywards as the nylon and synthetic fabrics melted and disintegrated in the heat.

She had been for an intensive session at the beauty parlour. A girl with make-up so thick that rocks could have been bounced off it had waxed her legs and other more delicate places. The fixed smile never left her face as she brutally hauled the hair-encrusted strips from Merrianne's legs. She surely had to have been employed for her truly sadistic streak. A stream of girls, reeking of heavy perfume, with thick make-up and pouting lips, had streaked her hair, leaving it silky smooth and glinting in the bright lights of the salon, plucked her heavy eyebrows and worked wonders with her grime-encrusted nails.

"Now at least you aren't going to put the dogs off their food," Derry had said, as she sashayed out into the reception area.

If she had found the brutal removal of her body hair excruciatingly painful, it was nothing compared to Derry's brutish ministrations. Supremely arrogant, fantastically egotistical, sulky as a small child when denied his own way, Derry was a nightmare to live with.

"Hurry up, can't you!" he bellowed from the bottom of the stairs.

Merrianne blew a kiss at her reflection and hurried to join him.

"Here," he said, tossing the car keys in her direction. "You can drive – the bags are already in the boot." He ran down the wide flight of stone steps that led to the gravel forecourt and jumped into the Jeep.

Merrianne followed, tottering slightly on the very high heels she was wearing. Derry, with a sigh of utmost pleasure, pulled the racing newspaper out from under the seat, lit a cigarette and settled down to while away the journey to the airport in comfort. Merrianne gingerly manoeuvred the big Jeep between the stone pillars and down the drive.

"Watch it, for fuck's sake," he snapped, glancing over his newspaper as she over-steered on a corner and careered over the grass for a few feet.

"Sorry," she said, breathless with the concentration of driving the unfamiliar vehicle – and in such high heels.

Derry let out a huge sigh and rustled the newspaper petulantly as he turned to the entries for the English Grand National. Sometimes he wondered if it had been a good idea to persuade Merrianne to move in with him. She really didn't compare with the class and incredible presence that Paris had. A bit like comparing a winning racehorse with a riding-school plod. But she was attractive, willing to do anything to please him, out of bed and even more so in it and she would undoubtedly tolerate his dalliances. Merrianne would fill Paris' place adequately. And she still had the good looks and reasonable intelligence to be an asset around the horse-owners.

Derry stalked across the carpark at Shannon airport, after throwing the bags onto a bent-wheeled trolley which he left Merrianne to deal with. She struggled after him, wrenching the trolley around as yet again it spun off in a different direction. It was hard to sashay on high heels and heave an unruly trolley around. The automatic doors swished open as Derry approached them, only to clang shut in her face, opening again reluctantly as if they didn't want her to enter. She hurried after Derry, high heels tap-tapping rapidly on the floor. The check-in girls were all smiles as Derry produced his tickets, their eyes flickering over Merrianne and dismissing her as unimportant. They were late – Derry didn't believe in wasting time sitting in airport lounges – but the stewardesses were all smiles as he took his seat. Behind her Merrianne could hear the hushed whispers of awe as the other passengers realised who he was.

"Is that Paris his fiancée, the top lady jockey, with him?" someone hissed.

"Nah, she was killed in an accident," said someone else in reverent tones.

If Derry didn't believe in hanging around in airports, he certainly liked doing it on racecourses, thought Merrianne, shivering in the misty predawn light as she watched Derry and Mary the groom tack up Pincushion, the horse that would later run in the biggest race in the world, The Grand National. Only a few short months ago she had been Pincushion's groom. Once Paris had been her boss. Now she was.... nobody. The big grey horse swished his thick black tail as Derry pulled his girths tight. He legged Mary up onto the horse and ordered the plump girl to ride the horse out onto the course.

"Horse has improved no end since he came from Paris," Derry said smugly as they followed the horse's muscular grey quarters out of the stable area.

Other horses that were running in the day's races were being exercised on the course. Wearing striped rugs over their quarters to protect them from the early morning chill, like medieval jousting horses, they bucketed over the turf, riders crouching low over their manes.

Derry, engrossed in watching Pincushion work, ignored Merrianne, and after half a dozen attempts to talk to him which were answered in monosyllabic grunts she gave up. Later, shivering with the cold, she tucked her arm through his. Derry shook her off as nonchalantly as if she were a fly that was buzzing around.

Danny Keogh, the horse's owner, wandered towards them, salt-and-pepper hair wild, bristle turning his square jaw blue. "What bloody hour of the day do you call this?" he snapped peevishly, his eyes bloodshot from a night's heavy drinking.

"The horse looks on great form," Derry ignored his complaints.

Yawning loudly, Danny stood beside Derry and watched the powerful grey horse charging through the murky grey morning, his black tail streaming like a banner behind him. "Will he win?" he asked, as Derry told Mary to take the horse back to the stable.

Derry put his arm companionably around Danny's shoulder. "Let's go and walk the course with the jockey, have a look at some of the fences, see if the going will be hard or soft." Without a backwards glance to see if Merrianne was all right, he walked away.

Merrianne could hear Danny's pleas long after they had vanished into the mist: "Will he win?"

The course began to fill up gradually, as people came from far and wide to soak up the heady atmosphere and ghoulishly watch the race to see the fallen horses and jockeys, downed by the enormous fences and phenomenal speed of the race. "At over four miles long, over some of the biggest fences, with the biggest field of runners in any race, this is one of the toughest races a horse and jockey can compete in," a television presenter was saying into his microphone, standing beneath the statue which marked the grave of Red Rum, the amazing horse who won the race three times. When he died he was buried at Aintree the site of his victories, beside the winning post. The presenter scowled as a little old lady, dressed in a drooping tweed overcoat and enormous hat adorned with peacock feathers, pushed past him to reverently lay a bunch of tulips on the grave of the horse.

Merrianne, her jacket adorned with a trainer's badge with Pincushion's colours, pushed her way into the parade ring where the horses were being led around. The security guard stood back respectfully and tipped his cap at her before moving back to guard the entrance.

Derry barely glanced in her direction as she made her way across the grass. "Had a good time?" he said, dropping a kiss onto her cheek, for Danny's benefit. "Wonderful," she kissed him back. There was no way that she was going to tell him that she had been sitting in the restaurant for most of the day, sipping cold coffee, sulking because he walked off without her.

"Will he win?" said Danny, coming across to join them. His salt-and-pepper hair had been smoothed down and he was clean shaven and reeked of Egotist his favourite aftershave.

The jockeys trooped out. Tony Mahoney, Derry's jockey came across to them, shivering with cold and nerves. His face was almost the same shade as the green striped silks that he wore.

"Will he win?" Danny demanded, shoving his face next to Tony's.

The bell rang and all hell broke loose in the parade ring. Horses, picking up the tension in the air, cavorted and kicked out in excitement. Grooms clung to their bridles, hauling them into the centre of the ring so that the trainers could leg the jockeys up onto their backs. Then a fanfare, guaranteed to make the hairs stand up on the back of the neck, rang out and the horses began to make their way onto the race track. Old horses, winners from previous races, frisked at the side of the grooms that led them, delighted to be back at Aintree.

Derry walked beside Pincushion, a huge grin splitting his face. A huge cheer rang out from the crowd as the announcer gave out his name.

After the parade the horses cantered down to the start. They milled around, circling, waiting, tension mounting until the starter came to begin the race. "It's up to the horse and Tony and luck now," said Derry, as he seized Merrianne's hand and gripped it with excitement. Merrianne entwined her fingers into Derry's, delighted to be with him. He did love her. He was glad that she was there. "They're off!" he yelled. Merrianne stole a glance at him – beneath his trilby hat his face was as excited and youthful as a child at Christmas.

Merrianne stood on tiptoe, but still she couldn't even see the huge television screen that was transmitting pictures of the race to the spectators. Instead she watched Derry, grinning with delight to be with him, hoping that everyone that she knew would see them together.

"Kilroy's down, Gaily Daily's run out," Derry chanted, his eyes wide with excitement, "Pincushion's still there, Pincushion's fourth, third, second!"

The crowds shifted slightly and at last she could see the television screen clearly: the final fence, Pincushion, exhausted, moving like a wooden rocking horse, lumbering over the obstacle. Pinky Nose, the other horse, was so tired that she didn't even take off at the fence but just ploughed through it, sending her jockey sprawling to the ground, where he sat up, beating the turf with his whip, furious at having lost the fame and glory of a win.

Tony cantered Pincushion over the line, standing high in his stirrups, whip flailing the air, a grin splitting his face from ear to ear.

"Has he won?" bellowed Danny, nearly deafening her.

Two enormous grey police horses, their riders red-faced with the heat beneath ceremonial plumed helmets, guarded the horse as he jogged high on adrenalin into the covered winners' enclosure. Derry, still clutching Merrianne's hand, shoved his way through the crowds until he reached his horse.

Behind her Merrianne could hear Danny, saying in bemused tones, "he won, he won."

Photographers crowded forwards to take pictures of the horse and his trainer and owner. Derry let go of Merrianne's hand but she shoved herself forwards, lining up beside the horse and Derry, almost squeezing Danny out of the picture.

"This is for Very Important People magazine!" yelled Andrew Casey, the photographer.

Merrianne grinned broadly. Now she truly belonged.

CHAPTER TWENTY-TWO

"Derry!" shrieked Merrianne, excitement making her voice several octaves higher. "Come and look!"

Derry sauntered casually out of the bathroom, wearing only a small towel around his waist and rubbing his wet hair with another. "What is it?" he asked, grimacing as the pitch of her voice made his teeth grate.

"Look," she said, pulling back the heavy damask curtains that cascaded in heavy folds from ceiling to floor. Derry abandoned drying his hair, threw the towel onto the bed and obediently went to the window and looked out. An enormous crowd had massed on the gravel forecourt, outside the house and lining the drive. They spilled out onto the lawns, trampling the daffodils and flattening the grass with their endlessly shuffling feet. Children hung on the post-and-rail fencing waving their hands at the foals that were out in the paddocks with their mothers.

"They're all waiting to welcome Pincushion home," Derry grinned delightedly. "We are popular all of a sudden." He moved so that he was standing behind Merrianne, and put his arms around her waist, drawing her close to him. His skin, still damp from the shower, was hot even through the silk robe that she wore. Merrianne leant back against him, revelling in the delicious feeling of his skin and the clean, soapy smell of him. Gently he bent his head and with one hand pulled the silk fabric down over her shoulder and nibbled at the tender flesh on her shoulder. Merrianne felt herself turn to liquid, she wanted him so much. His hand moved relentlessly upwards and slid inside her robe, fastening itself on her breast, his fingers seeking and then finding the eager nub of her nipple. Merrianne leant against him, feeling as if her legs surely wouldn't support her. His other hand slid down, his long fingers entwining themselves in her bush, tugging at the coarse hair, and then slid inside her.

"Turn around," he whispered, huskily, his head buried in her neck. She turned, the folds of the robe parting. The towel had vanished from his waist, she realised, as he pressed his hot body against hers. His mouth, tasting of toothpaste, closed on hers. She moaned into his mouth as he pushed her legs apart with his strong thighs, aware of how desperately she wanted him. As his hand slid around her thigh and lifted it to his waist so that he could push himself into her, she opened her eyes and gave a cry of horror, wriggling her leg out of his grasp.

"What the fuck!" Derry exploded furiously, his eyes flashing with temper at being thwarted just as he was about to push inside her.

"They can all see us!" she yelled, drawing back from the window.

"Don't be such a prude, darling," he hissed, grabbing hold of her and pulling her back towards the window.

"Derry, don't, not here," she wailed uselessly as he seized her wrists and pulled them above her head, holding them in a vice-like grip with one hand. The other he used to pull her robe apart, while his strong legs parted thighs that were clamped together like a virgin bride. As he shoved himself roughly into her, Merrianne wondered vaguely if it was her resistance or the fact that the majority of the crowd could have seen them if they had looked upwards that had turned him on so much. The thought only lasted for a moment for, as he twined his fingers in her hair and pulled her mouth down on his, she really didn't care anymore.

"You bastard!" she hissed, as she came, clawing at the thick folds of the curtains above her head. A moment later, Derry, abandoned his superb self-control and gasped with pleasure as he came, collapsing onto her shoulder.

His mobile phone rang as he eased himself out of her.

"Good timing," he grinned, crossing the room and grabbing the phone off the bed. "Great," he said into the receiver. "Be with you in a few minutes." He snapped off the phone, immediately back to business again. "Hurry and get dressed. The horsebox has just got to the village." He eased a checked cotton shirt over his long muscular arms and began to fasten it. "We have to meet them at the bottom of the drive and walk him up into the yard for our admiring public," he grinned, shrugging on his trousers and shoving his feet into leather brogues.

Merrianne dressed in the new yellow wool suit that she had bought from an exclusive little boutique in Dublin, hastily doing up the shiny pearl buttons. She was sure that they must absolutely reek of sex. Her make-up was ruined too, she thought looking at her face, the skin red and chaffed from the bristles on his chin. Hastily she slapped some foundation over the worst patches and hoped that everyone would be looking at the horse and not her and then ran downstairs behind Derry.

The crowd let out a huge cheer as they opened the front door. Derry, with a broad grin splitting his handsome face, ran lightly down the steps. "Fair play to you," yelled a balding man with a face like a rosy setting sun, as he waved a bunch of money in the air. Derry, ever chivalrous when there was a crowd to play to, opened the car door and helped Merrianne inside.

"Such a gentleman," said an envious lady, sighing with admiration at the lovely couple they made. Grinning manically and waving regally they drove the Jeep to the end of the drive where the horsebox was waiting. Pincushion had already been unloaded and stood on the grass verge, the noise of the crowd carrying over the parkland and making him dance in anticipation of another race.

"Thanks," said Derry taking hold of the horse's bridle. Mary gave Pincushion's muscular neck a final pat, laughing as the horse rubbed his head against Derry's stomach, delighted to be the centre of so much attention. Merrianne felt a twinge of pity for Paris. Pincushion had been one of her favourite horses when he was being trained at Redwood Grange. She must have been devastated when the horse won for Derry.

"Come on, Pincushion," Derry said, tugging the horse's reins. "We had better go and meet your admiring public."

A huge crowd had gathered around the horsebox, all wanting to welcome Pincushion home. A little girl ducked away from her mother and ran to Derry, thrusting a wilting daffodil at him.

"Thank you," Derry said, courteously, stooping to take the daffodil from her and drop a kiss on her cheek. Overawed the little girl burst into tears and ran, wailing loudly, back to her mother.

"He has that effect on all the girls," laughed a man in the crowd, his guffaws silenced by his wife who dug him in the ribs with her elbow seeing Merriane's stricken face. How long would it be before he made her cry too?

They set off up the drive, Derry walking in front, leading the horse, with Merrianne walking on the other side, struggling to keep up with him. The skirt on the yellow suit was much too tight for her to walk properly and so she had to take two tiny strides to his one larger one. And the gorgeous pale beige ankle boots that had looked so sumptuous in the shop were a nightmare to walk in. The heels were ridiculously high, forcing her to lean forwards as she scuttled along. She felt hot and uncomfortable.

Crowds lined either side of the drive, cheering, waving hand-made banners of congratulations. Pincushion walked proudly beside Derry, his ears pricked, accepting their adulation like a royal prince. Derry grinned broadly, stopping occasionally to let someone pat the horse, or to shake an outstretched hand. All along the drive, beneath the still pale leaves of the beech trees, people had gathered, spilling onto the drive to see their approach and then falling back to allow them to pass. Like Moses parting the Red Sea, thought Merrianne. A blister was forming on her heel where the boots had rubbed her. At last they rounded the final corner in the drive. Most of the crowds had gathered in the gravel forecourt of the house. A huge cheer rang out as they turned the corner. Pincushion, recognising the stables, let out a loud whinny of greeting to his equine friends. Derry led the horse to the front of the house, and a barrage of cameras went off, as the press surged forwards to take their pictures.

"Here, Miss," yelled a woman in the crowd, furiously waving a bunch of daffodils in Merrianne's direction. She went towards the woman, smiling, holding out her hand to take the flowers.

"Merrianne!" bellowed a familiar voice.

Merrianne started, her eyes scanning the crowd to see where the voice had come from. Then with horror she spotted Shula, dressed in some ridiculous brightly coloured patchwork jacket, an enormous red velvet beret perched on her head like a deadly fungus. Beside her was Charlie, deadpan, puffing on a thin roll-up. Hastily Merrianne grabbed the daffodils, pretending she hadn't seen her mother, too shaken to even thank the woman. She hurried after Derry who, dying to crack open the champagne, was taking the horse back to the stables. What the hell was her mother doing here? How on earth could she let Derry meet her? He would hardly want to have an aging hippy and her left-wing toyboy as company.

As the crowds began to disperse, Derry's friends began to arrive to celebrate the win in style. The stable lads, having hurried through their work, began to do justice to the barrel of Guinness that Derry had laid on. A harassed-looking bar man had been sent up from the village pub to dispense the drinks and was already red-faced and sweating. The dining-room had hastily been transformed, the long mahogany table pushed up against the wall, covered in a cloth and drink of every description crammed onto it.

Danny Keogh, his face puffy from the amount that he had drunk since the win, lurched through the crowds, a bottle of champagne in one hand and a pint of Guinness in the other. Merrianne escaped upstairs and changed thankfully out of the awful ankle-boots. When she peered out of the window the crowds had dispersed and to her relief there was no sign of her mother. She slipped into a pair of open-backed sandals and went back downstairs. The dining-room was crowded, the hum of conversation like the angry buzzing of a hornet's nest. Jockeys, looking uncomfortable in unfamiliar ties and jackets, were attempting to prove that they could drink more than the stable lads. The owners of the horses sipped champagne and tried to pretend that they didn't mind the vast sums of money that they gave to Derry to keep their horses running.

Merrianne threaded her way through the crowded room towards Derry. He was deep in conversation with Valerie Johnson, his dark hair almost touching her russet-red bob. Merrianne felt a surge of annoyance. She wanted to be with Derry, sharing his glory, not fighting off some middle-aged tart who thought that she had some claim to his attention.

"There you are," said Derry, not noticing her look of annoyance. "Get Valerie another drink, would you?" He removed Valerie's glass from her tanned hand and thrusted it nonchalantly in Merrianne's direction. Before she turned, Merrianne caught sight of Valerie's smug look of triumph at her having been sent away. Furious, Merrianne shoved Liam Tierney out of the way as she went to the makeshift bar to fetch Valerie's drink, wishing wholeheartedly that she would have the opportunity to spit in the glass.

The dining-room doors burst open and a very drunk stable lad staggered in leading a bemused-looking Pincushion who walked across the pale green carpet leaving dirty brown hoofprints.

"Shut up!" bellowed David Johnson, slamming a full bottle of champagne down onto the table to attract everyone's attention. His bald head glistened with sweat.

The hum of noise stopped instantly and everyone turned to him expectantly. "I think that we should drink a toast to our winning trainer, Derry Blake!"

"Derry!" yelled everyone, raising their glasses and showering themselves with drink. "Where is he?" David asked, peering around the room through the thick lenses of his enormous glasses. Everyone shrugged. There was no sign of Derry. Merrianne scanned the room too, feeling sick. There was no sign of Valerie either.

CHAPTER TWENTY-THREE

"Hello, could I speak to Paris O'Shea?" The male voice on the telephone had a strong Dublin accent.

"I'm Paris," she said hesitantly. Nowadays the telephone usually meant bad news. "This is Mick Lloyd from Racing Reports newspaper, I just wanted to get your reaction to Pincushion winning the Grand National."

The bastards, why could they never leave her alone, she thought, feeling her heart begin to pound. "Go away!" she stormed slamming down the receiver and then instantly regretting it. Now they knew how hurt and upset she was. If only she had said that it was great news and congratulated Derry!

How did they expect her to feel? One of her best horses had been taken away from her and given to the man who had broken her heart and he had won the biggest race in the world with it. "Oh, I'm delighted for Derry," she mumbled out loud, mocking herself. "The horse would never have won it if it had stayed with me. Derry is a far better trainer." Her throat seized up and the words became impossible to get out, but they went on and on in her mind. Then with a scream of temper she exploded, sweeping the half-read newspaper and her coffee cup to the floor. The cup shattered, the liquid oozing slowly over the newspaper, soaking into the words, mingling with the wet blotches where she had sobbed when she had read the report of how well the horse had run and what a wonderful trainer Derry was.

Weeping as if her heart would break, she slowly picked up the pieces of broken china. How easy it would be to shove one of these sharp pieces into her wrist, to watch the blood flowing out, slowly at first, then a torrent, covering the newspaper and those awful words. She stared at the piece of china for a long time, turning it over in her fingers. Then, almost reluctantly she picked up the rest of the pieces and wrapped them in the coffee-soaked newspaper, wrinkling her nose at the cloying smell of coffee and wet paper.

What a wonderful trainer Derry was. It had been she who had trained the horse. She had found the horse for Danny Keogh. She had just won a big race at Punchestown when he had come up to her, his wolfhound face fixed in a grin, and asked her to find him a horse and train it for him and then ride it. Winning the Grand National had been his dream. And she had promised him that she would make it come true. From the moment she had seen Pincushion she had known that he was the horse that she was looking for. A perfect chaser, tall, strong, with the most powerful quarters that she had ever seen and a great barrel of a chest, plenty of room for a big heart and lungs to give him the stamina that he would need. Danny had been horrified. The horse, skinny to the point of emaciation, and as nasty as a wife whose husband has had a fling with her best friend, had been phenomenally expensive. But to her great satisfaction the horse had proved her right. He became a total racing machine. He was a delight to ride, eating up the ground with his huge stride, taking the fences as if they were nothing and having the stamina to charge past all of the competition at the end of the race. She had been certain that he would take her safely around the awesome Grand National course and knew that there was a possibility that she could even win it and be the first lady in history to do so.

She had watched the race. She had not wanted to. She had been determined that she was not going to, yet relentlessly her feet had carried her inside when the race was about to start and her hands had switched on the television. The pain had been incredible, watching Derry being interviewed for television telling the reporters all about the horse. He was so breathtakingly handsome, arrogant, with his high cheekbones and long straight nose, and his favourite felt hat tipped over his dark eyes. And there beside him, simpering with triumph was Merrianne, transformed from plain stable girl into glamorous paramour.

She had been glued to the screen for every inch of the race, watching Pincushion leaping the enormous fences, almost mocking them as over and over again he soared into the air. Even at the final fence, when he must have been exhausted, he kept going, pounding relentlessly up the final stretch of turf. That should have been me, thought Paris, staring miserably at the screen, listening to the roar of the crowds, feeling the horse beneath her, nursing him home, gently up the final furlong and past the winning post. But instead she was at home, scarred physically and mentally, too broken in spirit to ride. Only alive because her body kept itself that way. If she could have told her lungs to stop breathing, or her heart to stop beating, she would have done so gladly.

She was glad that Paddy had gone out. It would have been unbearable to watch the race with him. His guilt at having lost the horse for her was immense. His hatred of Derry would have exploded as they watched the race, and while it was hard enough for her to cope with her own misery, it would have been torture to have to endure his as well.

Now, she straightened up slowly and shoved the sopping newspaper into the bin, then jumped violently as there was a loud banging on the door.

"Yes?"

A dishevelled man in a crumpled jacket stood on the doorstep. "Paris?" he smirked, his face splitting into a wolf-like grin revealing a row of tobacco-stained teeth, leaning at odd angles, like an abandoned graveyard. "Gerry Flaherty from the Racing Times. I wanted to get your comments on Pincushion winning the Grand National."

For a moment Paris stared at him, stunned into immobility. How dare he come marching into the yard and harass her at home? Her eyes roved over his predatory face, the rusty red hair thinning over a pate as freckled as a hen's egg, the protruding beer belly, out of place on his slender frame. An enormous camera dangled around his turkey-thin neck and his jacket pockets overflowed with tattered notebooks. "Why can't you leave me alone?" she snapped. Then as if something broke inside her, she gave a roar of temper and viciously shoved him off the doorstep.

"Oyy!" he yelled, moving rapidly backwards, used to hostility from his interviewees as he poked his long thin nose were it was never wanted, but suddenly afraid of her physical assault.

"Get away from here!" She shoved again, feeling his soft flesh, spongy beneath her fingers. She propelled him out into the stable yard. "Leave me alone!" she yelled, giving him a final shove.

"So," he mocked, dancing quickly out of reach, "I take it you aren't pleased that Derry won the Grand National with Pincushion."

She exploded into violent temper. "No, I'm fucking not pleased – that was my horse!" she wailed.

"Thanks then for your comments," grinned Gerry.

She realised then that he was lowering the camera. He had taken a photograph of her in full flight in a vicious temper. He sauntered off across the yard, whistling merrily, to a small, low-slung sports car, then drove off with a screech of tyres and a toot of the horn.

Pari sank down against the wall that separated the garden from the stable yard. How could she have let herself explode like that? Had she learnt nothing from her years of dealing with the media? You should never lose control in front of them. That was just what they wanted, some emotion to make a story out of. She should have just calmly told him to go away. "Oh fuck," she moaned, putting her head in her hands, was there no end to this hell?

"Well done," snapped Paddy the next morning, roughly shoving a rolled-up newspaper in her direction. "You made a fucking fool of yourself with that reporter yesterday." Sighing bitterly he went through to the kitchen. Paris could hear him switching on the kettle and the clatter of mugs as he made a cup of tea. "Could you not have just told him to go away? Shut the door in his face?"

Paris remained frozen in the centre of the room, his cruel words like blows to her. She hunched her shoulders as if to ward them off. Then, although she knew that she was not going to see anything good, she unfurled the newspaper.

Nothing could have prepared her for the awful sight on the front of the newspaper. The headlines read, That Was My Horse! and beneath it was a close-up shot of her face, contorted in rage, her mouth open, grimacing like a cornered lioness, her scar a deep angry red. She was still staring bleakly at the front page, holding it with trembling hands when Paddy came back into the room with two mugs of tea.

He put them down on the table. "Have you learned nothing?" he said bitterly. "Surely to God you should have learnt to keep your mouth shut around these leeches!"

Paris turned, slowly, biting her lip to stop herself from crying out, his anger was worse than anything.

"You've made a fucking idiot of yourself," Paddy said coldly, thrusting a

127

mug of tea in her direction.

Ignoring him, she fled from the room and out into the yard, taking deep gasps of breath as if she were coming to the surface of water after being submerged. She ran across to the field gate, banging into it hard to stop herself. Great choking sobs wrenched themselves from the depths of her stomach. She sank down onto the grass, head in her hands, and cried bitterly. He was right, of course. She had made a fool of herself. She was a fool. Just a useless piece of humanity.

Through the gate she could see Destiny and Daisy. The mare, contented and settled, with her small, fluffy companion grazed happily side by side. Each time Destiny took a stride Daisy followed her. As Paris watched, half-blinded by her tears, Destiny walked away to drink from the stream that bordered the field. Bleating anxiously the sheep cantered after her, nuzzling the horse's legs when she reached her as if to reassure herself that her enormous charge was safe.

A large silver car swept regally into the yard. Paris stared fixedly at the field, deliberately ignoring her mother who shouted a greeting as she got out of the car, clenching her hands into tight fists to stop herself putting two fingers up at her. "Lovely day, isn't it?" Elizabeth called across the yard.

Paris turned her back deliberately snubbing her. She would never, ever have anything to do with her mother, and the harder she tried to be nice the more Paris hated her. How could she really think that she could just waltz back into her life after all of this time? Paddy might have accepted her, but Paris would never. The hurt and bitterness ran too deeply. A few minutes later Paddy and Elizabeth came out of the house and got into the car, the sound of their cheerful banter carrying across the yard.

"Bye," they yelled in unison as they drove away.

The silence mocked her.

Everyone was happy except her. She was just a cowardly fool. She had lost Derry and had been so caught up in her own problems that she hadn't seen the trouble that Paddy was in. It was all her fault that they had lost Redwood Grange and had to live in this dump. All her fault that Derry didn't love her. She was going to spend her life beneath this black cloud, from which there seemed no escape. Life seemed pointless. What was the point of struggling, from day to day, being miserable, making everyone hate her.

She stood up. Enough was enough. She walked into the house, feeling as if she were sleepwalking. On the table the newspaper lay discarded, her picture mocking her. She walked past it to the sideboard and took a full bottle of whiskey out of it. Sobbing softly she unscrewed the top and put the bottle to her lips and took a long, choking gulp of the liquid. Then weaving slightly she went upstairs, her head spinning as the alcohol hit her. She clung to the banister, hauling herself up the stairs. In the bathroom cabinet there were rows of tablet bottles, painkillers, tranquillisers, dusty labelless bottles shoved in and forgotten about. The feeling of relief was immense. With a shaking hand she seized one of the bottles and opened it, giggling softly as she dropped the top. Then, with another large gulp of whiskey, she began to take the pills.

CHAPTER TWENTY FOUR

"What did you think you were playing at?"

Paris prised open her eyes, wincing as the bright sunlight sent darts of pain to her head. Vaguely she remembered someone roaring at her, hauling her around the yard, holding her head while she was sick, retching over and over again. "I think you call it trying to kill yourself," she muttered, bleakly.

She was in her bed, dressed in just her shirt, while Kane McCarthy sat at the end of the bed, his face etched with worry. She had no recollection of getting undressed. Presumably, she realised, with a growing sense of embarrassment that Kane must have taken off her clothes.

As if he could read her mind Kane said quietly, "you were sick all over yourself so I undressed you when I put you to bed."

Paris closed her eyes, trying to blot out the horrific image that his words conjured up. "Don't worry," he said, a tinge of humorous regret in his voice, "I didn't take advantage of you."

Paris was grey, her pinched face in sharp contrast to the startling white of the sheets, like a before and after advert for washing powder. Her eyes, smudged black beneath, were wide and afraid, like a deer cornered by the hounds. But at least she was alive. For days he had been wanting to come and see her again and decided to call casually by, ostensibly to ask how Daisy was getting on. He had thought that she was dead when he found her sprawled on the bathroom floor, surrounded by pills and an empty whisky bottle. It was obvious what she had tried to do. The liquid had spilled out all over the floor, spreading in a pale amber circle around her, making him choke with its pungent fumes. He had been unimaginably relieved when she had stirred and moaned, and even delighted when, as he had tried to haul her to her feet, she had told him to fuck off.

He had spent the night forcing her to be sick, almost heaving himself as she vomited up foul-smelling whiskey and the deadly combination of tablets. He was half hoping that Paddy would come back and help, but in the end was glad that he hadn't. No one should have to see another person in that condition. Then when she couldn't be sick any more he had walked her round and round the yard, breaking only to force her to groggily drink gallons of black coffee. As he walked, hauling her dead-weight around the dark yard, with the horses watching quizzically over their half doors, he reflected on the fact that he knew what to do because he had seen it on some television programme.

As dawn broke he had half dragged, half carried her up the narrow stairs and found what had to be her bedroom – a feminine pink silky quilt draped over a bed, the floor littered with catalogues for horse sales, smart wool suits crumpled and abandoned on a chair. It had been a relief to lay her down on the bed. His shoulders ached from supporting her weight through the long, dark hours of the endless night. And a greater relief when she opened her eyes. Even if it was to glare at him.

He looked like an enormous blonde teddy bear, she thought, glancing at him from under her eyelashes. His muscular body seemed to fill his shirt and jeans almost to bursting point.

"I couldn't even kill myself properly," she sighed, miserably.

Kane had to suppress a snort of laughter: it sounded ridiculous but she looked so pitiful, sitting up in the bed, knees drawn up to her chin, shoulders hunched over, her face a portrait of sorrow. "What the hell did you want to kill yourself for?" he asked quizzically, shaking his head in disbelief that anyone could be so stupid, or miserable, or selfish. He like everyone else got miserable at times. There was never enough money, or time, and farming was a tough, lonely business. Working day in day out from dawn to dusk with only your own thoughts to keep you company; your thoughts and a few hundred sheep. At times a great black cloud would descend, usually when he had drunk too much and had too many bills to pay. But to think of ending it all was incomprehensible.

131

Her face was blank, her mind gone to some far-off place that he couldn't reach. "Why?" he said softly, reaching and stroking the back of her hand. The skin was like parchment, stretched over her bones, a roadwork of blue lines clear beneath the pale flesh.

She looked at him. Kane could see her struggling to focus her mind, struggling with the demons that tormented her. Then she shook her head. One enormous tear spilled slowly out of the corner of one eye and trickled down her cheek before splashing onto the bedclothes. Life had just become too unbearable. She had only been able to see blackness ahead of her. Surprisingly now though, although her stomach ached from all the retching as if a horse had kicked it and her head felt as if it was going to split in two, she felt more positive, the darkness a little less black.

"I just didn't want to be alive anymore," she said bleakly. "I've lost everything – my home, Derry, I can't ride, my face ..." Her fingers gently touched the scar on her cheek as if to check that it was still there. "I can't ride," she repeated as if to confirm the fact to herself. The tears fell faster now, splashing in pools making the white cotton sheets transparent. "I can't ride," she repeated numbly she turned and stared out of the window. The myriad leaves in the palest of greens and silver danced in the sunlight, casting shadows on the freshly painted windowsill. "I've tried," she whispered, bitterly, "and tried, but I can't do it. I get on and I am absolutely terrified." She turned back to him, tears spilling rapidly down her cheeks. She made no attempt to check them. Kane itched to raise his hand to her cheek and wipe them away. "It was my life. Without racing, without riding, I have no life."

He was silent, unsure of what to say. He watched the shadows play on the bedclothes and the circular patches of salty dampness. "Your confidence will come back, you'll see. Be patient." The words sounded so useless and pathetic. He wanted to give her hope, tell her that it would be all right, that her fearlessness would return. But how could he tell her that when it might never come true?

"And this is a nice place," he said, glancing around the bedroom. It still smelt of fresh paint. She had worked hard to create a pretty refuge for herself, with pastel-pink walls and flowery curtains covered with delicate pink and lilac flowers. She had worked wonders on the rest of the house too. He remembered wild parties here when it was used to house the stable lads. Sometimes he would meet them in the village pub and the revelry would continue long after the landlord had thrown them out, back at Blackbird Stables drinking until the early hours of the morning. In those days there had been an awful orange carpet covered in disgusting red and green flowers, and hideous brown-and-cream striped wallpaper, peeling off where the damp had got behind the walls. Now it was all tasteful paintwork in pastel colours, long, luxurious curtains and beautiful furniture – the furniture they had brought with them from Redwood Grange.

Her lips twisted into a faint smile. "Yes, it is OK," she said, mechanically.

"And you will get your confidence back to ride again, you'll see." It was hard to imagine her being so scared of riding. She had been so brave. Her riding prowess had been legendary, competing against the men with daring and ease, flying over the huge fences on a powerful racehorse at thirty miles an hour. Fearless. It was hard to figure that she was now so scared that she couldn't even get on a horse.

"My face," she mumbled so quietly that he had to strain to hear the words. She looked away, as if even saying the words were too painful for her. She had been beautiful. Still was beautiful. The scar, now red and obvious, would eventually fade; it seemed to highlight her delicate beauty rather than mar it.

"That's nothing," he joked, rolling up his sleeve. "Look," he thrust out his arm in her direction. On the back of his forearm, a thin silver line ran through the tanned skin. "Fell onto a scythe." For a second he saw a spark of interest in her, a flicker of her old fire.

"That's nothing!" She pulled back the bedclothes and thrust a long, slender leg towards him, "Desperate Dan kicked me while we were parading for the 3 o'clock race at Punchestown." She indicated a small, puckered piece of flesh, almost invisible beneath the blonde hairs.

He shifted uncomfortably – her legs were glorious, she really had no idea of the effect that she had on him.

"Boy, did that hurt," she reflected, her eyes glazing with the memory.

"See," he said, slapping her leg gently, "you can still laugh."

She pulled the sheets back over her legs irritably.

"Please don't tell Paddy about this," she said then in a faltering voice. "He thinks I'm a fool as it is, making a show of myself for the newspapers."

Kane shook his head. "I won't. Don't forget though, no one really cares about the newspapers. That front page will be in the bin by this time tomorrow."

133

Paris nodded her head, considering his words. "You're right," she said finally. Then suddenly shoving back the sheets she leapt to the floor and began to dress. "Paddy will be back soon," she exclaimed. "He mustn't find me like this." She pulled the shirt over her head.

Kane averted his eyes. "I'll go downstairs." He got off the bed reluctantly. He would have loved to have watched her dress, seen the glorious body, thin though it was – that he had handled so gently the previous night, moving and alive.

He found the newspaper article laid out on the kitchen table, screwed it up and shoved it to the bottom of the bin where it nestled amongst the potato peelings and used tea bags. Only a fraction, showing Paris's glorious eyes flashing with temper, remained glaring up at him. He boiled the kettle and was pouring the water onto tea bags when she came into the kitchen. The memory of the previous night vanished. She looked serene and incredibly beautiful in a fragile, unearthly sort of way. She had washed and the sick smell that had lingered in her hair had gone, replaced with the smell of minty toothpaste and the delicate scent of woodland flowers.

"I'm really sorry for last night," she apologised humbly. She wished that he would go so that she could collect her thoughts. Trying to kill herself hadn't been the answer; she just had to pick herself up and make the best of things. She could train, be the greatest lady trainer in Ireland, in the world. Then maybe Derry would come back. "It's OK, I like mopping up vomit," he joked, seeing the smile fade from her eyes as she realised the mess that she must have seen her in.

Pride making her tetchy, Paris snapped. "Well, I'm sorry that I put you to any inconvenience." She glared at him, the untouched mugs of tea steaming on the table between them. "Maybe you should just leave me to it next time."

Kane, hurt, exhausted after his night-long efforts, shot back, "maybe next time I will just leave you on the bathroom floor to die." Then, almost shoving the table out of the way in his haste, he strode from the room.

CHAPTER TWENTY FIVE

Racing is supposed to be a glamorous sport, thought Merrianne, the sport of kings. Well it certainly wasn't very glamorous on a wet Tuesday evening at one of the small country race courses. Rain drifted lazily from the west, hanging in great sheets of fine mist that swirled around the ancient creaking wooden buildings. A strong wind gusted sporadically, making a corner of the plastic roof of the hamburger bar flap wildly. Merrianne pulled the edges of her mink-lined raincoat around her and shivered. What an awful day to have a horse running! Derry had only brought Valerie and David's horse because there were so few runners in the race today that their new horse, a rangy black gelding called Handsoff, might just stand a chance of winning. The rain was soaking through Merrianne's leather boots, and trickling slowly down the back of her neck, soaking into the mink collar, the fur sticking together like a cat that has just been dragged out of a river. This really was the back of beyond. She couldn't wait to be back in the luxurious comfort of the car, heading as fast as possible back to civilisation.

Her family had originated from the nearby town. Thank God, she pondered, they had all escaped south, all except Granny, who like her daughter Shula had her own way of doing things. Just the sight of the miserable, barren countryside, had made Merrianne shudder as she had driven to the race course with Derry. She had sat beside him reading the map and directing their route through the forlorn villages and farms that huddled beneath the malicious-looking low hills.

Derry had gone to declare the horse as a runner in the race. He had been gone ages. Probably gossiping with one of the other trainers. Merrianne grimaced as a huge drop of water, spilling off the guttering of the lean-to roof that she was sheltering under, splattered down on top of her head. She shuffled her feet, trying to warm them in the confines of the damp leather. She couldn't stand waiting in the rain any longer. She had to get inside. Derry had told her to wait for him by the owners' and trainers' stand. But he had been too long. She would go and shelter in the café – she would find Derry later. It wouldn't be hard. The rain had kept all but the most toughened of race watchers away. Only trainers, owners disappointed not to be able to show off their new outfits, stable lads and bookies walked around, hunched against the rain.

She went into the café. Inside, the combination of the wet weather and the heat from the cooking made the atmosphere steamy. Condensation ran from the walls and trickled in riverlets down the windows. Dine in style, thought Merrianne, wrinkling her nose at the institution-cream walls and the smell of boiled cabbage overlaid with frying. She got a cup of tea and sat down at a window table to look out at the rainswept buildings and empty tarmac. Puddles were rapidly becoming small ponds, the water splashing and bouncing onto the surface. An umbrella, torn from the hand of its owner danced gaily past the window carried on the wind. Merrianne sipped the scalding brew. It was supposed to have been tea, but in reality it could have been anything. It was merely a boiling hot liquid. She shovelled another spoon of sugar into it – at least it would taste sweet.

Merrianne sighed wistfully as she saw Morgan Flynn hurry past the window, his handsome face barely visible beneath the brim of a floppy waxed hat and the turned-up collar of his long waxed coat. He was gorgeous, in a dark, dangerous sort of way. Morgan and Derry hated each other with a vengeance, in spite of Morgan being married to Derry's sister. If the two men had horses in the same race, the atmosphere would be horrendous. They would snipe and argue with each other each other, before, during and after the race. She took another sip of tea and then almost choked, spilling a large amount down her chin in shock. Outside, huddled beneath an enormous umbrella was her mother, Charlie and her Gran. Of course, she remembered with a jolt: it was Gran's birthday. This must be her treat. Some treat, a day out battling the wind and rain to watch a few miserable horses churning around a few miles of mud. They had stopped, probably wondering about coming into the café. Merrianne lowered her head, hoping that they wouldn't see her. What on earth was that awful outfit that Shula was wearing? She raised her eyes slightly to look. Shula wore a hideous see-through plastic mac, beneath which she had one of her more flamboyant hippy creations. An ankle-length, flowing patchwork skirt in apparently a thousand pieces of brightly coloured scraps of silk and velvet was combined with huge clumpy boots and an Indian-style jacket and masses of cheap jewellery. Charlie, puffing furiously on a damp roll-up wore his ubiquitous combat trousers and jacket. And beside them stood Granny, standing out like a beacon in the grey weather in a threadbare purple wool coat that sagged at the hem above wrinkled beige tights. She had topped this creation with a red felt hat that was crammed over her tight perm. As they moved off Merrianne let out a gasp of breath and realised that she had stopped breathing in the panic of worrying if they were going to come into the café and want to sit with her. That was out of the question. What if Derry met them? Derry, to whom she had woven a tale of a wonderful childhood with wealthy parents, so elaborate that even she half believed it herself.

"Fucking Morgan Flynn's running one of his novices in my race," Derry fumed, storming into the café a few moments later.

Merrianne sighed, it was going to be a long day.

He drank half a cup of tea and then, grimacing with distaste at the disgusting liquid, jumped to his feet. "Come on, Valerie and David will be here any minute to watch Handsoff."

It was still raining when they went back outside.

"The horse should be in the parade ring," Derry yelled, his voice snatched away by the wind. He pulled a tweed flat cap over his head and set off. Merrianne trailed after him. Valerie and David. Great. What a way to spend a day, standing in the pouring rain, listening to Valerie Johnson's snide comments and trying to avoid running into her mother.

They ducked under the guard rail and walked across the soaking grass in the centre of the parade ring. The ring steward was muttering blackly about the race meeting being abandoned because the weather was getting so bad. Handsoff was being led around the ring with the four other entrants. Merrianne clutched Derry's arm to stop herself from shivering so much. She felt him stiffen with tension when Morgan Flynn ducked under the guard rail and came towards them.

"Hope your horse likes soft going," he called in mocking tones.

137

"Loves it," lied Derry.

The horses were walking around the parade ring, their backs hunched against the wind, ears laid flat back, furious at having been brought out of their warm lorries to race in the awful weather.

"Valerie!" Derry said in a delighted voice, reaching out to enfold her in a wet hug. Valerie flung herself into Derry's arms like they were long-lost lovers. "What rotten weather," she said, looking up at the sky and shuddering.

"It's always a good day when you are around," Derry told her. The famous Derry Blake charm had not been dampened by the weather. "Good to see you David," he added, cheerfully holding out his hand for Valerie's husband to shake.

"Hello, Merrianne," smirked Valerie, smugly holding onto Derry's arm. She looked at Merrianne as if she couldn't believe that she had the audacity to be around while she herself was swooning over Derry.

Merrianne hated her. Derry had told her that this was all part of the job. He had to tell the owners how wonderful they were, to charm then and make them feel part of the Westwood Park family, but still it rankled to see Valerie making calf-eyes at him and being with him. She acted so possessively, as if it was she that was Derry's girlfriend, not Merrianne.

"That's our Merrianne," she heard a voice say. Her heart thudded.

Her mother, Charlie and Gran were standing at the guard rail. She moved to the far side of Derry, out of their sight, but not before Derry noticed them, "Christ," he spat, contemptuously, "they've let the tinkers in!"

Merrianne shot a glance around Derry's shoulder. They were staring in her direction. Fortunately the horses went out onto the course and Derry pulled her away, so she was able to avoid their waves and shouts. This was ghastly. There was no way she would be able to avoid them, now that they had spotted her.

The race set off at the far end of the course, the horses invisible in the misty sheets of rain. Derry hurried to the owners' and trainers' bar, guiding Valerie with his hand in the small of her back. Merrianne trudged miserably after them, with many an anxious glance behind to see where her family were – but they had disappeared for the moment. David stomped beside her, grimly accepting his wife's open adulation of Derry. They watched the race from the relative comfort of the bar. A pitiful fire burned half-heartedly in the grate, its feeble flames not making the slightest bit of difference to the chilly room. Morgan stomped in afterwards and grabbed a seat at the bar. Merrianne crouched by the fire, trying to get some warmth back into her hands, while Derry fussed over Valerie and David, buying them drinks and gazing intently at the television that was relaying pictures of the race so that he could point out Handsoff to them.

The race began the television relaying pictures of dark shapes in the rain.

Valerie peered at the screen, her heavily made-up face intent, one hand, tipped with long red nails clutching Derry's arm as she yelled with excitement. "He's a great horse," she squeaked, her voice getting higher and higher as the horse began to outstrip the other runners. "He's going to win!" she yelled.

Merrianne saw Derry wince as Valerie's nails dug into his flesh. The horses slogged past the winning post, mud-splattered, exhausted with the heavy going that had dragged at their delicate legs, making every stride desperately hard.

"Oh Derry!" simpered Valerie, touching Derry's face with her hand and reaching up to kiss him lightly.

"Well done, I'm thrilled for you," Derry told her, looking over her wiry russet hair in triumph at Morgan.

When they went outside, the rain had miraculously stopped. They walked to the winners' enclosure. The jockey had just ridden Handsoff in. He slid off the drenched horse, whose body was a network of veins standing beneath his soaking coat. Pulling the saddle off, he gave his neck a pat and with a polite nod at them all walked off to weigh in.

"Let me lead him in," implored Valerie.

As she took hold of the bridle the loudspeaker above them announced that there was to be a steward's enquiry.

"What's going on?" Valerie demanded petulantly.

"Handsoff barged into Morgan Flynn's horse on the run up to the winning post," said a steward who was standing nearby.

"Could Derry Blake go to the Steward's Office, please," announced a voice over the loudspeaker.

His face like thunder Derry stalked away, leaving Valerie mouthing in disgust. Merrianne stared at her rain-soaked boots and bit her lip to try to hide her amusement. Valerie was so annoyed.

Derry returned a few minutes later shaking his head.

"The places have been reversed. Morgan Flynn's horse is the winner, came the announcement.

"Bad luck," mocked Morgan, as he led his horse into the winner's place.

Merrianne thought that Derry was going to explode. Never a good loser he stalked off the race course with Merrianne trailing in his wake, leaving David to pacify Valerie who was giving a great impression of a fishwife, screaming in temper at a bemused-looking steward.

As they headed for the exit, Merrianne saw Shula hurrying towards her. She quickened her pace but Shula ran and grabbed her by the arm. "High and mighty now, madam, aren't you?" she hissed.

CHAPTER TWENTY- SIX

The trip to Dublin was an annual tradition. For years, since they had left school and begun to earn a living, the week before the Irish Derby meeting at the Curragh Merrianne and two friends would go to Dublin and buy a new outfit for the occasion. "I'm looking forward to it," said Merrianne, as she arranged to meet Orla and Barbara beside the Molly Malone statue. And she was. For years Orla and Barbara had earned more money than she had. They had moved to Dublin after finishing school. Both had good jobs: Orla worked for a barrister and Barbara managed the children's department in a big store. Now Merrianne had the money: Derry gave her a vast allowance to buy clothes and keep herself beautiful with. As he said, he wanted her to look her very best at all times. Merrianne bubbled with excitement. Today she was going to give Orla and Barbara the day of their lives.

The two girls were waiting beside the statue as arranged. Orla, tiny and dark with a mass of curls cascading down her back, stood beside the chunky, Amazonian figure of Barbara, blonde hair, cut to an inch all over her perfectly shaped head. Merrianne could hardly contain her excitement - she had been looking forward to this day for ages. She pressed one of the vast array of buttons on the car door, the window glided down silently. Merrianne poked her head out.

"Going my way?" she shrieked, gesticulating wildly, just in case they hadn't noticed the enormous white limousine. Half of the passers-by turned to stare just in case it was some A-list superstar on a shopping trip. The other half tried to pretend that they hadn't seen it, feeling that it wouldn't be cool to openly admire such an exhibition of wealth and power. Orla and Barbara merely stared, open-mouthed in amazement. "Come on then," yelled Merrianne, pink with excitement. "The champagne's getting warm." She threw open the door. They were going to really enjoy today!

Orla and Barbara settled themselves in the squashy leather seats and took a glass of champagne each.

"Well," Orla whispered, shaking her head in astonishment.

"Fuck," was all that Barbara could repeat, as she pushed all of the buttons, examined the drinks cabinet and gazed out of the blacked-out windows. Merrianne watched them with delight.

The uniformed driver leapt out of the car and held open the door for them to get out right at the door of Ruby's, Dublin's newest and most exclusive restaurant. Merrianne had told them that Derry Blake was entertaining an important client. She had done such a good job that the staff were expecting at least one of the sheiks if not all of them to descend on the restaurant. The maitre d' looked down his long nose in distaste at Barbara's clumpy boots and the diamond stud that glistened on her tongue when she exclaimed, "I really fancied a McDonald's." Bristling with indignation he showed them to the table, wondering whether to dump the common girls in an obscure table out of sight and then deciding against it, just in case Derry turned up. He was a good tipper.

"Well, isn't this lovely," said Orla doubtfully, her eyes widening with shock as she glanced at the prices on the menu that a stunningly beautiful Italian waitress had handed to her.

"Now, girls," Merrianne enthused, stretching out her hands to touch both of her friends. How beautiful her hands looked with their gleaming white tips beside their bitten and badly painted ones! "Have anything that you want – this is on me!"

"Good job!" snapped Barbara. "These prices are way out of my league."

"So what do you think?" Merrianne asked, as their first course was dished up. She smiled around the table, waiting for their expressions of delight at the glorious way the chef had arranged three pieces of tomato, four prawns and a heap of lettuce.

Their reaction was decidedly cool, however.

"Lovely, Merrianne," said Orla politely.

Barbara shovelled a prawn into her mouth "They've charged twenty euros for this shit?"

Merrianne prickled with indignation. How dare Barbara criticise the meal after she had gone to so much trouble to get them a table!

"So, girls, how's life?" Merrianne asked, delicately forking a prawn into her mouth.

Barbara snorted. "Not as good as yours, obviously."

Merrianne grinned. Life really was good for her. She proceeded to tell her friends how wonderful it was to live at Westwood Park with Derry.

"And I'm going to have a new kitchen put in. Derry says I can spend however much I need," she sighed happily.

"Lucky you," Orla smiled tightly. "My boyfriend and I can't even afford to get a bedsit together."

"How's your mother, Merrianne?" growled Barbara, slamming down her knife and fork.

The atmosphere was decidedly frosty by the time they left the restaurant.

"I'll need a McDonald's in half an hour," grumbled Barbara, slumping down on the seat. "One tiny lamb chop and an anorexic's portion of vegetables isn't enough to keep me going."

"But it's a fabulous place," Orla, always the diplomat, said, "and I'll never get over the beautiful butt on the guy who brought us coffee!"

At that, they all fell about laughing, all half drunk on the heady white wine spritzers they had been knocking back during lunch.

Good humour restored, Merrianne directed the driver. "Let's go shopping."

Orla nudged Barbara viciously as she got out of the car and headed for McDonald's, staggering as if she were weak with starvation, "Behave!" she hissed, dragging the tall girl back to the shop window where Merrianne had her nose pressed up against the window, drooling over a Escada suit.

"I have to try this on," Merrianne said, looking longingly at the pink and yellow flowered jacket and skirt with a mass of sequinned flowers handsewn around the hem. Orla and Barbara trailed into the shop in her wake, Barbara wincing as the heavily made-up sycophantic shop assistant tottered towards them, holding open her arms and shrieking "Merrianne!" as if she were absolutely delighted to see her. Which she no doubt was, thinking of the commission she would earn on the amount of money Merrianne was likely to spend. Barbara collapsed giggling behind a pillar, making vomiting noises.

Orla, throwing her a filthy look, hissed reprovingly "Behave, can't you?"

"Well," snapped Barbara, picking up a price tag and giving a snort of disgust, "why can't she shop at Brown Thomas like the rest of us?"

Merrianne was having a great time. She tried on the suit; it fitted perfectly and the pastel colours brought out the tone of her skin and looked fabulous with her hair. "What do you think?" she said, sashaying into the shop, parading for Orla and Barbara to see.

"It's lovely," said Orla, furtively looking to see if the shop assistant was watching her as she picked up the price tag. "How much is it?"

Merrianne snatched her arm away. "Don't be silly! If you have to ask, you can't afford it," she said grandly, exclaiming with delight as the shop assistant approached her with an armful of clothes and a predatory expression.

An hour later Merrianne fished the credit card Derry had given her out of her handbag and handed it to the shop assistant who was virtually slavering at the thought of the commission she had made. Orla, mouth clamped tightly into a disapproving line, kicked Barbara on the shins. She had slumped to the floor and pretended to go to sleep leaning against one of the pillars.

"Fuck. I'm hungry," she complained bitterly, unfolding her long body as she got slowly to her feet.

"Now, let's go and find something for you two," Merrianne said, throwing her carrier bags carelessly into the limousine.

"Department store crap will have to do for us," snapped Barbara as she stomped down the street and into her favourite shop. She pulled a bright purple dress of a rail and held it against her body, eyebrows raised quizzically.

"Wow!" said Orla, pulling an admiring face.

Merrianne screwed up her mouth, "It just looks cheap," she said, smiling apologetically.

"Who the fuck does she think she is?" hissed Barbara, throwing the dress back onto the rail and turning her back on Merrianne. She stalked off to another rail and picked out another dress.

Orla followed miserably. "I think we'll shop when she's not around," she whispered, watching with relief as Merrianne wandered off down the shop, fingering the clothes with obvious distaste.

"Well I don't know about you, but I'm dammed if I'll let her pay for anything!" said Barbara. "In fact I'll pay for your outfit myself! I owe you one since that last time we went shopping."

Ten minutes later, Orla stood uncertainly beside Barbara at the checkout. Should she let Barbara pay? Merrianne was bound to be insulted if she did.

"Now what?" sighed Orla as she and Barbara stood at the checkout to pay for the outfits they had picked out. Merrianne was coming towards them with an armful of clothes.

"Just a few cheap bits for my holiday. Derry's taking me to Barbados," she said, heaving the clothes onto the counter. Barbara grabbed her credit card back from the shop assistant and snatched up her bag.

"Come on, Orla," she snarled, shoving past Merrianne. "I've had enough of this shit." Merrianne watched open-mouthed. What on earth had upset them?

Halfway down the shop, Barbara spun around. "Have a good holiday, darling!" she screeched, mocking the excited tones of the shop assistant who had been so pleased to see Merrianne. "Don't bother to send a post card!"

"Well, fuck both of you," muttered Merrianne, clenching her teeth to stop herself from sobbing. She's be damned if she was going to let them upset her. Friends! Well, if that was how they reacted to her good fortune it just showed the kind of friends they were! And if they didn't want to be friends with her then that was fine by her. They were just jealous of her. Jealous because she had a wonderful life, a gorgeous boyfriend and a fabulous home. Maybe it was time to move on. Really, as the fiancée, well, she would be soon, of a handsome, rich racehorse trainer, she'd have to get used to the fact that she couldn't be consorting with secretaries and shop girls. They didn't move in the same kind of circles that she did. They couldn't afford to shop in the places that she did. She had progressed, socially, she mused, as the car turned into the driveway of Westwood Park, as this shopping trip had proved.

As the car rounded the long sweeping corner of the drive that led into the forecourt of the house she gasped with shock. The forecourt was crammed with cars and jeeps. With a jolt, as if she had shoved her fingers into an electric light socket, she remembered. The dinner party. All of the horse owners had been invited to a pre-Derby dinner celebration. Black tie. Everyone would be in the house in their finery. She should be in there in the new ice-blue chiffon dress that lay, carefully folded and wrapped in layers of tissue paper by the shop assistant, but now thrown in temper at her feet on the floor of the car.

"Stop!" she shouted to the driver as he began to navigate through the parked cars at a snail's pace. The grabbing the bag with the dress in it and abandoning the rest of her shopping, she leapt from the car and tore around the back of the house, stumbling on the gravel. She dashed inside, through the kitchen door. Mrs McDonagh, the housekeeper, who hated Merrianne for keeping her nose firmly to the grindstone after years of just opening doors and spraying furniture polish inside to make it look as if she had cleaned the rooms, looked up from the dressed salmon that she was just putting the final touches to. "Derry's in a fine old temper," she smirked, maliciously, delighted that Merrianne was in trouble.

Merrianne hurtled past her, narrowly avoiding knocking down a tray of glasses that had been put ready for the port and brandy later on. She darted up the back stairs, heart pounding, her breath rushing in her ears, to the bedroom, unbuttoning her shirt as she took the steps two at a time. Fingers trembling with haste she wrenched off the shirt, slapped on some foundation, a smear of lipstick and mascara, daubed perfume behind her ears, slid into the dress and pounded back down the stairs, a pair of high heeled shoes in her hand.

From the dining-room she could hear the buzz of conversation. She shoved her feet into the shoes and strode to the dining room door. She paused there, hand on the doorknob and then turned it. She pushed the door open. Inside she saw the long dining-table, covered in a long, glaring-white linen tablecloth on which an antique dinner service bearing the Blake family crest was laid out. And around the table, dressed in their finery, the men in black dinner jackets, black bow ties and brightly coloured waistcoats, the women in cocktail dresses, glittering and shimmering with sequins and diamonds were Derry's guests. And there at the head of the table, a broad grin on his handsome face, wine glass to his lips was Derry.

He looked up as she came into the room. "Darling," he exclaimed in a delighted voice, "there you are!" He got up and came towards her. The smile was fixed on his face, but his eyes glittered dangerously. He took her shoulders and dropped a kiss on her cheek for the benefit of those assembled around the table. "You stupid little cunt!" he hissed in her ear. "How dare you make a fool out of me?"

146

CHAPTER TWENTY SEVEN

"Derry?" said Merrianne quietly closing the door to his office. Derry was sitting at his vast wooden desk, examining a horse's pedigree. He sat with his back to the huge window that looked out onto the front of the house. With the light behind him it was impossible to read his expression, but his voice was cold when he replied. "What did you want me for?"

She faltered, afraid of unleashing another torrent of wrath from him. Last night had been horrific. She had never seen him so angry.

After he had led her to the table, he had apologised to the guests on her behalf, saying she had been taken ill while on her way home from shopping but was now quite recovered. He had made no attempt to explain why she hadn't contacted him by phone. He had then been faultlessly polite for the whole of the dinner party and yet she could feel the pent-up tension and anger oozing from him. She had been beside him for the whole evening, smiling until her face ached with the effort, making conversation with his clients until her head was spinning. Even when the last guests announced that they were going to head home, Derry had solicitously draped a woollen shawl around her shoulders before they headed outside to wave them goodbye. He was still smiling when he bolted the big wooden front door as she waited beside him, expecting him to complain bitterly about her almost forgetting the dinner party. He slid the last bolt into place and then, quick as a tiger when it pounces, he sprang forwards and threw her bodily against the wall. Merrianne, the breath knocked out of her, was too shocked and frightened to cry out. "Don't you ever do that to me again!" he hissed, his face inches from hers. She watched his lips moving over his white, even teeth, as he spat out the words. Then as quickly he released his hold on her and, pulling loose his bow tie, walked calmly upstairs. Merrianne stood by the wall and watched the straight line of his back as he went, gasping as the breath came back into her body. She sank down onto the cold floor, as her legs gave way, sobbing with the suddenness of his anger.

Finally, shivering, she got shakily to her feet. Picking up the shawl that had slipped off her shoulders from the floor, she wrapped it around her, pulling the edges tightly around her for comfort and walked unsteadily back into the dining-room. With a trembling hand she poured herself a glass of brandy, slopping a good quantity onto the linen cloth. She sank down on one of the chairs, mindlessly fiddling with the abandoned dinner plates, twirling a heavy silver fork around in her fingers. How could she have been so stupid as to forget about the dinner party? Derry must have been worried about her. He was quite right to have been angry with her. She had expected a row, him telling how stupid she was, her apologising. He would sulk for a while, then she would win him around again. She hadn't expected the swift violence of his anger. She couldn't lose him now. She had to make him want her again.

She woke with a start. She had fallen asleep in the dining-room. Stiffly she sat up, shivering. It was bright outside and the birds were singing. The sound of footsteps going along the corridor and a door being closed told her that Derry was awake and was beginning his day's work. She must get him to forgive her. She had to.

Now, she approached his desk. "Please forgive me," she said.

"Don't ever make a fool of me again," he snarled, without raising his eyes from the paper.

Merrianne stepped towards him. Behind him, in a tall, brass stand were crammed antique whips, hunting whips with bone handles and long leather thongs, long canes used for side-saddle riding, and the shorter racing whips. The feeling of arousal came swiftly, Merrianne picked out a leather whip, slender, with a straight silver handle engraved with the Blake family crest. "You should smack my bottom for being so bad," she whispered.

She walked around to the side of the desk, the long dress that she still wore brushing the carpet.

148

Derry pushed his chair back from the desk and tossed the paper down. She put the whip down on the desk and stood in front of him. His face was immobile, impenetrable. For a moment she faltered. He reached out and fingered the whip, caressing it with his long fingers. "You *did* enjoy Fifty Shades," he said quietly, and to her immense relief she recognised the note of sexual arousal in his voice. He stood up, the wood of the chair creaked with his movement. His fingers were cool against her skin as he softly stroked the side of her face with the back of his hand. "So eager to please me," he mused, his eyes clouding with need. Merrianne could feel her heart pounding against her ribcage and hear her breath, ragged with desire. With one swift movement he tangled his hand into her hair and wrenched her head backwards, spinning her around so that she faced his desk. "You have a lot of making up to do," he said, quietly, his tone, oozing pent up anger. One hand held her head to the desk, the wood cool and smooth beneath her cheek while the other roughly pulled up the flimsy blue fabric of her dress and in one swift, violent movement pulled down her knickers.

"I hope so," she whispered, biting her lip to stop herself crying out as the whip lashed across her skin. A moment later he was pushing himself into her, rough in his haste.

It was fast and furious and within moments he was sliding out of her, brusque now his aggression was spent. "Now hurry and get dressed," he said, as he pushed himself away from her and zipped up his trousers. "We need to leave for the Curragh in an hour – the Derby meeting is very busy – I want to get there before the rush starts."

Relief flooded through her. The row was forgotten.

An hour later Derry was nodding his approval as she got into the car dressed in the new yellow and pink suit, throwing the matching wide-brimmed hat into the back seat. Derry looked terribly handsome in a dark suit, and striped cotton shirt. He smelt deliciously of aftershave. As the car swept down the drive shifted uncomfortably in her seat, trying to find a position to sit that didn't hurt. Derry glanced at her, his eyes twinkling at the memory of their encounter. His good humour was restored. Merrianne thanked her lucky stars for her inspiration about the riding-whip. She must remember that one for the future.

A grinning parking attendant, recognising Derry, directed them to the owners' and trainers' carpark.

Valerie and David were just getting out of their car, as Derry manoeuvred into a parking spot. "Isn't this exciting?" Valerie shrieked, tottering over on impossibly high heels to plant a kiss on Derry's cheek, leaving a smudge of crimson lipstick. "Oh hello, Merrianne," she said, sounding surprised, as Derry disentangled himself from her embrace.

"Next year we will have to see if we can get you a runner in the Derby," Derry said, scowling as Merrianne scrubbed at the lipstick on his cheek with a crumpled tissue.

"Wouldn't that be a great idea?" Valerie said, linking her arm into Derry's. "Do you have a horse in mind?" She steered Derry ahead of them, leaving Merrianne and David to trail behind. David smiled tightly at Merrianne, worried about what vast sum of money Derry was going to want for yet another horse.

The course was beginning to fill as they went in, gorgeous girls dressed in a month's wages worth of clothes sashayed around holding glasses of champagne, trying to catch the eye of a wealthy racehorse owner, or rich sheik. Hospitality tents, their awnings hanging limply in the heat, were buzzing with the noise of excited conversation like a swarm of angry bees.

David had organised a hospitality box overlooking the race track. Sliding glass doors led out onto a balcony that overlooked the course. Below them crowds wilted in the heat, cramming under the airless plastic awnings of the drinks tents, gulping chilled glasses of champagne to cool themselves off. Horses, tails flicking irritably at the flies, were led around the parade ring as sheiks and the impossibly wealthy wilted in their finery. David and Valerie had invited all of their important clients to join them. The room was filled with the loud, braying voices of insecure celebrities, all hoping that their collagen-enhanced and Botoxed faces would be photographed by the up-market magazine David had promised them would be coming.

Suddenly it all felt too much for Merrianne, her body felt raw from Derry's rough lovemaking. She wandered out and across the race course, weaving between the crowds of people. She was terribly hot in the jacket, but daren't take it off in case she had sweated onto the pink top and left dark stains on it. The enormous hat was a nightmare to wear, one man, busy on his mobile telephone had bounced into the brim, nearly sending her flying. Her hair would be plastered with sweat so she couldn't take it off. There was nowhere to go to get out of the relentless heat. The hospitality tents were stifling with the crowds and revellers were spilling out of them, pale Irish skins already turning red and freckly.

Merrianne turned a corner and walked bang into Orla and Barbara, weaving slightly from the amount they had drunk, arm in arm, dressed in co-ordinating purple and red outfits.

"Hi, Merrianne," Orla said, a small smile barely turning up the corners of her mouth. "Having fun with your rich friends?" hissed Barbara, looking down her long nose at Merrianne.

"Would you like to get a drink?" Merrianne asked tentatively, longing to be forgiven by her friends. She missed their raucous company and the easy camaraderie they had shared. Barbara snorted in astonishment as if Merrianne had suggested that she run naked across the course. "No thanks, you run along and enjoy yourself," she spat sarcastically. They walked off, Orla's high-pitched giggle ringing out above the buzz of noise.

Miserably Merrianne wandered back to the hospitality box. She had lost her best friends, but then again she had the company of loads of great people. Orla and Barbara were so spiteful she was better off without them. Everyone was crowded out on the balcony when she went in, watching the horses thundering up a race track, clouds of dust rising up from their flying hooves. Merrianne pushed her way through to Derry.

"Hi, gorgeous," he smiled, putting his arm around her shoulder and leaning down to kiss her, while his other hand was caressing Valerie's bottom. "I've just made three grand," he announced as Dermot Weld's horse powered past the finishing line ahead of the others. David looked boot-faced. None of the horses he had put money on had won. He should have let Derry pick out his horses. They wandered back into the box, where a black uniformed waitress was pouring glasses of champagne with a smug grin on her face. She had just been invited out by a member of the boy band that David had invited.

"Fetch us all a drink," Derry said to Merrianne, sitting down and scowling as the waitress, on a haze of happiness, wandered off to the other end of the room with her wobbling tray.

Merrianne got up with a sigh. Her feet ached. She grabbed four glasses and a bottle of champagne and brought them back to Derry.

"Merrianne, you are great," Valerie said patronisingly as she took the glasses from her. Valerie raised her champagne glass and said woozily. "You make such a wonderful couple, Derry – you should marry this girl."

Derry ran his hand leisurely up the back of Merrianne's thigh, under her skirt. "Maybe I will."

CHAPTER TWENTY EIGHT

"What a bitch I am!" Paris was suddenly wide awake in the middle of the night. Ever since the day she had watched Kane's car hurtling out of the drive in a cloud of dust a nagging feeling had played at the back of her mind. Now suddenly, through the bleary, slow-moving machinations of her mind, the feeling burst to the surface, brutally shoving her into wakefulness. She snapped on the bedside light, shoved two pillows behind her back and sat upright, shaking her head in amazement at her own brutality and insensitivity. How could she have been so nasty to the man who had saved her life? True, she hadn't wanted her life saved, but he had done it anyway. And now she was glad that he had. Life was a precious gift and shouldn't be thrown away over some worthless man.

Most people would have just called an ambulance and left her to get on with it. Left her to face the horrors of the hospital staff quizzing her sanity and the distress of Paddy when he discovered what she had done, hurt that she hadn't been able to confide in him. The memory of that night were so hazy, it was hard to imagine what he had done for her, holding her while she vomited, cleaning her up, walking around the yard for hours. It was hard to imagine anyone doing that, especially for a stranger. And all she had done was to be nasty to him, so nasty that he had driven off in disgust. She should make it up to him. Apologise for her rudeness and ingratitude.

Paris leant over and switched off the light, plunging the room into darkness. Shoving down the pillows she tried to sleep. But rest eluded her. She was haunted by the images of his hurt face as he drove away, remembering his kindness when he brought the sheep to help Destiny. It was hard to imagine Derry ever doing something so caring as trying to help a sick horse; he was all for shooting the mare, let alone bringing her a sheep to keep her company.

The harsh jangling of the alarm clock woke her some hours later. Sunlight was already streaming in through the windows. Somehow the work seemed easier today, without the ceaseless black gloom over her head to wear her out. Even Eddie, with his constant carping and passion for seeing the black side of everything couldn't diminish her new-found optimism.

When the stables were done and the horses worked she set off to find Kane. Now that the time had come she felt nervous of the reception that she would get. If he told her to clear off then she would have to accept that; she deserved it. She would have lost his friendship before she had even started to get to know him, but that would be all her own fault. Hopefully he would forgive her. He would accept that her nastiness was just a side effect of the black depression.

She drove slowly along the rutted track that wound upwards through the trees, away from Blackbird Stables. Really they must get something done about the drive. That was another day's work, she decided – there was no way that she was going to let anything get her down today. Once at the top of the drive she could look down over the tops of the trees. Blackbird Stables lay below her, surrounded by the sprawl of the stables and sheds, the black slate roofs shimmering in the sunlight.

Ignoring the nagging nervousness that tugged at her stomach muscles Paris headed for Kane's farm. The road curled upwards through the tree-lined valley, the branches straddling the road high in the air to create a green tunnel of leaves that filtered the sunlight into a thousand tiny shafts of light that danced in the breeze. Then as the trees ended she looked out on an endless carpet of countryside, spread like a page from a child's picture-book below her, the green patchwork of fields blurring into a blue haze where it faded into the skyline.

There far below her, surrounded by its impenetrable high wall, just like its owner's heart, was Westwood Park, tiny dark dots of horses scattered in the fields surrounding the imposing house. The faded cream stone of Morgan Flynn's home was nearby, surrounded by the stark lines of the enormous newly built sheds, that housed his ever-growing string of horses, testament to his ability as a trainer. In between the big stone house and the new sheds was a small cottage that had been his home when he was a struggling trainer. This was where he had first lived with Derry's sister Tara before he took on a partner and expanded to become the force that he was today. A river wound lazily through the bottom of the valley, a glistening silver strand fringed with willow trees.

A mile downstream she could see Kane's sturdy stone farmhouse. Looking as solid and dependable as its owner, the farm seemed to squat in the middle of the fields like a toy laid out for a child to play with. She shoved her foot on the accelerator and drove on. Time to face the music.

Amis Farm had been built by Kane's grandfather. A once-high wall bordered the farm. Now it was tumbledown, through lack of funds, patched with post-and-rail fencing. An enormous set of wrought-iron gates, testimony to the once-fabulous estate, were firmly closed. Paris heaved them open, drove through and tugged them shut again. A long drive, the gravel long covered by encroaching weeds curved through the overgrown grassland. Paris drove slowly, the sadness and air of neglect seeping into her. It was obvious that this had once been a fabulous estate. Age-old trees, soaring silver trunks of beech, the gnarled and twisted trunks of oaks held their heads proudly, beside others, dead, their leafless branches raised to the heavens in a silent plea.

She parked the car in a deserted yard. Blackbird Stables was positively modern compared to Kane's place. A long row of neglected sheds stood opposite the house, the doors sagging – leaning like Paddy when he came home some nights – against the rotting timber frames. The windows of the stone house staring out at her blankly. An old collie dog came towards her on stiff legs, barking hoarsely.

Then just as her courage failed and she was about to bolt, Kane came out of a shed, filthy and blood-streaked.

"Hello," he said shortly, wiping a blood-stained arm across his sweating forehead and leaving a red smear beneath his damp hair.

"I came to apologise," she stammered, but his blue eyes were cold and unfriendly. "Oh yes."

"For being such a bitch."

"Yes, you were."

"I am sorry – you were so kind to me. And I just acted like a total maggot."

"I said OK. I accept your apology. Now come and give me a hand." He turned and went back into the shed.

Paris followed him, frowning with curiosity. She had expected him to be hurt, sulky, that she would have had to work to win back his friendship. Just 'OK' came as a surprise.

Inside the shed sagging wooden timbers formed stalls. As her eyes became used to the dim light she saw Kane disappear into a stall at the far end of the shed. She went and peered over the partition. A black and white cow, her bulk filling most of the stall, was lying on her side, her eyes full of fear. She let out a deafening bellow of pain, heaving her great swollen belly. Kane, on his hands and knees behind her tail, was hauling at a pair of black, slimy calf's legs.

"Give me a hand, will you!" he grunted, panting with exertion.

Paris, used to helping the mares with their foals, grabbed one of the legs and, as the cow strained, pulled, helping Kane to ease the calf out. A moment later a dark muzzle appeared, followed by a dark head, a small diamond-shaped star in the middle of its forehead. "Once we get the shoulders out the rest will follow easily," Kane panted. "Steady girl," he grunted as the cow lurched suddenly to her feet, the calf dangling helplessly from beneath her tail. Then with one more bellow from its mother, the calf was expelled onto the straw at their feet. They gazed at it as it shook its head in bewilderment.

"Isn't it gorgeous?" sighed Paris. The miracle of birth was always amazing, no matter how many times it was seen.

Kane stood up, straightening his back with a grimace. Then as if oblivious to her presence he watched the calf begin its first attempts to get to its feet. He smiled as it lurched forwards and fell onto its nose, a furious expression on its small face.

Suddenly Paris felt tongue-tied. Had her forgiven her or not? She went outside the partition and leaned against it, watching Kane attend to the calf and mother.

"I'll make you some tea," he said, looking around as if he was surprised that she was still there.

She followed him across the yard and into the house.

"Cleaner's day off," he grinned, sweeping a pile of papers off the table. He stood with his arms full, looking for somewhere else to dump them. But not seeing a free surface anywhere he pulled out a chair with his foot and piled them on it.

As he switched on the kettle Paris looked shiftily around the kitchen, half afraid of what she would see lurking beneath the detritus of his life that littered every surface. This place was out of the Arc. An enormous pine table filled most of the space between a jumble of pine cupboards and an ancient range that lined the smoke-stained cream walls.

Kane caught her looking with horror around the room. "It's good to see you," he said, setting down two mugs of tea and slopping milk into them.

"I couldn't sleep last night," she confessed, "I was thinking about how good you had been to me that night. To stay up all night, looking after me."

Kane grinned broadly. "I stay up all night with cows a lot."

Paris sipped her tea, ignoring his joking jibe. Somehow, in spite of the awful kitchen, she was enjoying being with him. He had such an air of peace and gentleness about him. He was so easy to be with. She didn't need to try to humour him, like Derry. He accepted her for what she was. There was no need to be a brave racing superstar.

"I appreciate your friendship," she said humbly, meaning every word. He was like a big solid rock. Dependable. Something that you could cling to in a storm and know that nothing could hurt you.

"To friendship," he said, raising his tea mug and clicking it against hers.

"To friendship!" she responded and found herself smiling easily at him.

"Maybe we could go out for a drink sometime?" he said later, as she got into the car and slammed the car door shut.

Paris hesitated. What did he mean? Did he just mean a casual drink between neighbours or was he talking about a date?

He was staring at her, waiting for her response. She couldn't take the risk. Derry had hurt her too badly. There was no way that she was going to let Kane do the same. He was too good-looking, too charming – she would get hurt again.

"Kane," she said as coldly as she could. "I need to make something clear here. Since we are virtually neighbours I would like us to be on good terms. Please don't assume that I have any desire for anything else from you."

Kane grinned broadly, shoving his hands deep into his pockets. "Oh, hoity-toity all of a sudden! I think that you do want more. I think that you would love to go out with me if only you weren't so frosty and high and mighty."

"I can see that I made a big mistake coming here," Paris raged, shoving the car viciously into gear and letting out the clutch. The sound of his laughter drifted in through the open window as she hurtled out of the farm yard.

What a maddening, arrogant man! Who did he think he was? And when she had come to apologise! That was one mistake that she would never, ever make again.

CHAPTER TWENTY NINE

Paris pulled at the ragwort bush. Her fingers ached from tugging at the brightly coloured deadly plants, but already she had amassed a pile of them. Later she would burn them, and then someday she would create a garden out of this wilderness. She stood up, stiffly, easing her aching back.

Kane McCarthy was marching down the path that she had trampled through the undergrowth. What the hell did he want? Since the day she had made the mistake of going to thank him for saving her life they had seen each other on a few occasions and had settled into an uneasy truce, greeting each other with a polite coolness that had slowly developed into an easy familiarity.

"That's enough gardening for today," he growled sharply, grabbing hold of her wrist. "Come with me!" He yanked her after him.

"I'm busy," she protested, digging in her heels. "I want to get this patch weeded."

"You've done enough weeding," He steered her towards the house.

"What the hell are you playing at?" Paris snapped, jerking her arm away and glaring at him.

He ignored her and strode into the house. She had no choice but to follow him. He turned to face her. "It's time you went out and saw the world again."

Paris froze. She didn't want to go anywhere. She liked being here, busy tidying it up, making it into a home. Paddy could take the horses to the races; she could do the work here. She didn't need to go anywhere.

"Paris," Kane said, gently, "you can't stay hiding here forever, you have to go out, see people. Live."

"I don't want to go out," she hissed. Why couldn't he just go away and leave her alone? It was safe here. No one would look at her scarred face. Want to know why she wasn't riding anymore. Want to know why Derry had broken up with her. She had reached the very rock bottom of her world the day she had tried to kill herself. But if death wasn't the answer, then at least she could inhabit this life that she had created for herself, peaceful within the safe confines of home. She could train the horses. The lads that came to ride out were nice – they didn't ask stupid questions. They just got on with what she told them to do and went away again. Paddy skirted around her, taking the horses to the races, coming home drunk. His life went on as usual. He was taking out her mother, disappearing at odd times during the day, coming back looking radiant as if he had just discovered true love. They didn't talk about that relationship. Paris couldn't forgive her mother. Wouldn't. She didn't want anything to do with her. So Paddy conducted his relationship away from Blackbird Stables. It lay between them, unspoken, a festering sore that neither of them could bear to touch.

"You need to go out," Kane repeated gently. "You can't stay here forever."

"Why can't I?" she whispered.

"Because you aren't living," he said, taking her shoulders and turning her so that she faced the mirror. "You are just existing. Look at yourself for heaven's sake." He stood behind her and put one enormous hand on her forehead so that she couldn't turn away. Reluctantly she raised her eyes until she looked at her reflection. A tousle-haired, wild-eyed urchin stared crossly back at her. A smear of mud ran across her forehead where she had wiped away the sweat.

Wrenching herself out of his grip she moved closer to the mirror. Beneath her face, tanned from so many hours spent working outside, the scar that had slashed across her face was almost invisible. She put a grubby hand to her cheek, fingering the fine line of scar tissue. "I just want to be left alone," she said slowly. "Why can't you just go away?"

"Because I'm not going to let you just fade away. You're too special for that."

"Go and get in the bath," he continued brusquely as if embarrassed by his sudden show of emotion. "We're going out."

"B-but," she stammered.

"Bath," he said sternly, pointing up the stairs.

Paris went upstairs reluctantly and ran a bath. She found herself some clean underwear, then slid out of her filthy clothes and got into the water. She wasn't sure that going out was such a good idea, but Kane obviously wasn't going to give up. Maybe they could just go somewhere quiet for a bit of lunch and then come home and he would go away again. She soaped her body, letting the warm water soothe away the aches and pains from bending and pulling at the weeds.

As she dried herself the door opened and Kane marched in, one hand held dramatically over his eyes. He couldn't bear to see her undressed. He was in turmoil already just being with her. God only knew the havoc it would wreak if he saw her naked.

He went and rummaged in the wardrobe.

"Hey! What do you think you are doing?"

"Put this on," he said, shoving an elegant dress of dark silk covered with tiny specks of white in her direction.

Sighing with annoyance, Paris put her underwear and the dress on. If it wasn't enough for him to order around, now he was telling her what to wear.

A while later, after grumpily drying her hair and putting on make-up she went back downstairs. He was in the lounge, back to her, gazing out of the window at the garden that she was creating. As she came in he turned, and Paris gave a mocking cry of astonishment that disguised the real shock that she felt. He was dressed in a dark suit, with a pale yellow shirt and looked incredibly tall and handsome. Even from across the room she could smell the vaguest whiff of a heady aftershave. "You clean up well," she smiled unwillingly.

"So do you," he said. "Let's go." He led her out to the car.

"So," she said, pulling the car door shut, "where are we going?"

"Galway Races," he said, and seeing her look of horror he lurched the car forwards and hurtled out of the yard before she had time to jump out.

"I really don't want to go to the races," she said tightly.

Kane glanced at her white, pinched face, her eyes shining with unshed tears. "Do you good," he said quickly, wondering if he had done the right thing.

She was silent for the whole drive, lost in her own world. Kane had hoped that the day out would bring her out of herself. Now he wasn't so sure that it was a good idea, especially as they neared the race course, joining a long line of cars already queuing along the dual carriageway, and he noticed that her knuckles were white where they were clutching the car seat.

But it was too late to go back now. She was white-faced as she got out of the car and gazed fearfully towards the crowds.

"Come on, you'll be OK." He took her arm and led her towards the towering main stand.

As they walked across the tarmac a man, almost as wide as he was tall, waddled rapidly towards them with a swarthy leather-clad blonde man striding maliciously in his wake.

"Paris!" he shrieked in a high-pitched girly voice, holding out his arms and crushing her against the loud hand-painted silk waistcoat he wore.

"Milo McFadden, Kane McCarthy," Paris said, disentangling herself from his sweaty grasp.

"Lovely to meet you," Milo smiled, looking Kane up and down appraisingly. "I'm jealous," he hissed to Paris out of the corner of his fleshy mouth, raising his eyebrows devilishly. "I hope that you're coming to the party tonight!" Then, as his leather-clad boyfriend caught his eye, he clapped his hands in delight and waddled hastily away.

"He owns a huge castle, twenty miles from here," Paris explained. "He always gives a huge party on the day of the big race for all the racing people." The big race of the day was the Galway Plate with some of the best horses in racing, competing for the age-old prize and enormous prize money.

All the people they met were delighted to see Paris back at the races and slowly she relaxed and began to enjoy herself. He clever Kane was, she thought – to know how to bring her out of her misery.

Paris and Kane leant against the guard-rail and watched the horses parade for the big race. "Oh look!" she said excitedly, grabbing Kane's arm. "There's Morgan Flynn! His horse Change The Lock is one of the favourites."

Kane looked across the ring to where his neighbour, stood, almost unrecognisable in a smart suit, his pretty wife Tara looking frail but indescribably beautiful in a cream dress of finely woven lace, clutching their young son in her arms. "And there's Derry –." the words were out of her mouth before she realised it. She really didn't want to even acknowledge him.

Derry looked over and grinned in amusement. Merrianne, beside him, followed his gaze, glaring at Paris from beneath the huge hat she wore.

Derry's horse, Inter Net looked magnificent. There was no denying that he had come on since he had left Paris's yard and gone to Derry. He had matured, blossomed into a powerful, proud, racing machine, instead of the inexperienced, leggy horse that she had ridden over hurdles. Derry had decided that the horse would do better over the bigger fences. He was right. And the horse had gone from strength to strength, gaining confidence every time that he raced, winning race after race, to the delight of his owner Liam Tierney, who stood beside Merrianne, lips dry with excitement rasping over his jutting teeth.

Paris watched the race with the pride of a mother who has brought her son to football training every Saturday morning and stood on the touchline in rain and wind and who is now watching him play for Ireland against the best team in the world.

She was in another world, thought Kane, watching her as she watched the race, lips moving, whispering to the horse as it charged around the Galway circuit, leaping the fences as if he had wings. When the horse charged past the winning post, her scream of delight almost deafened him. He felt her mood sink as she came back down to earth. It would be Derry who was leading the horse into the winner's enclosure, not her.

"Come on," said Kane, when the last race of the day was over and the crowds were beginning to disperse. They walked across the concourse towards the carpark. Paris felt happier than she had done for weeks. Kane was easy company and she had enjoyed spending the day with him.

Suddenly Kane felt Paris freeze. He followed her startled gaze through the crowds. Derry was walking towards them, an excited Merrianne clinging to his arm and gazing delightedly up at him. Before Kane had time to drag Paris off in the opposite direction Derry was beside them.

"Hi, Paris," he said, looking her up and down appraisingly. "And its Kane McCarthy from Amis Farm, isn't it?" Derry glanced briefly in Kane's direction.

Kane itched to punch him. He was looking at Paris like a lion eyeing up a slender gazelle just before it pounced on it.

"Congratulations. Inter Net ran a really good race," Paris stammered. Derry had turned her knees and brain to jelly.

"Thanks, he's a great horse," he conceded. "Come and have a drink with us."

Kane felt like he was being led to the guillotine. The last thing that he wanted to do was to socialise with Paris's ex-boyfriend. She needed to get over him. Not spend time being with him. If only they hadn't bumped into him! If only he had taken Paris somewhere else to get her out of the rut she had got into. They went into one of the crowded hospitality tents and found a corner to stand in. Kane went to help Derry carry the drinks.

"Well," smirked Merrianne, "how things have changed."

"Haven't they?" Paris replied quietly, shoving her hands deep into her jacket pockets. "Who'd have thought that I would be with Derry," Merrianne said smugly, blowing a kiss at Derry who was walking back towards them, "while you ended up with some farm boy."

Paris was so dumbfounded at this that she made no reply, but she felt herself flushing with anger and humiliation. She accepted her drink from Kane and managed to force a sip down her tight throat. The icy liquid felt as if it would stick there.

Kane stood beside her silent, glowering.

Later as the parted, Derry dropped a kiss on Paris's cheek. "We'll see you at Milo's party – I assume that you are going?" grinned Derry.

His kiss turned her knees to jelly. Suddenly she forgot everything but the need to cling to him. She wanted to beg him to take her back.

"Make sure your farm boy hasn't got sheep-shit on his boots," hissed Merrianne maliciously as she brushed by Paris, her eyes glittering with mischief.

Kane and Paris made their way back to the car.

"Do you really want to go to this party?" Kane asked, wearily. He didn't want to spend another second anywhere near Derry, or his tart.

"I do," said Paris.

She had realised something: despite what he had down to her, she loved Derry Blake as much as she ever had. She just wanted to be close to him again. Even though she knew that the pain of seeing him with Merrianne would be unbearable, still she longed to be anywhere that he was. Maybe, just maybe she would find a way to get him back.

CHAPTER THIRTY

Milo McFadden' castle was twenty miles out of Galway. Set back from the road up a long, straight tree-lined drive the gothic castle had been built as a plaything for a wealthy factory owner over a hundred years ago. He had died, too busy having fun to marry and produce a son and heir, and so the castle was inherited by his nephew, a flighty lad who spent all of his inheritance and let the castle fall into disrepair. Milo had bought it for a song, in the eighties, returning from England having made a fortune, and lavished all his considerable wealth and taste on creating a superb home for himself and a long string of beautiful foreign boyfriends. Milo was popular on the racing circuit where his hospitality was legendary and the party that he held every year during Galway Races was unmissable. In the nearby Ferryman pub, the landlord was making great money from those who had been invited by Milo and who didn't know him well enough to know that any party he hosted always started two hours later than he said. The uninitiated crammed into the Ferryman, too embarrassed to hang around at the castle until the in-crowd arrived.

Telling Kane that she wanted to have a chat with Milo before his guest arrived, Tara left him to park the car and made her way into the castle, eagerly looking about to see if Derry had arrived yet. Milo came waddling along to meet her.

"Where's that gorgeous man?" was his greeting.

"He's gone to park the car."

"Lovely! I'll see him later then!"

"Milo, the castle looks fantastic," Paris said as she followed him into the castle. Already partygoers were descending on it, spilling out of cars, abandoned on the grass at either side of the drive. She looked around in amazement. The dark stone walls of the castle were festooned with flickering torches, casting bright light and dark shadows. A stone staircase wound languidly around the circular tower, dark, tantalising corridors led to opulently designed bedrooms which would later be filled with the noises of drunken lovemaking. A disco boomed out from the dungeons and at the top of the staircase, open to the elements, the castle ramparts had been laid out for eating, lit by brightly burning torches that had been placed all around the towers, giving an air of opulent splendour.

"Thank you, darling," beamed Milo, an enormous smile creasing his full moon face. "Now I want you to have the best time ever. Let's go and eat, otherwise I'll never get the chance later." He led her up the stone steps, to the castle ramparts.

The weather always looked kindly on Milo's party, and tonight was no exception. As they emerged into the open air at the top of the castle, the night air was still and balmy. Two long tables ran the length of the tower, laid with gleaming white cloths and a sparkling array of china and glasses, most of which would be broken by morning. Huge fires burned in the centre of the tower where a sweating chef, too hot in his white uniform and hat, slowly rotated a roasting pig, watched over by Milo's boyfriend. A dozen waitresses, picked for their beauty, stood beside the ramparts; later they would dish out drinks and collect debris.

Milo, waving the disgruntled chef to one side, proceeded to cut huge chunks of meat for Paris which he slapped with a flourish onto a plate. "Salads are that way," he said, pointing to a table which creaked under the weight of food – great bowls of lettuce, rosy tomatoes, dishes of potato salad, pasta, pickles all crammed together. Milo fished a smouldering potato wrapped in tin foil out of a clay oven behind him and shoved it onto the plate. "Eat, drink and get very merry," he commanded, handing her the plate, then began filling one for himself.

Kane then arrived and Milo began to ply him with food, while flirting shamelessly with him. Paris ignored the agonised looks Kane threw in her direction which were plainly pleas for help. Abandoning him to Milo, she went off to find a place to sit and eat at one of the long tables.

165

Familiar faces, old friends from the racing circuit, called out to her to join them. Paris pulled out a chair and took her place in between a trainer, who was sending out horses to the top races all over the world, and an ex-jockey who had broken his back in a fall riding in an obscure race held at a small country race course. All were delighted to see her once again. Racing people were used to the hard knocks that life sends along. They had all seen bad times, bad injuries and had to fight every day to keep their heads above water. All knew that even though they might be at the very pinnacle of their trade today, tomorrow could see them at the very bottom.

She looked about but could see no sign of Kane and Milo. Presumably Milo had lured him away to eat elsewhere. She knew how insistent Milo could be and Kane would be reluctant to offend his host. She shrugged. She had no doubt Kane could take care of himself, and despite his habit of outrageous flirtation, Milo was a perfect gentleman. The thought of an embarrassed Kane fending off Milo's advances raised a grin on her face. Serve him right, Mr Know-It-All and his wisecracks! She turned her attention back to the conversation.

As usual the talk was of racing and horses. The Tralee Racing festival was the next big event on the racing calendar, six days of racing with enormous prize money, as well as the competition for jockey who rode the most winners. The jockeys held their own private competition to see who could score with the gorgeous Roses who would be attending the races. The conversation faded to a dull hum as Derry walked out onto the open roof of the tower. Paris felt her eyes lock onto him, like a rabbit in the headlights of a car, fascinated by its deadly approach. Merrianne clung to his arm, possessively.

"He isn't worth it," boomed a lady trainer who was sitting opposite Paris and had seen her tortured expression. She glared across the tables at Derry, her face, lined and battered with years of standing out in harsh weather watching the horses work, crinkling with dislike.

Paris forced her lips into a smile, helplessly.

"Doesn't make it any easier though," the trainer continued, "I cried buckets when my husband ran off with that bloody jockey's wife. Just have to get on with it."

After the meal, heading off to one of the many bathrooms to patch up her make-up, Paris bumped into Merrianne. "Where's farm boy?" she hissed maliciously, presumably having seeing Paris eating alone.

Paris brushed past her, wondering how long she would get in prison for pushing Merrianne off the top of the tower.

Kane eventually escaped from Milo's grasp unscathed and Paris teased him unmercifully about the whole episode. In fact, he had got on very well with her old friend and had enjoyed his company, of not the company of the leather-clad boyfriend who had glowered at him jealously throughout their meal.

Much later, exhausted from dancing in the dungeon, Paris disentangled herself from the clammy grasp of a diminutive jockey and headed back up to the ground floor. Kane was happily engaged, dancing with a tall redhead, who seemed quite taken with him, judging from the way she was wrapped around him.

Halfway up the stone staircase was a window seat, the window open to let the night breeze blow in and cool the air. Her legs aching, Paris slumped thankfully down on the plump silk cushions that were scattered on the stone surface.

"Do you want to go down and dance?" said Derry's familiar voice, and footsteps came down the steps towards her.

"I'd rather feel a different sort of rhythm," Valerie replied huskily, her voice filled with longing.

Paris glanced out of the window seat to see Valerie and Derry on the landing above her. Derry opened a door and they disappeared into it. She heard Valerie's seductive giggle as the door closed firmly and the key was turned in the lock.

"Hey Paris, great to see you!" Morgan Flynn bounded up the steps towards her. "Come and have a drink with me and Tara!" He helped her off the window seat and they climbed the steps together.

"Tara, here's Paris," Morgan said, holding out a chair for her.

Tara's lovely face split into a broad, delighted grin when she saw the girl who had almost become her sister-in law. "I was so sorry when you and Derry split up," she said, earnestly. "You were so good for him. Better than her!" Tara threw a look of loathing towards Merrianne. Three drunk jockeys, taking advantage of Derry's absence, had homed in on Merrianne and were furiously trying to chat her up. "She's nothing but a gold-digger."

Paris spent a long time with Tara. After all, talking to Derry's sister was the next best thing to talking to him, she thought wryly.

The merriment continued. Bodies writhed to the music in the dungeons, drinkers and talkers sat out in the cool air on the roof, and mischief-makers locked themselves in the bedrooms.

There was no sign of Derry and Valerie.

When Morgan led Tara off to dance, Paris skulked about, hurt and smarting at the thought of Derry and Valerie together. She stayed out of Kane's way, no longer able to keep up any pretence of good humour.

The hours headed relentlessly towards dawn. Paris made her way up to the roof for some fresh air. Derry appeared a few minutes later, his face expressionless, not a trace of guilt marring his handsome features.

Paris couldn't understand herself. Even knowing he had just been with Valerie didn't lessen her longing for him. Before her accident she would have been too proud to accept such a thing, but now..... now, she had no pride left.

"Derry!" Paris put a hand onto his bare forearm, hoping that he wouldn't hear the desperate longing in her voice The skin was so cool beneath her hand, she ached to take off the rest of the shirt that he hadn't tucked back into his trousers after his exploits with Valerie.

"Enjoying the party?" he said, rolling down his shirt sleeves and beginning to do up the buttons.

"Not as much as you obviously are," Paris said, quietly, looking pointedly over her shoulder at Valerie, who after her entanglement with Derry had calmly walked across the rooftop dining-room to David who was asleep, his balding head resting on the food-splattered tablecloth, the shiny pate glistening in the light from the fires. Paris watched as Valerie, completely guiltless, shook him awake.

She laid her hand on his arm again but Derry shrugged it away. "Merrianne's fallen to sleep as well." At the far end of the castle roof, Merrianne lay slumped over the table, her blonde hair cascading over her face. Behind her a waiter was going around extinguishing the fires as the red light of the dawn chased the streaks of black from the sky.

"Shepherd's warning," mused Paris. "Weather is going to turn nasty. Just like Merrianne will when she finds out that you've been fucking Valerie."

"Hard to turn it down when it's offered so willingly," he shrugged, pulling on his jacket.

And suddenly, she cared after all. Anger came back in a rush. "You really are a bastard, aren't you?" she hissed, glaring as Valerie manhandled a wobbling David through the tables and, blowing a kiss in Derry's direction, went down the spiral stone staircase. "Were you such a two-timing shit when we were together? Are there more Valeries that I should have known about? Were there dozens of women nudging each other and giggling behind my back, knowing that you had been fucking them while I was away?"

Derry pulled out a chair and sat down, looking for a long while in Merrianne's direction. Then he shook his head, his eyes boring into hers. "I was never unfaithful to you."

Paris gave a snort of laughter. "I don't believe that for a second."

He pulled out a chair and gestured at it for her to sit down. Paris sank down. She had never hated him more at that moment.

"It's true," he said, reaching across the table and taking her hand.

Paris looked down and saw her hand, dirt engrained into the lines, the nails bitten, lying in his clean, smooth one, like a dead thing.

"You were the only girl I ever loved," he said gently, never taking his eyes off her face. "I could never have looked at anyone else while I had you."

As if it had a will of its own Paris felt her hand move and her fingers entwine with his. Merrianne, Valerie, Kane, all forgotten, the world spun dizzily on its axis until only she and Derry and the fierce red rays of the dawn existed.

"But you changed," he said in a quietly accusing voice. "I loved Paris, but she went away from me and I was left with someone I didn't know."

Paris breathed out a huge sigh. She had changed. She had lost her nerve, she couldn't ride any more, but under it all she was still the same person. Maybe her riding ability would come back. For a moment she contemplated galloping a horse towards a fence and felt the now-familiar surge of fear grip her stomach. The image was too horrific to contemplate. "But I'm still Paris," she implored. If only she could have him back, everything would be all right again, she was sure.

Derry shook his head, closing his eyes; then he opened them again, looking at her as if she were a stranger. "No," he said, vehemently. "You're not. You're a stranger, I wanted to marry Paris, have her forever, have a family. Sons."

Even in her distress Paris smiled at his macho arrogance, assuming that they would have only had sons.

"I'm still me," she argued furiously.

Derry sighed bitterly. "Prove it then."

"How?"

"Start winning races again."

"I will. I promise." She almost convinced herself that she could.

Derry snorted with derision. "Win my favourite race, the Galway Plate, next year and I'll marry you within the month."

A movement nearby made them jerk apart. Merrianne stood at the end of the table, her face a picture of fury. She had heard every word.

CHAPTER THIRTY ONE

At least Paris had the decency to look embarrassed, thought Merrianne, clutching the chair-back to prevent herself exploding with rage. Derry merely looked amused.

"You have woken up then, Sleeping Beauty," he said smoothly.

Dawn was breaking over the castle, the sky already a hazy blue as the sunlight began to break through. It was going to be another scorching hot day. The rooftop dining-room was virtually deserted, the tables and chair abandoned, with the debris of the night's revelry strewn carelessly around. A pool of red wine, from an upended bottle, spread slowly across the concrete floor, trickling into the cracks. The skeleton of the barbeque lay grey and cold, an enterprising fly crawled on the carcase of the suckling pig. At the far side of the rooftop a group of exhausted partygoers were gathering up their belongings, hurrying to catch a few hours' sleep before racing began again, their drunken giggling loud in the still morning air.

"It looks as if you were busy while I was asleep," Merrianne spat. "What the hell is going on?"

Paris got to her feet, two spots of bright colour burned in either cheek. "I had better go. Bye, Derry." She stared fixedly at a spot on the stained tablecloth.

"Yes," snapped Merrianne, glaring at her rival, her mouth clamped into a tight angry line, "I think that you better had."

For a moment Paris was frozen to the spot, her mouth opening and closing as if she wanted to speak, but couldn't quite form the words.

"Off you go then," ordered Merrianne. Derry was with her now. And Paris was no one. Once she had been Merrianne's boss, able to tell her what to do. Now the tables were turned. She was telling Paris what to do. And it felt very good.

Paris glared coldly at Merrianne, who glared back across the table with equal animosity, like two prize fighters trying to psyche each other out before a big fight. Paris dropped her eyes first and her gaze shifted slowly to Derry, softening to a look of pure longing, like a child with its nose pressed up against the toyshop window at Christmas. "Derry?" Her pleading voice was scarcely more than a whisper.

"I'll see you around, Paris," he said with careless nonchalance.

Merrianne noticed with great satisfaction that Paris seemed to reel at his brusque dismissal, as if he had hit her. Then Paris turned, slowly, like a sleepwalker and, lurching first into a discarded chair, she walked away. Merrianne glared after her. Paris, her back hunched as if she carried a heavy load, walked across the rooftop and finally disappeared down the steps into the castle. Only then did Merrianne turn her furious gaze back to Derry.

Thoroughly unrepentant, he stretched as leisurely as a cat, and yawned loudly. "Fuck, I'm tired," he grinned, sidling around the table to seize her around the waist and pull her against his shirtfront.

Merrianne breathed in smoke and perfume from the fabric of his shirt. "What the hell was going on there?" she spat, wriggling furiously out of his grasp.

Derry, performing mental acrobatics as furiously as a salmon caught on a hook, side- stepped her question. "Let's go home. I want to go to bed."

Merrianne, trembling inside, wished that she could have remained squashed against his shirt front, cocooned in the delicious feeling that he belonged to her. Now that had all evaporated. He was chasing Paris. He still wanted her. She wished that she had never heard his words: "Win The Galway Plate and I'll marry you within the month." If only she had stayed asleep, with her head on the table, she would have never heard him. And would still feel that delicious safe feeling of being in love. Now it was gone. Replaced by a bitter feeling of betrayal and doubt. "I'm not going anywhere with you," she sobbed, tugging a tissue out of her handbag. Her mascara would run if she started to cry. "You still want Paris!"

Derry, a crafty liar who, before his relationship with Paris, had spent years side-stepping one betrayed woman after another, burst into uproarious laughter. "I don't want Paris!" He moved around the table to Merrianne, pulling down the arms that she had folded protectively across her chest. "How could I want Paris when I have you?" He pulled Merrianne gently against him, one hand stroking her hair gently. It was true. He didn't want Paris. Not the current Paris. He wanted the old, fiery, brave Paris. He had no time, or desire to be cosseting and cajoling a nervous woman full of self-doubt. Merrianne, for all her failings, at least loved him and would do anything to please him. He felt her soften against him and smiled triumphantly.

Merrianne turned her face to him, her sweet blue eyes gazing lovingly into his, until, with a blow that would have stunned a prize fighter, she slapped him across the face. "Liar!" she hissed. The face that had seconds previously looked so gentle and full of love, was contorted with rage, spittle flying from the mouth that he had been about to kiss as she roared, "you fucking bastard! I know that you still want her!" She shoved him violently away and stalked off.

Derry put his hand to his stinging face, glaring after Merrianne as she snatched her jacket from the chair-back where she had left it and, swinging it over her shoulder, marched away without a backwards glance.

Slow hand-clapping came from the group that had been about to leave. When the argument had begun they had watched, silent and open-mouthed, not wanting to miss a second of the performance, which would later be rehashed and told to everyone at the races.

"Nice to see you getting your comeuppance!" shouted one of the girls, bitter because Derry had once turned her down flat when she had very blatantly offered to have sex with him in the back of his horsebox.

Derry smiled tightly and, always a slick performer, walked towards the group. "Perhaps I should have done that to you when you tried to seduce me while your boyfriend was being carted off to hospital." He ran lightly down the stone steps into the dark interior of the castle, giggling softly at the thought of the havoc he had just wrought. Served the little bitch right!

"You told me you were there all the time I was unconscious!" The indignant words of her boyfriend floated down the tower, as the young jockey remembered a fall at Thurles where he had been knocked out cold by the horse's hoof as they had cartwheeled together along rock-hard ground.

"I was! I was!" wailed the girl.

Merrianne ran down the stone steps, her footsteps echoing in the now empty tower. Dirty glasses littered every surface and the uneven stone-flagged floor was littered with cigarette-ends. A forgotten handbag lay forlornly propped against the crumbling stone in the deep recess of a window. At the bottom of the steps the tower opened out into a large circular hall. Milo lay asleep, sprawled on the red upholstery of an opulently carved sofa. One plump hand resting across the swell of his belly, the other draped over the shoulder of his boyfriend who sat on the floor beside him, smoking. "Hi," said the leather-clad man, in his heavy French accent, glancing briefly in her direction as she passed and exhaling a plume of thick smoke as he spoke.

Merrianne turned the wrought-iron handle and pulled open the door. Light and fresh, warm air flooded into the damp tower, the scent of summer flowers mingling with the smell of stale alcohol, smoke and sweating bodies. Then she was outside, walking down the drive away from the castle, the scent of the cherry blossom wafting towards her in the breeze.

Even before the Paris episode, Merrianne hadn't enjoyed herself, in spite of being invited to one of the most prestigious parties on the racing circuit. She had hoped that Derry would spend the evening with her. She had looked longingly at the other partygoers, lovers entwined together, eating, chatting, dancing, while she had been dumped unceremoniously almost as soon as they had arrived. Derry had always said that he had to look after his clients, keep them happy, but he certainly seemed to make a meal out of looking after the clinging viper, Valerie Johnson. And yet when she had chatted to Mike McInerney, a jockey who had sometimes ridden for Paris, and then danced with him, she had caught Derry's look of fury and left Mike, afraid of Derry's wrath. She had eventually fallen asleep waiting for Derry; it had been his voice that had woken her. And she had opened her eyes to hear him telling Paris that he would marry her.

Feet aching, she moved onto the long grass at the side of the drive. Leaning against a fence she slipped off her shoes, and holding them in her hand walked barefoot, the dried-out grass prickly beneath her feet. As she reached the end of the drive, she knew that she had made a terrible mistake. What had she thought that she was going to do? Walk home? And to which home? If she had fallen out with Derry, she could hardly go there. But she certainly didn't want to have to go banging on Shula's door. Shula would be delighted to see Merrianne down at rock bottom again. Probably in a minute Derry would come after her. He wouldn't go back with Paris. He had said so. And she would make sure that he wanted her more than he could ever want to be with Paris. She would make him love her so much that he would never want another woman. She must have misheard what he was saying to Paris. She would forgive him. What choice was there? She thought of the beauty of Westwood Park, the line of expensive clothes in her wardrobe. And Derry, beautiful, desirable, unattainable. He would come after her. He had to. They would have great fun making up. She would make him sweat for a while. Not forgive him immediately.

She heard the car before she saw it, the powerful engine purring down the drive behind her, the wheels crunching aggressively on the tarmac. Merrianne tilted her head higher and swung her hips. She would make him sweat. The car swept past her, stopped at the end of the drive and then turned out onto the road, the engine roaring with power as Derry shoved his foot on the accelerator. Merrianne's heart leapt from her throat to her boots, sinking with shock and disappointment. He had completely ignored her. She had told him to fuck off and now he had. She was alone. Barefoot, penniless and alone. Furiously she shoved her shoes back on and stomped painfully and miserably along the road.

The sports car was pulled up onto the grass verge around the next corner, its engine running. Derry watched her through the rear-view mirror, chuckling with malicious pleasure at how her distraught face suddenly wreathed into a smile of delight when she saw him. For a moment he toyed with the idea of driving off again, but he decided he had taught her enough of a lesson. She wouldn't flounce off again in a hurry.

Merrianne hobbled painfully towards the car with as much dignity as she could muster. She wrenched open the heavy door.

"Would you like a lift?" he said, raising his eyebrows sardonically. Merrianne looked longingly at the cool leather seats, music from the CD player hummed quietly. Derry grinned disarmingly. "Get in. I think it's time we organised that Barbados trip." Merrianne got into the car, sinking thankfully down into the cool leather, feeling the blast of cool air against her aching feet. He was a bastard. But then what was a girl to do?

CHAPTER THIRTY TWO

The party atmosphere on the race tracks continued as the beautiful people headed south, like fabulous birds migrating in search of the sun, descending on Tralee for the racing festival. Derry had horses running in the festival. The Snooty Fox, Liam Tierney's highly strung bay horse was entered for the big race of the festival, the Kerry National. Derry read a report about the race as Merrianne drove down to Tralee. He sprawled in the front seat, newspapers strewn everywhere, looking up only to criticise her driving.

"Ollie Molloy's new trainer, Charlie Coyne, has entered Our Racehorse," he snorted, indignant that the rough, abrasive man would dare to compete against the best horses around. "He'll be in for a shock when the rest of the horses leave his bloody mule standing at the start." He rustled the newspaper irritably as he turned the pages. "And Paris has got that old nag Red Arrow entered. What does she think she's playing at? That old thing couldn't win a donkey derby!"

Paris. Merrianne prickled at the mere mention of her name. She would have to keep her eye on Derry if Paris was around. She would have to keep an eye on Derry if Valerie was around. In fact she would have to keep an eye on Derry all of the time. If she had forgiven Derry for his conversation with Paris, she still hadn't forgotten it. The words sprang into her mind like an enormous neon sign being switched on: "Win and I'll marry you." Just a joke, he had said, Paris had been crying, begging him to take her back. He hadn't wanted to have anything to do with her, but what was he supposed to have done? Thrown her down the steps and run. They had been together for a long time. She wasn't over him. But there was no way that he would marry her. That was silly. She couldn't even ride anymore, so there was no chance of her ever winning a race again – yet alone a prestigious, highly competitive race like the Galway Plate. He had even joked that if Merrianne won the Galway Plate then he would marry her. Convincing arguments, especially when said lying on a sun-lounger outside Liam Tierney's opulent villa in Barbados. With Derry beside her twenty-four hours a day, lounging in the sun, swimming, shopping, it was easy to believe that he meant every word.

But now that they were back, Merrianne wasn't so sure. Paris was bound to be at the races, looking at Derry with those pleading eyes, looking like a calf in the back of a lorry off to slaughter. In her angry flight from the castle Merrianne had come to realise two things. She didn't want to give up Derry. No matter what a bastard he was, she was hooked completely. She loved him, desperately, fascinated by him like a small animal trapped in the mesmerising gaze of a deadly cobra. She could no more walk out on him than fly. And the other thing that she had learnt was that if she pushed him too far, Derry would walk away from her without a backwards glance. It was a strange balance of power. She had burnt her bridges, made him her life, her friends, her home. She shuddered at the thought of ever having to return to Shula's. Derry was all that she had now.

"In here!" Derry waved his hand to indicate that Merrianne should turn in through an enormous pair of intricately decorated, soaring iron gates. Stepping hard on the brakes, she turned the car up a long drive that wound leisurely through immaculate parkland, where fat, glossy mares and foals grazed. The avenue turned and then, laid out before them, like a picture in a glossy advert, were the sleek white lines of an enormous mansion.

"Welcome to Ballycross Hall," said Derry, folding up his newspaper. "It's very kind of Alex Ivan to invite us to stay. He's not often here – he spends most of his time in Hong Kong. He trains horses there. This is where he breeds the horses. Most of these will end up racing in Hong Kong."

Merrianne stopped the car on a wide sweep of gravel in front of the house and gazed in awe at the opulence that surrounded her. Westwood Park was magnificent, but this was a world apart. The whole place reeked of money. Three gardeners tended a lawn as smooth as a billiard table. The formal gardens stretched into the distance, tiny lines of box hedges containing a riot of coloured flowers, paths meandering between regimented lines of trees, cleverly designed to give glimpses of secret fountains and statues half hidden behind curtains of leaves.

A tall man, stick-thin, his pinched face almost hidden behind huge round glasses ran down the steps towards them.

"Alex," smiled Merrianne, holding out her hand to shake his hand.

"That's the butler," hissed Derry, nudging her roughly in the ribs.

Merrianne hastily withdrew her hand, a pink flush flooding over her cheeks. The butler took their bags and led them up a flight of stone steps through a pair of wide columns that guarded the double doors and into the house. Setting down the bags, he stalked along a bright, airy corridor, with Merrianne and Derry following. Merrianne had never seen so many priceless-looking antiques, they jostled for space with the intricate carvings and marble statues.

Impassively the butler threw open a set of double doors and stood back for them to enter. Merrianne followed Derry into the most magnificent room that she had ever seen. Light flooded in from huge windows that looked out over paddocks bordered with double fences of thick timber rails, down to the wide sweep of a river that glistened in the mid-day sun like the diamond on the ring of the man that rose to greet them. "Derry and – ?"

"Merrianne," Derry cut in quickly.

Alex Ivan pumped Derry's hand. "Good to see you," and then turned the full force of his charm on Merrianne. He was thickset, with a thick thatch of very dark hair and eyes as black as sloe berries. A wide boy from the East end of London, Alex had made good. Very good. He had dragged himself out of the gutter, clawing and fighting. A professional gambler by trade he had turned his considerable finances and business acumen into hotels and casinos and finally began to train horses in England and then, more recently in Hong Kong. He took hold of Merrianne's hands and looked at her appraisingly. "Derry is a lucky man," Alex had a deep gravelly voice, all trace of the East End long since vanquished.

Merrianne caught a whiff of woody aftershave and the distinctive tang of money. She felt his eyes rove approvingly over her body. He was gorgeous, exuding power and delicious danger. "Peter will show you to your rooms. Come down when you are ready and we'll eat," Alex shot a bawdy wink in Derry's direction. "Don't rush."

Their bedroom was above the room that they had first been shown into, with the same magnificent view. As the solemn-faced Peter padded slowly away Merrianne gave a whoop of delight, rushing around the room, as excited as a child at Christmas. The deep pile of the pale green carpet caressed her aching feet as she leapt onto the enormous bed, stroking the pale cream silk cover and running her hand over the intricate Chinese carving of the bed-head.

"Derry, come and feel how gorgeous this bed is," she said huskily, lying back, feeling the cool silk beneath her body and twining her hands into the wooden carvings. "Don't give me ideas!" Derry climbed onto the bed and ran his hands over her stomach. "Come and see what I've found."

Taking her by the hand, he led her into the bathroom. A huge Jacuzzi filled one corner of the marble-tiled room. Merrianne fingered the pale beige towels chosen to pick out the cream lines in the marble while Derry filled the bath. Alex Ivor must be incredibly wealthy.

"Where's Mrs Ivor?" she asked a few moments later, clambering into the bath, and lowering herself onto Derry's cock that sprang jauntily out of the bubbles like a periscope.

"There isn't one," he said, gently rubbing soap over her breasts. "Just a mistress in every country."

"Would you like me to help you pick some winners?" Alex asked, helping Merrianne out of the Rolls Royce as they arrived at the races.

Yes, I would, thought Merrianne, shaking her head in refusal. "No, thank you. Derry will do it," she said, with more than a tinge of regret.

"Lucky Derry," Alex said huskily, his eyes locked onto hers, and Merrianne could see the naked desire in the dark depths. She looked quickly away, afraid that he would see the attraction in her eyes. It was Derry that she wanted.

The races were already underway, but such was the charisma of Alex and the beauty of Derry that the crowds parted magically before them.

"Henry Meargh has invited us to his box," Alex said leading the way across the tarmac.

Inside the box a sweating cameraman from Important People magazine was lining the rich and famous up against the wall, snapping them with his imposing camera, hissing their names into his recorder and nattering on the mobile phone that was pressed to his ear.

Merrianne took the ice-cold glass of champagne that was thrust into her hand, awestruck, recognising faces from the television and magazines.

"Look, there's ...." Merrianne began to say to Derry, turning to discover that he had wandered off to talk to the Rose contestants who were circulating through the celebs. It was hard to believe that she was actually here. Part of this glamorous group. One of them. She had arrived. This had to be the only way to live.

A while later Merrianne went down to the parade ring with Derry to watch the horses. Paris's horse Red Arrow shambled around the ring like a mule, shuffling his feet and swishing his tail angrily.

"Great to see you again," Derry told Paris, joining her in the parade ring. Paris blushed furiously and hurried away, while Merrianne seethed inside. It was as if he enjoyed tormenting the two of them.

Paris stood at the far end of the ring, her eyes concealed behind dark glasses, glaring at Merrianne who stood possessively beside Derry.

The Snooty Fox bucked and cantered sideways, trying to yank the reins away from his handler. "Looks well," said Liam Tierney, his owner.

The Molloys were out in force. Our Racehorse was led around the ring by the eldest Molloy, a surly spotty-faced youth who chattered constantly on his mobile phone. Ollie, his shirt open to his waist, red moon face beaming with pleasure beneath a straw hat, told everyone who would listen that the horse was sure to win. The jockeys trooped out, pale faces clashing with the garish silks and near-transparent breeches they wore. As the jockeys were legged up onto the dancing horses, Merrianne caught sight of Tamara Cunnigham, her broad backside spilling out over the tiny saddle, enormous beside the emaciated forms of the other jockeys.

"Poor horse," Derry spat in disgust as Tamara's horse jogged past him. Yet there was something eye-catching about the girl rider, blonde hair tied up into a swag that bounced beneath her skull cap. She rode with a careless elegance laughing companionably with the other riders, aware of the surprised stares of the spectators.

In the distance the starter climbed his podium and the flag fluttered down. The race began.

Red Arrow, as if determined to show the younger horses what he was made of, shot straight to the front of the runners, legs pounding furiously. Our Racehorse refused to start, running backwards until the steward cracked his hunting whip at him. Red Arrow made it as far as the tenth fence, where he ground to a halt, digging in his toes resolutely. His grinning jockey rode him slowly back to the parade ring. That was a good performance for the contrary old horse. The rest of the field continued on, hurtling over the fences, ears flattened against the roar of the crowds. The Snooty Fox cruised over the line two lengths ahead of Tamara's horse.

As he went to fetch the Snooty Fox to bring him into the winners' enclosure, Derry shook Tamara by the hand. "Great riding – you are some girl!" he said, gazing up at her admiringly. Merrianne felt the familiar tang of jealousy clutch her stomach. It would be wonderful if Derry looked at her with such admiration.

The nagging thought had been at the back of her mind for days, swirling in the myriad of images that zipped through her mind every day. It was her that Derry should be marrying. They were so right together. Glamorous. Beautiful. The perfect couple. The thought grew and grew until it took shape and burst into life, like a flower, a tiny closed bud, opening as the sunlight shines on it. She should ride in races. Make him admire her like he did Tamara and had Paris. She had to ride in races. She was going to win the Galway Plate and make Derry so proud of her that he would want to marry her. And then he would forget all about Paris. Forever.

CHAPTER THIRTY THREE

Another sleepless night. Paris reached over and snapped on the bedside light. What was the point of lying awake, replaying Derry's words over and over again: "Win and I'll marry you." The impossibility haunted her. She could never ride again. The very thought terrified her. She had tried again after Milo McFadden's party. Bolstered up on a tide of hopefulness, she had been convinced that her nervousness would have vanished. She would ride, she would race again; she would win him back from Merrianne.

Kane had driven her home after the party. He had stopped the car in the yard and turned off the engine.

"Thanks for a great night," he had said, turning towards her.

Paris was miles away, lost in thought. "What?" she said, dragging herself reluctantly back to reality. "Oh, that's OK." She wished that he would go and leave her alone with her thoughts. Derry wanted her back. If she could ride. She would get on a horse and ride over to Westwood Park. It was all so easy. "Look, I've got a lot to do. I'd better go and make a start," she said, easing herself out of Kane's Jeep, trying not to notice the naked hurt that she could see in his eyes.

In mid-summer the dawn came early and the sun was already climbing above the treetops as she marched jauntily across the yard to change. The horses looked out over their half doors, whickering softly, surprised to see anyone so early in the morning and hopeful that she might feed them. Without giving herself time to think Paris went inside. Paddy's snores reverberated around the house as she walked upstairs into her room. She changed hurriedly into a pair of jodhpurs and sweatshirt, tugging on the familiar clothes, the smell of horse-sweat and muck engrained into the fibres and remaining in spite of just being freshly washed. Snatching up her riding hat from the top of the press in the kitchen she went outside. The cover of the hat was dusty from sitting unused in the kitchen. Outside it was cool, the sun not yet sending the temperatures soaring. Diamond drops of dew glistened on the grass, the air smelt fresh and clean. She breathed in the heady scent of the white jasmine that clambered determinedly around the arch of the garden gate, overpowering even the straw and clean smell of hay that drifted from the stable yard. The birds sang, like a chorus of musicians serenading a conquering hero.

In a moment she would be riding again and everything would be all right. Derry's challenge had been just the catalyst that she had needed.

Grabbing a saddle and bridle from the tack room she had gone into Sausage's stable. The horse had yawned and rolled his eyes in astonishment to see anyone so early. A martyred look spread over his kind bay face as she shoved the bridle on, banging the bit on his long yellow teeth in her haste. Buckling up the final strap of the girth she led the horse outside. She wiped her hands on the back of her jodhpurs; for some reason the palms were sweating. An evil stitch gripped the side of her stomach and she hoped that she hadn't eaten anything rancid at the party. Gathering up the reins, she lifted her foot and shoved it in the stirrup. Then nothing happened. She physically couldn't lift herself into the saddle. Normally, to mount, the rider bounced on the ball of the foot still on the ground and then sprang into the saddle, but her legs wouldn't work. They were frozen, paralysed with fear. Slowly she withdrew her foot, easing the muscles that had tightened up with panic. Burying her head in the warm, silky hair of Sausage's mane she began to sob. Why on earth had she put herself through that? She had known that she couldn't ride again. The hope that she might have been able to cut like a knife through her emotions. It was all a dream. An impossible dream.

She toiled through the day, the dreadful knowledge weighing heavily on her shoulders. She would never get Derry back.

Now, a squally shower of rain drummed petulantly on her bedroom window. Outside the wind tore at a loose guttering on one of the sheds, slamming it incessantly against the stone building, the clanging of metal against stone echoing in the darkness. From the other side of the house echoed Paddy's contented snores. He was sleeping as peacefully as a baby, after a night out with Elizabeth. High on a tide of new-found love he had come upstairs singing tunelessly and was snoring a few minutes later.

Three o'clock. She was wide awake, all hope of any rest gone. Sighing, she reached for her book. Lying in bed trying to sleep with fears and regrets pressing down on her mind like lead weights was dreadful. She opened the book, an easy-to-read, familiar tale that she knew she could lose herself in. Then, out of the well-thumbed pages fluttered a photograph, used as a bookmark. One enormous tear rolled gently down her cheek and splattered on the ancient T-shirt she wore for bed. The photograph was of her and Derry, taken when she had won a big race at Punchestown. They were grinning at the camera, his arm around her shoulders. She was filthy, her silks and face splattered in mud. A fleeting moment of intense happiness, long gone, but still with the power to hurt her. She shoved the photograph to the back of the book and forced herself to look at the pages. Losing herself momentarily in the story, the bleak horizon of her life was forgotten temporarily.

Shivering in the pre-dawn cold Paris reached down the bed and grabbed the sleeve of the jumper that she had discarded the previous night. She drew it towards her and pulled it on over her head. She might be suffering from insomnia, but she wasn't going to shiver as well. Suddenly she froze. Instinct born of a life-time with horses instantly alerted her to an unusual noise. She listened intently. There, over the sound of her own breathing, Paddy's snoring and the squall that raged outside, a dog was barking. Wild, excited barking – not a stern, 'don't come near my yard' warning bark to warn off a stealthy fox or shifty trespasser. And then above the hysterical barking came the plaintive, terrified bleating of sheep.

A dog was in amongst the sheep chasing them.

Kane had delivered a trailer-load of the woolly creatures with their curious amber eyes and bemused expressions, a few days after the party. He had obviously been looking for an excuse to come and see her. "I've brought you some sheep to improve your grass," he had said as she crossed the yard to greet him. He slid out of the Jeep. Paris tried and failed to stop herself watching the way his muscles worked beneath the fabric of his shirt as he opened the trailer and let out the sheep. It really was ridiculous the way her stomach fluttered every time he smiled at her. It was Derry that she loved. Derry that she wanted. All that mattered was getting him back. She wasn't going to get involved with anyone else.

Now, fingers fumbling in her haste, she pulled on a pair of jeans and ran downstairs, yelling for Paddy to wake up. His befuddled voice followed her downstairs.

"Wake up! There are dogs in at the sheep," she roared, darting into the kitchen in search of a torch. Tugging open drawers she rummaged around for a torch, clumsy in her haste, only to finally find it where it should have been, on the windowsill. Shoving her bare feet into Wellington boots and pulling an old coat on, she wrenched open the front door, gasping as a blast of icy rain hit her in the face. "Paddy!" she roared again, hopelessly. The peaceful sound of his snoring reverberated down the stairs as she slammed the door behind her.

The storm had whipped itself up into a frenzy. Raindrops flung themselves across the yard in thick sheets of glistening diamond drops, slamming onto the concrete yard and bouncing high into the air with the force. A plastic bucket, left out by accident flew across the yard, wedging itself into a bush where it writhed, trapped by the leaves. At the extreme edges of the pale torchlight the trees thrashed menacingly, their frenzied branches seeming to claw at the air as if they wanted to reach out and seize her. Head bowed against the ferocity of the storm, she ran across the yard, splashing through the lakes of rainwater that had collected on the uneven surface. Slipping and sliding on the glassy surface of the mud, Paris wrenched the field gate open and went inside, shining her torch through the rain, crying out in horror at the destruction before her.

Two dogs, a black and white collie and an enormous shaggy mongrel of uncertain origins, had wrought an orgy of destruction. One sheep lay between them, her terrified eyes shining in the torchlight, a curve of shiny mud slicked where her legs had thrashed in her desperation to escape. The collie was tearing frantically at the fleece on her neck, while the mongrel tugged feverishly at the wool on her back.

"Get off," Paris yelled, hearing the hysteria in her voice as she ran like a woman possessed towards the snarling dogs. The mongrel, the more cowardly of the two, released his hold and gambolled gaily away into the darkness, leering at her over his powerful shoulder. The collie momentarily halted his obsessive destruction and glared at Paris, his mouth open in a mocking semblance of a grin, his long front fangs glossy with blood. Paris kicked him sharply in the ribs. He yelped and danced out of the way, then darted back to renew his attack on the sheep. Paris launched into him with her boots, finally sending him flying with a kick that jolted her weak leg and made her cry out with the sudden pain. At last the dog's courage failed and he abandoned his prize and galloped after his companion.

Paris shone her torch bleakly around the devastation that the dogs had wrought. At the far end of the field huddled the terrified sheep, bleating pitifully, pressing against each other in a desperate attempt to hide from the dogs. The rest of the field was a horrific image of destruction. Clumps of wool torn from the sheep littered the field, blown against the tufts of long grass, as if a feather pillow had exploded. The sheep that had been caught by the dogs lay prone on the grass. Numbly, scarcely feeling the rain soaking through her clothes and trickling down her neck, Paris wandered through the prostrate bodies. Three were dead, massive wounds torn in their necks, the dark stains of blood mingling with the rain and mud.

One sheep was alive, lying on her back, legs paddling mechanically. Paris heaved her upright. With a frantic bleat she hurtled back to the others. Four were injured: one had a gaping wound in her neck, the others, in the eerie light from the torch, were covered in nasty bite-marks where the wool had been torn away and the dogs had sunk their teeth into them.

Paris went back and fetched the Jeep, bumping slowly over the rain-slicked turf, then hauled the limp, impossibly heavy sheep into the back of the vehicle.

She bedded down a stable with clean straw and heaved the sheep into the shelter, examining them properly in the light and tending to their wounds. She would have to break the news to Kane in the morning. Suddenly exhausted she sank down onto a bale of straw, grimly surveying the chaos that the dogs had wrought. Then, with an awful jolt, she realised Destiny and Daisy were in the field.

CHAPTER THIRTY FOUR

Paris shot back outside, slamming the stable door shut. The sheep would have to wait. She had to find Destiny. Plunging through the puddles, squinting against the driving rain, she cursed herself. Why on earth had she left the mare outside? The evening had been so warm as she had looked at the mare, grazing contentedly with Daisy her sheep beside her, sharing the field with the other sheep, but aloof from them, Daisy proudly guarding her enormous equine friend. She had known that she should bring the two of them into the safety of the stables, but, since Derry, the misery that numbed her made every task seem exhausting. She crawled through the day as if she was swimming through thick treacle. And so she had left them out. All that she wanted to do was to go inside, to seek the oblivion of watching a mindless television programme and then to seek the solace of a sleep that never came. And then, when it had started to rain she was too miserable, sunk in her own despair, longing for Derry and a life that had slipped out of her grasp, that she hadn't bothered to go outside and bring Destiny in. There was plenty of shelter in the field. She had assumed that she would be all right. She and Daisy would huddle crossly beneath the shelter of the high hedges and grumble together about their lazy mistress.

Now she was paying the penalty. A thousand grim images swirled around in her imagination as she ran, each one worse than the one before. She tugged open the field gate and went inside, shining the torch into the darkness.

The sheep, huddled miserably beneath the shelter of the hedge, eyed her suspiciously, one of them bleating a plaintive warning. Pulling the gate shut behind her Paris shouted her mare's name, the wind taking the sound as soon as it came from her mouth, making her gasp as the breath was torn from her. She began to run, shining the torch from side to side, seeking out the dark corners and hollows of the field where the pair might be sheltering. Or lying injured. A movement, at the far end of the field caught her eye. She shone the torch, the bright beam of light searching like a spotlight seeking the performers on stage. Illuminated in the light, jerking frenziedly like a marionette, was Daisy. The sheep, terrified by the frenzied attack by the dogs had tried to push her way through the hedge. Her fleece had caught on the thick briars and whitethorn bushes, trapping her. Almost exhausted by her efforts the sheep thrashed compulsively, trying to free herself. Beside her gaped a hole shoved in the thick hedge. The mare had pushed her way out of the field to flee from the onslaught of the dogs. Beyond lay an enormous ditch, with steep sides that would trap a panic-stricken horse.

Paris hurtled down the field, sliding and stumbling on the rain-slicked grass. Stumbling over a clump of rushes she sprawled headlong, sliding on her front, the torch spinning into the air, before landing, the light extinguished in the rushes. Paris scrambled to her feet, the front of her jeans soaked, the fabric heavy and unyielding. Sobbing with frustration she searched for the torch, raking her fingers into the thick strands of the rushes, until with a gasp of relief, her fingers closed around its smooth shaft. She shook it, and a pale glimmer of light oozed reluctantly from the bulb. She hurried on towards the panic-stricken sheep, heart pounding with the effort.

Daisy bleated pitifully, trapped in the clinging briars by her fleece.

"OK, girl," Paris said gently, grabbing hold of the sheep to stop her futile thrashing. Reaching into the pocket of her jeans she withdrew the knife she always carried, to open bags of feed and the strings on haybales, and slashed hastily at the thick strands of the briars that clung viciously to the sheep. The sheep gave a final leap and pulled herself free from the remaining stands, trotting indignantly up the field before coming to a halt, bleating for Destiny.

Paris shoved her way through the remnants of the hedge, the pale light of the torch shining on the long grass of the bog. Destiny lay belly-deep in the mud in the ditch.

"No, please, no!" Paris prayed. Destiny gave a deep whiney of recognition and thrashed furiously trying to free herself from the clinging mud. "Woah, steady girl!" Paris grabbed the mare's head-collar, stroking her rain-soaked, mud-splattered face. She slid down into the ditch. She had to keep the mare from panicking. She was only going to sink deeper into the mud if she thrashed around. With a final plaintive flutter the torchlight extinguished itself, plunging them into darkness. Destiny was still, her rapid breathing loud over the patter of raindrops. Paris knelt on the ground beside her, feeling the water from the ditch oozing through her already soaked jeans, chilling her skin further.

Suddenly Destiny gave an explosive leap, trying in vain to free herself. Knocking Paris flying with her flailing hooves, she landed back in the ditch, her front legs firmly trapping Paris beneath. Paris felt the rain beat in a fresh squall against the skin of her face. They were going to die here. Trapped together, sinking irreversibly into the black, stinking mud. The mare, as if sharing her feelings rolled onto her side, with a load moan of resignation. As she rolled Paris felt one leg come free. Wriggling desperately, clawing at the mud for a grip and hauling at the rushes she pulled herself free from under the mare's legs.

She had to get Destiny out of the ditch. Eventually Destiny would become exhausted and give up the fight for life. Then death would come quickly. She had to get help. There was no way she could do it herself. Kane. She needed Kane. Throwing the torch down in disgust she began to run. Weak with the effort of getting out of the mud and the weight of the water clinging to her jeans, she ploughed onwards to the house.

"Fucking dogs!" Kane swore an hour later, leaping out of his tractor. The first grey light of dawn was filtering slowly through the murk. The rain had stopped, the hedges dripped, sagging beneath the weight of water that had clung to their branches. A dark trail where the enormous wheels of the tractor had squashed into the wet ground led from the gate to the gaping hole in the hedge.

"The owners don't know any better," Paris complained, bitterly, as he handed her a thick nylon rope.

"Don't care either. They just let their dogs roam all over the place, not caring what they do!" He shook his head at such stupidity. He shoved his way through the gap in the hedge. "Fuck," he swore softly, looking in horror at the exhausted mare. In the pale light, the situation looked hopeless. Destiny lay on her side, her dark coat soaked with sweat and rain and streaked with mud. It was plastered in her mane, flattening the silky hair to her neck, clinging to her ears, caked around the velvet soft skin of her muzzle.

"Get her out," pleaded Paris, her voice rising in panic. The mare would die of exhaustion if they didn't free her soon. She scrambled through the hedge and crouched beside the mare, fitfully scraping the clinging mud from her face. "Kane, get her out," she sobbed, her voice rising to hysterical pitch.

Kane hauled Paris to her feet and put his arm around her shoulder, pulling her towards him. As she leant on him for support he gently enfolded her in his arms, feeling the shivers rack through her thin frame as the cold and terror set in. "Don't worry," he said, with more conviction than he felt. "We'll soon have her out of there." He sent Paris to fetch a shovel out of the back of the tractor and crouched down beside the mare. He let out a low whistle of despair. She was in an awful predicament. If they could get her out it would be a pure miracle. "Thanks," he said, taking the shovel from Paris. If he could get the ropes underneath the mare's chest they might just be able to drag her free with the tractor. Pushing the shovel into the peaty earth he began to work. Paris had been dealt such a rough deal with her life recently. If only he could save the mare. She deserved a bit of good luck. And maybe it would help her to see how much she needed him in her life.

Having dug a small channel under the mare, behind her front legs, he tried to thrust the ropes through it, but the soft mud kept filling it up again. He tried again, shoving his arm through the channel up to the shoulder.

"Right Paris!" he gasped. "Can you grab the ends?"

She clawed the mud away with her hands and pulled the ropes through.

Kane knotted the ropes firmly around Destiny and tied them to the tractor. Then, saying a silent prayer, he got into the cab and gently eased the tractor forwards. The rope tightened as the deadly mud clung to the mare, trying to hold her, and then with aching slowness she emerged from the ditch. She began to plunge as she felt the mud release its deadly grip on her body and almost stood up and then fell sideways, exhausted by fear and exertion.

"Yeees!" Paris screamed with delight as the mare finally slid free from the mud. Elation gave her new energy and she jumped up and punched the air.

"Thank you, thank you!" She flung her arms around Kane's neck and planted a huge kiss on his cheek.

"Hang on, we've got to get her up to the yard yet," Kane said. He unzipped his mud-caked rain-jacket and, gently sliding his arms around Paris, he pulled her against his warm chest.

Paris felt all the tension drain from her body, as she leant against Kane, feeling the warm, safe comfort of his body against hers.

Destiny lay sprawled on the rain-soaked grass, her sides heaving, legs paddling slowly, her head outstretched, nostrils flared with red. Paris, brought sharply back to earth by the sight, began to cry. She had pinned all her hopes on freeing the mare, but now she looked as if she was going to die from exhaustion and the sheer terror of her ordeal. She wrenched herself sharply from Kane's arms.

"Get up, Destiny" she pleaded, heaving on the mare's head-collar, hauling her mud-caked head a few inches off the ground. "Please try!" The mare thrashed furiously, trying to get up, then fell exhausted back onto the grass and lay still. "She's going to die!" Paris closed her eyes and covered her face with her muddy hands, unable to bear the loss of her beloved mare.

Kane nearly wept with frustration. He had wanted so desperately to be able to save the mare for Paris.

Then, with an almighty effort, Destiny pulled herself upright and staggered to her feet. With a cry of delight Paris leapt forwards and grabbed her head-collar, as she swayed unsteadily, legs outstretched like a new-born foal.

Slowly they led the mare up the field towards the stable yard. It was fully light now, the rain had stopped and a pale sun was trying to force its way through the last remnants of the silver clouds. The air smelt fresh, the dust from the heat wave washed away in the storm. Destiny stumbled and half fell through the doorway, but at last she was safely home. Paris shook fresh straw around the walls, creating deep soft banks that would cushion the mare if she fell again. She bustled around making the mare comfortable until she remembered Kane. He was standing in a corner of the stable, looking at the filthy mare in wonderment.

"Thank you," Paris said quietly coming to stand in front of him. He was filthy, mud caked over his shirt front and jeans. Then on impulse she reached up and wiped a smear of mud from his cheek, and a moment later she was in his arms, pressed against the warm, safe bulk of his chest. She felt him tilt his head seeking her lips and raised her mouth to meet his, twining her hands in his thick blonde hair. His lips felt delicious against hers, his hands were roaming everywhere over her body, turning her insides to liquid. A sudden noise made them jump apart, startled. With a bleat of annoyance at having been forgotten, Daisy trotted purposely into the stable, fixing them with a baleful glance from her yellow eyes. "What a lovely couple," Kane grinned.

Paris wasn't convinced that he was talking about the animals.

CHAPTER THIRTY FIVE

Derry began to laugh. He shook with laughter so hard that the spoon of sugar he was transferring from the sugar bowl to his cup spilled out all over the marble-topped table.

Merrianne glared at him. How dare he laugh!

"What the fuck do you want to ride in races for?" he said, when he was able to talk. He folded the newspaper that he was reading, put it down slowly on the table and leant back against the squashy cushions of the sofa, resting one arm along its back and raising his eyebrows quizzically.

Merrianne sat on the edge of the chair opposite him, the sunlight filtering through the long leaves of the wisteria turning her blonde hair to burnished gold.

Derry thought that since Merrianne had come to live with him she had blossomed. Nurtured by his wealth and the ministrations of the beauty parlours and exclusive dress shops she had turned into a stunning beauty. Perfect for him, always eager to please, in bed and out of it.

He knew perfectly well where her ridiculous idea had come from: she was scared that he would go back to Paris if she ever got herself together again. He knew that he would, if she did. Paris was – had been - his soul mate. Beautiful and independent. He sighed at the memory. He had moved on. Paris was old territory. She would never ride again, never be the same gorgeous creature that strutted through the race course aware of her beauty, acknowledging the stares of admiration from men and women, yet belonging solely to him.

Merrianne was clutching her hands together, twining the fingers as if she could not contain her excitement. "Well," she explained, wistful as a child explaining to a parent why she needs the biggest doll in the shop window.

Derry looked past her, studying an antique oil painting on the wall behind her, to stop himself laughing at her ridiculous suggestion.

"I always wanted to race," she lied. She had lain awake every night for the past week trying to come up with an argument that would convince him. "I was about to get my chance to ride in a race when I worked for Paris, when the yard closed." She sighed wistfully before adding, "it's my dream."

Derry reached forward and picked up his coffee cup, stirring the liquid thoughtfully. "No other reason?" he asked silkily.

Merrianne sighed.

"You told Paris that if she won the Galway Plate you would marry her."

"I told her that to get rid of her when she was begging me to take her back at Milo's party."

"Well, will you tell me that you will marry me if I win the Galway Plate?"

"Definitely," he lied, in a serious voice, looking at her solemnly. There was about as much chance of Merrianne winning the Galway Plate as Elvis winning the Eurovision Song Contest. At least telling her that would shut her up. She would soon get tired of the idea. And even if she ever did ride, she would soon discover what hard work it was and decide that shopping was a far better option.

"Stop taking the piss out of me!" Merrianne raged, leaping to her feet, sending Derry's half-drunk cup of coffee sloshing violently in its cup as she shoved the table out of the way and flounced from the room.

Derry puffed out his cheeks, sighing as he mopped the spilt coffee with a silk handkerchief. Women were so hard to please. He had said that he would marry her - what more did she want? He gave a snort of amusement, remembering how eager she had been, just to win him finally from Paris. He drained the last cold dregs of the coffee. She didn't have to prove herself to keep him. He was quite happy with her. As long as she looked after him and made his life easier and didn't complain too much about his infidelities, he was happy.

But Merrianne's eagerness had touched him and, feeling guilty, he went upstairs after her. She was in the bedroom, sitting in front of the dressing-table. Her expressionless face reflected countless times in the three mirrors that stood on the antique table. Merrianne watched him through the mirror as he came into the room. It was hard to believe that he belonged to her. He was so handsome. He sat down heavily on the bed, looking at her reflection in the mirror. Immensely hurt by his mockery; she fought back the tears that were threatening to fall.

"Look. I'm sorry," he said, "if you want to start to ride, you can. There are a couple of point-to-point horses you can ride to get the experience and we'll see how you go on from there."

Merrianne rested her elbows on the glass top of the dressing-table and cupped her chin in her hands. Her eyes met his in the mirror, hard as the glass that reflected them. "Are you sure?" she said finally, her voice cold.

Derry got to his feet and padded across the thick carpet to stand behind her. He dropped a kiss on the top of her head. "Quite sure."

She leapt to her feet and flung herself into his arms. "Thank you," she said, her voice muffled against his shirt front. "And you will keep your promise?"

Derry pushed her away, holding her at arms' length, "Of course," he grinned, mustering the most sincere voice that he could. "You win the Galway Plate and I'll marry you."

No one was more disgusted by the news that Merrianne was going to ride than Mary, Derry's head stable girl.

"What the fuck does she want to ride in races for?" she snapped, that afternoon, wriggling back into her jeans and pulling a strand of straw from her hair.

"She thinks I'll marry her if she wins the Galway Plate," mused Derry, running his comb through his tousled hair and surreptitiously checking his shirt front for lipstick. Mary scowled, her thick dark eyebrows almost joining in the middle. If Merrianne came down to the yard on a regular basis it would severely cramp the time that she could spend in the barn or the lorry with Derry.

"And will you?" she whispered, seductively, beginning to unbutton his shirt again. "Maybe," he said huskily. It would do Mary good to be kept on her toes.

The following morning Merrianne made her way down to the stables with Derry. She had forgotten how awful it was to get up at such an ungodly hour of the morning. And if she hadn't been so determined, she could have quite easily rolled over and gone back to sleep when his alarm-clock went off. Instead she got up, dressed in the brand new jodhpurs that she had bought the previous day in a flattering shade of brown that she knew showed of the taut line of her bottom and followed Derry down to the yard. Mary, the head girl, was a surly creature. Merrianne had taken an immediate dislike to the short, plump girl whose wiry brown hair frizzed around her scowling face.

"Hi, Mary, it's good of you to let me ride out," she said, determined to be friendly to the girl.

"S'OK," snapped Mary, glaring at Merrianne.

The first string of horses was almost ready to go out on exercise.

"What horse are you putting Merrianne on? – asked Derry, already looking at the feed charts that he had worked out with Mary.

"Picasso," Mary said coldly, meeting Derry's look of astonishment impassively. She was going to make sure that Merrianne wouldn't want to ride out any more.

Derry led Merrianne to Picasso's box. The small, grey gelding snuffled his pockets eagerly looking for mints. Derry had been surprised at Mary's choice. Picasso was a pig to ride; quiet and sluggish on the lanes he became an unstoppable monster on the gallops. Hopefully Merrianne would soon get sick of the idea of wanting to ride. Perhaps Mary's was a good idea.

"You can ride out with the first lot of horses – they're going to be schooling the horses over fences, so we'll see how you go on." He legged Merrianne up.

She looked at home on a horse. Used to riding the horses on exercise when she worked for Paris, Merrianne was delighted to be back in the saddle. Picasso felt small, compared to the horses that she was used to, his tiny grey ears seeming to be right in front of her face.

The horses began to work, walking round and round in the yard to settle them and stretch delicate legs that had been standing in the stables all night. Then they all went out onto the road, a long caterpillar of expensive horseflesh. The gallops were a short ride away. Merrianne had to thump her heels against Picasso's unresponsive sides to get him to keep up with the others. Mary had obviously put her on the quietest horse in the yard. As they turned onto the gallops, Picasso perked up, pricking his tiny ears and capering sideways.

"I think Merrianne's racing career is about to end before it begins," Derry said with amusement, parking his Jeep at the top of the hill, his vantage point for watching the horses work.

"Picasso is completely unstoppable," giggled Mary wickedly. This would teach Merrianne to try to muscle in on her territory.

The horses began to canter in pairs along the sandy track that went around the field. Then they moved faster into a gallop.

Picasso, suddenly waking up, hurtled along the sandy track, his grey legs going like pistons, rapidly outstripping the chestnut horse he was supposed to be working with and hurtling off to catch up with the pair of horses that were galloping ahead.

"I can't watch," Derry laughed, lighting up a cigarette.

Mary gave a snort of amusement as Picasso shoved his head between his knees and gave an enormous buck.

"She's off," she said with satisfaction.

Merrianne was scrambling to her feet as Picasso, bucking with delight at having rid himself of his rider, galloped into the distance..

"Right, let's see you do some fences," Derry said impassively, sometime later, when Picasso had finally been caught and Merrianne had been heaved back into the saddle, her bottom lip quivering with the effort of stopping herself from crying.

They turned the horses to the fences. The chestnut horse sailed over in the lead. Picasso, galloping flat out, suddenly dug in his toes and dropped his head. Merrianne flew over the fence landing with a thud the other side.

"Oooo!" winced Mary. "That must have hurt!" she giggled, as Merrianne scrambled to her feet, brushing the sand from her backside.

One of the other lads caught Picasso and legged Merrianne back into the saddle. She turned the horse and this time he sailed over the fence like an old hunter and galloped meekly after the chestnut. Mary, who had given up smoking at Christmas reached into his packet, withdrew a cigarette and lit it, sucking on it in temper. She stole a look at Derry. He was transfixed by Merrianne's determination. Damn, she had wanted to make Merrianne look a fool, to scare her off wanting to ride. Now Derry thought that she was the next champion lady jockey.

"Well, she's certainly got some guts," he said, looking at Merrianne with pride.

CHAPTER THIRTY-SIX

Merrianne sat in the passenger seat of Derry's jeep and shuddered. Months of work, riding out on every nasty, difficult or downright dangerous horse that Mary palmed off on her, learning how to stay on, to get the best from the horses. All for this. A Sunday afternoon in the middle of a rainstorm in the most godforsaken corner of Ireland at a point to point. Her first race.

The Jeep slid sideways, its wheels spinning, trying to get a grip on the rainslicked ground. With a lurch the tyres found a purchase and shot forwards, showering a car parking steward with mud. He shook his fist angrily, at them, wiping the chunks of dirt from the front of his florescent vest. Slowly the Jeep bumped over the ground. It had rained constantly all night, and pools of water had collected in the hollows in the ground and washed away the wood chippings that had been laid in the gateways to stop them getting churned up.

Behind them a tractor was towing Derry's blue and gold lorry across the mud; it was so heavy that it had sunk into the mud as soon as Mary had driven it onto the field. Trailers and lorries were abandoned everywhere, up to their axles in mud, all waiting for the harassed tractor-driver to rescue them later.

"I hope that stupid cow is careful with my lorry," Derry snapped petulantly, glaring at the lorry which was lurching over the ground, Mary's worried face pressed up to the windscreen as she concentrated on following the tractor. "Well, here we are," Derry added, with more than a touch of sarcasm in his voice. The wipers spun across the rain-slicked windscreen, clearing it momentarily. Merrianne had a chance to grimly survey the miserable landscape before the rain obscured her view again.

The Ballywest Hunt had held their annual point-to-point race on the sloping windswept hillside at Ballycrua for the last twenty years. The uneven, land, dotted with prickly gorse bushes belonged to the bent-kneed old hunt master, who, always convinced that he knew best, refused to move the venue to more suitable land.

The weighing tent stood at the crest of the hill, exposed to the bitter winds that swept from the west. The flimsy cream-coloured tarpaulin sheets flapped listlessly in the icy wind, and a great pool of water had collected on the roof which sagged inwards threatening to drag the roof down. Beside the weighing tent was the parade ring. Half a dozen miserable-looking horses were walking around the roped-off square of grass, their ears laid back against the wind, swishing their tails miserably, longing to be back in the comfort of their stables. The refreshment tent had been pegged in the only sheltered spot in the field. Farmers clutching glasses of whiskey huddled in the doorway of the tent, watching the proceedings while their wives sat on rickety benches inside, sipping tea and relating the latest gossip in hushed tones.

"What a dump," complained Valerie Johnson, leaning through the gap in the front seats to peer through the rain-soaked windscreen. "Remind me. Why the hell are we spending a perfectly good Sunday afternoon sitting in the middle of a field?" she moaned, looking down her long nose as a small boy, dressed in drenched jeans and a coat several sizes too big hammered on the Jeep door trying to sell them a race programme.

"This, my darling," explained Derry patiently, letting down the window a few inches and handing the boy a twenty-euro note, "is racehorse kindergarden. Some of the best National Hunt horses will begin their careers at these sorts of events. And buyers will be here to check out the talent." He pulled the rain-soaked programme in through the window, refusing the change, which the boy shoved in his pocket with a grin. He thumbed through the form guide, gingerly prising open the wet pages, so they wouldn't tear. "Merrianne is riding today to get the experience she needs to compete in steeplechases. So that she can win the Galway Plate. And her mount is a horse that I have brought especially for her to give her that experience. He has run in dozens of these things, never won anything, but is as safe as a riding-school pony to ride."

His sarcasm was lost on Merrianne who was too miserable to notice. She was shivering so much from nerves that she wondered if she would ever be able to sit on a horse, let alone ride in a race. As they watched, the jockeys came out of the flapping tarpaulin sheets of the weighing tent, slashing their whips against thin leather boots and trying to look as if they were totally unconcerned about riding in the awful conditions. In the centre of the ring a small man, totally swamped by the enormous waxed coat that he wore, rang a brass bell. At his signal, the jockeys surged forwards and were legged up onto the horses and rode out onto the course.

"Come on," said Derry. "We had better declare the horse."

"I'm staying here," Valerie said, drawing the collar of her mink-lined waterproof coat dramatically around herself and shuddering, She poked Richard with a long, red-tipped nail, jolting him from the delicious dream that he had been having about his secretary. "What the –." He snapped crossly, he had just been about to remove Sandra's lacy-topped stockings as she lay half naked on his desk, her eyes dark with desire.

"Wake up, we're here," Valerie said, reaching into the back of the jeep for a flask of hot tea.

Merrianne shoved open the jeep door, and a strong blast of wind blew it from her hand, jerking her fingers.

"Hurry up and shut the door," complained Richard, pulling his cloth cap further down over the round dome of his forehead and shutting his eyes. Perhaps he would just have time to imagine opening Sandra's blouse before Valerie forced him to drink scalding tea.

Merrianne slammed the door shut, a sheet of rain splattered against her, soaking straight through her jodhpurs and trickling down inside her new leather boots.

"Run!" yelled Derry, his voice lost on the wind, as he put his hand on the small of her back, guiding her as they ran, slithering on the wet ground and bursting into the weighing tent.

"Derry Blake," simpered the Secretary, looking up unsteadily at Derry. The legs of her chair kept sinking into the soft ground when she moved and this was made perilous by the fact that she was unsteady anyway due to the huge amount of white wine she had drunk at the lunch that the hunt masters gave beforehand. "Sartaj, number thirteen," she said, studying the horse's documents and then handing Derry a white number cloth with the numbers sewn crookedly onto it in red.

"Unlucky for some," he said with a grin, crumpling the white cloth into his pocket. "Make sure you bring it back here afterwards," the Secretary said sternly.

Derry ignored her. "You go that way," he said to Merrianne, in the patient tones reserved for small children, steering Merrianne towards a gap in the canvas through which she could see the naked torsos of the male jockeys as they changed.

Clutching the leather overnight bag she had brought especially for the occasion in front of her like a shield, Merrianne made her way tentatively into the inner recesses of the weighing tent. Crammed into the warm, steaming atmosphere were the riders. Some were changing, shivering as they stripped out of jeans and warm jumpers into the paper-thin nylon breeches and brightly coloured silks. Others were shrugging off filthy, wet clothes after they had ridden. Low benches lined the four sides of the tent that had been sectioned off as a changing room. Merrianne averted her eyes as a jockey, completely naked, his drenched clothes discarded in a heap on the grass, lolled on one of the benches, rubbing his crotch with a towel and chatting into the mobile phone that was clamped to his ear. A low wolf whistle shrilled out over the hum of conversation.

"Come and help me unbutton my jeans," yelled a male voice.

"I'll help you change, darlin'!" roared another.

Merrianne, frozen uncertainly at the entrance to the changing room, felt colour flood into her face, staining her cold cheeks.

"You can change over here," said a female voice.

Merrianne flickered her eyes over the lecherous mass of maleness until with relief she saw another female face.

"Don't mind them," said Tamara, grabbing Merrianne's bag and leading her to a corner of the tent. "They wouldn't know what to do with a real woman if they got one." She shoved Merrianne's bag under the bench and turned to face her, pushing a wiry strand of blonde hair out of her eyes. "I'm Cindy Knightly" she said, thrusting out her hand. "We're riding in the same race."

Merrianne shook her hand, grateful to have found a companion.

"We had better get changed," Tamara said, nonchalantly shrugging off her mohair jumper, oblivious to the lusty stares of the jockeys.

Merrianne, shy at the thought of them staring at her, turned her back and then pulled off her jumper as fast as she could, wriggling hastily into the stiff board-like back protector that everyone had to wear. As she buttoned up the silks, made in Derry's blue and maroon colours she began to shake, nerves gripping her stomach in a vice-like grasp. What the hell had she let herself in for? She couldn't do this. Three miles of galloping over the undulating course, over the awful fences. She had walked the course the previous evening with Derry. The fences had seemed enormous. Now they seemed impossible. The downhill fence where Derry had told her to be careful seemed like jumping off the side of a house. She couldn't do it.

She sat on the bench feeling sick. The roar of noise and happy camaraderie from the jockeys made her head spin. She was sure that her legs wouldn't support her if she got up.

"Come on," said Cindy. "We have to weigh in."

Feeling as if she was in a dream, Merrianne got up. As if from a long way away she saw herself getting her tiny saddle out of the bag and walking out of the changing area. She stood on a set of bathroom scales as a woman clad in a huge woolly hat and brightly checked tweed coat marked down her weight, shoving lead weights into her saddle-cloth to bring her to the required 12 stone. Then all too quickly they were all trooping outside into the rain, like Christians going out to meet the lions, thought Merrianne, looking miserably at the faces that ringed the parade ring.

Somehow she found Derry.

"All you will have to do is sit on the horse. He is an armchair of a ride. Safe as a house," Derry was saying, his voice coming as if from the end of a long tunnel. Sartaj looked enormous, his huge ears towering way above her. Derry legged her up onto his broad back. The tiny stirrups felt different lengths, the saddle too small, the reins too thick for her numb fingers. The rain stung her face as it fell. The horse shied violently as the wind blew up a loose flap of the canvas tent, and she clutched his mane to stop herself from falling. What the hell was she doing this for?

The steward rang his bell and the horses were led out onto the track. Sartaj lurched into a canter as Mary released his bridle, loping after the others to the start of the race. Merrianne was aware of the white guard rails, swaying gently in the wind, the faces of the spectators craning to watch. Cindy was speaking to her, but Merrianne couldn't make out what she was saying, she was aware only of the length of the horse's neck, his ears stretched out into the distance and the track, stretching out in front of her, the grass churned up, brown mud lying in chunks where the horses hooves had torn it up in previous races and the first fence, enormous, and intimidating.

Then the horses were running. Merrianne stood in the saddle, feeling her horse moving beneath her, the smell of the churned-up earth and horse-sweat and leather filling her nostrils and the dead-sounding thud of hooves on the ground and swearing of the jockeys as they jostled for position loud in her ears.

The first fence loomed up, a vast swathe of brown that reared high and solid into the air. She clutched his mane as the horse rose to take the fence. She had done it. A whoop of sheer delight exploded involuntarily from her. She heard one of the other jockeys laugh.

Four jumps later a horse fell in front of her. The horse shot sideways out of the way of the flailing hooves. Merrianne flew through the air alone and landed with a thud that knocked the wind out of her. A first-aid man hurried across the track hoping that he would have to give her the kiss of life. Merrianne struggled to her feet, watching the horse, riderless, charging after the others. Shaking off the attentions of the First Aid man she began the long uphill walk back to the weighing room. Her new boots were agony, rubbing at her heels. The rain had soaked through her silks and they clung to her body, her hip hurt from where she had landed.

But Merrianne couldn't contain the huge grin that spread over her face. She had done it. She had raced and she couldn't wait to do it again.

CHAPTER THIRTY-SEVEN

Paris drummed her fingers crossly against the pine surface of the table, trying to fight the impatience that was gnawing at her stomach.

Kane was late. Above her, on the wall, the hands of the clock slid relentlessly around. He had been supposed to pick her up twenty minutes ago.

Kane had grown on her in the weeks since the night of the storm, after he had helped her with Destiny. He had been so calm that night, so in control of the situation, made her feel so safe and protected. And when he had put his arms around her it had felt so right. She still longed for Derry, still hoped that he would come charging into the yard to reclaim her, but somehow Kane had softened the pain. Every time that she went out with him she spent the evening determined that this would be the last time. She still loved Derry, longed for him with every fibre of her body and soul. It wasn't fair to sit drinking with Kane, laughing with him, knowing that at the end of the evening he would want more, knowing that she was being unfair to him to let him think that they could have any sort of relationship. She loved Derry, and yet at the end of every evening out she would relent and agree to go out with Kane again. He was so solid, gentle, considerate, the complete opposite of Derry.

The party at Hopton Cross had been due to start at nine o'clock. Of course everyone knew that meant ten. People would then begin to pour into the enormous ballroom of Gerry Leary's home for the annual ball, one of the biggest bashes on the racing circuit. Gerry was famous for his hospitality. His parties were as formal as Milo McFadden's were wild.

Kane had been supposed to pick her up at nine thirty and now it was ten and he still hadn't arrived.

She was so determined to make Derry see what he was missing that she had spent ages getting ready. She ignored the gnawing worry that she would never ride again, never race again, and that was what Derry really wanted from her, but at least she knew that he was still interested in her. He didn't really love Merrianne, she was sure of that.

She had splashed out on a new dress – black, high at the front, it plunged daringly low at the back clinging to the curves of her waist and hips and then flaring out in graceful folds to the floor. She had put on weight since her suicide attempt, so now instead of looking like a famine victim she merely looked slender and fragile. The hairdresser had worked hard to give her a completely new look, streaking her hair with blonde and cutting it so that it fell in soft waves around her face and shoulders. She had spent hours in the bath, scrubbing and exfoliating, using every potion and body lotion that she found in the bathroom cabinet, the dumping ground for years' worth of unwanted girly Christmas presents. She had even put on long false nails, painted in a pale pink. It was these that she drummed on the table, taut with impatience.

The telephone rang, making her jump. She dashed into the hall, just beating Paddy who was hoping that it was Elizabeth telephoning for him. She snatched up the receiver. It was Kane.

"'Lo," he said, thickly.

"Where are you," said Paris, and she could hear the exasperation in her voice.

"Ugggghhhh," he groaned pitifully. "I've got the most terrible cold. I've been dosing myself with everything to try to get myself right, but nothing's working. I'm not going to make it. I'm really sorry."

But why in God's name didn't you let me know in time? Paris wanted to scream. "That's terrible," she said aloud, feeling disappointment settle over her. That was the evening ruined.

"I'm really sorry I didn't tell you earlier," he sniffled, breaking off the conversation in a spasm of coughing, but to be honest, I didn't want to disappoint you and I kept hoping I would be able to stage a miraculous recovery.

"Fine, no problem," Paris felt tears of disappointment prickle at the back of her eyes. She had been looking forward to seeing the approval in Kane's eyes when he saw her new dress. And looking forward to seeing Derry.

"Get well soon." She put the receiver down. It rang again almost immediately.

Paddy hurtled down the hall and snatched it up. "Hello!" he exclaimed in an excited voice, a broad grin breaking out over his face. "Yes, I would love to come out." He walked off to fetch his coat as if there were springs under his feet, barely conscious of Paris slumped on the stairs. She glared after her father, annoyed at his betrayal. How could he have anything to do with her mother after what she had done to them? Bloody, bloody men. They always let you down.

"See you later," Paddy said, slamming the door. He wouldn't have noticed if she was sitting on the stairs stark naked, he was on such a high with his new-found love for Elizabeth.

Paris listened as Paddy drove away and silence descended on the house. The clock ticked relentlessly in the kitchen, time slipping away. Time that she should be enjoying herself. Feeling desperately sorry for herself, she wandered into the kitchen. The gold-edged invitation card for the party lay propped on the window-sill, mocking her. Paris picked it up, turning the thick card over in her hands. How she had been looking forward to this party! To show everyone that she was fighting back. But most of all to show Derry how stunning she was and what he was missing. Damn it, she thought, snatching up her handbag from the table. She would go anyway. It wasn't as if she needed Kane to look after her.

The vast gravel forecourt that served as a carpark was already crowded when Paris arrived. Enormous spotlights concealed in regimental rows of trimmed yew trees lit up the pale façade of the huge house. The front of the house rose, four square and three stories high, huge towering windows looking out over the acres of formal gardens. At either side of the house single-story buildings had been added, spreading out from the main house like vast extended wings of an exotic bird. These housed a pool room and, on the far side, the vast ballroom where the party was being held. All of Ireland's wealthy and famous would congregate in the ballroom and later the party would spill into the poolroom where expensive dresses would be ruined with frolicking in the water.

Paris went inside. A vast hall, carpeted in red for the occasion, led the way into the depths of the house. Glamorous waitresses circulated, holding silver trays with tall glasses of champagne. Paris took a glass and wandered into the house, looking for a familiar face to talk too. Room after opulent room was filled with dinner-jacketed men and women dripping diamonds. Paris caught sight of Derry, Merrianne clinging possessively to his side. Her breath caught with the pain of seeing him and her longing for him. She took another deep swig of her champagne, feeling the comforting numbness of the alcohol washing over her.

Lonely, she pretended to admire the vast array of oil paintings that crammed the walls.

"All on your own?" a familiar voice said silkily.

Her heart pounded. It was Derry.

"Looks that way," she snapped. The pain of losing him was so intense that she couldn't bear him near her. It would be easier if he had died, then at least she wouldn't have to go through a life knowing that he lived with someone else. His eyes roved over her body, taking in her slenderness, the new haircut. She felt a pang of satisfaction that at least he had noticed. Over his shoulder she saw Merrianne glaring coldly at her. "You had better go back to your girlfriend," she snapped, jerking her head in Merrianne's direction.

Derry smiled shortly. "I'll talk to you later."

The party raged on. Paris, seeking the numb carelessness of being drunk, gulped champagne as if it were water on a hot day. She ceased to care that she was alone, wandering between clusters of people chatting and smiling a bright false smile. She had been a fool to come; she had only wanted to come to show Derry what he was missing. A vain and very stupid attempt to show him that she was better than Merrianne. But somehow without Kane she felt vulnerable and lonely.

Finally, stumbling against a table and almost sending an ornate vase flying, she realised that she was very drunk. She needed to go home. She left the groups of people, heading to the front door.

Suddenly Derry's arm blocked the way. Paris leant back against the wall, facing him. "You look gorgeous," he said, his eyes bored into hers.

"Thank you," she said, feebly. Derry's face was inches from hers. He must be very aware of the havoc that he was wreaking on her. She could smell his heady aftershave, the whiskey on his breath. His teeth were very white, his lips infinitely kissable. Paris closed her eyes to blot out the image of him. He turned her to liquid, she longed for him so terribly much.

"I'm still hoping that you will win the Galway Plate," he murmured softly.

Paris could feel the heat from his body. She could barely stand up, her knees were like jelly, she quivered with longing for him. "I miss you," she whispered.

"I miss you too," he said silkily, as he gently fingered the flesh of her exposed shoulder, then trailed his hand slowly down the length of her body, lingering on the curve of her breast, circling the bud of her nipple, sending delicious shivers down the length of her spine. "Merrianne's busy on the dance floor. Let's get some fresh air," he said. It was a command rather than a suggestion.

The entrance hall was deserted as they crossed it, their footsteps silent on the thick red carpet. Derry pulled open the door and led her outside. The night air was cold and Paris shivered, leaning instinctively on Derry for warmth.

"Here," he said, shrugging off his jacket and putting it over her shoulders. He took her hand, twining his long fingers in hers. Paris fought to blank out the thought of what his fingers could do to her body, but all she could focus on was the feel of his skin touching hers. She ached with longing for him, for the blissful release of the pent up desire that was building deliciously somewhere just below her navel.

The thumping bass of the disco boomed out through the open windows behind them as they walked across the deserted carpark. Paris was silent, thoughts flashing through her mind, the delicious haze of alcohol fading in the icy air. Derry was with Merrianne now. She had Kane. This was wrong, she was being a fool. Derry stopped and backed her gently against the bonnet of his sports car. All of the thoughts stopped. She wanted him so badly. He put his arms around her and drew her into the warmth of his body, sliding his hands down her back, gliding softly over her skin before descending into the dress to cup her buttocks and draw her closer to him. Withdrawing his hand he lifted her onto the bonnet of the car, spreading her legs so that he could press himself against her. Unable to stop him even if she had wanted, Paris felt him slide his hand up her thigh, lifting the flimsy fabric of her dress, sliding over the top of her stocking-tops and inside her knickers. She gasped as one long finger plunged inside her.

"So wet," Derry whispered, his voice harsh with desire as he bent his head to kiss her, twining his tongue into her mouth.

She heard herself cry out as he shoved the delicate fabric aside and plunged himself into her. She twined her legs around his hips, wanting to pull him deeper and deeper into her. He shoved her back against the bonnet of the car, running his hands over her breasts, as she cried out, oblivious to who might hear.

With a shudder she came, opening her eyes to see the look of concentration on Derry's face as he exploded inside her.

As he slid out of her, Paris felt him withdraw mentally as well. He zipped up his trousers, smoothing back his hair, pulling down her dress, his expression akin to a small boy who has been caught shoplifting. "I had better go back —Merrianne will be wondering where I am," he said, hauling Paris to her feet. With that, he dropped a small kiss on her forehead, pulled his jacket from around her shoulders and walked away without a backwards glance. Paris leant against the car and watched him go. He had used her. Taken her love for him and used her in the cruellest way possible.

CHAPTER THIRTY-EIGHT

"What's this John Moore like?" Joe McHugh said, squinting at the race programme. "He's very good," Paris heard herself say, reassuringly. She struggled to focus her attention on Joe. His beloved horse was running in a few minutes with a new jockey on board; she owed it to Joe to assure him that Red Arrow was in safe hands.

Paris wished that she were anywhere else than in the middle of a busy parade ring watching the horses walk around at the start of a race. All around were the owners of the other horses that would be running against Red Arrow and the trainers. The hum of noise had become a blur, and Paris felt as if she were watching the proceedings from the end of a long tunnel, watching herself act out the role of a racehorse trainer, saddling the horse by remote control while in reality her real self had gone somewhere else. She longed to be alone, to collect her thoughts; try to make sense out of the turmoil that was churning around inside her head.

How could she have let herself be used by Derry like that? He had taken her outside, fucked her in the most perfunctory way possible and then walked blithely back to his girlfriend. And yet she had known that was what was going to happen and had still wanted him.

Paris felt her breath catch as Derry walked across the ring, Merrianne beside him, obscenely glamorous in a cream wool coat that just skimmed the top of her soft brown suede boots. A wide-brimmed brown hat and co-ordinating handbag made her look like a supermodel. Paris felt hatred, bitter as bile, rise in her throat. How everyone had enjoyed telling her about Merrianne beginning to ride in races! Merrianne was becoming everything that Paris had once been. Merrianne had everything that Paris wanted. Derry and success.

Paris could hear Joe's voice, but it was as if she were under water, the sounds muffled and indistinctive. Paris met Derry's eyes. They bored into hers, making her feel as if she were stark naked.

As he and Merrianne passed he raised one eyebrow sardonically. "Paris," he smirked in greeting.

Paris knowing that he was thinking about lying her on the bonnet of his car - the way she had opened her legs, her longing for him so dreadfully urgent, not caring about anyone else, betraying Kane's kindness - felt an angry flush of colour spread over her cheeks.

"Paris?" Joe's usually kind voice had an edge of annoyance to it as he tugged on her coat sleeve to drag her attention back to him. "Don't you think that Red Arrow is looking great today? He is really enjoying his day out."

The jockeys came out, spilling from the weigh room jostling with each other like naughty puppies.

"Jockeys up!" roared the steward.

At his words the grooms stopped walking the horses around and pulled the horses into the centre of the turf, waiting for the jockeys to come and get on them.

Paris's jockey walked towards them, his hand outstretched to greet Joe.

"Didn't you ride Sunny Boy for Tony Williams?" Joe asked, grasping the jockey's hand and launched into a stream of concerned enquiries.

Paris sighed with relief as Paddy walked across the parade ring towards them. He could look after Joe, stop him worrying about Red Arrow.

She scowled as she saw Elizabeth duck under the white guard rail and hurry across the grass after him, looking like a woman half her age she glided across the turf, her high heels hardly sinking into the turf, her dark blue coat swirling around her like a cape.

"Hello, Paris," said a voice beside her. Paris spun around to face Merrianne.

"Hello," she replied shortly, her eyes darting around the parade ring, looking urgently for an excuse to escape.

"Don't you just wish that you were riding?" Merrianne's eyes glittered maliciously as they swept over Paris's face.

"Maybe," she shrugged, turning away before she stopped fighting the urge to punch Merrianne. The stewards would take a pretty dim view of a trainer cat-fighting in the parade ring.

"Oh, you must miss it," goaded Merrianne, striding alongside Paris, her long coat brushing against Paris's legs. "Now that I've started racing I'm finding it amazing, the buzz is – .better than sex,"

"Derry must not be fucking you properly if you think that," Paris snapped, turning on her heel and leaving Merrianne open-mouthed trying to think of a smart reply.

Paris watched Joe walk happily away with her parents. She had no desire to be part of their little circle.

The horses went out onto the track, Derry's horse, Starfire, bucking madly as Mary released the bridle, sending the other horses scattering as they got out of the way of his flailing hooves.

Red Arrow, unconcerned by all the fuss, trotted after them, stoically ignoring the thumping heels of his jockey who was trying to get him to canter. Finally as the lad belted him down the shoulder with his whip, he lumbered into a canter a mulish expression on his face.

Paris walked away down the course through the public areas. She had no desire to go onto the owners and trainers stand. If seeing her parents nauseatingly loving with each other wasn't bad enough, she would also have to put up with Derry and Merrianne who seemed to have their tongues down each other's throats at every opportunity. The concourse was crowded, spectators seizing the opportunity to come racing on the mild autumn afternoon. Paris wandered past the huge umbrellas and bulging money bags of the bookmakers, immune to the cries of the bookies as they gave out the odds for the horses, grabbing money from the outstretched hands of gamblers. She found a quiet spot by the guard rail in front of the main stand and leant on the rail watching the horses circling at the start, a far-off blur of colour in the distance. Everywhere around were couples, huddled together, laughing, walking arm in arm, in love, arguing, picking the horses out, just together. She began to long for Kane, wishing that he were there, his huge bulk as secure as a battered old teddy bear. Guilt gnawed at her like an open wound, guilt and annoyance at her own stupidity for letting Derry use her.

The race started, distracting her from the thoughts that thrashed in the back of her mind. Red Arrow loped along after the leaders, slithering over the fences, as if he did not want to lose contact with the ground. Starfire was in the lead, his sturdy legs pounding like pistons along the turf.

"Isn't Red Arrow going well?" said Joe, coming to lean on the guard rail beside her. Paris shook her head in astonishment, as the horses turned towards home. Red Arrow had slowly been improving each time that he had run recently, but this time he was really excelling himself. The horses thundered past the stands, as the crowds yelled roars of encouragement.

"He's going to win me a race, you know," Joe continued, gazing with undisguised affection at the pounding quarters of his horse as, swishing his tail with annoyance, he thundered around the track.

Paris shrugged. "Maybe he prefers being in a small yard." At Redwood Grange Red Arrow had just been one of a huge number of horses. Maybe he enjoyed the individual attention that he was getting at Blackbird Stables. Certainly she had the time to spend in his stable, grooming and talking to him. She had rather made a pet of the old horse; he would stand for hours tugging at his hay while she leant against his neck, seeking the warmth and solace of his presence. Until Daisy arrived, Destiny never liked company; like many mares she was stand-offish and aloof, preferring her own company, not like the soppy geldings who revelled in love and affection.

"He's never gone this well before," whispered Joe, reverently, gazing in awe at the caterpillar of horses that were moving swiftly around the track. As the horses turned for home Red Arrow was still running, lumbering along the track, ears laid back in distaste, huge hooves slamming into the ground.

"He's going to finish third!" Paris yelled in excitement. She gripped Joe's arm, feeling the frail flesh beneath her fingers. As the horses thundered over the line Paris stole a look at Joe's transfixed face. Tears were coursing down his withered cheeks. "Bless you, Paris," he breathed, crying unashamedly. "Bless you."

Once Red Arrow was safely in the lorry ready to go home Paris went to the owners and trainers bar. Joe had begged her to join him for a drink. The bar was crowded as she treaded her way through to Joe and her parents. Paddy, purple in the face, was saluting Joe with a glass half full of whiskey. Paris ordered a coke and clinking glasses with Joe sat down, smiling shortly at her mother, but taking care not to sit close by. Now she tolerated her mother's presence, an uneasy truce existed, but though Paris would never forgive her, she made no secret of the fact that she resented her. She, Elizabeth, had caused too much pain. She had walked away without a backwards glance.

Paris had seen her father crumble, literally brought to his knees by grief. She had been helpless to stop his pain and could only stand by and watch as he slowly took up the reins of his life again, his pain numbed by the alcohol that he had sought solace in. Elizabeth had destroyed her childhood. Paddy might have forgiven her, might have been so weak that he let her wheedle her way back into his life, but Paris would never forget what she had done. And she would never forgive.

She stole a look at her mother as Paddy lurched to his feet, sending glasses flying and reeled off to the bar. Elizabeth's immaculate face was set in annoyance. Paddy lurched to the centre of the bar announcing loudly that he was going to sing. In loud, drunken tones he proceeded to slaughter 'The Fields of Athenry'. Paris cringed as a huge circle opened around him as everyone moved out of his way. Some malicious person handed him another whiskey which he downed in one before caterwauling another verse and then slowly sinking sideways. He fell over a table, sending the glasses flying to shatter against the tiled floor, and the table gave way, the legs shooting in different directions like a newborn foal. He landed in the tweed-clad lap of a whiskery-faced old lady whose mouth pursed in disapproval as she shoved him away.

"Take me home, darlin'," he roared, holding out his hand to Elizabeth as she walked past him on her way out of the bar.

Paddy shuffled downstairs, looking green. He groped his way into the kitchen, heaving disgustingly over the sink. How could he drink so much he had to pass out? Why could he not stop when he felt himself getting drunk, like everyone else? He pulled out a chair, wincing at the noise of the legs scraping across the stone floor.

"Tea?" Paris asked shortly, glaring at her father from across the room. Without waiting for his reply she slammed tea bags into the pot and banged the lid down, noisily. He raised his head and, with an awful jolt, she realised that tears were streaming down his craggy face.

"Elizabeth told me it's over. She can't cope with my drinking. I've lost her again," he sobbed.

CHAPTER THIRTY-NINE

Merrianne had come a long way in a short time. Her determination to race had impressed even the unimpressionable Derry. He had thought when she had fallen off on the first day that she had raced that she would give up. She had trudged up the long hill back towards the parade ring, drenched and muddy, rain dripping from the silk cover on her skull cap, making her breeches transparent, clinging to her legs. She looked impossibly sexy and bursting with excitement. One of the spectators caught the horse and led it back to her. He legged Merrianne up and, letting her legs dangle by the horse's side, instead of putting them into the impossibly short stirrups, she rode back to find Derry.

If Derry had expected her to cry with temper and pain he was wrong. She slid off the horse, a grin splitting her face from ear to ear.

"I loved it," she cried, clapping her hand against the horse's muscular neck.

"You did?" said Derry in astonishment.

Mary sullenly threw a rug over Sartaj and led him away.

"It was totally amazing," she breathed, eyes shining with the memory of flying over the fences, the speed of the horses. "I'm entered again next Sunday, aren't I?" she said, excitedly, taking off her wet gloves and taking hold of his hand.

"Uhhh-uhhh ..." Derry steered her towards the jeep, which was parked on the hill far above them, his quicksilver mind taking in all that she was saying. This was an unexpected turn. He had never expected her to enjoy it so much. He had been surprised that she had learnt to ride the horses so well on the gallops, but riding at home was completely different from racing. Out on the race course it was every man for himself – no one was going to pay any attention if your horse jumped wrong, or slow down for you if you were scared. This was a tough game; falls hurt, jockeys and horses got injured, sometimes badly. He knew from his own experience the enormous adrenaline rush, the pre-race nerves, and the indescribable feeling of riding a good horse over fences, in front of the competition. Merrianne had caught the racing bug.

"You haven't forgotten our bet, have you?" Merrianne said as they walked up to the jeep. "When I win the Galway Plate …"

Derry fought down a snort of laughter. She really was unbelievable – she had just managed to jump four fences in a nondescript point-to-point, now she was talking about winning one of the best steeplechase races in Irish racing. "When you win the Galway Plate I will marry you," he told her solemnly.

The following weekend she fared a little better. Bulled up by Derry's pep talk and a week spent being bullied mercilessly over fences on every single one of the horses in the yard, she learnt the hard way how to stay on.

"You are a good rider," Derry had told her, picking her up yet again from the sandy surface of the gallops after she had fallen off yet another of the horses, "but you need to find that survival instinct.".

Yet every day she felt herself becoming better, her balance skills sharpening, staying on the horses when they stumbled on landing, or did awkward jumps, learning through sheer determination how to help the horses, to haul them back up, balance them when they stumbled. She was delighted with herself to actually finish the race. The pace had been blistering, the fourteen men riders all experienced and determined to win. They had rapidly outstripped the placid horse that Merrianne rode, leaving her a fence behind, to gallop resolutely through the finish line last and alone. Slowly she improved, driven by her determination to succeed. Week after week they journeyed to a point-to-point, for Merrianne to change in a draughty tent pitched in the corner of a field and then race.

"I've got a surprise for you," Derry told Merrianne as she rode back into the yard after exercising the horses.

A new horse looked eagerly out over the open half door, surveying the scene, neighing in greeting to the other horses as they were ridden into the yard. "A new horse for you to point-to-point," Derry told her as she came across the yard to look at the newcomer. He opened the box, took her hand and led her inside. The horse was an absolute beauty. He was dark bay, with a coat like a shiny conker, a thin white stripe running down his face and four long white socks. "Meet Water Babe," he said, grinning at the look of delight on Merrianne's face. "He's yours."

Merrianne gently touched the horse's silky coat as if she couldn't believe that he was real. He was the most beautiful horse that she had ever seen. "Really mine?" she whispered, completely awestruck.

Derry nodded, feeling like a benevolent uncle, dispensing gifts.

Merrianne shot across the stable and threw her arms around his neck, pressing her lips against his. Derry pushed her gently back against the stable wall, the horse regarding them with solemn eyes. He undid the buttons of her shirt, exploring her mouth with his tongue as she pressed eagerly against him. He fingered each rosy nipple that sprang to attention beneath his touch. Then abruptly he pulled away.

"You can show me how grateful you are later," he said.

The horse had cost him virtually nothing. A distraught lady had telephoned him a few days ago. Her husband had left her. His business had failed and he had bolted, apparently to Australia, leaving her to clear up the mess that he had caused. The horse had been in training on the Curragh and the trainer wanted his bill settled. She had read about Derry in the newspapers and had telephoned him to see if he would buy the horse and help her out of a tight spot. Derry, when he heard the horse's name, recognising it from point-to-point results, had brought the horse for a song, clearing the trainer's bills and leaving her with a little money left over.

Now feeling terribly altruistic he gave the horse to Merrianne. If she was determined to race at least she had better have a really good horse to do it on, so that she didn't embarrass him by finishing the race behind everyone else. Merrianne was totally dumbstruck. She rode the horse out into the paddock, walking it slowly around. He was like being put into a flashy sports car after only ever having driven a tatty old banger.

"Come on, let's see some action," said Derry climbing onto the fence and watching as she kicked the horse into a trot and then a canter.

The horse bounced along. He was the most powerful thing that she had ever ridden – every stride he took ate up the ground.

"Let's see how he jumps!" yelled Derry.

Merrianne turned the horse towards the fence. He pricked his ears, shortening his stride beneath her as he saw the fence. She eased the reins and his pace increased, hurtling towards the fence and flying over it like a bird.

"Brilliant," said Derry, frowning. The horse really had got talent. He was already regretting giving it to Merrianne – he could have sold it to any other of his clients for a large sum of money.

She rode back to the stable yard, awestruck. She couldn't believe what had happened. Derry had brought her this magnificent horse, this horse that could win any race. He had given it to her to ride. Her horse. He must want her to win. He really must want to marry her.

A few weeks later Merrianne had her first race on Water Babe. She stood alone in the parade ring, shivering with cold and nerves. There was no sign of Derry. He had gone off a while ago with Valerie who had been complaining of needing a brandy to warm herself up. Merrianne started as a hand touched her arm.

"Hey, gorgeous!" She turned and found herself face to face with Alex Ivor. "What on earth are you riding in races for?" His dark eyes were full of concern.

Merrianne shrugged off his arm. "Because......" her voice trailed off, it was too complicated to try to explain why she had to ride.

"If you were mine, I wouldn't let you ride," Alex touched her face gently. "I wouldn't risk you getting hurt."

She stepped back out of his reach. "Derry likes me to race," she said, confused and embarrassed at his attentions.

Alex laughed softly and shook his head. "Derry doesn't deserve you."

It was flattering and yet disturbing at the same time.

Merrianne rode out onto the course. The new horse felt impossibly lively, his long ears pricked sharply, head held high, staring goggle-eyed at the brightly coloured mass of balloons that a tradesman was selling.

The race starter walked out onto the course, holding his flag like an orchestra conductor about to start a concert.

"Line up!" he bellowed and the horses began to form a ragged line in front of the starter, plunging coiled springs full of energy waiting to begin the race.

The flag fluttered down and the horses thundered down the course. Merrianne stood in her stirrups, looking intently through the horse's sharply pricked ears. The first fence came up quickly – they were with the leading horses, the whole lot going over the fence in one mass of movement. They galloped past the tents, the beer tent and the weigh room. Merrianne had a vague glimpse of people standing in the doorways watching. Past the parade ring, the runners for the next race being led around, their grooms turning to watch. Then they were galloping out into the countryside, silence all around except the thud of hooves on the ground and the loud crashing of breaking brushwood as they leapt the fences. Beside her Merrianne could see the rider of a small grey horse that was running with its head up – he was, grim-faced, wrestling to control the horse. Drunk on excitement, it ran straight at the line of big round straw bales that had been placed to steer the horses around the course, cannoning straight into one of the bales, cart-wheeling, sending its rider sprawling.

"That fucker's mad!" yelled one of the riders, to no one in particular.

Beneath her Water Babe felt powerful, full of energy, his gallop eating up the ground, every fence giving her more and more confidence. She heard the steward ring the bell at the side of the course: there was one more lap to go, five more fences. They sped around the course, Merrianne kicking the horse on, his long stride eating up the ground, full of running. The horse beside her was not going so well; tiring with the fast speed, he plunged wildly at the next fence, skidding over the top of it and sprawling on the ground. There were two horses ahead of her, just ahead. She could see the glint of their iron hooves as they churned the ground, their tails whisking over the fence just in front of her. She was going to come third. Merrianne felt a surge of happiness. She could picture herself walking down the aisle in a dress of creamy silk, while Derry, impossibly handsome, waited in a grey morning suit at the altar.

With two fences to jump Merrianne lashed her whip down Water Babe's shoulder, feeling him redouble his efforts, valiantly trying to draw level with the other horses. They reached the final fence neck and neck. Three horses leaping in mid-air together, Merriane touched knees with the riders on either side of her. They swooped in to land together. Her horse put down slightly in front of the others. Spurring him on with her heels and whip, she rode as if her life depended on it, urging the horse on. She glanced over her shoulder: the two other horses were behind her. The winning post flashed by. She had won. Her scream of delight echoed around the fields. She had done it. She had won a point to point. Now Derry would have to let her ride in steeplechases. She was on her way to winning the Galway Plate. On her way to marrying Derry.

CHAPTER FORTY

Paddy was drunk again. Paris couldn't stand it. It was one thing to get drunk at night and reel off to bed, but to be drunk in the middle of the day was too much to bear. In the months since Elizabeth had dumped him again he had sunk into a deep despair, and deep into every bottle that he could find. Paris had tried everything to stop him, pleading, shouting. All to no avail. It was as if he had given up on life. Now he was lurching down the lane leading a young horse, supposedly helping with moving the horses to new pasture.

Paris walked down the lane, leading Destiny. The mare, as bad-tempered as ever wrinkled her nose and lay her ears flat back against her head every time one of the other horses came close to her. Paris had started training the mare again – the lads were riding her out. Soon she would be ready to race. If Paris couldn't ride any more, at least she could have the pleasure of training the mare and seeing her running. Daisy trotted contentedly beside Destiny, as happily as an old dog. Kane hauled an unwilling and very cross yearling along.

Kane had taken to turning up unannounced at the farm, hanging around, chatting to Paris, making himself useful. Paris tolerated his presence. He wasn't Derry, but she was never going to get him back, so she just had to make the best of things. At least Kane was easy company, and useful to have around the place.

The first leaves were beginning to spring into life on the hawthorn bushes, bright yellow daffodils waved their trumpet heads. The honey smell of the yellow gorse flowers wafted towards them, mingling with the heavy smell of the sheep who grazed in the fields beside the road, the first lambs hurtling in packs around their staid mothers, leaping and twisting in the air in delight at being alive.

"What is Paddy doing now?" Paris looked back over her shoulder. Paddy, having lurched into the bank, had stopped to examine a half-built bird's nest that had caught his eye in the hedge, not yet concealed by the leaves. He was oblivious to the yearling, which furious at being separated from its companion, plunged furiously, snorting with temper, trying to get away from Paddy, its fine legs flailing in the air, dangerously close to his head which was pressed into the hedge, immersed in wonder at the miracle of nest-building.

"Come on Paddy!" Paris yelled, sighing as she hauled on the lead-rope to bring Destiny to a halt.

Paddy, as if he had just remembered where he was, stumbled off the bank, and carried on after them up the road.

"The gate's here," she told Kane, handing her lead-rope to him as she waded through the long grass to the rickety wooden gate, which was held together with baler twine. Watching her struggle with the heavy gate, Kane finally said, "you hold these horses, I'll open the gate".

Kane heaved the heavy gate free of the briars and long grass that clung to its lower rungs and shoved it open. Paris led Destiny, with Daisy trotting at her heels, and the yearling into the field. She slipped the head-collar off the yearling, watching as it galloped away from her, delighted to be free.

Then she looked back and saw with horror, that Paddy had slipped on the road and let the other yearling go. It was galloping excitedly up the road, its tail kinked high over its back, snorting with terror at finding itself suddenly separated from its companions.

Kane grabbed Destiny's lead-rope and clung to the mare as she plunged, excited by the antics of the young horses.

Then, as they watched, powerless to do anything, the yearling pushed his way into the hedge in a vain attempt to get to his friend. The hedge gave way and the yearling exploded into the field, but then to her horror she saw that hidden in the hedge was a rusting line of barbed wire, which was now stuck around the yearling's neck, unravelling as it hurtled across the field, maddened with panic.

Paddy clambered slowly to his feet and lurched into the field in a vain attempt to catch the panic-stricken yearling.

"Oh my God," Paris whispered under her breath as horrified, she watched the yearling turn, the barbed wire streaming after him like a deadly bride's train. Paddy stood in its path as the yearling raced, blind with panic, trying to free itself from the clinging wire. It knocked him flying as it galloped past, and Paddy was caught by the spikes of the wire, entangled in it and dragged along the ground. For long horrific moments when time stood still, they could hear the hiss of his body as it scraped along the ground, bumping over the turf as the yearling galloped. Then as the yearling changed direction, the wire broke free and he galloped off to join his companion.

"Daddy!" shrieked Paris, hurtling across the grass to towards the still form of Paddy who was draped across the turf like a doll abandoned by a child.

Paddy lay still. Blood poured from a multitude of gashes that tore across his body spreading like spilt ink across a blotting paper into his clothes, staining them dark red. "Daddy," Paris sobbed skidding to a halt and crouching beside him. His eyes were closed, his face still, relaxed as if he were sleeping. "Daddy, wake up!" She shook his good arm, praying that he would open his eyes, get up, walk away.

"We need to get an ambulance," Kane's gentle voice said, touching her softly on the arm. "Run up the lane to the house."

"It's miles," she sobbed, feeling panic rising. Why the hell had she come without her mobile phone? The battery had been low and she had left it in the kitchen charging up. "He's going to bleed to death!" Her voice rose in desperation. Then as if on autopilot she rose slowly to her feet. "Morgan Flynn's is closer if I go across the fields." She took Destiny's lead-rope from Kane, quickly throwing it over the mare's neck and tying it on the other side of her head-collar, to make reins. "Quick, leg me up,"

"But –" began Kane

"Hurry!" Paris said, and Kane took her leg and threw her onto Destiny's warm, smooth back. She looked down at him. "Try to look after him, I'll be as quick as I can." She wrenched on the lead-rope, hauling the mare around and kicking her onwards.

Fleetingly she had time to remember that she was too afraid to ride, but now she was on Destiny, riding, without a tinge of fear. Saving Paddy was more important than anything. The mare moved beneath her, her legs pounding across the pasture, Ahead she could see the grey slate roof of Radford Lodge, Morgan Flynn's home, glistening invitingly in the spring sunlight. She would ride there and get him to ring for an ambulance. The yearlings, seeing Destiny galloping across the field streaked after her, their spindly legs flying across the turf. She glanced to the side to see them neck and neck with Destiny, their necks outstretched with the effort.

At the far end of the pasture a stone wall marked the end of the field. Gritting her teeth she kicked Destiny, feeling the mare's muscles bunch beneath her thighs as she powered forwards towards the wall. She swooped over the wall, the yearlings grinding to a halt, daunted by the impossibility of jumping the wall. They stood and watched Destiny stretching her long legs as she hurtled towards Radford Lodge.

A herd of black and white cows scattered in panic as Destiny galloped through their field, Paris crouched low over the mare's flying mane, her heels urging her on to greater speed. They plunged through a shallow stream, Destiny stumbling and almost falling as she scrambled up the bank at the other side. Paris clung on, her thighs gripping the mare's sweat-soaked sides.

Then they were off again, galloping flat out over the uneven turf. Radford Lodge was close now – she could see the shining green metal of the huge barns that housed the racehorses and the pale sand-coloured stone of the mansion that Morgan had so lovingly restored. Then she hauled on the lead-rope reins. A tall hedge separated her from Radford Lodge. Rising over six feet, the hedge was solid and impassable. A wide ditch gaped in front of it. Paris galloped along the hedge, her eyes raking the boundary, looking for a gate. Seeing one she kicked Destiny towards it, then hauled on the lead-rope to stop her. The gate was padlocked. Turning Destiny once more, Paris took a deep breath and dug her heels into the mare's sides, feeling her power as the mare leapt forwards, springing lightly over the hedge and ditch as if it were nothing, hurtling down the final field.

Morgan Flynn stood looking out of the bedroom window. Behind him, stretched out, her body trailing languidly across the sheets, lay his wife, Tara. She slumbered, sated after a long lunch-time spent in bed. The staff had all gone home for the afternoon, until it was time for the evening stables the nanny had taken their son out for a walk and Morgan and Tara had taken advantage of the silence to creep off to bed for a while. Morgan buttoned his shirt, slowly, relaxed by the loving caresses of his gentle wife, smiling at the thought of how he could still rouse her to such delights. A movement caught his eye. Far away across the fields a horse and rider were coming towards the house, flying over the grass, galloping flat out. He watched as they jumped a low wall, hurtled through his cattle, scattering them in all directions. Morgan scowled. Who the bloody hell was the idiot riding like that? As the rider came nearer, changing from a mere dot on the horizon to a face that he recognised, he saw it was Paris, riding her mare. He opened the window, craning out to watch, a leaden feeling of tension slowly growing in the pit of his stomach. She wasn't riding as if the very devil himself were after her for no reason. Something was very wrong. As he watched she paused, trapped by the huge hedge that bordered the paddocks close to the house. He saw her searching for a way out, then watched dumbstruck as she set the mare at the hedge. He felt his hands grip the edge of the window-sill, aware that his own breathing had stopped as he watched the mare hurtling towards the hedge and flying over it. What a horse! Then before he had time to reflect on the magnificent jump, he hurtled downstairs to meet Paris and see what had caused her desperate flight to Radford Lodge.

He reached the yard just as Paris slithered to the ground. "Morgan, I need an ambulance to the field at Cusheen, Paddy's had a terrible accident." The words came rapping out like machine-gun fire. She was as white as a sheet, trembling from head to foot, the mare dripped with sweat, her veins standing out like cords beneath her coat. Her sides heaved.

"I can ride," Paris whispered.

Morgan grabbed Destiny as Paris slid slowly to the ground in a dead faint.

CHAPTER FORTY-ONE

Paris opened her eyes. She had drifted off to sleep. She lay on the sofa in an airy wood-panelled room. She shifted, then squirmed upright in panic, throwing off the tartan blanket that had been draped over her. Paddy. She had to get back to him.

"It's OK, the ambulance is on the way." Tara thrust a glass, half full of neat brandy, into Paris's hand. "Morgan's rung for it." Her pretty blue eyes raked over Paris's face, full of concern.

Paris took a gulp, spluttering as the fiery liquid hit the back of her throat. "Is Destiny OK?" she croaked, the brandy making her eyes water. She had abandoned the mare in the panic to get the ambulance after she had come around with her head between her knees sitting on the front doorstep of Radford Lodge.

"One of the lads is looking after her. Morgan will get her brought back to you in the lorry later on."

"We should go over to Crusheen," announced Morgan, marching into the room. "That was some jump!" he couldn't resist saying.

Paris, despite her worry about Paddy, grinned in disbelief, "I was too scared to ride after my accident," she said, laying the empty brandy glass on a delicate hexagonal table beside the burgundy leather sofa that she had been lying on. She shook her head, "I guess needing to help Paddy cured me."

"Naturally it would," said Morgan. "We had better get over there - the ambulance won't take long."

Paris followed him out of the room, along a dark corridor and out into the sunshine. "I'll be back as soon as I can," Morgan said to Tara. Even in their rush he still had time to drop a kiss onto her lips.

She clung to him for a moment before stepping backwards. "I hope everything is OK, Paris," she said, he mouth twisting into a grimace of concern.

They got into Morgan's Jeep. Tara backed into the doorway of the house and raised her hand. She remained, framed in the greenery and pale flowers of the climbing roses that wound their way around the metal arch around the front door.

It was a lot further by the road than it had been across country on the back of a horse. But Morgan drove quickly, slamming the gears to power the big vehicle around the corners and up the hills. "That mare of yours is brilliant," he said, swerving into the grass bank to avoid an oncoming tractor.

"Isn't she?" Paris grinned in spite of herself. She had loved the mare for so long, and hoped and dreamed that she might be a great horse, a potential champion, that even the worry about her father couldn't dampen her enthusiasm. "I was starting to train her for some point to points, then maybe some novice chases and then ... who knows ..." Morgan nodded. "You will be able to ride her in races now."

Paris was silent. That had been her ambition. Until the accident. When she had started training Destiny again she had assumed that another jockey would ride her in races. But now that she had ridden, maybe she would be able to race again.

She fell silent as they approached the field, not wanting to see the horrific image of Paddy lying cold on the ground. He had driven her mad, but she loved him so much. She had no one else. If he died she would be totally alone. She began to shake, the shock of the accident sinking in.

"Here." Paris showed Morgan where the field was with a wave of her hand.

He drove the Jeep onto the grass verge and switched off. It jerked forwards to a halt as he forgot to take it out of gear.

They got out. The siren of an ambulance could be heard wailing in the distance, hurtling towards them. Paris ran back into the field. Paddy lay motionless on the grass. Kane was kneeling beside him, his face grim. The two yearlings grazed close by, as if they didn't want to miss out on any of the excitement. Paris could see a long gash on the leg of the one that had been stuck in the wire, but he would have to look after himself for now, she had more important things to attend to.

"How is he?" Paris whispered, crouching beside Kane. He took her hand in his enormous warm one and chaffed it gently. "He's still with us anyway," he sighed, shifting his position. He had taken off his wax jacket and draped it over Paddy, whose face was relaxed as if he were sleeping, the skin pale, ghostly. "He must have knocked himself out when he was being dragged," Kane said, his fingers gripping Paris's. "And he's lost a lot of blood."

Paris clung to his hand as if her life depended on it. He was so warm and strong and safe. She couldn't bear to lose him.

"Please save him," she sobbed hysterically to the ambulance crew as they crouched over Paddy a few minutes later. "Oh God, please save him!"

"Paris," Paddy whispered, hoarsely, as his eyes slowly focused on her. His face was grey against the snowy whiteness of the hospital pillow. Paris wiped her eyes, trying to stop the tears of relief that were spilling down her cheeks. He was going to be OK. "I've got to stop drinking. It's going to kill me if I don't." He shook his head, his face crumpling. "And Elizabeth won't have anything to do with me until I give it up."

Paris felt the muscles of her jaw clench. He would give up drinking for Elizabeth, the woman who had dumped him and her child when she had sloped off with some jockey, but he wouldn't give it up for her. She had begged him countless times, pleaded with him. Tried to make him see the harm he was doing himself. But he never did anything about it. Not even when he had lost their home through his drinking. But Elizabeth snapped her fingers and he would do anything for her.

Paris took hold of his ice-cold hand where it lay like a dead thing on the pea-green hospital blanket. What did it matter what the reason was? If he was going to try to give up drinking she would help him.

Paddy was stitched up, checked out and deemed fit for release a few days later. He was very subdued as she helped him into the car, not looking forward to the days that lay ahead. He was determined to go cold turkey. To stay at home and with Paris's help get the booze out of his system.

"This isn't going to be much fun," he said, wryly as they drew into the yard at Blackbird Stables, thinking of the nightmares and sweating and cramps that had been predicted for those who were giving up the demon drink. The doctor had recommended that he go to a proper clinic to be dried out, but Paddy had known countless drinking comrades that had spent fortunes in rehab and still failed. He was determined to go it alone. Paris was given the job of making sure he didn't take a drink, ever again. It would be tough for a while, he told her, but things would get easier and it would all be worth it in the end. Paris knew what he meant. He would get Elizabeth back.

"Here we go then." Paddy swallowed hard. It had been easy to talk about not drinking but now, faced with the actual reality, the prospect seemed grim.

"Wait," said Paris, opening the car door. "I've got something to show you first." Paris sprinted over to Destiny's stable. She had left her bridle and saddle in a corner when she had done the mare earlier on. Hastily, her fingers trembling with excitement, she slid the bridle over Destiny's head and buckled the saddle into place. Then she led her out into the yard. Paddy had got out of the Jeep and was leaning up against the low wall that bordered the garden, raising his grey face to soak up the pale rays of the sun. He looked as she led the mare towards him. He was shaking like a leaf blown in a gale.

"Watch this!" Paris quickly got on the horse, scrambling as nimbly into the saddle as she ever had done before her accident.

Paddy's face split into a broad grin, which crinkled the corners of his eyes and folded the lines of his craggy face. "You're riding," he said, in amazement.

"Now watch this," Paris grinned and hauling the mare's reins kicked her into a trot. Then, her iron-shod hooves sliding and sending showers of sparks, she began to canter on the concrete surface, then, with a whisk of her tail she flew over the low stone wall out of the yard into the field. Paddy let out a whoop that echoed around the yard.

"That's put some heart in me," said Paddy a few minutes later, when she had put Destiny back into her stable and was carrying his bag into the house. "But I'm not looking forward to this."

"You can do it, I know that you can," Paris replied, propping the door open with her bottom to let him come into the house moving slowly and stiffly. The wounds from the barbed wire that had criss-crossed his legs had been stitched, the flesh tightly pulled together, making it difficult to walk. He stood uncertainly in the kitchen, looking around as if he were a stranger in a new environment, shuffling his feet and picking up objects and putting them down again minutes later in a distracted way. "So we just have to wait now," he muttered, examining a tea cup nervously, a tense expression flitting across his eyes. Paris shook her head; she was as nervous as he was. Afraid of the terrible time that he was going to have to go through to rid his body of the burning desire for the alcohol that it so desperately needed. Afraid that she would give in when he begged her to let him have a drink. And at the same time, afraid of the person that he was going to become, the stranger that was her father without his senses dulled with alcohol.

The days were long. The nights even longer. Time blurred into a constant mire of nightmares, hallucinations, sweating, vomit and abuse. At times he didn't seem to know who she was, or where he was, only aware of the constant, desperate need for a drink. Paris locked the doors to prevent him getting out, sat in an armchair as he slept fitfully. Waiting. Thinking. She could ride again. She had another chance at life. A chance to get Derry back and live the life she once had. She would race again and win. Derry would marry her as they had once planned and then... She pushed her feelings of guilt about betraying Kane with Derry at the party to the back of her mind.

Outside, life went on. The lads came in and told her how things were in the yard. Destiny was working well. Red Arrow seemed to have been given a new lease of life. The yearling that had caused Paddy's accident was healing well. Its scars would hardly be visible in a few months' time. The concern about Paddy's wellbeing was etched on their faces together with sympathy for Paris, who they knew was now itching to get back riding again. She watched enviously as they rode out of the yard every afternoon to exercise the horses. At least though, soon she would be able to go with them.

The lads had just brought back the horses from their exercise when there was a knock on the door. Thinking that it was one of them Paris threw the door open. Elizabeth stood on the path, immaculate as ever in pale blue trousers and matching jumper. "Paddy telephoned me to say that he was trying to get off the drink. He really is determined to get me back," she said smugly, marching past Paris into the house. "I'll look after him now."

CHAPTER FORTY-TWO

Kane's jeep was in the yard when she got home from the feed merchants. Paris drove into the yard and parked beside him. The yard was deserted, the horses hanging their heads sleepily over the stable doors. The tips of Daisy's white ears were just visible over the top of Destiny's stable door, turning like radar to investigate what was happening outside. The kitchen hummed with noise and laughter as Paris went down the corridor towards it. She swung open the door and the noise stopped. Paddy sat in the armchair, a vast mug of tea, his new tipple, cupped in his hand. Kane had folded his bulk into one of the wooden chairs at the table opposite Elizabeth who was plying him with fruit cake and biscuits and batting her eyelids at him like a coquettish schoolgirl.

"Paris," said Elizabeth, leaping to her feet and grabbing a mug from the draining-board. "Sit down. Kane's come to see us." She spoke with the wariness of a woman caught playing house in someone else's domain.

"Hi," Paris said irritation at her mother's presence making her short-tempered.

"We were just going to take some fresh air," Elizabeth said pointedly, shooting a glance in Paddy's direction.

"I just wanted to hear about –" Paddy's words froze on his lips under Elizabeth's frosty glare. "I'll get my coat."

Obedient as a child Paddy levered himself out of the armchair, laid his mug solicitously in the sink and went out, with Elizabeth on his heels.

A long silence settled on the kitchen, broken only by the interminable slow ticking of the clock. Kane stirred his tea and cleared his throat.

The silence hung between them again. Kane shuffled, wriggling in his seat like a small boy with a secret to tell.

"I've bought a new place, I wondered if you would like to see it," Kane blurted out, stirring his tea so furiously that it spilled out, sloshing over the table.

Paris watched the liquid spreading slowly over the pine surface.

"I'd love you to see it," he started again, meeting her eyes for the first time, looking at her imploringly.

Paris grinned in spite of herself. She had so much to do on the yard, but it was hard to resist him.

Kane heaved open an old iron gate, dumping it into the thorny branches of the hedge. He got back into the Jeep, and drove through the open gate.

"It's about a mile down here," he said shoving the Jeep into gear and bumping down the rutted track. Paris thought that her teeth would be shaken out as the jeep jolted and bumped along. The deep bumps made the vehicle sway alarmingly, jolting her sideways so that she cannoned off his strong arm. "The border is that hedge over there." Kane pointed into the distance. Grassland stretched in either direction, long and unkempt as a tramp's hair. "It hasn't been grazed for years," Kane explained. "The bachelor that owned it died and they were years locating his relatives. They found his only living relative, a niece living in Australia, and she wanted it sold as quickly as possible." He paused, halting the Jeep at the top of a small rise. Below them the farm stretched, the overgrown grassland encroaching into the tangled hedges and tumbledown walls. Kane stared, so enrapt in its beauty that he forgot about Paris, sitting equally awed beside him. "I bought it thinking that it would make a great place to settle down. Raise a family," he said wistfully. "It's near enough to my home place to use all of the land. Expand, maybe rent out my house, rebuild the one here."

"It's like paradise," breathed Paris.

Below them wound the silver thread of a river, bound by willow trees that bent their delicate branches into the water, like strands of wet hair, and there, tucked into a hollow, half way up the hillside was the abandoned cottage, built of grey stone, surrounded by tumbledown buildings, huddling together as if for warmth. Kane shoved the Jeep into gear again and drove towards the farm.

"Can I go and look around?" Paris asked, getting out of the Jeep. The front door of the farmhouse swung open lazily in the breeze as if inviting her to go and explore.

"In a minute," said Kane, putting his hand gently on her arm. "Come and see this." Enthralled by the magic that the peaceful farmstead wrought over her, Paris followed him up a steep path that led out of the farm yard. As it wound through a steep hill behind the farm she grabbed his arm, letting him drag her along over the rough grass and steep incline. Finally they reached the top of the hill. "Come here," said Kane, leading the way to a long low rock that crouched in the grass, like an animal waiting to pounce. He took her hand and pulled her down beside him.

Paris let her hand stay where it was. "Oh Kane," was all that she could say. From their vantage point it looked as if they could see the whole of Ireland, a green patchwork of fields, silver threads of streams, grey roads, blurring into the blue horizon.

"I love this place," he murmured, then slowly getting to his feet he pulled Paris upright. They stood inches apart. Paris could feel the heat from his body, his lips were inches from hers. "And I love you," he whispered, gently, shyly dropping a tentative kiss on her lips.

Paris stiffened instinctively. His love was the last thing that she wanted. How could she want him when she still loved Derry?

Interpreting her stillness as encouragement, Kane slowly wrapped his hand around the back of her neck and drew her closer towards him. His lips were delicious. Gentle on hers, his tongue plying against hers, lowering her resistance, until she put her arms around his neck and kissed him back, desire flaring deep within her.

"Let's go down to the house," he said hoarsely taking her hand and leading her back down the path.

Halfway down the path it began to rain, huge drops pattering from the sky, soaking through their clothes. They dived in through the open door of the cottage, laughing hysterically.

"You're soaked," said Kane, gently sweeping the tangled, wet hair off Paris's face.

"So are you!" She ran her hand along his arm, where the wet fabric clung to his skin. "I'm going to light a fire," he said, turning away abruptly. Old furniture littered the rooms of the cottage, Kane broke up a chair, found some newspaper, and as Paris sat on the windowsill and watched, soon coaxed a fire into life.

Kane walked slowly towards Paris. He pulled her to her feet and slid his hands around the slender span of her waist. "I've wanted you for so long," he whispered burying his face in the nape of her neck.

Paris fumbled with the buttons of his shirt, finally managing to undo them as he deftly undid her buttons and unhooked her bra, her breasts spilling out of the fabric. Kane moaned as she spread back the sides of his shirt and sliding inside, pushing herself against his chest. His skin was cool against hers. Paris let her hands rove over his taut torso, the muscles of his stomach were hard beneath her fingers.

Kane moved his hands over her skin, relentlessly moving over her breasts, caressing her nipples. His fingers were deliciously cool against her skin which seemed to burn with longing for him. He bent his head, his hot mouth finding and nipping at her skin. Paris moaned, feeling herself turn to liquid at his touch.

Kane shrugged off his jeans, then locking his eyes onto hers began to slowly take off hers. When the agony of waiting became too much she shrugged off his hands and began to remove her jeans herself, but he seized her hands. "Wait," he commanded, recommencing his leisurely teasing. When finally her jeans lay in a heap on the floor Kane steered her back to the windowsill, spreading her legs gently with his hands.

Just as Paris thought she was going to explode with expectation he slid slowly to his knees, parting her labia with his fingers and began to slowly tease her clitoris with his tongue. She leant back against the window barely half aware of the cool, smooth glass on her back and of the storm, lightening scudding across the darkened sky.

His tongue teased, bringing her closer and closer to the orgasm she so desperately needed, until finally he stood, enfolding her in his powerful arms as his cock slid deliciously into her. She cried out, a harsh, animal cry of sheer longing as his lips found hers. She could taste herself on him, she moaned with pleasure, writhing wanting, needing him deeper and deeper inside her. Not until her orgasm built and then finally exploded into waves of pleasure did he give into his own. For a long while they stood together, skin against skin, sated with pleasure until slowly Kane eased himself out of her. Smiling tenderly he cupped her face in his hands, kissing her lips softly.

236

"I wanted so much to do that to you." he said as he tenderly stroked her hair and the contours of her face.

Long moments passed as they stood together. Paris watched the flames flicker in the grate and listened to the rain pattering on the roof slates, the cold gradually seeping into her body as slowly she descended into the full horror of her actions. How could she have been such a fool to get carried away with the romance, her longing for another person? She had led Kane, made him believe that she was interested in him. He was nice. Gentle, kind. The lovemaking had been wonderful. Really wonderful, but it had been a mistake. She must never let it happen again. It wasn't fair to Kane to let him think that he would ever mean anything to her. He was too nice. He would find himself some cute farm girl that would make him a good wife. Her life was headed in a different direction. She had to race again, start to win. She had to have Derry. He was the only thing that mattered. She lay in Kane's arms and wished that he were Derry.

CHAPTER FORTY-THREE

Morgan handed Paris a glass of whiskey and stood with his bottom resting against his desk. "Cheers!" he said, raising his glass in a salute to her. "That's some horse you have there."

Paris felt her face split into a broad grin. "And at last I can ride her again."

"I was amazed to see her jump that hedge behind the house," he said, shaking his head at the memory. "And you riding her bareback."

"Amazing what you can do when there's no choice," Paris replied.

The horses from Morgan's stables walked gracefully past the window, their riders lolling casually in the saddles, smoking cigarettes and chatting, on their way back from the morning exercise. For a moment Morgan was absorbed in the sight. He went to the window and stared out, looking at each horse, his eyes taking in how well the horse looked, noting any problems, his instinct telling him if any of them were unwell, or not performing as they should be.

"So," said Morgan as the horses went around a corner of the yard and were lost from sight. "What are your plans for her now?"

"I want to start racing her as soon as possible," she told him, swigging a huge mouthful of whiskey and almost choking. "She is entered in her first race next month. Sean McGrath, who has been riding her for me at home, was due to race her, but now I can take the ride."

Morgan was silent for a moment, his eyes flickering over the wood-panelled room, as he considered his reply.

Paris, interpreting his silence as being bored and wanting her to go so that he could get on with his work, knocked back the remaining dregs of the whisky and put down the glass. "I'd better let you get on, you must have a lot to do," she said, shuffling her bottom to the edge of the leather sofa in readiness for getting up. "I just wanted to call to thank you for helping with Paddy."

"No problem," Morgan said, his voice distant. "How is he now?"

Paris snorted. "Oh fine," she said, unable to keep the edge of sarcasm out of her voice. "He's off the drink and madly in love with my mother again. The two of them are revolting, wandering around like lovesick teenagers."

She didn't feel able to tell him how truly awful it was at home. Paddy and Elizabeth were unable to keep their hands off each other, having decided to make a real go of their relationship now that Paddy was well and truly off the drink. He had finally got over the terrible cravings, and spurred on by his love for his ex-wife and the knowledge that she would walk away from him if he lapsed and started to drink again, he had stuck to his vow with grim determination, and was spurning alcohol as fiercely as any Pioneer. There had been many uncomfortable moments as Paris had marched into rooms to find them entwined on the sofa, or lain awake listening to the creaking of the bed. Their new-found love had only made her more aware of her longing for Derry and her confusion about Kane.

Making love to Kane on the afternoon of the storm had only heightened her feelings of confusion. Derry was the man that she wanted. Letting Kane think that he was anything more than a friend had been a mistake. A terrible, cruel mistake. She had avoided him ever since they had driven home in stunned silence: he, delighted that Paris was his now and over her relationship with Derry; Paris, cursing herself for getting carried away with the romance of the moment and her longing for the physical touch of another person. Since then she had managed to avoid Kane. Fobbing off his telephone calls, telling him that she was too busy to see him, putting off the inevitable confrontation when eventually she would have to tell him that it was Derry that she wanted. Not him. Not ever.

"Don't go," Morgan said, focusing on her for the first time since he had been lost in his own world, pondering the fantastic mare that Paris owned.

Paris slid her bottom slowly to the back of the sofa. "You've nothing good to work that horse against, to see how good she really is. How about bringing her over here a few times a week, work her with some of my horses?

Carna Boy maybe, he's nearly ready for Cheltenham. That will give you a good idea of how good she is."

"That would be brilliant," Paris enthused. She had been worried how she was going to really get the mare fit. It was easy to gallop her with the other horses that she was training, but none of them had her power and speed. Nothing would really test her.

"She has done all her fitness work," she explained to Morgan. "She's ready to be put to the test now."

She drove home feeling delighted. And terrified. Now she really was going to race again. Riding was one thing. But racing was another. Would she be able to cope with the speeds when racing, jumping again surrounded by loads of other horses? And what if she fell again? Would her fragile confidence survive another fall? Or would she lose her nerve again?

Her delight at being able to ride again rapidly gave way to a dreadful feeling of panic when she thought about racing again. It was quite one thing to ride out with the lads on the horses. Walking along the lanes was safe, and held no fears for her. It was wonderful after all the months of longing to be able to sit on a horse, to be able to feel the graceful movement of the horse's body beneath her, hear the clip-clop of their iron- shod hooves on the ground, hear the creak of the leather saddlery as they moved.

Galloping the horses stretched her frail confidence to its limits. She felt movements that she had never noticed before - how fast the horses went, the feeling of immense power, how the horse stretched low beneath her as it began to gallop, legs powering over the turf, eating up the ground, which flashed beneath the hooves. And jumping. Popping over small fences on her own was easy, manageable. She could control the pace that the horse jumped, there was no unstoppable rush of power as the horse lurched towards the fence, no split-second hesitation of worry that the horse could stop, fall and so could she. But jumping with the other horses beside her was another thing altogether, even over the low brushwood fences that they had placed on the sand surface of the gallops. The horses, excited by the presence of the others fought for their heads, huge powerful quarters thrusting them at the fence and into the air, no chance for error. A mistake and you were falling. Falling beneath the hooves of the other horses. Only sheer determination kept her going, tears streaming down her face, longing to stop, to turn the horse and go back to the stables, never try again. Only the dream of winning Derry's love back spurred her on. She had to succeed.

Whatever it cost.

Gradually it got easier and she stopped closing her eyes as the horse took off over a fence, her legs stopped turning to jelly in the last few strides before the jump. And she stopped clutching a handful of silky mane to balance herself as the horse flew into the air. Day after day she forced herself to the limits of her confidence, gradually eroding the nagging fear. Even coping with galloping Destiny on Morgan Flynn's gallops, riding against the famous Carna Boy who was going to Cheltenham again to have another attempt at the Gold Cup. The handsome grey horse was impressive, powering along the gallops, his long ears sharply pricked, powerful quarters moving like a magnificent machine. But Destiny had kept up with him. Matching him stride for stride along the sand surface, flying over the fences as if they were nothing. She had even felt as if she could have passed him, but Paris daren't say that to Morgan. Paris had gone home thrilled with herself. She had truly conquered her fears about riding. Now she just had to race again.

All evening Paris felt her fingers itching, longing to tell Derry that she was riding again, that she was going to race again, that the Galway Plate was within her grasp. She longed to get the house to herself so that she could telephone him, but Paddy and Elizabeth lingered resolutely over their dinner, holding hands over the table and gazing into each other's eyes across the flickering light of a candle. Paris, escaping from the table as soon as she could, fled to her room to escape the unspoken waves of passion. Usually they wandered off after dinner to get some fresh air. Tonight, because she wanted them to go out, of course, they lingered longer than usual. Paris sitting in her room, watching her small portable television with the sound turned right down so that she could hear them when they did go out, constantly hovered by her door, willing them to hurry up.

Eventually she heard the sound of their chairs scraping across the stone tiles of the floor and finally the front door slammed and the house was silent. Paris picked her mobile. She got halfway through punching out the once-familiar number when she paused. Derry would think that she was crazy. She pressed the off button; it would be madness to telephone. But she so desperately wanted him to know that she was riding again! He mustn't marry Merrianne before she got her chance to win him back. She snatched up her telephone again and punched in the number before she had time to bottle out. Derry answered on the third ring. "Westwood Park," his familiar voice was as delicious as warm chocolate.

"It's me," she said, before thinking what a stupid thing that was to say, he would have seen her number come up on his telephone.

"Paris!" he shouted her name, the delight in hearing her voice obvious.

Paris could hear Merrianne's muffled angry voice.

"Hello, Derry," she said, "I just wanted you to know that I have started riding again."

"Uhh uhh!" came his surprised reply.

"Yes, and I'm racing again next week. I hope that you haven't forgotten our bargain." Paris stared at herself in the mirror; her scar, once livid and red, had faded to a pale line, almost invisible against the weathered tan on her face. Being able to ride once more had given her a new confidence; she looked alive again. Triumph glittered in her eyes.

"Most definitely not. Thank you for letting me know."

Over at Westwood Park Derry turned off his mobile. Silently he looked across the room at Merrianne, curled with her legs beneath her on the wide cream sofa, her blonde head buried in the glossy pages of one of her fashion magazines, no doubt looking to see what hideously expensive creations she could spend his money on next when Paris had rung.

Now she was staring across at him expectantly, anger glittering in her eyes. "What did she want?" she snapped petulantly.

A malicious smirk slowly turned up the corners of his mouth. Merrianne would be furious when he dropped this bombshell. "That was Paris," he said, unable to keep the amusement out of his voice at the two beautiful women's rivalry against each other — all for him. "She rang to say that she is riding again. You are racing against her next week."

CHAPTER FORTY-FOUR

Merrianne stared fixedly at the glossy pages of her fashion magazine, determined to show Derry that she wasn't rattled by his words. She had been reading a report on the fashions shown in the big annual show in Milan. Black apparently was the new black. And hemlines were creeping upwards again. That had been good news. She had great legs, long and shapely with finely defined calves and ankles as delicate as a thoroughbred foal. It was a shame to hide legs like hers under long swathes of fabric. And then the telephone had rung, and shattered her peace of mind. Paris was riding again.

Derry pushed himself out of his armchair and went to the sideboard where an array of every drink known to man was assembled. Merrianne watched surreptitiously, pretending not to care, as he seized a bottle of whisky and then put it down, sifting through the bottles distractedly as if he couldn't decide what he wanted to drink. Merrianne had never seen him so bothered. He had endured steward's enquiries, unruly horses, militant staff, suicidal owners and never turned a hair. Now one phone call and he was in bits.

Derry abandoned his shuffling of the bottles and stared out of the window. Merrianne watched as he shook his head from time to time, as if involved in an inner conversation that she had no part in. Beyond him she could see the pale leaves of the trees, bursting into life with the new spring, shifting gently in the breeze. Life continuing while hers froze. As if feeling her incredulous gaze, Derry dragged himself back from wherever his mind had taken him to. He grabbed a bottle of gin and poured himself a generous measure, before unscrewing another bottle and tipping a generous slurp of brandy in on top of it. Merrianne winced at the revolting concoction. "Drink?" he asked, adding ice cubes.

Merrianne shuddered. "No, thanks!" She didn't think that he would want to drink that either when he realised what was in it.

He sat back down opposite her, setting the glass down untasted on the glass-topped table in front of them. He lit a cigarette, puffing deeply on it before laying it in the ashtray and leaning back in the armchair, hands behind his head and blowing out a great plume of smoke at the ceiling.

"Well, this is a turn-up for the books," he eventually mumbled, contemplatively, shaking his head, "Paris riding again."

"That's great." Merrianne forced herself to smile, pretending she didn't realise what his words meant. She had competition. Paris intended to win the Galway Plate to marry Derry. Just like she did. "I'm really pleased for her," she added, closing the magazine. There was no point in pretending that she could see what was written on the pages any more – the words had blurred into a meaningless jumble.

"Are you really, darling?" Derry raised his eyebrows quizzically, an edge of sarcasm to his voice. "I would have thought that it was the last thing that you would want. A bit of competition in the race to win my hand in marriage."

Merrianne scowled. Of course he was right. She had wanted to ride to make him proud of her. To make him want to marry her. Now bloody Paris was back on the scene, slinking around like a cat waving itself around your ankles when it was hungry, yowling for attention. Having Paris on the scene was the very last thing that she wanted.

Derry yawned and stretched. "I'm going to do the night-time rounds do you want to come?"

Merrianne nodded eagerly. The night-time stroll around the stable yard, checking that the horses were OK had become a treasured part of her routine. Derry took a long swig of his drink, grimacing and nearly gagging as the dreadful concoction hit his taste-buds. He dumped the glass on the table. Paris had really got to him.

"I'll fetch my coat." Merrianne leapt to her feet and hurried away.

Derry shoved the window open and tossed the repulsive liquid out over the roots of the lilac tree that grew close by. Hearing Merrianne coming back he scowled. He could have done without her company tonight. Now he would have to wander around the stable yard, her hand in his, tucked into his pocket, half listening to her constant chatter. He desperately wanted to go alone. Then he could have hurried across the yard to the little cottage at the far end of the walled garden where Mary lived. Always obliging and always touchingly delighted to see him, he could have sought solace in some mindless fucking.

Derry shrugged on the long wool overcoat that Merrianne brought from the cloakroom for him. She had already put hers on, tied the belt jauntily to one side, changed into a pair of sensible shoes and fastened a silk scarf around her neck. There was a full moon, dusting the whole park with silvery light, casting long dark shadows in the shrubbery and the tall trees beyond. They set off down the drive, their footsteps crunching on the gravel, then quietening as they turned off towards the arched entrance to the stable yard. The fox-shaped weather vane on top of the clock tower pointed east, frozen in the still night air, like a fox waiting to pounce on his prey. One of the horses, hearing their approach, neighed in greeting, another got quickly to his feet, his hooves scraping on the concrete surface of his stable as he scattered the straw out of the way with his scrambling feet. Derry unlatched the gate. In the far distance, he could see the lights from Mary's cottage glinting invitingly.

"What do you think Teddy Bear's chances are at Cheltenham?" asked Merrianne, increasing his longing for the quiet adoration of Mary. Since she had started to race Merrianne thought that she had become an expert, constantly annoying him with questions about the fitness and ability of the horses, driving him mad with her opinions about how he should work the horses or where he should run them.

"Very good." He stood back to let her pass through the gate and shut it behind them. "He's eating well and is working well on the gallops, he's about as fit as he is ever going to be."

"What about Phone Me, the trainer from Galway, Richard Kirwan's horse, is he much competition? How will he go on the soft ground?"

Derry gritted his teeth, aware that a muscle was twitching in his cheek. Merrianne was very beautiful, wonderful in bed, an asset in every direction, but sometimes he just wished she would butt out. His head reeled with worrying about the horses all day and night. Now he just wanted peace and quiet, to stroll around the stables, admiring his horses, checking that they were happy, dreaming of a rosy future for each one. The last thing that he wanted was to have to answer Merrianne's questions.

Merrianne, wanting to be a perfect girlfriend, interested in her man's career, began again. "Do you think it would do the horses good to have some of that supplement, Run Well, in their feed?"

To shut her up Derry pushed Merrianne up against the wall and kissed her, pushing his tongue hard into her mouth. Now she really had to shut up.

"Fuck me here," she hissed, nibbling his earlobe seductively, shoving her pelvis against his. She dropped her hand, running it down the front of his shirt and then trailing slowly down the front of his trousers, tugging the zip undone. Her fingers were icy cold, making him gasp as she reached inside his trousers. She sank to her knees, taking him in her mouth, the sharp contrast between her icy fingers and the hot wetness of her mouth divine. Twining his fingers in her hair, he jerked her to her feet, shoving her roughly back against the stone wall of the stables. He pushed open the sides of her coat, hauling her skirt over her hips. Sliding his hand over her stocking tops he encountered soft, bare flesh and then the soft, springy hair of her bush and sticky, enticing wetness. "Naughty," he said hoarsely, sliding a long finger inside her, "no knickers."

Merrianne pulled his face towards her, sliding her tongue inside his mouth as she clamped her mouth over his. Eagerly she guided him inside her, moaning with pleasure as he entered her.

"You really are the best fuck ever," Derry gasped in between thrusts. With a final burst of thrusts he came, collapsing against her shoulder, resting his sweat-drenched forehead on the cool rough stone. He eased himself out of her as Merrianne wriggled her skirt back over her hips and ran her fingers through her tangled hair.

They wandered around the stables in a companionable silence. Derry in his après sex stupor had become increasingly monosyllabic until finally Merrianne stopped trying to show an interest in his work and be an entertaining companion. Perhaps being wild sexually was enough.

It was a beautiful night, the bright moonlight making the old buildings seem even more enchanting. Even the dung heap, in the far corner of the yard, close to the walled garden, was made beautiful. The horses, always curious, poking their heads out over half doors, looked like mythological creatures from another world with the dark shadows casting an eerie glow on their coats. They wandered around the long oval of immaculately manicured turf, looking in over each stable door, checking the horses, stopping to adjust a rug in one stable and run a hand slowly down the back of a delicate foreleg in another, checking for any signs of damage that would mean that the horse wouldn't be able to race. Merrianne loved these moments. Derry was at his most relaxed, away from the constant demands of the staff and horses and owners and the insistent incessant ringing of his telephone.

Water Babe was asleep in his stable, stretched out, flat on his side, long delicate legs sprawled across the straw. He lifted his head, blinking in annoyance as Derry snapped on the light. Merrianne followed Derry inside. "Hey, boy," she said softly, moving forwards. Water Babe heaved himself up so that he lay with his long legs tucked beneath him. Merrianne went to his head and crouched down so that his head was level with hers and gently scratched his gleaming white blaze. Water Babe wriggled his soft nose with pleasure as Merrianne scratched the side of his face with a long fingernail. Derry leant against the stable wall, watching with a half-smile playing on his face as Merrianne moved around to the side of the horse and sat on his back as he lay in the straw. Merrianne really was enchanting; she tried so hard to please him.

Merrianne ran her hand slowly along his neck, looking through his ears as if she was riding him. His muscles were hard beneath her fingers, the skin soft and pliable. He was fit, ready to take on the world, a super racehorse. He was one of the best horses in the yard. And he belonged to her. On this horse she would win races. On this horse she was going to win the Galway Plate. She had nothing to fear from Paris. All she had to do was get the best out of Water Babe. The race was on. Let the best woman win.

CHAPTER FORTY-FIVE

"Tilt your head down a little," said Manny Conley, the photographer for Glamorous Ireland magazine. "Keep that look."

Merrianne tilted her head down, letting her blonde hair fall over her right shoulder like a golden waterfall and looking seductively at the camera. Manny clicked the camera, giving little orgasmic cries of delight every time he took a photograph. Then he lay down the camera, clasping his hands together like a delighted child. "Gorgeous, darling," he cooed, tossing his thick mane of wavy jet-black hair with a flick of his head. "You're wasted riding horses - you should have been a model."

Merrianne eased herself slowly down off the top rail of the fence. She had been sitting there for so long posing for Manny that the sharp wooden rail had dug into her thighs, cutting off the circulation. She rubbed her bottom as the blood began to rush back, sending prickles of pins and needles throbbing through her bottom. Being photographed for the magazine had taken hours. Manny had draped her along the gold damask fabric of the sofa in the library, she had lain seductively on her tummy on the white lacy bedspread, sat with a Waterford crystal glass raised to her lips in front of the long dinner-table, laid out with the best Blake china, and sat for hours on Water Babe, grinning at the camera until her face ached.

The team from Glamorous Ireland had descended on the house at an unearthly hour of the morning. Derry, as always wary of journalists and the way that they always twisted reality to create a more interesting story, headed off to the stables, to take his temper out on the staff, leaving Merrianne to deal with the invasion.

Merrianne had been thrilled when Eileen Freeman, the editor, had telephoned and said that they were interested in doing a feature on her, portraying her as the glamorous jockey girlfriend of the famous trainer Derry Blake. Plum French, the features writer, had flounced in first, listing alarmingly to one side, dragged down by the weight of the enormous leather bag that was slung from one shoulder. Her hair, dyed in an alarming dark shade of her namesake was cut so that it fell in wispy spikes over her rouged cheeks, making her look like a wayward fairy peeping out of the leaves of a Virginia Creeper plant. An army of make-up artists, a lighting specialist, like a bondage club on its annual outing, all clad in tight leather draped with silver chains, trooped in behind her. Manny Conlan brought up the rear, sweeping his tanned head around as he scanned the house looking for possible locations to shoot photographs.

"Dar-Ling!" Plum shrieked, grasping Merrianne by both of her wrists and bumping her breasts against Merrianne as she air-kissed on either side of her face. Merrianne almost choked on the cloying smell of her perfume and the sickly odour of her heavy foundation. "So good of you to let us interview you. What a fabulous house!" Plum bounded off into the house with Manny on her heels, pushing open doors and peering inside, both exclaiming with delight at the photo opportunities that lay inside. The make-up artists, three identikit blondes with short spiky hair and lashings of make-up, hovered in the enormous hall, dumping their silver make-up cases thankfully down on the bottom of the curved staircase. They cast surreptitious glances in Merrianne's direction, assessing which make-up to use on her and what look they wanted to create. Kevin Alexander, who was as bald and wrinkled as an old tortoise, scowled aggressively peering into each dark corner, his thick lips thrust out petulantly as he worried about the lighting for the photographs.

Now, the photographs taken Plum came forward. "Dar-ling we'll go and do your interview now," she screeched, grabbing Merrianne's arm and leading her towards the house. The make-up artists, lighting man and Manny piled into Manny's enormous American car and headed off to the pub, leaving Plum to follow them later when she had prised an interesting story out of Merrianne.

Mrs McDonagh, who had spent the morning bringing cups of tea and biscuits and trying to get photographed, bustled around scowling and tutting at the rings they had made on the furniture by carelessly dumping their cups and equipment on the surfaces she had spent hours polishing.

Plum settled herself in the depths of one of the armchairs in the conservatory, opposite Merrianne, and switched on the voice recorder that she had laid between them on the marble-topped coffee table. "Now," she said, leaning forward, wriggling as she hitched down her tight black leather miniskirt that had ridden up as she sat down, giving Merrianne a rather alarming glimpse of plump thighs spilling from her stocking tops. "What's made you decide to start to ride in races?"

An hour later, Plum, having exhausted her store of questions, switched off her voice-recorder. "Wonderful, Merrianne, I think that I've got everything that I need. I'll telephone you if there are any further questions." She shoved the voice-recorder into the depths of her bag.

Merrianne walked her to the front door and watched as she heaved her enormous bag into the passenger seat of the sports car and then folded herself into the driver seat. "The feature should appear in next month's issue," she shrieked, leaning across the seat to yell out of the passenger window as she reversed the car. Then waving her hand out of the window, she shot out of the forecourt and hurtled down the drive, narrowly avoiding the stable cat who was heading into the shrubbery with a mouse that he had just caught.

Derry, who had been watching from the stable yard, emerged as soon as the coast was clear. Merrianne, delighted by the attention of the magazine, was disappointed that Derry didn't share her excitement.

"They are all vipers," he muttered darkly, sitting down to his lunch. "They will build you up into something wonderful and then the next minute they will pull you to shreds." He opened the newspaper and began to read, shovelling food into his mouth distractedly. "Now this is something that you should read," he said, giving a snort of amusement. He turned the newspaper and shoved it in Merrianne's direction, tapping an article with his finger.

Merrianne pushed her plate away. Suddenly she wasn't hungry any more. 'Back in the saddle'– the headline was emblazoned across half of the page with a old grainy photograph of Paris galloping across a finish line. Scowling, Merrianne began to read, her eyes flickering rapidly over the text. "Paris is riding one of Morgan Flynn's horses in the same race as me."

Derry took another mouthful of food and chewed thoughtfully before saying, "I saw that Flynn had a horse entered, but he hadn't named the jockey. Nice for you to have a bit of female companionship."

Merrianne closed the newspaper. That was the last thing that she wanted. And he knew it.

Merrianne and Paris were racing in the fourth race of the day. The race course was already crowded as they came out of the weigh room. Merrianne was glad to get outside, the atmosphere in the changing room having been extremely tense. Paris, white- faced and visibly shaking, had changed in silence. Walter Bollinger, one of the other jockeys had done up the buttons on her silks as her hands wouldn't work.

"You shouldn't be racing. You might fall again," Merrianne said maliciously, watching as Paris's face turned a funny shade of grey. "Derry's going to marry me, so you might as well give up now," she continued.

Paris suddenly shot across the room. "Don't bank on it, Merrianne," she spat, her face inches from her rival's.

There were ten horses in the race, all being led around the parade ring by their lads and lasses, their coats glistening with health in the pale sunlight.

Merrianne went down the steps towards the mass of people, her eyes searching for Derry. Out of the corner of her eye she saw Paris find Morgan, then Derry was in front of her, looking fabulously glamorous in a camel-coloured overcoat with a velvet collar. Alex was beside him, his face wreathed in a huge smile.

"Well," smirked Derry, complacently, "the race is on to see who will win my hand in marriage." He turned away to talk to another trainer.

"This is madness," snapped Alex, seizing Merrianne by the arm and pulling her towards him. "You shouldn't have to prove anything to win Derry." He released her abruptly, then gazed at her for a long moment. "What do I have to do to win you?" he asked quietly.

Merrianne stared at him, feeling her insides churn with sudden emotion. Tears started to her eyes at the respect and gentleness in his tone, the sincerity in his eyes. Respect, gentleness, sincerity: had she ever had any of those from Derry in all the time she knew him? She suddenly felt an impulse to fling herself into the arms of this near-stranger, to beg him to take her away to a quiet place where she could forget all this strain.

She shook her head. What was she thinking of? She hardly knew this

251

man. Derry, with all his faults, was what she wanted. And it was Derry that she was going to win.

Alex was still waiting silently: his question had not been a casual one.

Just then the steward rang his bell, the signal that it was time to mount. Merrianne started. "Alex," she said, "I must go – I'll see you – after – after the race." Then she turned and fled from this man with his kind eyes who was demanding something from her that she had no interest in giving.

In the parade ring, Mary, her mouth screwed up in temper, dragged Water Babe into the centre of the grass in the parade ring. Derry threw Merrianne up into the saddle. "Save him until three fences from home and then –" Derry's words of advice were lost as a cheer rang out from the crowd as the result of the previous race was confirmed.

As they circled before the start Merrianne stole a glance at Paris. She looked green, her complexion clashing horribly with the red and yellow striped silks that she wore. Merrianne could see that her legs were trembling even across the parade ring. Then they lined up and the race was underway.

Paris forgotten, Merrianne concentrated on Water Babe, feeling the powerful horse pulling at the reins, fighting for his head, wanting to rush away in front of the other horses. She held tight onto the reins. If she let him go to the front too quickly he would tire himself out and have no energy left for the finish. Each fence flashed by, Water Babe skimming over them gracefully, eating up the ground easily between them. As they whisked over the third last fence, Merrianne grinned with delight, Water Babe felt like a fresh horse, oozing energy. She slapped him once down the shoulder with her short whip and he surged forwards.

Water Babe began to draw away from the other horses, his long stride eating up the ground. The winning post flashed by. She had won. Merrianne raised one hand in a power salute and gave a loud whoop of delight. Now let Paris see who was the best rider. She might as well give up now. She just hadn't got the same edge that she had before, the same determination to win whatever it cost. And Merrianne had.

The spectators were going wild as she rode Water Babe into the winner's enclosure, ahead of Walter Bollinger and John Kelly.

Alex shoved his way through the crowds to place a warm hand on her leg as she rode by, "I think that this is madness, but you rode a great race."

"Thanks!" Merrianne scanned the crowds for Derry and caught sight of him looking at the race programme with Valerie huddled close to him. He hadn't even come to congratulate her.

The two lads rode into the stalls for the second and third-placed horses and a huge cheer rang out as Merrianne rode into the stall with a winner sign placed above it. As Merrianne posed for photographs she caught sight of Paris walking away with Morgan Flynn, the exhausted horse between them. Merrianne slid from her horse and was grabbed by the photographers again, who positioned her beside Water Babe and a grinning Derry who appeared just in time to share her glory.

Merrianne unbuckled her saddle and went to weigh in. Mary stomped away with the horse. Derry had disappeared. The changing room smelt of stale sweat and horses. Averting her eyes from the painfully thin naked limbs of the jockeys who were changing, Merrianne made her way to the area that had been reserved for the lady jockeys. Paris had already showered and was wriggling her way into a pair of jeans while trying to hold a towel together around her breasts.

"You rode a good race," Paris said, as Merrianne nonchalantly shrugged off her silks. Merrianne immediately felt herself prickle with annoyance, Paris was patronising her. She might have ridden in more races than Merrianne, but Merrianne was every inch as good as she had ever been. And probably better.

"Of course," she snapped shortly, sliding out of her breeches and marching into the shower. She didn't want to start a conversation with Paris. As far as Merrianne was concerned, Paris was her rival. Enemies in battle.

Merrianne showered and changed into her jeans and a smart jacket and went out to find Derry.

As she walked across the crowded concourse Plum French hurtled towards her, shrieking with delight. "Darling, how great to see you again," she yelled, holding out her arms and darting forwards as fast as her high heels and the weight of her bag would allow her.

Merrianne stopped, a grin of delight spreading across her face, hoping that everyone would know that she was friends with such an important journalist. But as she opened her arms to greet Plum, the journalist hurtled straight past her. Merrianne spun around to see Plum launch herself, like a lost puppy finding its owner, straight into the outstretched arms of Paris.

CHAPTER FORTY-SIX

Paris was so scared that she wondered if she really had got her nerve back. She glanced at her alarm-clock: four thirty. Two hours before she had to get up. There was no way that she could go back to sleep again. Not that she was even sure that she wanted to, the nightmares were too frightening. Hooves flashing past her face, knocking her over and over again, rolling faster and faster along the rutted turf. Then falling into water, the hooves thudding down on top of her, forcing her head under water, and she couldn't breathe, she was drowning. She had woken with a jolt as ice-cold water gushed into her lungs.

Rain thundered on the roof, battering in squally showers against her bedroom window. Paris shivered. In twelve hours it would be all over, she would have ridden Red Arrow in his race and be on her way home. How she longed for that moment, when she would be able to get into the lorry and heave a sigh of relief that she had done it. The first race on Morgan Flynn's horse had been bad enough, but she felt worse this time. Excitement at actually being able to ride again had bolstered her through the run-up to the race, but this time the feelings of fear were far more acute.

Morgan had been very kind when she had trailed in at the back of the ten runners, Merrianne had been riding into the winners' enclosure before Paris steered her horse slowly over the finish line. There had been no one left to watch except her parents and Morgan.

"Great job," Morgan had said, seizing the horse's bridle. "This horse is a long way from being fit - you did really well to finish with him."

Paris hadn't been able to speak. The tired horse had done a really bad jump over the last fence, screwing in mid-air, his hindlegs scrabbling through the brushwood as he floundered trying to stay upright as he landed. She had almost fallen off, sprawling forwards, the horse's bay ears alarmingly close to her face, and catching her thumb on the hard muscle that ran down the length of his neck, the pain shooting up her hand. She was terrified. Only the fact that the horse had continued to gallop had kept her in the saddle. If she had fallen at that moment she would have been finished – her confidence was shaky enough.

Paris snuggled down beneath the quilt again and pulled it around her shoulders, shivering with cold and nerves. Why the hell had she let Joe persuade her to ride Red Arrow? He had been so thrilled with the horse managing to finish a race that he was convinced that great things lay ahead for him.

She must have dozed off, for what seemed like seconds later the buzzing of the alarm-clock woke her. She snapped off the insistent noise. She was exhausted. Groaning, she pushed back the covers and got up. It was still raining, drumming down onto the roof in irritable squalls. Great. Now the ground would be horrible for the races, mud that would cling to the horses' hooves, dragging at their legs, and making the fences harder - the take-off point before would be slippery and the mud deep.

A nagging pain cramped her stomach. She massaged her side, trying to ease the muscles that had clenched with fear. She just made it to the bathroom before she was violently sick, retching up acid-tasting orange bile. She raised her head, looking with horror at her reflection. The effort of retching had brought out two bright red spots of colour on her deathly white complexion. Her teeth were chattering so hard that they were a blur of white in the mirror. She washed, struggled into her clothes and went downstairs. There was no sign of Paddy and Elizabeth. No doubt they would be curled up in bed, lying in each other's arms like two young newlyweds. Paris snapped on the kettle, opening the cupboards as it boiled. There was nothing that she would be able to eat. Even the thought of a bowl of cereal made her heave. Finally she settled for a digestive biscuit, dunked in the hot tea she had made. She could at least get some food down without having to chew. Only the thought that Derry would be at the races stopped her from going back to bed and giving up on the whole thing.

"It's great that you are riding again," he had said, putting his hand on her leg as she sat on Morgan Flynn's horse a few weeks previously. "I haven't forgotten my promise."

Paris had hated him for those words. And herself for wanting him back so desperately that she would do anything to prove to him that she was worthy of being his girlfriend.

Forcing herself to swallow the last bit of the biscuit, Paris pulled on a long waxed coat and went outside into the yard. She had finished the work before Paddy and Elizabeth finally emerged from the house, blinking like moles surfacing from underground. Red Arrow was loaded onto the box, waiting to leave, resting a hind leg, ears lolling, a patient expression on his whiskery old face.

"We'll follow you," Paddy told her, unable to resist pinching Elizabeth's bottom as she walked to the car. Paris scowled as Elizabeth giggled coquettishly like a school-girl. Life at home was like being caught between the devil and the deep blue sea, she either had Paddy drunk and no Elizabeth, or Paddy sober and had to suffer Elizabeth being around. If only it could be Paddy sober and no Elizabeth. But from the way they were acting it looked as if she would have to suffer Elizabeth for a while longer. At least once she had won the Galway Plate and married Derry she would have her own home.

The rain had collected in huge puddles on the race course. Paris sloshed through them on her way to the weigh room, feeling like a prisoner going to the gallows. She declared Red Arrow as a runner and went to get ready. The changing room buzzed with noise, as the young jockeys teased each other, the friendly banter tossed backwards and forwards. Merrianne sat in the corner that had been partitioned off for the ladies. Tamara Cunningham sprawled nonchalantly on the opposite bench. Merrianne was immaculate, her blonde hair scraped back into a pony-tail, her face impassive beneath the layer of make-up she wore. She looked calm, composed and completely unafraid. Tamara, with her mobile phone clamped to her ear, began to change, completely unabashed by her nakedness as she shrugged off her jeans and slid into a pair of breeches. Her presence made Paris tremble at the memory of the terrible accident the last time that she had ridden against Tamara. She began to change, turning her back to the other girls so that they wouldn't see how much her hands were trembling, and then sat on the hard bench seat, trying to force herself to breathe. Their fearlessness made Paris more afraid; she couldn't compete with them.

She felt no better when she went out into the parade ring. Red Arrow looked enormous; she should never have started riding again. Paddy legged her up into a saddle that felt too small and slippery. The horse's ears seemed miles away, the reins cumbersome between fingers that were wet with sweat inside her gloves.

They went out onto the course, the horses shooting past Red Arrow as he cantered as gently as a riding-school pony to the start line. He stood patiently at the start line, ignoring the frenzied plunging of the other horses as they frantically waited to start running. Paris swallowed hard, trying to remember to keep breathing, trying to ease the cramp of panic that gripped her stomach.

Merrianne grinned maliciously at her. "You haven't the guts for racing any more. I can see you trembling from here."

The tape flew up. Red Arrow bounded forwards, taking charge of his nervous passenger, whisking her gently over the fences, powering through the deep mud as nimbly as any young horse. Paris, having grabbed a handful of mane as they went over the first fence didn't relax until they rounded the home turn, the horses packed together in a bunch, exploding over the fences together. She let go of his mane.

And then she realised that Red Arrow had his long nose in front of the other horses, gamely charging forwards, moving with grim determination. He could win.

And with that thought she sat still, all fear forgotten, willing the horse home as he surged in front of the others, skimming over the final fence alone and powering towards the finishing line. With a laugh of sheer delight Paris glanced back over her shoulder to see the surprised faces of the other riders. For a split second her eyes locked with Merrianne's. Naked fury was written all over her face.

Red Arrow thundered past the winning post.

"We won!" yelled Paris, slapping Red Arrow on the neck with delight. Paris felt tears of joy stream down her face. She raised her arm, waving her whip furiously as the roars of the crowds echoed in her ears. Suddenly Red Arrow lurched forwards, as if he had stumbled. His legs gave way beneath him and he fell sideways. Paris rolled off to the side, just getting her leg out of the way before his massive weight crushed it. "Red," she sobbed, the tears of joy turning to despair as the faithful old horse gave a final desperate attempt to rise, his legs paddling as if he were running and then his head fell back onto the mud, as his brave heart stopped beating, his final breath rushing out in a low, rattling groan.

The rest of the horses charged past, mud flying up from their hooves, splattering against his wet coat. Paris, covered in mud, lay over the hump of his back, her tears falling onto his mud-stained coat. He was still warm, the steam from his body rising gently into the rain. She reached forwards and stroked his kind old face. His eyes were still open, the raindrops pattering slowly into their unseeing brown depths. Paris ran her hand over his eyelid, pushing it closed.

"Come on, love. You're doing no good here," a steward said in a kindly voice, hauling her to her feet. Paris leant against him, her legs wouldn't hold her up any more, and sobbed uncontrollably. Poor Red Arrow, he had given the best performance of his life. He had proved Joe right. He had won a race. And died in the attempt.

A crowd of ghoulish spectators gathered beside Red Arrow, leaning on the rails gawping unashamedly as the stewards began to unbuckle his saddle. The other horses in the race walked past the prone form of the horse on their way back to the stables, their jockeys calling out kind words of sympathy to Paris. Paris stared fixedly at the ground, watching the hooves go past, too upset to meet anyone's eyes. A horse stopped. Paris dragged her eyes reluctantly upwards past the horse's mud-splattered white socks, the black tops of his legs and on upwards to the triumphant face of his jockey.

Merrianne's mouth twisted into a malicious smirk. "You should give up now, before you hurt yourself again," she said.

CHAPTER FORTY-SEVEN

Walter Bollinger was very small and very angry. "You're a real nasty bitch," he spat, jabbing his finger at Merrianne's chest. She backed away rapidly, in fright at his sudden outburst, colour flooding into her cheeks with embarrassment as the crowded room froze into expectant silence, all watching the scene unfold. The odour of unwashed and very sweaty-smelling clothes made her gasp as she found herself pressed up against the wall pegs where the jockeys hung their belongings when they changed into their racing silks. She had just come into the weigh room to get ready for racing. The last thing that she had expected was to be set upon by 5 foot of pure fury. Walter had been waiting for her to arrive, sitting on the bench, tapping his feet, already encased in wafer-thin leather boots, in impatience.

"I'm going to sort that bitch out for what she said to you," he had told Paris importantly when she came into change.

"It doesn't matter, Walt," she had told him, placing a cool hand on his arm.

"It does to me," Walter had muttered, feeling very protective towards Paris, who he had always had a soft spot for. He had been fuming since Merrianne had been so nasty to Paris when Red Arrow had died. Walter liked Paris, she had always been kind to him, given him rides on good horses when she was training, giving him a place to stay when his father finally kicked him out for good. Walter wasn't going to stand for anyone being so cruel as to mock someone whose horse had just died. Racing was a tough enough game without being rotten to each other.

"What you said the other day was pure evil!" His eyes were almost level with Merrianne's chin.

Taken aback, she looked down at the top of his head. His wiry dark hair was standing up at different angles, as if he had just got out of bed, and she could see flakes of dandruff in the zig-zag parting. "All I said was –" she began.

Walter leaned closer. She could smell bad digestion and whiskey on his breath. Walter jabbed his finger into her chest to punctuate the words. "You. Leave. Paris alone," he snarled, flecks of spittle pattering against her cheeks.

"Right, fine," spluttered Merrianne, wriggling away. The best thing to do was obviously to humour the poisonous little dwarf. Her relationship with Paris had nothing to do with him. "Little prick," she muttered furiously under her breath. How dare he try to make her look a fool in front of all the other jockeys! She stalked away, glimpsing Paris out of the corner of her eye, watching the scene, a supercilious smile turning up the corners of her mouth.

Everyone turned away hastily, no one meeting Merrianne's eyes as she stalked over to the ladies' changing area. Merrianne wrenched her clothes off, trembling with self-righteous anger. How dare Walter talk to her like that? And embarrass her in front of everyone. Success is the greatest revenge, she fumed silently. Water Babe was going brilliantly. He could easily win the race today. That would show them all; she would win and walk away with her head high.

When everyone was changed, the steward called for them to wait by the door that led out into the parade ring. They gathered in the corridor, like schoolchildren waiting to go into class, giggling together, joking, some silent, contemplating the race nervously. No one spoke to Merrianne, who stood apart from them, ostracised from the friendly camaraderie. The security guard opened the door and let the riders in from the last race. Red-faced with their exertions and mud-splattered they walked past the waiting riders, to much back-slapping and banter. "OK," grinned the Security Guard, holding back the door as they all trooped out.

As Merrianne walked across the parade ring, Alex Ivor fell into step beside her. "Please stop this madness," he said with the utmost seriousness. "Derry is just playing the two of you along. He doesn't want you. He's just getting his kicks out of letting the two of you fight for him."

"Leave me alone, Alex," pleaded Merrianne. She didn't want him to see the confusion that his presence created in her.

"Merrianne – stop!" He caught her arm and halted her. "Just listen to me one moment!"

"What are you doing?" she exploded angrily, pulling her arm away! "I have a race-"

"One moment!" he interrupted.

She glared at him but didn't turn away.

"Merrianne," he said urgently. "I have an instinct about people that has served me well all my life. I look in your eyes and I know you are a good person at heart – but I believe you hardly know who you are any more. Your desire for Derry Blake has made you spiteful, even cruel. Let me-"

"That's enough!" she raged at him. "How dare you! Are you deliberately trying to upset me before the race?" With that she turned on her heel and strode away from him fuming.

Derry looked quizzically at her flushed face when she reached him and Water Babe. She turned away from him to hide her face and saw Paris, gazing so hard at Derry, almost fall over a camera bag that a photographer had dumped on the ground as he took pictures of the horses. Merrianne deliberately planted a huge kiss on Derry's cheek to annoy her.

The bell rang and the jockeys mounted their horses. Derry threw Merrianne into Water Babe's saddle.

Paddy was still valiantly trying to shove Paris onto Destiny, while Morgan Flynn clung to the mare's bridle, his face impassive, giving Paris calming words of advice. She was green with nerves. Kane, his face filled with adoration, like a puppy, watched her every move from the edge of the parade ring.

The horses went out onto the track. "Hope your mare doesn't fall again!" Merrianne hissed, riding her horse alongside Paris. Alex's voice echoed in her mind: 'spiteful, even cruel' She shook her head to banish the voice.

She screwed her mouth up into a semblance of a smile as Walter Bollinger scowled at her. She wasn't going to be cowed by a little jerk like him. Paris should fight her won battles. She'd show them! Water Babe was going to win. Derry had told her that he was the favourite with the bookies. She would show Paris once and for all who was the best rider.

Then they were off.

Water Babe hurtled along, full of running, skimming over the fences like

261

a bird, his ears sharply pricked, thoroughly enjoying himself. Merrianne crouched over his withers, the silky hair of his mane whipping against her face, revelling in the glorious feeling of power from her horse. He was going to win easily.

The race passed in a flash. As the second fence from home came up she was in fourth place, the ideal spot to take the lead and charge to the line in front. Tommy Swaine and Robbie Walsh were in front, the powerhouse quarters of their horses pounding like pistons in front of her. But as she began to pull Water Babe around to pass them Walter blocked her way, his face set, staring fixedly forwards.

"Move over!" roared Merrianne.

Walter ignored her. Fury and panic mingling uncomfortably, Merrianne glanced over her shoulder: two other horses were right behind her, making it impossible to pull back and go around Walter. They were deliberately blocking her in. Using their horses to stop her getting to the front.

"Get out the fucking way!" she yelled again, hearing the hysteria rising in her voice. They had jumped the last fence and were charging towards the finish line. Walter shot her a glance of pure malice. Merrianne, mouthing with fury, saw Paris urging Destiny forwards on the outside of all of the horses, passing the winning post in third place.

Merrianne was still bristling with temper after she had showered and changed. The lads in the weigh room had been delighted that Paris had done well in the race, feeling it made up for the awful death of Red Arrow. But they seemed even more delighted that their evil plans to block Merrianne in and not let her win had worked. There was a lot of nudging and stifled laughter as Merrianne had stalked, puce with temper, back into the weigh room.

Even Derry had been unsympathetic. "You have to know what is going on everywhere in the race, behind, to the side, not just in front," he told her, licking his handkerchief and scrubbing away a smear of mud from her cheek that she had missed in the shower. Merrianne shrugged off his hand and stalked away towards the owners and trainers bar. She needed a drink. And a large one at that.

"Hello, Merrianne," said a familiar voice, bringing Merrianne to a halt as if she had run into an invisible brick wall.

Shula blocked the way, looking for all the world like a mutated peacock in a brightly coloured patchwork coat and enormous hat that sagged beneath the weight of fake flowers stuck on the brim.

"Oh fuck," she hissed under her breath as Derry caught up with her.

"I thought I'd see if you remembered me," said Shula, smiling triumphantly. "I'm Shula - your mother."

Merrianne felt her heart sink as Derry, with a broad grin, stuck out his hand. "Hello," he said silkily, shaking Shula's hand solemnly. She shuddered inwardly as she noticed the dirt engrained in her mother's finger-nails.

"Merrianne," he reproved sternly, his face mocking as he turned to face her, "why haven't you introduced me to your delightful mother before?" Merrianne closed her eyes in horror. Derry was going to enjoy tormenting her over her scruffy, hippy mother. At least, she thought, bleakly, Charlie was nowhere in sight, that was one blessing.

"We were just going to the owners and trainers Bar – please join us, I'm sure Merrianne would love to have you there." He took Shula's arm and, darting a glance of great amusement at Merrianne's discomfiture, marched towards the bar. Merrianne followed, squirming with embarrassment.

"And where is your husband today?" Merrianne heard him say as he led Shula across the betting-slip-strewn tarmac. Merrianne didn't even want to hear her reply. She had certainly never had a husband. And Merrianne doubted that she could even remember who had sired her daughter. Heaven knew what Shula was telling Derry.

They made an incongruous couple. Derry, tall and impossibly elegant, from the top of his felt fedora to the tips of his hand-made shoes, oozed class and wealth. His tweed jacket and corduroy trousers looked bizarrely out of place beside Shula's vividly coloured patchwork coat. It swirled around her ankles, the hem-line rising and falling like a heart-beat chart, above clumpy lace-up boots. Merrianne shuddered to think what dreadful creation she had on underneath the coat.

To Merrianne's utter horror Valerie and David were propping up the bar. David was deep in conversation with a tweed-hatted trainer and didn't glance up. Valerie was halfway across the room, ready to launch herself at Derry in greeting when the sight of Shula brought her up short. As she shuddered to a halt in front of him, Derry, guiding Shula with his hand on the small of her back, introduced her.

"Valerie," he smirked, "this is Merrianne's mother, Shula."

"Oh." Valerie for once was lost for words, her mouth forming a perfect circle as she gazed in amazement at Shula. Merrianne cringed.

"We'll grab a table," Derry said. "Merrianne, order the drinks, will you? I'll have a whiskey, gin for Valerie and David and I'm sure you know what your mother drinks."

Merrianne went to the bar and ordered the drinks. She took the loaded tray and headed back to the table. Valerie had recovered her composure and was busily snooping into Shula's life with the fascinated dedication of a zoologist discovering a new species. Merrianne sat down and handed the drinks around. Shula was pink with excitement and had taken off her coat to reveal a black velvet top that scooped so low over her ample bosom that Derry could probably see her toes if he peeped down it.

"Where has Merrianne kept you hidden all this time?" Derry said.

Merrianne glanced up and saw to her utter horror that he was gazing at Shula in utter fascination.

CHAPTER FORTY-EIGHT

As Destiny launched herself into the air at the final fence Paris knew that she was going to win the race. They were two lengths ahead of the rest of the runners and the mare was still full of energy. Then, as Destiny landed, she stumbled, falling onto her nose, ploughing a deep furrow in the wet earth with the soft, velvety skin of her muzzle, her legs floundering in every direction as she fell. Paris was pitched forward with the momentum of the fall. She caught a glimpse of Destiny's ears, still sharply pricked, way below her, then the turf rushed up to meet her. Instinctively Paris curled into a ball, rolling as she hit the ground, with a thud that knocked the breath out of her. The horses behind thundered over the fence, as Paris tucked her head into her knees, tensing against the agony as a hoof caught her, or even worse trod on her. Then there was silence. After what seemed long minutes but in fact was probably only split seconds, Paris uncurled herself and got slowly to her feet. Her shoulder ached where she had landed.

Destiny had got straight to her feet and carried on running with the rest of the horses.

She passed the winning post with an embarrassed look on her face, realising she had forgotten Paris. Paris didn't know whether to laugh or cry. At least she was safe, she hadn't hurt herself in the fall, and nor apparently had Destiny, but she had been so certain that she was going to win, the disappointment was hard to take. That was one of the funny things about racing, or horses even, that no matter how good you were, or how convinced of victory you were, the horse would always conspire to prove you wrong. So many races had been lost at the final fence, or in the run up to the winning post. Paris trudged slowly back to the weigh room, feeling terribly conspicuous on the vast expanse of turf, churned up by the horses as they ran. It was hard to walk in her stiff leather boots, and she kept tripping over the rutted turf. A bright horseshoe, lost in the last race, glinted mockingly at her. It pointed back at her - the luck running out, she thought, just like my luck.

As she reached the concourse Paris ducked under the white guard rail and walked across the turf towards Morgan. Hers had been the last race of the day and everyone was now leaving.

"Never mind, Paris," said Morgan, putting his arm gently around her shoulders. "She was going great – she just made a mistake coming into the last, she will be all the better for it, give her a bit of experience."

Paris smiled tightly. "Thanks."

Morgan gave her arm a brief squeeze. "See you soon - come over in a few days and we'll school her over some fences at my place." Then he was jogging away, hurrying to get back to his own horses.

Eddie, who had come to help for the day to get away from his wife, had caught Destiny. He was waiting in the parade ring, holding the mare, who was spinning around him wildly, whinnying madly, terrified of being alone now that the other horses had all gone. "I'm sure she's injured her leg," Eddie grumbled. "See, she's lame!" He walked a few strides, leading the mare. "She's probably damaged a tendon," he added dramatically, giving Paris the full benefit of his pessimistic nature. Paris bit her lip; the last thing that she wanted now was doom and gloom from Eddie. The mare did look a bit stiff when she walked though. Paris took off her gloves and ran a hand down the back of each of the mare's forelegs feeling for any telltale heat or swelling that would indicate serious damage. She stood up; her shoulder was really throbbing now and her head was beginning to ache – there was a sore spot just behind her left ear where her skull cap must have dug in when it hit the ground.

"There's nothing serious, Eddie," she said, tiredly. "Come on. Let's get her home." Paris walked away towards the weigh room, leaving Eddie to take Destiny back to the lorry and have her loaded up by the time she had changed.

"This horse will be dog lame in the morning - she's damaged her tendons,"

Paris could hear Eddie muttering to himself as he walked away.

She reached the changing rooms. All of the jockeys had changed quickly and shoved off to the pub. Only Tommy Swaine remained, huddled into a corner, still in his silks, sobbing pitifully. A bit embarrassed Paris went into the ladies' area and showered. Then dressed in jeans and a sweatshirt came back out. Tommy hadn't moved.

"Are you OK?" Paris sat down beside him.

Tommy shook his head angrily. "Fucking stewards have just given me a thirty-day ban for using the whip too much on the fucking dog of a horse that I was riding today. Now I'm going to miss the big race at Punchestown."

"Shit, that's rotten," said Paris sympathetically.

Tommy was to have been riding one of the favourites, now he would have to sit on the sidelines and watch someone else ride the horse in a race that he had been dreaming about for weeks.

Eddie poked his head around the door. "Destiny's loaded. She looks very sore. Sooner she's home the better," he snapped, as usual convinced that no one knew better than he did.

"I'm sorry," said Paris, patting Tommy gently on the hand. He began to sob again as she got up and followed Eddie out to the lorry park.

The next morning, Destiny, although certainly stiff when she moved, showed none of the desperate lameness that Eddie had been convinced she would have.

"I'm going to turn her out for the day," Paris told him, in a voice that even he daren't argue with "That should do her the world of good. Then I'll hose her legs with cold water when she comes in and see how she is tomorrow." She led the mare across the yard with Daisy following on her heels, bleating in a worried tone if the mare got more than two strides away, like a concerned nanny.

Paris led Destiny into the field and let her go. The mare, having been confined to her stables when she was not racing or being exercised was delighted to get a spell of unaccustomed freedom. She galloped away across the field, bucking madly without a trace of the stiffness that had so concerned Eddie. Daisy ran after her, like a matronly nanny running after a wayward child.

The following morning however, the stiffness was there again - nothing too terrible, just a barely noticeable shortness in Destiny's stride. Paris tacked up the mare and rode her out, hacking her quietly around the lanes, but still a gnawing feeling of worry nagged at the back of her mind. What if something was seriously wrong with the mare and she didn't get better? She had been so certain that she would be able to ride her in the Galway Plate. She didn't have the money to buy another horse if Destiny was too lame to run and she knew that Morgan's horses were all being ridden by other jockeys.

In panic she set off for Radford Lodge. Morgan would know what to do with the mare. Of course Paris had as much experience as he did in dealing with horses, but sometimes it was nice just to have someone to talk to and discuss the various treatments that she could use.

Morgan was in the yard when she arrived, showing off the new horse that he had just bought to Tara. "What do you think of my Warchester Hurdle prospect?" he asked Paris, unable to keep the pride out of his voice.

"Very nice," she told him, looking at the tall black gelding, who was looking around himself warily. "I wanted to ask your advice," she said, running an appreciative hand down the gelding's muscular neck.

Morgan turned his mouth down, in an expression of surprise. "You had better come inside then," he told her, gesturing to Kate, his groom to take the black horse back to his stable. "I'm ready for a cup of tea anyway," he said, looking hopefully at Tara.

"I get the hint," Tara said, sliding down from the wall where she had been sitting and walking into the house ahead of them.

Morgan led the way into his office and gestured at an armchair beside the empty fireplace and sat down opposite her, stretching his long legs in front of him. "So, what can I help you with?" he asked.

"It's Destiny," began Paris, pausing as Tara came in with a tray full of tea things.

"Is that the mare that you jumped the hedge on bareback?" asked Tara, pouring tea into two mugs and scattering biscuits onto a plate.

"Yes,"

"So, what's wrong with her?" Morgan said, picking up his mug.

"Well, nothing to serious," Paris began, wishing that Tara would go away. How could she explain to Morgan that she needed to get her horse right so that she could steal Tara's brother from his new girlfriend? Tara and she had always been good friends, but friendship was one thing, trying to oust his girlfriend was another thing. For all Paris knew, Tara and Merrianne could be bosom buddies. Somehow she doubted it, but still …

There was an uncomfortable pause.

Tara, sensing that she wasn't wanted, took the tea tray off to the kitchen.

"But?" said Morgan quizzically, leaning towards Paris.

Paris shrugged. "Well, after she fell the other day she has been pretty stiff, I've been cold hosing her legs, but I just wanted to sound off on you. See if you had any other ideas."

Morgan puffed out his cheeks. Paris knew how to care for her horses as well as he did. There must be a real concern behind her coming to ask his advice. "Well, you are doing all that I would do. There are some good massage people around, but you know of them already. Maybe I'd bring her to the sea for a few days – the salt water is the best miracle cure I know."

Paris took a long swallow of her tea. "The sea," she mused, "Maybe that would be a good idea."

"What's the rush with her?" he asked. "Surely a few days off won't make much difference to her?"

"She has to be right for the Galway Plate," Paris exclaimed. "I need to –" Her words faded into oblivion, uncertain of Morgan's reaction.

Morgan scowled; something wasn't right. Paris was buzzing with a frenzied excitement, high spots of rosy pink colouring her cheeks. "Why are you so desperate to win the Plate?" he asked.

He saw her start, as if he had dug too deeply. Her eyes flickered around the room, like a trapped animal looking for an escape. "Why, Paris?" he said again.

"For Derry," she confessed, the words coming out so quickly and quietly that he could barely make out what she said, or, he wondered later, it might have been that he didn't want to hear.

"What?" he snapped, incredulously.

"I have to win the Galway Plate. Derry said he will dump Merrianne and marry me if I can start winning again. He told me that he would marry me if I won the Galway Plate," she said, slowly this time, a half smile of wonder flickering across her face.

She was unprepared for Morgan's reaction.

"For Christ's sake, Paris," he exploded. "If Derry thought anything of you at all you wouldn't have to be risking your neck trying to win a race to get him to love you. Morgan slammed down his mug of tea onto the floor beside his chair in fury. "Kane McCarthy is desperately in love with you. Any fool can see that. For Christ sake, Paris, you have a wonderful man who wants you and you have to go risking everything for that bastard. Don't be so bloody stupid! Derry isn't worth it!" He spoke with a bitter hatred for the brother-in-law who had almost cost him his marriage, by tearing Tara apart with his machinations, trying to prevent her from being happy with Morgan.

"I have to get him back," Paris said, dully. "I love him."

"I won't help you anymore." Morgan shook his head sadly at her. Something inside him suddenly snapped, exploding into a violent temper at her sheer stupidity and the twisted, sadistic manner in which Derry manipulated everyone. "You want to get Derry Blake back; you can do it on your own."

CHAPTER FORTY-NINE

"I'll come with you," Kane said, when Paris announced that she was bringing Destiny over to the sea at Silver Cove to see if the sea water would help with the stiffness. Paris scowled. She couldn't spend any time with Kane. She knew how attracted to her he was – and, admittedly, how attracted to him she was, and didn't want to risk any chance of making the same mistake she had in the cottage on the day of the rainstorm. He was too attractive. Too dangerous. He distracted her from what she wanted. Derry.

"What a good idea," Elizabeth smiled. She never missed an opportunity to throw the two of them together. She had given up trying to tell Paris that she was a fool for running after Derry Blake and that she should make a go of it with Kane. It was obvious how much he thought of Paris. Even today he had been sitting patiently at the kitchen table waiting for her to come in, his face lighting up like an old faithful dog when he heard her footsteps coming up the path.

Paris, sensing that she was being backed into a corner, shrugged. "Whatever." At least Kane could help her to put up the heavy lorry ramp.

Early the following morning she loaded Destiny into the lorry. Daisy came along as a matter of course. Kane was outside waiting before she even got up, no doubt making sure that she couldn't go without him.

"Her tendons are damaged, she needs time off," grumbled Eddie, his bottom lip jutting forwards like a petulant child. "No good bringing her to the sea - it's rest she needs."

Paris slammed up the ramp, drowning out his words. Kane had already settled himself in the passenger seat when she climbed up into the cab. A flask, which she assumed contained hot tea, lay on the seat beside him. Paris shook her head, wryly. "You will make someone a lovely wife," she said, sarcastically. She wasn't even half as organised as he was.

"I'd make you a lovely husband," Kane said, quietly.

Paris ignored him pointedly.

The beach at Silver Cove was approached by a long steep narrow lane that wound between tumbledown walls to a small carpark. After Paris had pulled right up the grass bank twice to let cars coming away from the beach drive past her, they were near enough to the beach to see that it was packed, "Shit," she fumed. "Bloody children everywhere - they must all be on holiday or something,"

"The carpark is full too," Kane told her, totally unnecessarily.

"Yes, I can see that," said Paris through gritted teeth. What a waste of time this had been. Two hours in the lorry and now they couldn't even bring the mare into the sea. It wouldn't be safe to bring Destiny out amongst all the cavorting children, even if they could find space in the carpark to unload her. It looked as if a full-scale game of football was being played on the beach. She could never take Destiny on there; the mare was so fresh she could buck or kick out at one of the children.

Paris felt herself getting redder and redder with the heat and irritation. The carpark was so full that there was barely room to turn the lorry around. All of the holiday makers were gawping at her.

"Having trouble?" said a short fat man, whose face glowed deep red with the sun. "I wanted to ride my horse in the water, but it's too crowded and now I can't find enough room to turn," she sighed.

"I'm just leaving.," He marshalled a horde of children into the back seat of his small car, "You should just be able to turn in my spot. If you want somewhere quiet there's a bay further on. You have to park on the beach, just watch out for the tide though". Paris gave him a thumbs-up signal in thanks.

"Just go back onto the main road and turn left, carry on there for another mile and you'll see the sign for Coral Cove, just after Kelehan's bar. It should be pretty quiet – everyone comes here because of the carpark."

Coral Cove was easy to find. A brown fingerpost with the beach symbol on it pointed the way down a short stretch of boreen just past the pub, as

272

the man had directed. Paris turned the lorry and drove slowly down the rough boreen, bumping over the pot-holes and wincing as the thick briars that grew on either side scraped against the painted sides of the lorry.

"Look at that," exclaimed Kane in amazement as they reached the end of the boreen. "What a perfect beach," replied Paris, awestruck by the beauty of the place. Ahead of them, framed between jagged black rocks, was a wide sandy bay. Golden sand stretched down to the sea, a blur of turquoise blue in the distance. Paris drove slowly onto the beach past wooden boats lying on their sides, cumbersome as whales washed up by the tide.

"There must have been a bad storm to wash the seaweed as high as this," mused Kane, as Paris bumped over a line of dark seaweed, tangled with bits of green nylon rope and plastic bottles. She steered the lorry along the shoreline; a field of cows on their left came and watched their progress curiously standing against a barbed wire fence strewn with lines of seaweed and bits of nylon fishing net.

"That looks like a good spot to unload," she said, pointing to a flat area of beach that stood at the top of a little rise. Just before it the sand dipped down, scooped into a hollow, like a dried riverbed and at the other side a beautiful flat area stretched out.

She stopped the lorry, drinking in the noise of the seashore now that the dull throb of the engine had gone. Seabirds cried, as they wheeled in the sky above, their sound like that of a baby abandoned and hungry, bees buzzed lazily in the gorse that dotted the grass and far away in the distance the dull thunder of the sea as it crashed onto the beach.

"Come on then," Paris said, shoving open the door and letting in a salty blast of sea air, tinged with the scent of warm grass and cows. She slid out of the cab, feet crunching onto the sand.

"This is beautiful," said Kane, turning his face to the sun, "and so are you," he caught her around the waist and dropped a kiss on her forehead.

"Come on or the day will be over before I've been in the sea," said Paris, uncomfortably, wriggling out of his arms. She couldn't risk getting close to him again.

They pulled down the lorry ramp and Paris saddled Destiny and then led her out, shutting Daisy back inside the lorry where she bleated indignantly, furious at being separated from her companion. The horse stood with her head high, eyes full of curiosity, ears sharply pricked, eager to explore her new surroundings.

Kane threw Paris up into the saddle.

"See you in a while," she said, as Kane sat down on the warm grass.

"Don't hurry," he yawned, stretching out in the grass and closing his eyes.

It was wonderful on the beach, the sand thudded softly beneath Destiny's hooves as she rode. At first the mare was afraid of the sea, which moved and shot over her legs, covering them with ice-cold foamy water which bubbled and then receded on the sand. But gradually she got used to the waves and went deeper into the water, pawing at the sea with a front leg, sending salty water showering all over the two of them. Paris walked her up and down in the water, going so deep that the water almost reached the soles of her boots. After an hour she turned the mare and went back to the lorry. The sea water had crept higher up the beach trickling further onto the sand with each wave. Kane still dozed on the grass, his arms tucked behind his head, a lazy smile playing on his handsome face. Paris stopped the mare and stood looking down at him, wishing that she could get Derry out of her system.

Then suddenly he opened one eye and grinning broadly got to his feet. "Had fun?"

He took the mare's bridle while Paris undid the buckles of the saddle.

"It was wonderful," she told him, heaving the saddle off the mare. "If it wasn't so far away from everywhere I'd love to live out here."

They put Destiny back into the lorry, to Daisy's joy and relief, and slammed up the ramp.

"Let's go and get something to eat. I'm starving," said Kane.

Paris shrugged. "OK, why not? We'll walk up to that pub. There didn't look to be too much of a carpark outside and the road was very busy. The lorry will be safer here,"

They walked up to the pub. An old man passed them on the boreen,

"Tide's coming in," he said, gesturing with his head at the sea.

"Good," said Paris, with a giggle. Funny people out here, they didn't say hello like normal people.

They got a sandwich in the pub and a glass of Guinness each and then wandered back to the lorry as the barman closed for the afternoon. The old man stood at the end of the boreen and, as they got closer, Paris realised with a jolt like a thousand volts of electricity passing through her that the sea water was lapping against his feet. Feeling sick, she gave a yelp of horror and hurtled down the boreen, skidding to a halt beside him Kane at her heels.

"Tide comes in here very fast," he commented, not addressing them particularly.

Paris felt sick. The bay where she had ridden only a short time ago was entirely covered and the lorry, parked on that little rise, stood axle-deep in water.

"Fuck!" said Kane in amazement.

"Oh God, how far in does it come?" cried Paris to the old man. "My mare and a sheep are trapped inside."

"They'll be grand," said the old man, poking at a bit of seaweed with his foot. "Tide will start to go back out soon. Tis nearly high tide already. You'll have to wait till the tide goes out – it will be too deep in that dip to drive through but your lorry will come to no harm there."

Gritting her teeth, Paris glared at the lorry. Why the hell hadn't she moved it off the beach?

"Don't worry," Kane said gently, putting his arm around her shoulder. "The water's not deep enough to cause any damage to anything."

Paris bit her lip. Well, they'd just have to take the old man's word for it and be patient.

"I'd better go and check on the animals," Kane said.

"I'll come too," Paris said, worried about Destiny.

They picked their way across the rock-strewn grass and then pulled off their boots, rolled up their jeans and waded through the sea, gasping at the icy water.

They hauled themselves up into the cab and went through to the back where the animals where. Destiny stood unconcerned by their predicament, gently nibbling hat her hay-net, with Daisy beside her chomping at the fallen strands of dried grass. "Come here," said Kane. He lay on his back on the narrow bed behind the lorry cab. When Paris, hesitated he said gently "I know I rushed you before. I won't touch you until you want me." Paris burned with the memory of the afternoon they had spent together during the storm. She couldn't let that happen again, the feelings he wrought in her were too confusing.

"Come on," he repeated. "Lie down, we may as well have a nap."

She lay on the bed beside him, tucking herself under his arm and resting her head on his chest, warm and comfortable. She smiled to herself. If Derry had been here he would have been absolutely freaking out now, going wild about getting stuck in the sea, the time they were wasting. And it would be all her fault. She closed her eyes, relaxing against the warmth of Kane's body. If only Derry were more like Kane.

CHAPTER FIFTY

Paris never knew if it was the sea water that cured Destiny's stiffness, but she was soon sound enough to go back into full work again. Paris though did know that she had been thrown into confusion. She had thoroughly enjoyed being with Kane. When the lorry had got stranded on the beach they had lain in each other's arms and dozed contentedly until the sea water had receded. She couldn't rid herself of the thought that if she had been with Derry the incident would have resulted in a huge argument: him furious at her stupidity for parking on the beach in the first place, she angry at him for not telling her not to park on the beach. There would have been lots of shouting, swearing, vicious hatred and then a violent, passionate making up afterwards. She had enjoyed the peacefulness that she had found with Kane. Life ticked gently along on an even keel, with none of the heart- breaking highs and lows that she had with Derry.

Yet still, like a bomb set to explode, she couldn't be turned off her course, she had to have Derry back. Yes, life with him was tempestuous, but that was because they were so passionate about each other. What she had with Kane was more like a wonderful friendship.

Destiny was entered in the Rocher Chase, one of the big races in the four-day racing festival at Killarney. She was loaded into the lorry before dawn, Daisy in attendance, to begin the long journey south to the beautiful racecourse. The first light was streaking the sky with silver and the palest blue as they left Blackbird Stables. Rain was falling as they reached Killarney.

"I hope this doesn't last." Paris snapped on the windscreen wipers, scowling as they swept away the water that was lashing against the lorry. Destiny wouldn't like the soft ground, she ran best when there had been no rain.

"It won't," Kane said, wiping the misted windscreen with a cloth. "I listened to the forecast last night, there should just be slight showers early on in the day and getting hot again this afternoon. You will get your good ground, don't worry."

Kane was so organised, so very different from her. Left alone she would have been driving now worrying about the rain falling and wondering if she should turn back and not even bother trying to run the mare if the ground was going to be too soft. He even kept her calm, prattling mindlessly about his new farm and the work he wanted to do to it.

She would have been surprised to know what was actually going through Kane's mind.

While he prattled on, Kane was worrying if playing it cool and slow was working with Paris. He wanted to hold her, to smother her with passion, spend hours in bed with her, one day maybe marry her. He had a glorious dream of her suddenly realising that he was the man for her and would see Derry Blake for the rat he was. Then he could make her his own. His new farm would make a perfect training stables. That was one of the reasons that he had brought it. He had thought of Paris the minute he had seen the place.

The buildings could all be converted, extended to create a beautiful stable block, the sloping land would make the ideal place to train horses. And the little house where they had made love could be extended, rooms put on to house them, maybe even a nursery for their children. He stared out of the window. Paris would probably throw him out if she knew what he was thinking. He had rushed her too much that day that they had made love in the cottage. Since then he had felt her drawing away from him, as if she was scared to let her feelings go. He had cursed himself for rushing her. He was back to square one again. One false move and she would rush away like a frightened deer.

They reached Killarney right on schedule. He had been right, the rain had stopped. Paris was grinning. "This place is so beautiful, I always forget how gorgeous it is until I come here again," she was saying, gazing out of the window at the wooded slopes that rose above them.

They met a traffic jam as they neared the town, and he saw her face change as they pulled to a halt behind Derry Blake's lorry. Damn that man! Why did they have to arrive at the same time? Of all the lorries to be stuck behind! Derry's lorry was unmistakable, painted in dark blue and gold, with his racehorse logo and his name emblazoned across the back of the ramp.

Paris became silent, all the joy gone out of her day. "Bloody Merrianne's riding her horse, Water Babe," she sighed.

Kane stole a look at her. She had gone inwards, her face closed and expressionless. The two women were both giving their horses a last run before the Galway meeting in two weeks' time. Now the two horses were virtually at the peak of their performance. Today would be the final run which would bring them to that peak.

The traffic jam shuffled relentlessly forwards. Then suddenly the road cleared and the traffic began to flow again. Moments later Derry's lorry pulled out of the line of slow traffic at a wide place in the road and shot away, making a car coming towards him swerve out of the way with much flashing of lights and honking horn.

"Jeez," Kane shook his head, "Derry Blake is some prick! He nearly made that car crash into the bank!"

Paris was silent. Kane wasn't even sure if she had heard him. Normally he was guarded when referring to Derry.

A short time later they pulled onto the race course. Derry's lorry was already parked. Mary his buxom groom was unloading Water Babe. "Poor thing's probably seasick after all that swaying about," Kane tried again.

"Yes," said Paris in a voice that made Kane think that if he had asked her to give him a pink elephant she would have still made the same reply.

She pulled the lorry into a parking spot, stalling it as she stopped.

She was really wound up, thought Kane. Silently she went off to get ready, leaving him with the horse. "I'll get the horse ready, dear, see you in the parade ring, dear," he muttered crossly to himself, wondering how he was going to manage to part Daisy from the horse on his own.

Paris smiled bleakly at the Security Guard who let her into the weigh room. She couldn't face another episode of verbal abuse from Merrianne.

"I hope that yoke of yours will manage to stay on its feet today," sniffed Merrianne cattily, her nerves jangling from all of the ragging that Derry had been giving her about Shula. He was still laughing about how Merrianne's wealthy parents had turned out to be nothing better than an aging hippy mother.

"I hope you don't get stuck in traffic," Paris snapped back, reminding Merrianne of when the jockeys blocked her in with their horse.

"Now ladies!" John Kelly, always the peacemaker, said sternly.

Paris glared coldly at Merrianne. She couldn't wait to see her face when Derry told her to shove off and that he was back with Paris now. With a toss of her blonde hair Merrianne turned her back on Paris and began to change.

At last it was time for the jockeys to go to the parade ring. Paris found Kane, his handsome face was full of concern. "I hate you doing this," he said, adjusting the collar of her silks. "I'm frightened of you getting hurt again."

Paris looked away, afraid that she might throw herself into his arms and walk away from the race. It would have been so easy to do. Kane would have never wanted her to prove anything to him. He accepted her unconditionally. But she still had to prove to Derry – and herself – that she was a winner.

When the time came, Kane legged her up, giving her thigh a gentle squeeze. "Please be careful." Once she was on the horse Paris felt better. Merrianne might have Derry at the moment, but she was the better rider. She felt like an adder poised for the strike. Two more races and Derry was hers.

As she walked past Derry, he met her eyes. His smouldered with unspoken passion, as he raised his hand in greeting. Paris saw Kane scowling at him, but then she was out on the track, standing high in her stirrups as Destiny bucked with the sheer pleasure of being fit and healthy.

"No gouging, no hitting below the belt," John Kelly wise-cracked, quoting the boxing referee's words before a fight at the two girls.

"Shove off," hissed Merrianne, pulling Water Babe away from him roughly, hauling on the reins in temper.

Paris giggled. John was always good at seeing the funny side of any situation.

Destiny got a good start. Galloping along the track with the leading horses, sweeping over the fences. But Merrianne was beside her, the two horses neck and neck. Paris stared fixedly at the track, determined not to let the presence of Merrianne bother her, but still it rankled and she felt herself pushing the mare to make her go ahead of her rival. Yet still Merrianne was resolutely beside her, grinning like a banshee.

280

They rounded the home turn and all of the jockeys kicked their horses on, increasing the pace, every one determined to win. Four horses took the second last fence together, cruising into the air as if they were welded together, Destiny touched the ground first, her ears pricked, thoroughly enjoying herself. Paris slapped her down the shoulder with her whip, gritting her teeth with determination, driving the horse towards the winning post. Ignoring every rule that she knew about race riding and jumping carefully, she went at the last fence like a mad thing, and the mare took off too soon, stretching desperately in mid-air to clear the fence. But they were in the lead and with Merrianne and the two other jockeys hot on her heels Paris set off to the winning post as if the devil himself were on her heels. She urged the mare on with her hands, thumping her heels against the mare's heaving sides and Destiny responded, somehow finding the energy to charge past the winning post in front of the others.

Paris punched the air with a victory salute, looking around to see Merrianne's face set in fury as she passed the post in second place. Paris hauled on her reins and Destiny dropped thankfully to a trot and then a walk. She steered the exhausted mare off the course, a long line of people crowded at either side to cheer her home, a long tunnel of faces and noise. A hat flew into the air as its owner tossed it in delight at having won a huge amount of money on her win.

Kane ran towards her grinning from ear to ear, and hugged her leg, the closest he could get to her, "Brilliant race," he yelled over the noise of the crowd.

Paris looked down and saw the naked pride in her achievement shining in his face. She looked away and stared fixedly between Destiny's sharply pricked ears. Why couldn't she let herself love him. He would be so hurt if he realised why she had to race.

She rode into the Winners' Enclosure, feeling a surge of pleasure as Merrianne made her way miserably into the second-place stall. She slid off. Destiny was drenched with sweat, it dripped from her belly, collecting in a puddle on the floor beneath her. The photographers surged forwards, taking photos of her as Kane threw his arms around Paris in delight. Then she wriggled out of his grasp. Derry was there. With a cry of delight she launched herself at him.

Kane backed away from them, feeling sick, Destiny almost knocking him over as she rubbed her sweaty, itching head on his arm. He smiled mechanically as another photographer arranged him next to the mare. "Winning horse Destiny, photographed with her groom," he was saying into a tape-recorder.

"That was a brilliant ride, my darling," Derry was saying, his arms around Paris. She was looking up at him, her face filled with wonder and happiness.

Kane, surrounded by the joyous scenes, felt bitter tears of disappointment prick at the back of his eyes. Derry was stealing her in front of his eyes.

CHAPTER FIFTY-ONE

Merrianne had never been so angry in her life. Derry had been all over Paris, congratulating her for winning the race. He had barely given her a second glance. She pulled the saddle off Water Babe and smiling valiantly so that Mary wouldn't notice how bothered she was by Derry. Then she stalked off to the weigh room.

Then her heart sank. She could see Alex Ivor standing waiting for her. Alex was the last thing she needed now.

She walked past him with a curt nod, but he fell into step beside her.

"I'm really glad that Paris won," he said. "Let her have Derry. Give up this madness." He grabbed hold of her arm and pulled her around to face him. Merrianne jerked her arm free. Alex towered over her, his sloe-black eyes full of concern.

"Alex," she said through gritted teeth, "this is getting to be a habit with you. Are you stalking me or what? Why? What's in it for you?"

"I'm worried about you, Merrianne."

"But why do you care? Do you have a grudge against Derry? Are you trying to steal me from him out of spite?"

Sighing he shook his head. "You're unreachable, aren't you?" With that he turned and walked away.

Merrianne stared after him, surprised that she felt an urge to run after him. How easy it would be, she suddenly thought, to throw herself into his arms and forget all this heartache. But she loved Derry. He had promised that he would marry her if she won. And that was what she wanted.

In the changing room she stripped off and went into the shower, watching bleakly as the water ran down her breasts and stomach, black from the dirt that had been thrown up during the race. The rain during the morning had wet the surface of the ground, creating sticky mud. Flecks of the mud stuck to her face, the gritty texture scraping her skin as she rubbed at them with the soap, turning to rivulets of black that poured down her body. Derry was slipping through her fingers like the water she held in her cupped hand, relentlessly going back to Paris, now that she was winning again.

She dried herself and dressed. Paris was at the opposite end of the room, changing with the male riders, unabashed by changing in front of them. Through the lines of clothes that hung on the hooks above the benches that were arranged in lines down the length of the room, Merrianne could see her. She was lit up with happiness like a Christmas tree. What did Derry see in her, she thought bleakly, studying her rival surreptitiously. She was no great beauty, compared to Merriane's eye-catching good looks – attractive, maybe, with her high cheekbones and wide eyes. Even from across the room, Merrianne could see the pale line of the scar that crossed her cheekbone. Merrianne brushed her long blonde hair, letting the hot air from the hairdryer play on it. Derry couldn't prefer Paris to her. The thought of that was too awful to contemplate. What if Derry did go back to Paris? What would become of me, thought Merrianne. It was a terrifying thought. She had got used to living the good life as the girlfriend of the famous Derry Blake. But as well, at the bottom of it all, she loved him. And she wasn't going to give him up without a fight.

Merrianne flung her hair-drier into her bag and stood up. Casting a last look around her to make sure that she hadn't forgotten anything, she went towards the door. Paris was changing, buttoning up a wrinkled pink shirt that she had pulled from her battered bag. The colour clashed horribly with her face, flushed a deep red from the shower. At least she had the decency to look guilty as Merrianne passed her.

"Bad luck," Paris said softly.

Merrianne jerked to a halt, "What did you say?" she spat.

Paris carried on buttoning her shirt "I said bad luck - you rode a good race,"

Something inside Merrianne snapped. "I don't need your commiserations, you patronising bitch," she raged.

284

Paris shrugged. "Suit yourself." She turned away pointedly.

"Don't you turn your back on me!" Merrianne grabbed Paris's shoulder and wrenched her around.

"Cat fight," yelled one of the jockeys, delighted to see a spat between the two women. There were often fist fights and rows between the jockeys, but two women fighting was something not to be missed.

"I'm sick of you trying to steal Derry," snarled Merrianne.

"He was mine in the first place," retorted Paris, her face inches from Merrianne's.

"Until you lost him. I'm sick of you simpering around him, conniving your way back into his heart like some bitch on heat. Keep your hands off him!" She shook her hand free and swung at Paris. There was a satisfying loud slapping noise as her palm hit Paris across her cheek.

Paris reeled back in shock, clutching her hand to her burning cheek. "Derry doesn't want you," she hissed, grabbing her bag and shoving past Merrianne. "He'll be glad to see the back of you." The door slammed shut. A round of slow hand-clapping broke out from the jockeys who had gathered around to watch.

"Fuck off all of you," snarled Merrianne, glaring at the excited faces, "or you'll all get the same!" The group melted away silently.

"He'll be glad to see the back of you," Paris had said. Merrianne clenched her teeth together so hard that her jaw hurt. She was going to prove the bitch wrong.

Derry was sitting outside the weigh room on a wooden bench seat, his legs stretched out comfortably in front of him. "There you are," he said, getting to his feet. "I thought that you had gone around again."

Merrianne forced herself to smile. She put her arm through his. "You seemed very pleased that Paris had won that race," she said, trying to keep the edge out of her voice.

"Of course," Derry replied, smoothly. "I'm glad that she can ride again. It was a shame she had such a bad accident and lost her nerve. She rode well. She deserved to win,"

Merrianne bit her tongue. What about your loyalty to me, she fumed silently, but she kept her anger to herself, she wasn't going to cling like a vine to him, he must never know how much she cared. How much it hurt her to see him chatting up other women, dancing attendance on Paris.

Changing the subject as easily as a bullfighter slips out of the path of a charging beast, Derry sidestepped. "Come on, I want to call in at Valerie and David's on the way home – we've been invited for dinner,"

Merrianne groaned inwardly. She ached all over, all that she wanted to do was to go home and lie in a hot bath and soak away the stress of the day. Now she would have to spend the evening watching Derry sucking up to Valerie and her making cow's eyes at him all evening, while she had to listen to David bragging about his chain of shops.

David and Valerie lived in a sprawling red-brick bungalow at the end of a long drive, which, Valerie never tired of telling people, the architect had designed to blend into the landscape. Built on many different levels to fit into the slope of the woodland that surrounded it, the house even had a stream that flowed underneath a section of the floor, which had been made in thick glass so that they could sit in the lounge and admire the fish swimming in the stream. Inside, as she remembered from previous hellish visits was a mismatch of styles and colours dragged back from their holidays to be arranged in what Valerie thought was stylish fashion around the pale wood floors of the house. Turkish furniture mixed with Chinese rugs, and animal skins brought back from Africa before it became illegal. It was a horrendous place to get drunk: the furniture made you feel sick and the differing levels of the floors, joined by low steps was horrendous when drunk as you kept forgetting the steps were there and sprawling up them.

They pulled into the fancy tiled courtyard at the back of the house. Surrounding the house were garish red-brick flowerbeds, overflowing with ornamental shrubs. Beyond the courtyard, reached by a honeysuckle-covered archway, was a double garage, where David kept a lot of the goodies that he found for the shops.

"What the fuck is she doing here?" Merrianne couldn't believe her eyes, for, emerging from the garage was Shula. She had abandoned her hippy clothes and was dressed very elegantly in a plain pair of black trousers and cream-coloured T-shirt. She was giggling coquettishly at David as they came across the garden, their heads close together, looking very companionable.

"Oh hi, Merrianne," sang Shula, as if it was the most normal thing in the world to emerge from David's garage and see her estranged daughter standing open-mouthed on the lawn.

"What are you doing?" exclaimed Merrianne furiously. As if she hadn't had a bad enough day already, to find her mother here was too much. At least, she noted with relief Shula didn't look her normal hippyish self.

"David's commissioned me to do some pottery for one of his shops," Shula grinned, looking at David as if he were an angel. "Isn't he wonderful?"

Merrianne could have thought of something to say, but she bit her lip.

"You'll stay for dinner?" David said, taking Shula's hand as if he couldn't bear to see her go.

"Great," Shula preened herself. "If you are sure Valerie won't mind."

"Course not," David said firmly. "She will be delighted."

"I bet she will," hissed Derry as they followed them into the house.

"Oh," said Valerie, emerging from the leopard skin-draped lounge in a black cat-suit, "I didn't know that you were coming in." She looked Shula up and down slowly in distaste.

"I wanted to discuss the new pottery lines," David cut in quickly.

Valerie closed her eyes slowly and sighed, her mouth twisting down like a big trout. "Fine," she snapped, then recovering her composure led the way to the other side of the house, up and down steps and along corridors until she opened a door to a dining- room.

Merrianne, who had been there for dinner on numerous occasions, closed her eyes in readiness for the assault on her optic nerves.

"David, it's beautiful," swooned Shula, waltzing into the room, ignoring Valerie and running her hand along the silk sari fabric that had been draped in thick swags on the walls.

"I got all of these in Goa," David said, visibly swaggering at Shula's admiration. "And the furniture in China," he told her, running a hand lovingly across the black table, inlaid with Chinese designs in white mother-of-pearl.

"I once went to Goa," mused Shula. "Great hippy colonies out there."

Dinner was an uncomfortable meal. Valerie made countless trips to the kitchen, returning with platters of smoked salmon, whole lobsters and a dish of crisp salad and tiny new potatoes, swimming in butter, which Merrianne spurned. She had brought a new dress for Derry's birthday party and she didn't want any unsightly bulges to mar its lines. Shula tucked in as if she had never been fed before, wolfing down huge slivers of smoked salmon and sucking the lobster claws noisily. Derry twitched with suppressed laughter, Merrianne squirmed with embarrassment, Valerie looked as if she was going to explode and David watched with an expression of adoration on his face.

287

Valerie ate nothing, but merely sat at the head of the table, gulping down wine from a glass that would have comfortably held goldfish, seething with anger.

"So you're designing some pots for David's shop?" Derry asked, suddenly turning his mega-watt charm in Shula's direction.

"Uh uhhh," Shula said, licking lobster from her fingers. "He's commissioned me to do some earthenware vases." She tilted her head on one side, regarding Derry through sultry, half closed eyes.

Merrianne twitched with irritation. As if it wasn't enough for her mother to turn up and embarrass her, now she was flirting with Derry.

"You must show me what you can do some time." Derry said, his eyes boring into Shula, undressing her with his eyes.

Valerie slammed a coffee pot down on the table. "Coffee," she snapped, twitching with anger that Derry had turned his attention from her to this middle-aged hippy who had muscled in on her territory.

Derry leant back in his chair, grinning broadly, fully aware of the effect he was having on Shula who was licking her lips like a hungry dog. And the effect he was having on Merrianne.

It was driving Merrianne mad. Having to suffer him chatting up other women, usually in front of her, as if she didn't matter was bad enough, but flirting with her mother!

"What a fiasco," snapped Merrianne when the evening had finally ground to a halt and she was driving Derry home.

Derry who had drunk far too much, let the back of the seat down and closed his eyes. "Fiasco! I didn't think so," he said. "Your mother is something else! We ought to get her over for dinner some night. I want to get to know her a lot better."

CHAPTER FIFTY-TWO

There was no way that Derry was even going to think about Paris tonight, thought Merrianne sliding into a deep bath, filled with all the skin-softening and toning products that she had found on her latest shopping expedition to Dublin. She was going to look so gorgeous tonight that Derry would want to be with her always.

His birthday party – she had looked forward to tonight for ages – it was going to be a really special night.

As she lay in the bath, the catering staff were putting the finishing touches to the buffet supper that was laid out in the dining-room. The silver candelabra glistened, reflecting the china platters of delicious food that she had spent hours selecting with the catering manager. Derry although aware that a party was being held for his birthday had been shipped off racing for the day to Tipperary so that he was out of the way while she organised the party. There were no horses from Westwood Park running, so the day would be relaxing for him, spent in the bars and hospitality boxes, chatting to friends and enjoying the racing without having to look after tetchy jockeys or irritable owners.

A marquee had been erected on the vast lawn at the back of the house, stretching from the French windows of the dining-room to the formal flowerbeds filled with delicately scented lavender and the satin soft petals of the rose bushes. A wood floor had been laid down on the lawn so that the tables that had been arranged in the marquee wouldn't sink into the soft turf. A disco had been set up in one corner, where a shaven headed DJ had arranged a vast selection of music. He had shoved the tables further back, complaining that they were encroaching on the dance floor.

After soaking her skin, Merrianne got out of the bath and applied her new skin purifying mask, slapping the china clay all over her body, then mooching around in the bathroom until it dried, white and cracking, making her look like an Egyptian Mummy dug up by archaeologists. She got back into the bath, washing off the purifying mask. She stroked her skin and was delighted to find that it felt as soft as a peach. Satisfied at last she got out of the bath, dried herself and then spent another two hours applying her make-up, blow-drying her hair into a sleek shiny cascade down her back setting off the air tan that had been done a few days previously, her blonde hair contrasting beautifully with the coffee shade of her tan.

Ready at last, she slipped the delicate creamy-coloured satin dress over her head. Cut on the bias it fell to the floor clinging deliciously to every curve and contour, making her look slender, but womanly. Examining her reflection from every angle in the mirror she was at last satisfied. Ready for the night to begin she opened the bedroom door, took a deep breath and then, head held high, walked graciously downstairs.

She wandered through the downstairs rooms, and as time passed, becoming more and more irritated. There was still no sign of Derry. The party was due to start in an hour – he should have been back by now, to get ready to receive the guests with her. Everywhere looked beautiful. Mrs McDonagh had excelled herself, managing to supervise a team of girls hired for the day from the village. They had scrubbed and polished everywhere until the whole house gleamed.

Merrianne rang Derry's telephone. It rang for ages until he finally answered it. There was noise and laughter in the back ground. He was on his way back, he told her. He would be there in a few minutes. Merrianne poured herself a glass of gin, clinked a few chunks of ice into it and sloshed a token amount of tonic water on top, to calm the irritation that was gnawing at her stomach. Her fingers clenched and unclenched as she walked around the house, unable to stay still, unable to concentrate. How the hell could he let her down like this? It was his birthday, she had gone to all the trouble of organising a special party for him. Now he should be here.

The catering staff shifted uncomfortably as she wandered down the buffet table, criticising and complaining for the want of something better to do. They were delighted when Mrs McDonagh, red-faced with the wine that she had been swigging all day came to tell Merrianne that the first guests were arriving. Sighing with temper, Merrianne slammed her glass down on the nearest table and stalked to the front door, pasting a smile on her face. She would have to greet the people alone until Derry arrived. How embarrassing would that be?

"Oh, where's Derry," were Valerie's first words as she stalked in, almost clad in a long red velvet dress that plunged to the level of her buttocks and to her navel at the front. She threw her mink coat at David, who was so busy craning his neck to peer down the front of her dress that he didn't see the coat and it fell to the floor.

"He will be back soon," Merrianne said through gritted teeth. "He got delayed."

"I see," smirked Valerie, pointedly, looking sideways at Merrianne to see if she could see the lines made by any underwear beneath the satin folds of the dress.

"Why don't you go in and get a drink?" Merrianne said, with a wave of her arm. David, having rescued the coat from the floor and taken it to the cloak room, came back looking peeved. "What's wrong with you," he snapped at Valerie.

"We're the first here," she said, in a disappointed voice. She had been looking forward to a grapple with Derry.

People began to arrive. A line of expensive cars and Jeeps crawled up the drive cramming into the gravel forecourt and then onto the manicured grass at either side of the drive. Merrianne stood in the increasingly cold night air greeting the guests as they arrived. Behind her the guests crowded into the reception rooms, shuffling uncertainly to help themselves to drinks and then out into the marquee. Merrianne writhed with temper. Derry should have been here to help greet the guests, organise drinks, show people the way out to the marquee. Instead she stood alone while Derry's guests made their own party behind her.

Alex arrived, looking impossibly handsome in a tuxedo, with a bunch of red roses in his hand. "You look gorgeous," he told her, handing her the roses. "You would love living in Hong Kong," he whispered wickedly in her ear as he bent to kiss her cheek. "I go back after Galway Races. You should really think about coming with me."

"I'll be marrying Derry then," Merrianne said firmly, twisting the roses in her hands. But she had to smile – he just wouldn't let up!

"So...." he continued, "where's Birthday Boy then?"

"He – has been delayed," she said shortly.

With a hollow laugh, he walked past her into the party. "He really doesn't deserve you."

Merrianne put the flowers down on the table beside her. Alex was right. She tried so hard to make Derry happy and all he ever did was hurt her. Maybe she should just tell him to get lost and walk away with Alex. But maybe she was better with the devil that she knew. What did she know about Alex after all? She wanted to be married. To start a family. Have security. Alex probably just wanted another mistress.

She rang Derry's telephone again and got the same reply: he was on his way home. He sounded drunk. Merrianne, determined not to show how annoyed she was in front of the party guests, switched off the phone. She wanted to run up to her bedroom, cry the bitter tears that prickled at the back of her eyes. Finally the line of guests trickled to a halt and Merrianne closed the front door. Then, taking a long swig of her drink she tilted her chin and glided into the house.

A crowd of people looked in her direction as she glided towards them a happy smile turning up the corners of her lips.

Tara who had come alone, came towards her with a sympathetic smile. "You have done a great job," she said, looking around the room. "Everything looks wonderful."

Merrianne dragged her eyes back to the girl who she had hoped would one day become her sister-in-law.

"Don't worry. Derry will be here soon," Tara said sympathetically. "He probably got held up somewhere."

Merrianne smiled tightly; she would like to string him up somewhere.

There was a sudden blast of cold air and everyone turned towards the door. A hush fell on the room as Derry staggered in, eyes crossing with drink, his tie askew, shirt billowing from his trousers, a broad grin splitting his face. But worst of all, Paris was under his arm, obviously as drunk as he was. Paris held onto his waist swaying gently, a drunken smile leering on her face.

"Hi, everybody!" he yelled, raising a bottle that he held in greeting and saluting them before taking a long swig. "Say hi, Paris," he said, his arm around Paris's neck, swinging her around like a rag-doll.

"Hi," grinned Paris, her eyes unfocused, staring around herself.

Merrianne felt as if she had been thrown at force into a brick wall. She clutched the table beside herself to prevent herself from falling. There was a rushing sound in her ears. How could Derry bring Paris here, flaunting her at his own birthday party?

Then, with a huge effort, she pulled herself together. Amazed at what she could do, she went forwards and kissed him softly on the cheek. "Glad you could come," she hissed. "You are very welcome, Paris," she said dully. "What can I get you to drink?" she wasn't going to show everyone that she was upset by Derry. Pride kept her from breaking down in tears, and rushing from the room.

Paris wandered away without answering Merrianne, leaving her alone with Derry. "How could you?" she hissed bitterly.

"Don't nag, baby," he mumbled drunkenly, nibbling gently on her ear. Taking her hand he led her into the crowd, everyone coming forward to wish him a happy birthday.

Merrianne seethed inwardly. Tomorrow she would give Derry a piece of her mind, but for now they were on show. Smiling they glided onto the dance floor, as the DJ put on a slow number. Derry took her in his arms and they swayed together. As they moved around the dance floor she glimpsed Alex, leaning in the doorway watching her. She met his eyes and saw immense compassion in their dark depths. He smiled tightly and then turned away.

Later Shula arrived, looking incredibly glamorous in a long black dress. Merrianne frowned, what on earth had wrought this change in her mother's style? She had never seen Shula in such a dress before, and where had she found the money for something so obviously expensive?

Derry raised his hand in greeting. Merrianne glared at her mother as she blew a sulty kiss in Derry's direction. Then she was swallowed up by the crowds and Merrianne couldn't see her any more.

One of the waitresses came and fetched Merrianne, telling her that the food was ready to be served. Derry announced at the top of his voice that everyone should go and eat. Hand in hand he and Merrianne led the way to the dining-room.

"Baby, you've done a brilliant job," Derry said guiltily, as he looked at the dining-table laden with food.

After they had helped themselves Derry and Merrianne wandered together into the conservatory to eat. It was quiet in there, the rest of the guests eating out in the marquee.

"I'm so sorry," he muttered. "I just got drinking, and I met Paris at the races," he confessed.

Merrianne knew that was the closest that she would get to an admission of guilt from him.

Paris leant miserably against the wall, watching Derry and Merrianne. Merrianne, seeing her watching, clung harder to Derry's arm, smiling up at him, very deliberately. She would show Paris just who Derry belonged too.

They went back into the marquee. It hummed with life, everyone wanting to speak to Derry. Merrianne held his hand possessively as they walked together, the earlier incident pushed to the back of her mind. They went back to the dance floor, swaying together in time to the music. Derry grabbed a bottle of champagne and a glass from a table as they danced by. He filled the glass, his arms draped behind Merrianne's back; she could feel icy drips of the liquid landing on her bare back as he poured.

"You deserve a drink," he said, steering her gracefully to the edge of the room and handing her the glass.

Merrianne gulped the champagne gratefully. She was hot and thirsty, her nerves fraught with the earlier tensions. "Lovely," she said, holding out her glass for Derry to refill, seeing with dismay that his eyes were already scouring the room.

She saw Shula and Paris standing at opposite sides of the room, both smiling invitingly at him. Merrianne snatched the bottle and walked away, pouring another glass of champagne. The party was a nightmare. She had worked so hard to make it a special evening for Derry, but all he wanted to do was chase women. The pain was unbearable, and Merrianne stumbled away clutching the bottle. At least getting drunk would stop her caring … too much.

CHAPTER FIFTY-THREE

Paris woke with an almighty hangover. Something had died inside her mouth, she was sure of it. Her head felt as if she had been banging it against a wall for the night, a throbbing pain surging behind her eyes. Her stomach churned with waves of nausea. The bathroom was a long way away, down the corridor, past the bedroom where Paddy and Elizabeth slept. She moved to the edge of the bed, which began to spin, like some fairground ride. Edging her legs closer, she wondered if she would be able to make the bathroom before the nausea got the better of her and she was violently sick. She lowered her legs out of the bed, and levered herself upwards, holding onto the edge of the bed for support. Even in this painful state she registered that her feet were on a cold floor, not the carpet that she usually put her feet onto. Gingerly she prised her eyes open. And then shut them again quickly. She was at Westwood Park. She didn't recognise the bedroom, polished wood floor, antique metal bed with a lacy white cover thrown over it and heavy antique furniture. But she did recognise the view from the window. She was in a bedroom at the back of the house, looking out over the stable yard. "Fuck," she winced, squinting against the light that was flooding in through the windows as she prised her eyes open for the second time. "Oh no," she groaned. How had she got here? Vague memories of the previous night and the previous day flooded back. Walking into the hall the previous evening, hardly able to stand, a sea of faces. Derry's birthday party. Clearer was the memory of meeting Derry at the races and being thrilled that he was on his own and that he had asked her for a drink with him.

She remembered the sea of faces, staring at them, impassive, angry, stunned, amused when they had arrived drunk to the party. And then she remembered a final face. Merrianne's, white and set as she stared at her boyfriend, swaying beside the front door with his ex-girlfriend propped under his arm. Paris suppressed a giggle, which quickly turned to a groan. As much as she loathed Merrianne it had been a pretty horrible thing to do.

She had disgraced herself in front of the whole racing community.

She noticed, breathing a silent prayer of thanks, that at least she was fully clothed. If someone had dragged her upstairs and raped her then they had obviously gone to the trouble of dressing her again afterwards. She slid a tentative hand between her legs; her knickers were still in place. Holding out her wrist, she moved her head backwards until she could focus on the dial of her watch. And then swore again. Ten o'clock. She should be at home, helping Eddie to clean out the stables. Kane was supposed to be arriving in half an hour to give Daisy some injection. Paris fell back onto the pillow with a sigh. It was all too much. She could already imagine the self-righteous anger oozing from Eddie when he found that she had dumped all the work on him while she cleared off to some party. And Kane, too. Paris pulled the pillow around her face. He would be like a puppy that someone had whipped, the terrible hurt reflected in those lovely green eyes. Well, she couldn't change it now.

She raised her head again. It was no good, she couldn't hide up here all day. She had to go and face the music at home. The thought of walking downstairs and meeting Derry, or worse, Merrianne was dreadful. Derry would think it hilarious that she had got so drunk that she had passed out in a bedroom. He was used to that sort of behaviour from his raucous friends, Merrianne though was a different kettle of fish. She would be furious that Paris had dared to gate-crash Derry's party and disgrace her publically.

Maybe she could get out without anyone noticing her, she thought. If she could get out of the house and get down the drive she could phone Paddy and get him to collect her. She stood up shakily. The room was swaying uncomfortably, but the urgent feeling of nausea had subsided. She padded across the wooden floor, unearthed her shoes and handbag from beneath a chair, and opened the door. The noise of arguments and wailing carried up the wide staircase, which was at the end of the corridor. Wincing at the noise and at the certainty that she was going to be seen as she made her escape, she padded, shoes in hand towards the staircase. Every step hurt as if she had been through the spin cycle of a washing machine. For some strange reason she kept bouncing off the walls at either side of the corridor, ending up with her shoulder landing against the stern portraits of Derry's long-forgotten ancestors. They had no need to look down their long noses at her, thought Paris, standing back to focus on whether or not she had straightened one of the portraits; they had all spent half of their lives in a similar state to hers.

A wave of nausea rose from her stomach; she was going to have to be sick. There was a bathroom somewhere along this corridor, she remembered, shoving open door after door, finding only Merrianne's tasteful bedrooms, a growing feeling of panic rising as the need to vomit became more urgent. Sour-tasting bile rose at the back of her throat. She couldn't keep it in any longer. Shoving open a final door, she dashed into the bedroom and threw up in the hand basin beside the window. Stars danced before her eyes and a cold sweat broke out on her forehead. How had Paddy done this to himself day after day? Paris doubted that she was ever going to drink again. She retched again, every muscle taut as her stomach tried to rid itself of the poisonous alcohol.

"Good morning," Derry's voice said slickly behind her.

Great, he had found her, bottom facing the door, with her head halfway in the hand basin, heaving her guts up. Very glamorous.

"Oh, hi," she smiled, wanly, horribly aware that there were beads of sweat on her forehead and that her face must be purple with the strain of vomiting.

"Sleep well?" Derry asked, as if it were the most normal thing in the world to find your ex-girlfriend throwing up in one of the guest rooms.

"Fine," she nodded, prickling with annoyance. He looked as immaculate as ever, only a faint line of red beneath his eyes gave any indication of the state he must have been in when he went to bed. A wave of aftershave hit her, making her more aware of her own dishevelled state; she must reek like a polecat.

"I have to go." She made an attempt at shrugging her shoulders blithely.

"Of course," he smiled, enjoying her discomfiture.

"Things are a bit tense downstairs," he said with a grin, "Merrianne's in a foul temper. Apparently I was chasing her mother and you all night."

Paris pulled a sympathetic face. "I'd better go," she said again, starting towards him. Derry remained in the doorway, making her have to squeeze past him. For a horrific moment she thought that he was going to try to kiss her, and however much she wanted that she doubted that he would have enjoyed running his tongue around her stinking mouth. She pressed against him, feeling the warmth of his body where hers touched him. He was doing this deliberately. Then she was past and out on the corridor. She bolted down the corridor as fast as she could weave.

Paris reached the bottom of the stairs. Just a few steps and she would be outside. Halfway between the stairs and the door she froze.

"Leaving so soon?" Merrianne's voice came from behind her. Swallowing hard, Paris turned slowly to face Merrianne who was standing in the doorway of one of the rooms, glaring.

"Busy day," Paris attempted, managing to force a bright smile on her face, as if this scene were nothing out of the usual.

Merrianne exploded from the room, blonde hair flying behind her, still dressed in the gorgeous cream-coloured dress she had been wearing the previous night. "How dare you come here," she spat, her face inches from Paris.

"I had every right," Paris drew herself to her full height. "Since Derry asked me, and this is Derry's house." Then, leaving Merrianne mouthing in anger, she turned and stalked towards the door, with as much dignity as she could muster in her dishevelled state.

Paris slammed the door behind her and leant on it, breathing the warm summer air. The scent of roses drifted up from the bed at the bottom of the flight of stone steps. Thankful to have made her escape she shoved her feet into her shoes and teetered down the steps. She began to feel better now that she was outside in the fresh air. Fishing in her handbag she unearthed her mobile phone and rang Paddy, arranging for him to collect her from the end of the Westwood Park drive.

If Paddy was angry he didn't betray the fact. Like Father, like daughter, thought Paris, as she leant against the high stone wall at the end of the drive, waiting for him. Paddy had no right to give out at her for getting drunk and ending up miles from home. He had done it often enough. She had lost count of the times that she had abandoned everything to go and fetch him back from some house miles away.

"I stayed the night," she said by way of explanation getting into the car.

"So I see," Paddy said shortly. He was clean-shaven, smartly dressed and smelt pleasantly of soap and clean clothes. "Kane's been waiting for you at home," he told her, not taking his eyes off the road.

Paris could feel the disapproval emitting from him. "Derry asked me to his party," she said sulkily.

Paddy grunted. "Derry fucked up your life once, you've a chance to make a go of things with Kane and you are letting Derry fuck things up for you again. Derry doesn't want you. He's just stringing you along."

Paris stared fixedly at the road ahead. What did he know? Kane wasn't the man for her. Derry and she belonged together.

She was glad when they pulled into the yard at Blackbird Stables. Anything was better than sitting in the car with the tense atmosphere. She had managed to bite her lip and not fly off the handle and tell Paddy to keep out of her life. She felt too ill for an argument.

But then she would have gladly gone on riding in the car, with Paddy giving out all day instead of what she found at the yard.

Paddy stopped the car and went wordlessly into the house. Paris struggled out of the passenger seat. She longed to go and lie down. She slammed the door and leant against the sun-warmed panels of the car for support, looking in agony as Kane descended on her from across the yard.

"I've done Daisy's injection," he said pointedly, before adding sarcastically, "did you have a nice evening?" He had obviously worked out where she had been last night.

Paris shook her head, too bleakly aware of Kane's furious expression to say anything. She slowly raised her eyes, wincing at the pain she saw reflected in his eyes.

"You were with that bastard," he said accusingly.

Paris was silent, longing to slide into his arms and beg forgiveness, make him understand what a fool she had been. Tell him that she wanted him, not Derry.

"Why do you have to chase after him!" Kane spat, as if he were unable to let Derry's name past his lips.

Paris looked away. "I....." she began and then the words died on her lips. How could she explain to him that the pain of losing Derry, and not being able to ride had hurt her more than she could ever imagine. She had to prove to herself that she was still the same person that she once had been, and to do that she had to win races and get Derry back.

Kane slumped back against the car. "I've chased you enough." He spoke as if he were exhausted, as if each word was an immense effort. "I've hoped that you would see how much I loved you. How happy we could have been together. Hoped you would realise...." His words trailed off into silence.

Paris closed her eyes, fighting back tears. She did know how much he loved her. Did know how happy they could be together. And, in that moment, she felt that it was only her pride that kept her relentlessly locked onto this course.

She opened her eyes. Kane was walking across the yard to his Jeep.

"Kane...." she whispered.

"I hope he makes you very happy."

She heard the catch in his voice.

Then he got into the car and drove away.

She stood in the yard watching the Jeep until she could see it no longer, and still she remained, unable to move. How could she have let him go?

CHAPTER FIFTY-FOUR

Kane had gone. She had lost him, through her own stupidity. Chasing after Derry was pure madness. He had dumped her in the cruellest way possible just when she had needed him most and then said he would have her back only when she could prove herself to him. No one should have to do that. If he really loved her, he would have never let her go in the first place. Kane had always been there for her. Had loved her no matter what. And now she had lost him. It was hard to imagine life without him. But it was too late now. She had lost him because she had wanted Derry. There was no alternative now but to win Derry back, otherwise she would have paid a huge price for nothing.

Destiny came to stand at her stable door, pushing her head out over the closed bottom half of it. She neighed in greeting when she spotted Paris.

At least the mare still loved her. "Back in a minute," Paris called across the yard to her. "Or two," she added, quietly to herself, going into the house.

An angry silence emitted from the direction of the kitchen. Paris went upstairs. No point in saying anything more to Paddy; or Elizabeth, who was doubtless lurking in the kitchen, ready to bitch about her to Paddy. Least said soonest mended, Paris thought to herself.

After swallowing painkillers to dull the fierce pain that throbbed at the back of her eyes, she changed into a pair of jodhpurs, throwing the smoky-smelling clothes that she had worn the previous day into a heap on the floor – she would shove them into the washing machine later. Then, pulling a sweatshirt over her hair, she dragged a brush through the worst of the tangles, grimacing in distaste as she looked in the mirror. Her green cheeks had mascara streaked down them, the remains of her lipstick was smeared over her chin. God! Derry, Merrianne and Kane had seen her like this! To say nothing of Paddy. She wiped away the old make-up and applied a fresh coat of mascara, with a trembling hand. "Beautiful," she said, wryly, examining her handiwork in the mirror. She still looked green, decidedly ill, with puffy bags under her eyes.

Then slowly she went downstairs. Hunger gnawed at her stomach; maybe she would feel better if she ate something. Torn between facing the wrath of Paddy and Elizabeth and feeling sick and dizzy all day, she decided that she needed to eat. She would just say nothing if they started on her about Derry.

The contented scene of domesticity rankled though as soon as she went into the kitchen. Paddy sat at the kitchen table the newspaper spread out before him, his glasses perched on the end of his nose, mug of tea cupped in his hand. Behind him Elizabeth was wiping the breakfast dishes that she had just washed.

"Morning," said Paris, sullenly.

"Morning, darling," Elizabeth said, rather too brightly, anger emitted from the set line of her shoulders.

"I'm going to meet Joe," Paddy said, suddenly getting to his feet. He drained his mug and set it down solicitously in the sink. "We're going to look at a horse that he wants to buy to replace Red Arrow."

"Why don't you sit down, Paris," Elizabeth said. It was a command.

Paris pulled out a chair and sat down, folding her arms in front of her aggressively; she was in no mood for a row with Elizabeth.

"You could probably do with some breakfast." Elizabeth began to busy herself putting bread in the toaster and brewing a fresh pot of tea. The air reverberated with the silence.

Finally Paris could bear it no longer, "I only went to a party," she said, holding out her hands palms upwards in a gesture of helplessness.

Elizabeth spun around and put her hands on top of a chair, leaning down towards Paris. "It was whose party you went to that concerns everyone," she hissed.

Paris stared at her mother's hands. The fingers were long, white where they clenched around the top of the chair, with the blue lines of the veins clear under the papery skin.

"Don't lose Kane," Elizabeth said,

Paris glared at her, not quite able to meet her eyes. Instead she concentrated on her mouth, the pale pink lipstick moving over a line of white, even teeth. "Derry's not right for you," she continued, turning to rescue the toast from the toaster.

"How the hell do you know what's right for me?" Paris snapped. She was thoroughly sick of everyone assuming that the one man who she had always loved was wrong for her and that Kane was the answer to all her problems. "How dare you!" She heard her voice rising alarmingly as her temper flared.

"Because I'm your mother," Elizabeth said, flinging the toast onto a plate and thumping it down on the table.

Paris snorted with laughter. "What a joke! You might have given birth to me, but you cleared off and left me. Remember? You walked out on your duties as a mother." She saw Elizabeth's lips press tightly together. "You have no right to say that you know what I need out of my life. You don't even know me," Paris reached for a slice of toast. She scraped butter over it viciously, the knife scraping deep into the brown surface.

Elizabeth filled the teapot with water from the boiling kettle and put it on the table. Then she put a mug down, filled a jug with milk and put it beside the mug. The silence lengthened. "I don't need to be a mother to see that Derry Blake is only going to hurt you again. Whatever you think about me, the next time he breaks your heart Kane won't be there to stop you taking another overdose."

Paris almost choked on a mouthful of toast. Kane had betrayed her. She had asked him not to say anything about her suicide attempt. He had obviously told Elizabeth. She had known all the time. Paris lurched to her feet, throwing the toast down on the plate and dashed from the room. She couldn't breathe. How dare he blab about that night to Elizabeth?

Grabbing her skull cap from the shelf in the hall, Paris shoved her feet into her jodhpur boots and went outside. She wanted to get as far away from Elizabeth as possible. The yard was immaculate. Eddie had worked hard. No straw blew across the yard, the buckets were stacked tidily in the tack room. Amazing what he could do when there was no one to gossip with, she thought furiously. The lads would be here to ride out soon. Paris couldn't face them. She wanted to get away, ride high into the hills where no one would bother her. Maybe things would have calmed down when she returned. It wouldn't hurt Destiny to be ridden out instead of working her on the gallops. Maybe she would bring her to the forest where there were long sandy tracks that were perfect for galloping on anyway.

She grabbed her saddle and bridle and took it into the mare's stable. Pulling off her rug she stood back, admiring her beautiful mare. She looked fabulous, gleaming with health, hard muscle bulging from her powerful hind quarters. Daisy, seeing the saddle and bridle, observed Paris balefully, chewing indignantly at some hay, knowing that her companion was about to leave her. Paris put the tack onto the mare and led her outside. As she went to slam the door Daisy, furious at being left behind shoved the door with her head, catching Paris off-guard and muscling her way into the yard.

"No you don't," she growled. Ignoring the sheep's bleat of temper, she grabbed the sheep by her thick fleece she pushed the door open with her toe and shoved the sheep back inside the stable. Then she got on the horse and rode out of the yard. Daisy's head and front legs emerged over the top of the door, her mouth open bleating plaintively for Destiny to come back.

As she left the yard Paris looked back to see Daisy scrambling over the stable door and dropping smugly into the yard, where with a bleat she trotted after the mare.

"Go back, Daisy," growled Paris, pushing the mare into a trot. She looked back over her shoulder to see the sheep break into a lurching canter, following them. As soon as her hooves touched the grass at the side of the drive Paris kicked the mare, making her go faster. She sprang into a canter, her ears sharply pricked, delighted to be going on an excursion, but with her ears flickering back constantly, alerted to the plaintive cries of the sheep. Daisy would soon give up - she couldn't keep up with the mare's speed. She would stop and graze in the fields until the mare came back. Paris made it to the front gate ahead of Daisy and had time to dismount and pull the gate shut before she arrived. The sheep shoved her head through the bars of the gate, furious at having been left, her yellow eyes glaring at Paris.

"Go home," Paris yelled, waving her arm, making Destiny jump away in alarm.

She got back on the mare and trotted away, listening to the plaintive bleats of the sheep loud above the clattering of Destiny's iron-shod feet on the road. A hundred yards up the road she turned right, going off down a narrow lane that led to the forest. Just then, there was a squeal of brakes behind her.

Paris turned, just in time to see Daisy, halfway across the road, being hit by a large Jeep which accelerated rapidly away. The sheep was knocked flying, landing at the far side of the road, her legs paddling as she lay on the grass. Paris leapt from the saddle and dragged Destiny back to the junction. The sheep raised her head and bleated softly as she heard the sound of the mare approaching. She tried to rise and couldn't. Paris looked at her, feeling sick with guilt. One of her back legs lay at a horrific angle.

Paris felt sick. She had seriously injured, perhaps even killed Daisy, Kane's beloved sheep. She should have gone back, shut Daisy in properly. Now she was badly hurt, could even die of shock. All because she loved the horse and wanted to stay with her. Destiny nudged the sheep with her nose, whickering in alarm. Paris pulled Daisy as gently as she could to the side of the road and got back on the horse. She would have to go home and fetch the Jeep.

Back at home, the mare, without the comforting companionship of her guardian, whinnied frantically, dashing around the stable in a frenzy, sweat already pouring from her flanks. What had she done? Paris cursed herself. Kane's other sheep had gone back to his farm a month ago, otherwise she would have used one of them to calm Destiny.

The lads were just arriving to exercise the horses. Yelling at them to come and help, Paris leapt in the Jeep and led to where she had left the sheep. To her relief Daisy was still conscious, though obviously in great pain. They carefully lifted her into the back of the Jeep, supporting her broken leg as much as possible, and set out for the vet's surgery.

Paris's first concern after she returned from the vet's where she had left a sedated Daisy awaiting her operation, was to quieten Destiny who was still frantically banging about in her stable. She had to get another sheep for her as a matter of urgency, otherwise she might do herself an injury or lapse into a depression again and not be able to race. And Destiny must race. She must race and win the Galway Plate.

She would telephone Kane. He would help. He would get her another sheep. He had plenty wandering around doing nothing.

"Hello," he said sullenly, obviously having seen her number come up on his mobile telephone.

"Kane, it's me," she said unnecessarily.

"Yes," his voice was cold.

"Daisy has broken her leg – she got hit by a car. I've taken her to the vet's, she's going to be OK, but I need –"

"What happened to her?" he asked urgently.

Paris swallowed hard. "She followed me when I was exercising Destiny. A Jeep...."

"Poor little Daisy...." His voice was a whisper over the telephone line.

"She's going to be fine. But, erm.....I need another sheep to keep Destiny company, otherwise she won't be able to race and –"

"Damn you and this bloody obsession with winning races!" Kane snarled. "Talk to Derry – you obviously prefer him to me."

And the line went dead.

CHAPTER FIFTY-FIVE

Paris slammed the phone down. Bloody men, they were never there when you needed them!

"Let Derry sort you out," she mocked Kane's stiff tones. "Right, I will," she said out loud, picking up the receiver again and punching in Derry's mobile number.

He answered on the second ring. "Paris," his voice was filled with delight at her telephoning. "And to what do I owe this pleasure?"

"Derry," Paris could hear the panic in her voice growing as the pitiful whinnying from Destiny reached her ears and the sound of the mare throwing herself against the wooden door to get out and find her friend. "I need a sheep."

Derry gave a snort of laughter. "Darling, surely you can get yourself a boyfriend, no need to resort to sheep. But won't Farm Boy oblige?"

"No," she said, ignoring the snide remarks. "Destiny had a sheep for a companion but it got injured this morning. I need one urgently to replace it. She's going mad without it."

She heard Derry sigh, "I can't help you. I'm stuck in the yard sorting out paperwork. I hardly dare go into the house. Merrianne's still off her head with fury. Maybe I should get her a sheep to keep her calm. All that arguing and recrimination is doing my head in. Sorry I can't help."

And he replaced the receiver.

Paris felt hot tears spill down her cheeks. How could she have been so stupid? She had hurt Kane so terribly badly, all for Derry. And Derry was never there for her.

She turned on the office computer and typed 'sheep breeders' into the search engine. If those bastards couldn't help her then she would have to buy a sheep for herself to keep the mare happy.

Elizabeth came out of the kitchen with a mug of tea, which she put beside the computer for Paris. "I heard what you were saying," she said, standing uncertainly beside Paris. "That's bad luck. Is there anything that I can do?"

"No," snapped Paris, starting fixedly at the computer screen. She didn't need Elizabeth's help. Or her sympathy.

Each telephone call she made, the answer was the same. No one had any sheep for sale, although there was a sale in a nearby town in a few days time. A few days was no good. Unless she kept the mare calm and relaxed she wouldn't eat, she would lose weight, or she could injure herself dashing around the stable in such a frenzied way. She rang a neighbouring farmer. He was out, his wife said, but she didn't think that he would mind selling her a sheep. The wife would telephone his mobile number and get him to ring Paris. Paris put the receiver down again. Bloody woman, could she not just give his mobile number? Eventually the farmer rang her back – yes, he would sell her a sheep, but the price was ridiculously high. But then the mare set up another bout of frenzied whinnying and Paris made the deal. She would pay anything that he asked. She would come and fetch the sheep immediately.

Slamming the phone down, knowing that she had been conned by a sharp farmer, taking advantage of her desperation, Paris went outside. She reversed her jeep and drove out of the yard, slamming on the brakes to avoid colliding with Kane who was hurtling into the yard from the other direction. Pink with fright at the near accident, Paris reversed.

She got out and walked across to him. "Hi," she said, subdued. She had treated him like dirt and yet still he had come to her rescue.

"I brought you another sheep," he growled, shortly, still fuming, slamming the door of his jeep and moving around to the back door and tugging it open. "Try not to hurt this one," he muttered, in a bleak attempt at humour, reaching inside the Jeep and pulling out a wriggling sheep which bleated indignantly.

"Yes, I …" the words froze on her lips as with horror she heard the sound of another Jeep, hurtling down the drive. Only one person ever drove as fast as that. Within seconds a bright red Jeep exploded into the yard, confirming her worst fears but making her mouth split involuntarily into a grin of delight. "Derry," she breathed.

The jeep came to an abrupt stop and Derry emerged, smartly dressed, clean shaven, smelling deliciously of aftershave, his eyes dancing with amusement as he looked at Kane with distaste as he wrestled with the squirming sheep. The comparison between the two men was blinding. Kane was filthy from spending a day working on the new farm, his blonde hair tousled and filled with dust that dirtied his face, clinging to the stubble that darkened his chin.

"Ah, two Sir Galahads dashing to your rescue," Derry said sardonically, a smile of amusement twisting up the corners of his wide mouth. "Or did Farm Boy bring his new girlfriend to introduce to you?" He raised an eyebrow in Kane's direction. "She suits you. As advanced a level of conversation as you are capable of." He smirked. "Fuck off," snapped Kane, heaving the sheep back into the Jeep and slamming the door violently. Then slowly he turned to face Derry, his eyes blazing in his dirty face. "I'd always thought that you were a bastard to Paris," he said quietly, looking from Derry to Paris, his eyes were dead and cold. Paris quailed under the force of hatred that emitted from him. "But I've changed my mind. I think that you two suit each other. You are both cold-hearted selfish bastards." He glared at them silently for a moment and then turned and got into the Jeep. Paris could see the pain etched on his face as he drove away.

For a moment they were silent, then Derry shrugged.

"Farm Boy's rather touchy isn't he?" he said smugly, staring after Kane's jeep as it bounced up the track rattling and belching out black smoke.

The thought that Derry had gone to all the trouble of getting her a sheep meant a lot to Paris, but somehow she wished that he hadn't arrived just at that precise moment. She would have liked to have made up with Kane, but now that wasn't going to happen. She tore her eyes away from the trail of smoke that was being left in Kane's wake. "I've brought you a sheep," Derry announced, as if he were bringing her the crown jewels. "I rang my farm manager and he selected this one personally as being a suitable companion for a top class racehorse." He flung open the back door of his Jeep and blinking with distaste at the strong sheep smell that assailed his nostrils he reached in and dragged a small and very angry sheep out. "Actually," he added with a grin, "this was the first one that his sheepdogs managed to corner in the field." He dumped the sheep in the yard, where it lay thrashing helplessly, like a fish that has just been landed, front and back legs bound with rope to stop it jumping around all over the Jeep. "I'll open the stable door for you," he said, leaving Paris to haul the sheep across the yard and into Destiny's stable.

As he flung open the door Destiny shot to the back of the stable, regarding them fearfully, her eyes looking beyond them to see if her sheep was with them. A circular track of churned-up straw ran around the edge of the stable where the mare had paced in her frenzy. Paris hauled the sheep into the stable, untied its legs and stood back. It scrambled to its feet, shaking itself indignantly at the rough treatment and shot immediately to a pile of hay that had fallen from Destiny's manger and began to eat. The mare stopped quivering and looked at the sheep as if she couldn't believe her eyes. Then she visibly relaxed, moving forwards with bright eyes and pricked ears to sniff the sheep, scenting the familiar odour. The sheep looked at her balefully and then carried on eating.

"God, if only women were so easy to calm down," Derry commented, his eyes raking over Destiny.

Proudly Paris undid the mare's rug and pulled it off over her muscular quarters. Derry turned his mouth down in a gesture of approval. "She looks brilliant," he said, running his hand down the mare's body, and down over her muscular quarters. Paris watched him as if hypnotised. There was something sensual about the way his hands slid over the mare's shining coat. She wished it were her body that his hands were sliding over. As if he could read her mind Derry turned to her, one eyebrow raised quizzically. "I'd like to be doing that to you," he said softly.

Her breath caught in her throat.

"Come here," Derry commanded.

She hesitated. Kane was right: Derry was a selfish bastard. Slowly, reluctantly, she stepped forwards into his arms.

He began to unbutton her jodhpurs, pulling her towards himself. Paris could feel the heat from his body. He slid his hands inside the back of her jodhpurs, cupping her bottom in his hands. "Take these off," he commanded, already sliding the fabric over her hips. She pulled them off as he watched, then he pulled away, spreading the mare's rug over the straw. She slid her sweatshirt off over her head, shivering slightly in the cool air of the stable. The mare turned her back indignantly as Derry's hands slid over Paris's body, while the sheep chewed hay, oblivious to what was happening.

He pounded into her, making her cry out with pleasure, not caring who could hear. His mouth locked onto hers, his tongue halfway down her throat. It was hard to breathe. All of his weight pressed down on her body as he thrust himself into her. Then with a rapid staccato of movement he came and then was still. Then he was easing himself out of her and pulling up his trousers. "I hope that you win the Galway Plate. You really are such a good fuck."

CHAPTER FIFTY-SIX

Shula spent breakfast time wilting, drooped over her bowl of cereal like the head of some exotic flower that is past its best. Merrianne chewed her bowl of fruit salad thoughtfully, annoyed with her, wishing that she would hurry up and clear off back to her own home. Charlie, unable to cope with the change in Shula, now that she was mixing with the smart racehorse set, had dumped her and cleared off with a dirty-looking teenager with studs in her tongue and heaven knew where else. Merrianne thought that she was making too much of how upset she was. Shula, beneath her hippy exterior, was as hard as nails, as tough as any businesswoman - she just lacked the smart suit and mobile phone. She wouldn't be upset for long. She would soon replace Charlie with some other lover. Shula was never alone for very long.

Derry was behaving in the most irritating fashion towards Shula. Merrianne had expected him to be grumpy, growling at her to get rid of Shula. Instead he was unusually attentive. Solicitously pouring her tea, patting her hand gently when she sniffed miserably. Finally he said that he would take her to the stables and show her the horses and then maybe they would take a stroll around the garden, to cheer her up.

"Then you really ought to think about going home," Merrianne said pointedly.

They went out, creeping out like naughty schoolchildren as if they were aware of her wrath.

Merrianne finished her breakfast, huffily. She wanted her mother gone. She was monopolising Derry, sobbing on his shoulder, spending hours closeted in his office telling him about how awful Charlie was. Merrianne was only amazed that he hadn't exploded and told her to get rid of her mother. His patience and tolerance was amazing.

The doorbell rang. Mrs Mcdonagh was upstairs savaging the carpets with the hoover.

Sighing at the intrusion on her thoughts, Merrianne went to the door. Alex was on the doorstep.

"Hi, gorgeous," he said, leaping forwards to enclose her in a big bear hug before she could escape. He smelt deliciously of clean laundry and soap. "I've got an appointment with Derry," he said, stepping past her into the cool hall.

As always she was painfully aware of the effect that he had on her. And clinging to her loyalty to Derry she turned her thoughts elsewhere. "He should be back in a minute," she said, leading Alex into the lounge.

"If I were Derry I wouldn't leave you alone for a minute," he said quietly, his dark eyes glinting, his hand touching her arm.

Merrianne shook her arm free. In fact, she thought wryly, she seemed to spend all her time in his presence just shaking him off. "Don't," she snapped.

Alex moved to the window, then turned and fixed her with his gaze. "I haven't been able to stop thinking about you."

"Alex, stop, please. I'm Derry's girlfriend," she said, sternly.

Alex gave a snort of laughter, shaking his head. "Derry treats you like shit. You deserve better than him."

"I'll go and find Derry," said Merrianne, shifting uncomfortably under Alex's scrutiny.

"That's probably a good idea," he answered, his eyes raking over her face.

She tore herself away and walked somewhat unsteadily out of the room. She closed the door behind her and leant against the cool wooden panels, holding onto the curved brass door handle for support. She couldn't deny the strength of the attraction she felt for Alex any longer. Every muscle quivered with the feelings he aroused in her. She mustn't even think about it. She had Derry now. She had messed around for long enough, flitting from one man to another. Derry was the one thing that she had striven for. Here at Westwood Park she would make her home. Make a life with Derry, marry and later have children. She was determined not to end up like her mother, like some whore, flitting from whichever man caught her attention to the next. Alex was gorgeous and he had made his feelings blatantly obvious but she wasn't going to mess up what she had with Derry with some careless flirtation. She would prove to herself that she wasn't like her mother.

Derry and Shula were probably down at the stables. Shula seemed to have acquired a sudden interest in the horses since she arrived. Merrianne perched on the edge of the desk and picked up the telephone; the receiver smelt of aftershave and whiskey. His mobile telephone lay abandoned amongst the papers on his desk so Merrianne punched in the number for the stable yard telephone, drumming her fingers on the wooden surface of the desk as she waited for it to be answered, imagining Mary scowling at the intrusion, running across the yard, abandoning whatever she had been doing, maybe hoping that it would be Derry on the end of the line.

"Hello," Mary said breathlessly.

Merrianne scowled at the hope in the other girl's voice. Girls were always chasing Derry. It made her sick. He belonged to her, but they all assumed that they could steal him, pushing her out as they jostled to give him their telephone numbers, the blatant sexual invitations shining in their eyes.

"Is Derry there?" she asked, shortly.

"No, I haven't seen him for ages,"

Merrianne could hear the delight in Mary's voice that she should be searching for him. Merrianne slammed down the receiver without bothering to say goodbye.

A blast of cool air wafted into the smoky room. The French windows swung open, lazily pulled by a slight breeze. Derry must be walking Shula around the garden. Shaking her head in annoyance, Merrianne went out into the garden. It was pleasantly warm, chilled only by a slight breeze that blew lazily from the west, playing with the flower-heads, making them bob gently up and down. She went down the steps onto the lawn. Her heels sank into the damp turf, so she kicked them off, dumping them at the bottom of the steps. The short, manicured grass felt deliciously warm and damp beneath her feet. There was no sign of Derry, or Shula in the formal gardens close to the house. Merrianne walked on towards the tall, ornamental lines of yew trees. Derry had probably taken Shula to see the new ornamental pond that he was creating at the far end of the gardens. It was cool and dark and mysterious inside the tunnel made by the branches of the trees, they closed over her head, blocking out the light. The yew leaves were prickly under her feet as she walked, the grass unable to grow where there was no light.

She emerged from the tunnel, feeling impatience prickling at the back of her mind. She should hurry, Alex was alone in the house. It was rude to leave him alone for so long. She opened her mouth, about to call his name again when she heard voices from within the arbour. The iron curve of metal was covered with a sweet-smelling honeysuckle which trailed lazily over the curved arch. Inside was a magic kingdom, a circular area, paved with old stone slabs filled with antique statues of naked nymphs and small plants that grew in the dim light. She pushed back a trailing branch of honeysuckle and went forwards.

She froze as she entered the arbour, never having suspected she would see such a sight as now confronted her. At the far side of the arbour was a curved stone bench, set beside the sweet scented jasmine plants that trailed up the iron pillars behind it. There on the stone bench, lying on her back, legs up in the air was Shula. Derry was between her legs, his face contorted with pleasure, both oblivious to her presence.

Merrianne reeled backwards as if she had been punched. Then she was running back to the house, her breath loud and rasping, her heart feeling as if it was about to explode. She shot up the steps and into Derry's office like a hunted deer, half falling into his chair.

How could he do that to her? With Shula? Her own mother! After all that she had done for Shula! She was nothing but a cheap tart! She had stolen the one thing that she knew was important to Merrianne. Taken it and abused it in her own home. And Derry – what a rotten, filthy, cheating bastard he was! He was totally without morals.

Her instinct was to dash upstairs, throw her clothes into a suitcase and walk out, head held high. But where would she go? She had no money of her own, no talent for any job. And she had got used to living a good life. She would have to make sure Shula left; she would never tell them what she had seen.

She remembered Alex, sitting in the lounge. She had to go and put on a brave face, pretend nothing had happened. She got up slowly as if every muscle hurt and slowly went down the corridor to him.

"There you are," Alex said, his face creasing with delight.

"There's no sign of Derry," she smiled shortly. "He must have gone off

315

onto the gallops."

"Ah," grunted Alex. "Strange, his Jeep's still outside – I saw it when I pulled up and I didn't hear him leave."

Merrianne closed her eyes. There was no end to this nightmare. How could she tell Alex that she had just caught her mother shagging her boyfriend?

"Alex, I..." She struggled to speak.

Alex shook his head and yet again she was aware of his deep scrutiny. "What's wrong, Merrianne?" he asked, crossing the room and standing in front of her. Merrianne lowered her head so that he wouldn't see the tears that were threatening to spill down her face. She started as his gentle fingertips touched her face, tilting it so that he could look at her.

"What are you doing with a bastard like Derry?" He shook his head.

Merrianne made her mouth twist into a small smile – it hurt her cheeks with the effort. "I love him," she whispered.

Alex let go of her face and walked away. "Merrianne," he said sternly, "people in love don't walk around looking as if they have just witnessed a murder."

Merrianne looked at him, startled. "Is it that obvious?"

"What is it?" he asked again.

"Derry," she said in a small voice.

"I assumed that much," he answered shortly,

"He's out in the garden fucking my mother."

"Ah," said Alex, shaking his head slowly. "Good old Derry, comes up trumps again."

Merrianne sank down onto the sofa as if her legs wouldn't hold her any longer.

Alex crouched beside her. "Why on earth do you stay with him? He's nothing but an out and out bastard. However much you love him, he will always hurt you. Leave now."

Merrianne looked at him, a bitter smile twisting her face. "That's easy for you to say. If I leave him what do I do? Get some grotty flat, a job in a supermarket? No money ..." Her voice trailed off.

Alex shook his head. "Stay here until he makes you bitter and wretched. And then he'll throw you out." He sat on the sofa beside her. "Come with me. I think the world of you."

Merrianne looked at him as if he had suggested that she fly around the room.

"I would make you happy, care for you, I wouldn't treat you like Derry does."

Merrianne smiled. He was the kindest, sweetest man that she had ever met. She shook her head. "I can't think straight," she whispered.

Alex shrugged, "You don't have to decide now. Think about it. I'm there waiting for you if you want me."

Merrianne felt as if she were walking through a thick fog. "I can't think about anything until after the Galway Plate. I have to win that race and prove to Derry once and for all that I am as good as anyone else."

CHAPTER FIFTY-SEVEN

Merrianne sat in the Jeep silently. Derry, assuming that it was nerves, left her alone. Merrianne couldn't bring herself to speak to him. Behind them, Shula, looking dreadfully glamorous in a new cream wool dress, knitted in a delicate and tiny pattern, with a wide-brimmed cream hat decorated with a enormous bouquet of cream and pale pink flowers, chattered constantly about the outfits that the other racegoers were wearing. Merrianne couldn't bring herself to speak to her either. It was obvious now where her new outfits were coming from – Derry.

"This is it then, your big day," Derry said, pulling the handbrake.

"Yes," said Merrianne shortly. She was terrified. All of her hopes and dreams had been pinned on this day for so long. She was going to race against the top jockeys, risk her life, and for what? For a man who thought so little of her that he had seduced her own mother while the two of them were living in the same house. But it was too late to back out now. And more than ever, she wanted to show Paris once and for all that she was the better rider.

Merrianne clamped her sweating fingers tighter around her leather bag, wishing that the race were already running. How much longer did she have to wait before she could get on Water Babe and ride out onto the course. She got out of the jeep, smiling tightly at Derry, and clutching her bag walked through the carpark. The security guard let her in, grinning and wishing her luck. Already the changing room was busy, jockeys having had too much of the famous Galway hospitality were sweating it off in the sauna. Others draped themselves around the bench seats, changing, the room filled with the usual banter and gossip.

Merrianne closed the door behind her, and walked, grinning, trying to avert her eyes from the scrawny flesh that was displayed around the room. Paris was already changing as Merrianne went into the section that had been reserved for the ladies. The two scowled at each other. Today was judgement day.

Paris buttoned up her silks with trembling fingers. The old panic was returning. What the hell was she doing here? Why did she have to push herself to the limits? What if she fell again? She felt sick. There was no point in going to the toilets though – she hadn't managed to eat and there was nothing left in her stomach to come up. The muscles at the side of her stomach ached with retching.

Then she was ready. There was nothing left to do except listen to the commentary on the races that were being run, wincing at the falls, the feeling of panic growing stronger with every passing minute.

One of the riders was carted off to hospital in the ambulance. The news made Paris panic even more – what if she fell again, or was brought down by another rider? She wished that she were on Destiny - then she would feel confident again. What if she couldn't get on her, what if Paddy went to throw her up into the saddle and her legs refused to work?

The steward signalled that it was time for the jockeys to come out. Paris followed the line. Merrianne was in front of her, laughing and joking with one of the other riders. How could she be so confident? The jockeys from the last race came in, the security guard swinging back to let them pass, patting one on the back, giving a look of commiseration to another. He went from racecourse to racecourse, constantly travelling, and knew all of the jockeys, shared their joys and sorrows.

Then the door swung back and the jockeys trooped out into the parade ring. Merrianne sauntered out ahead of her, walking confidently towards Derry and her horse.

Paris looked desperately for Paddy and Destiny. For a moment she couldn't see them, as she walked around the ring, barging into the people that crowded in there, conscious of a mass of faces peering over the guard rail. The spectators were five deep in places, crowded onto the wooden viewing stand looking at the jockeys. Paris found Paddy, by accident, blundering blindly into the parade ring in panic. All of the other jockeys were mounted and beginning to ride around the parade ring. Destiny tried to pull away from Paddy, restless because the other horses were walking around the perimeter of the ring.

"Where have you been," snapped Paddy, as wound up as she was and longing for a drink. Only the calming presence of Elizabeth, like a jailer at his elbow, kept him from slinking into the bar for a restorative whiskey.

He legged Paris up onto Destiny. The saddle felt slippery, her stirrups too short, she was certain that they were different lengths, her skull cap felt too tight around her throat, the wide nylon strap cutting into her. Paddy began to lead the mare around the parade ring. She could see a sea of faces staring at her, curious, not sure if she was a girl or not. She glanced across the ring. Merrianne sat astride Water Babe, her reins loose, oozing confidence.

The horses began to go out onto the course, the grooms leading them through the gate and letting them go. In a few minutes they would be riding back, through the same gate, and it would be all over. The direction of their lives would be decided by this race.

"Good luck," said Paddy, slipping the lead-rope from Destiny's bit.

The mare bounded forwards with a whisk of her tail, delighted to be racing, if her owner wasn't.

Merrianne clenched her fingers around Water Babe's reins; she could feel the horse prancing beneath her, eager to be racing. She kept one eye fixed on the white flag, waiting for it to sweep downwards to signal the start of the race. The horses were packed tightly together, legs moving as they pranced, muscular quarters coiled ready to spring forwards like cats at the signal. The flag fluttered down. Merrianne drove her heels hard into Water Babe's sides, feeling the muscle move beneath her boots as he sprang into life, ears flat back against his neck. The horses in the race burst forwards in an explosion of motion, their hooves thundering on the ground, hurtling in a mass towards the first fence. Hayden O'Connor was launched high into the air as his horse The Dun Romin hurtled straight into the fence in its excitement and then stopped dead. He landed with a thud that was audible even over the sound of the horses' hooves.

The horses began to spread out, four running in a group in the lead, followed by Water Babe. Out of the corner of her eye Merrianne could see

Paris, her face white and set, crouched over Destiny's withers. Behind them came the other eight horses, strung out along the white guard rail like a giant centipede. Fence after fence they jumped, Merrianne concentrating only on the horses in front of her, ready to turn Water Babe if one of them fell, alert to anything happening in the race, and aware of the looming presence of Paris, breathing hard down her neck. The falls and refusals and horses that had run out of energy and were being stopped behind were all irrelevant. All that mattered was to keep Water Babe going and when the moment was right to move to the front of the runners and pass the winning post in the lead.

The horses passed the stands for the first time. Merrianne was aware of a sea of faces and a roar of noise as they hurtled past and then the silence descended, broken only by the thunder of hooves and the crashing noise as they burst through the brushwood fences. They galloped downhill, the sea a blur of blue on the distant horizon. The dual carriageway flashed past, a line of cars still waiting to come into the race course, then above her, on the right, the ruined stone tower and the marquees. Two fences left to jump. The horses in front were beginning to tire, their hind quarters moving mechanically, the jockeys urging them on with their hands and heels.

Merrianne glanced across at Paris. Their eyes locked for a second, the unspoken challenge clear in their faces. Paris kicked Destiny on, driving her past the four leading horses. Merrianne followed. Water Babe was full of energy, powering up the track towards the blur of colour that was the concourse. Water Babe matched Destiny stride for stride. Merrianne was aware of her horse's intense power: she was going to win easily. Destiny had tired as soon as she had got to the front of the runners, her head bobbing up and down tiredly as she used every bit of her energy to run. Merrianne turned Water Babe's head. Ahead of them was clear turf. Nothing lay between them and victory.

But what was she fighting for? Alex was right. Derry was a bastard, she didn't really want him. The race had been to prove to herself that she was capable of winning it.

The winning post was looming up fast. Beside her Merrianne could see Paris urging her mare on desperately, driving her heels into the mare's sides, cracking her down the shoulder with her whip, the mare's nostrils flaring red as she charged to the finish. Merrianne stopped pushing Water Babe. He slowed imperceptibly, ears flickering backwards and forwards, curious at why she was easing up on him when he should be straining every muscle to pass Destiny.

Paris was welcome to Derry. If she wanted him so badly she could have him. He meant nothing but heartache to any woman. The winning post whipped past, Destiny's long tail whipped Merrianne's boot as she past the post in front of Water Babe.

Merrianne turned to Paris as they slowed.

Paris's face was alive with happiness, a broad grin splitting her face from ear to ear, her cheeks bright red with the effort and the wind. "I won," she said, incredulously.

They rode slowly up to the winner's enclosure, the crowds parting magically in front of them. Merrianne could hear the incredulous high-pitched tones of the commentator as he raved excitedly about the race. "We have had ladies win the race before, many of you will remember the brave Sarah Cullen who won the race on her father's horse, now we have two ladies, coming first and second." The words faded as they moved away from the tannoy.

Merrianne saw Derry shoot forward, bursting out of the crowd to grab Destiny's bridle. He shot Merrianne a tight smile. For a second she felt the pain of losing him. She had deliberately lost the race, given him to Paris. He was such a bastard they deserved each other. Yet still she felt the loss, the pain raw deep within her. The pain of losing him and of losing the race. The glory should have been hers. Could have been hers. If she had wanted it.

They rode into the winners' enclosure. Derry led Paris into the larger winner's place while Merrianne walked into the second place. There was a huge cheer of delight as Paris jumped off Destiny. Merrianne slid down from Water Babe. He was exhausted, his sides heaving like bellows, nostrils wide and red. Merrianne slid her saddle off the horse; it was soaked with sweat. She wound the girth straps around the saddle and began to walk to the weigh room. Someone tugged her arm.

Merrianne spun around to face Paris, her mud-splattered face alive with happiness as she said, "I won. You had better start packing."

CHAPTER FIFTY-EIGHT

Merrianne wrenched open the dressing-room door, unsuccessfully stifling a sob as she snapped on the light and looked in on all of the clothes that she had accumulated during her stay with Derry. The spotlights lit up the room, shining on the rows of ball gowns, smart dresses, skirts, suits that she had bought for attending the races, all hanging from a rail, the doors to the press unable to close and encase the fabrics. At the far end of the room were drawers, crammed full of shirts, sweaters, silk lingerie. Running the height of the room were a double row of open-fronted boxes, designed to hold her shoes. Each hole was crammed with shoes and handbags of every shade and style.

Packing seemed to be such a momentous task. Bleakly she wandered out of the room, her fingers brushing along the line of fabrics, the different textures brushing against her fingers. The bathroom too was crammed with her belongings, jars of creams and lotions, boxes of expensive make-up in their beautiful packaging filled the drawers.

Merrianne drifted back into the dressing-room, wrenched open a cupboard door and heaved out two enormous suitcases. She heaved them into the bedroom and manhandled them onto the bed and laid them side by side. She undid the catches on one and lifted the lid. She had to start her packing.

A wave of sadness washed over her. Her life with Derry was over. And she mourned for it. Alex had been delighted that she had lost the race and even more delighted when she confessed that she had let Paris win. There would have to be a stewards enquiry to explain why she hadn't tried harder to win, but she would face that later. He had taken her into the bar after the race and brought her champagne to try to numb the feelings of loss. Derry had come in with Paris grinning delightedly beside him. There was no sign of Shula.

"Well, looks like Paris got what she deserved," Alex said, glancing in Derry's direction. "And so did you."

Merrianne looked at him quizzically.

"Me!" he grinned, clinking his glass against hers. "Here's to a new life!"

Grabbing a handful of clothes from the rail she carried them back into the bedroom, tripping and stumbling over the fabric as it trailed around her feet. She laid them on the bed, wrenching a dress off its hanger and folding it carelessly. Then as she placed it in the suitcase, she noticed a small heap of sand collected in the lowest corner of the case.

She smiled sadly, gently touched her finger to the grains of sand and lifted them to her face. Sand from the beach when they had been away together. The bitterness of the memory tightened her throat. How she had loved him! How happy she had been with him, so proud of him! Now all of that was gone, evaporated like an early morning mist. And only bitterness remained. Merrianne wiped the sand slowly and deliberately on the red silk cover on the bed, watching the tiny grains trickle down and fall into the carpet. They would probably remain there forever, part of her memory.

Although the suitcases were huge they were soon filled with her possessions and still an enormous amount remained. Sweating under their weight, Merrianne humped the cases downstairs, putting them down on the stone-tiled floor of the hall with a bang that echoed around the house. Then, head held high and teeth clenched to stop herself from crying, Merrianne marched to the kitchen and then stopped again. She loved this room. She had taken ages to re-do the kitchen, getting the wooden fronts of the units tastefully distressed in cream paint, rubbed away to show a faded green beneath. The black marble tops gleamed beneath the concealed spotlights that had been positioned beneath the units and in the ceiling. They had spent many cosy nights eating together in the kitchen. Sitting at the scrubbed wood table, discussing the horses, her racing career. It had all been a complete farce, he had never loved her. She had just been a convenience, someone to cook for him and keep his bed warm at night and do the myriad of tiny jobs that a valet could have done. Now Paris was going to cook in this kitchen, drink wine at the scrubbed table. Thinking was too painful. Merrianne crossed the room and wrenched open a drawer, grabbed a thick roll of black dustbin bags and shot out of the kitchen, slamming the door behind her. She ran back upstairs and into the bedroom, tearing off sections of the black bags, tugging at the plastic to open them and then shoving armfuls of clothes and shoes and jewellery into them.

"You don't have to go today," Derry said, slinking quietly into the room.

"Yes, I do," Merrianne snapped back, trying to tug open another plastic bag and failing. With a cry of frustration she threw the bag to one side and ripped off another. "Where's your new girlfriend?" she snarled as the silence lengthened.

"Which one?" he joked, his grim attempt at black humour failing miserably. Merrianne ignored him, wishing that he would go and leave her in peace, leave her the luxury of tears and misery instead of standing over her gloating. "I'm not going to pinch the silver," she snapped. "You don't have to stand over me."

Derry raised his eyebrows sardonically. "Can't be too careful."

"You really are a bastard," Merrianne hissed, turning to face him. "It's not enough for you to make me risk my neck to have to keep you, riding in a race to prove that I was good enough to be considered the girlfriend of the great Derry Blake. You have to fuck my mother as well!"

He had the grace to look guilty for a split second, before he laughed. "She offered it to me. You were too obsessed with winning the bloody Galway Plate to notice what I was doing."

Merrianne felt as if her head was going to burst, the pain was too great. "Where is she now?" she snarled, wanting to throttle her mother.

"She cleared off this morning, when she knew that you wouldn't be staying on. Has to find herself a new boyfriend, just like you do."

The hatred coursed between them, as heavy and as oppressive as a thundercloud. Merrianne tugged the drawer from its runners and tipped the contents into the black bag.

"Make sure you take everything," he said, nastily.

Her possessions all out of the bedroom, Merrianne dragged the black bags downstairs, packing them into her car as Derry lolled in the hall, watching, a smug smile playing on the corners of his mouth. "I'm keeping the car," she told him, shoving the last bag onto the back seat. "It was a present."

Derry gave a short laugh. "Fine by me, I doubt Paris will want your cast-offs."

It was Merrianne's turn to give a snort of laughter. "Really, you do surprise me, Derry," she spat. "She wants you."

Her mobile telephone rang, and Merriane spoke briefly into it before snapping it off. "I'm going to the stable yard," she said. "Would you care to join me?"

Derry scowled. "There's nothing there for you," he said, sullenly.

"I think that you are wrong, darling," Merrianne retorted. "Don't forget Water Babe is my horse. I'm the registered owner of him. I have plans for that horse." She had the satisfaction of seeing naked fury course across his face. "In fact," she said glancing down the drive to where a large pale green and gold lorry was slowly coming towards them, "that's the lorry to collect him now."

Merrianne solicitously locked her car.

"Wouldn't like to get it stolen," she hissed, glaring at Derry. "Would you like to come and say goodbye to Water Babe?" She walked with great dignity down the drive to the stable yard, Derry striding beside her, fury emitting from every pore.

"That's Alex Ivan's lorry!" he blurted out as they rounded the corner into the yard. Alex's name was emblazoned along the side of the lorry in dark blue lettering.

"My goodness, Derry, you are sharp," Merrianne growled.

They reached the stable yard just as the driver of the lorry was lowering the ramp. It slid electronically to the tarmac surface with an expensive-sounding clunk. The surface of the ramp was covered in rubber matting, which led up into the inside of the beautiful horse box. Even Derry in his fury couldn't help but stop and admire the box. Inside every panel was pale mahogany, with brass fittings gleaming softly in the dull light.

The driver fetched a thick leather head-collar from a peg and came towards Merrianne. "Which is the horse, madam?" She led the way across the yard.

"You've sold him to Alex," Derry spat incredulously. "How could you sell him to Alex? You know how much I think of that horse – he has a great career in front of him, all the biggest chases. You knew that I would have bought him off you. How could you sell him to Alex?" Derry shook his head in disbelief, so thrown that he was hanging onto the stable door for support. If the situation hadn't been so sad, Merrianne would have felt delighted that she had wrought such anguish on him.

"You are heartbroken about losing this bloody horse, aren't you?" she hissed, her face inches from his, as the driver went into the stable and put the head-collar onto Water Babe.

She watched as the driver led the horse to the bottom of the lorry ramp, undid the buckles on his rug and pulled it off. Then after folding it solicitously he opened a locker set into the bottom of the lorry and pulled out a brand-new green and gold rug, which he laid gently over the horse and then led him into the lorry. He came back down the ramp, pressed a button and the ramp glided slowly into place.

"Heartbroken about the horse and you don't give a damn about me," Merrianne said, bitterly. "Shall I tell you something?"

Derry was glaring at the lorry as it reversed slowly in the confines of the yard.

"I haven't sold the horse, I'm going to live with Alex, and the horse is coming with me."

Derry looked at her as if she had walloped him with a baseball bat. "When did you arrange all this? For fuck's sake you talk about me being a two-timing rat! You must have been seeing him all the time."

Merrianne shook her head. "Actually no. Unlike you I have some decency and so does Alex. He asked me to end my relationship with you when he could see what a bastard you were being and I wouldn't. I clung to the belief that there was some good in you. And you proved me wrong."

"Good old Alex," snapped Derry. "Coming to the rescue of a damsel in distress. I wish you both the best of luck."

The lorry drove slowly out of the yard. Merrianne walked slowly up the drive back towards her car. Derry still strutted beside her taunting and bitching. Suddenly she felt very tired, she longed to get to Alex, to start a new life, safe in his arms. To see what future they might have together. Leaving Westwood Park was awful, the pain almost unbearable. She had such dreams of her life here with Derry. But he had destroyed them and nearly destroyed her with them. Suddenly she wanted to be far away, to never see Derry Blake and Paris again, to escape from the shackles that her love for him and his home had put on her. "I'm glad to be going," she said, reaching her car and shoving the key into the lock. "Paris is welcome to you."

"She proved that she was the better rider. It was she who won the Galway Plate. You were second," he spat cattily, leaning on the roof of the car to glare at her.

Merrianne shook her head slowly, pulling open the car door. "No, she didn't win. I decided that she was welcome to you. That I was better off without you. I let her win that race."

Then, as his mouth dropped open, Merrianne got into the car and drove away, waving out of the window, the sound of her triumphant laugher drifting back towards Derry.

CHAPTER FIFTY-NINE

Paris opened her eyes.

"You're back where you belong," Murmured Derry, closing his mouth over hers. When they parted he leant up on his elbow, looking at her. "This is the Paris I love. The Winner." He softly stroked her cheek, moving his fingers gently over her scar, as if he were examining a horse. "We'll have to get you off to a plastic surgeon as soon as possible, do something about this scar. I don't want people to say 'Look, that's the trainer with the scarred girlfriend' now, do I?"

Paris turned her face away to hide the hurt she knew must be in her eyes. Derry could be so insensitive. The thought sprang into her mind: Kane had hardly even remarked on her scar. But Derry's reason for suggesting surgery: he didn't want to be seen with a woman with a scared face.

"How about some tea for your beloved?" Derry said, heaving the bedclothes off her. Paris slid her legs out of bed and stood up. This was what she had longed for during the time that she had been without him. To be with him, wake with him, be with him during the day, sleep with him, share his life again. Why then did she feel so uneasy? What was the matter with her? She should have been feeling nothing but bliss, but there was a nagging feeling at the back of her mind all the time, like an aching tooth.

On the whole, however, she had slid back into her old role comfortably, as if she had never been away, except for the house, newly decorated, reminding her at every turn of Merrianne.

Paris padded quietly down to the kitchen, Merrianne had done a beautiful job of redesigning the room. It was like being in the set for an interiors magazine, mused Paris, idly opening and shutting drawers searching for the cutlery, which she eventually found in a concealed drawer in the work surface.

She made tea and wandered back upstairs to Derry. They lay in bed, watching the sun climb higher over the trees in the park, letting the life in the yard go on without them. Paris relaxed: this was more like it. This was how she had imagined it when they were apart. She snuggled under his arm, luxuriating in the warmth of his body.

In a week's time they would be married. Then they were heading off to Kentucky where there was a horse that Derry wanted to buy. A gorgeous dress hung in the wardrobe at Blackbird Stables. She had chosen it herself. She hadn't wanted any help from Elizabeth. Though, from her mother's reaction to the wedding announcement Paris doubted if she would have offered any help.

Elizabeth and Paddy had been less than delighted when she had told them of her plans to marry Derry. Her announcement had met with an icy silence. It had made it worse that Derry hadn't even bothered to come and tell them with her. He had gone to the sales. Which, as Paddy had snapped, was very convenient as it gave him the ideal escape from their anger.

"I ought to get dressed," Paris said, glancing guiltily at her watch. She had been away from home since early evening the previous day and really ought to go home and check the horses. It wasn't fair to leave all the work to Paddy. After she was married he would have to cope with the few horses that were in the yard, but for now she still felt as if she ought to be there.

"Don't worry," Derry drawled, "surely even your father can manage those rundown old nags you've been training?"

Paris felt a prickle of annoyance. Just because he had the best horses that money could buy in his yard, he always assumed that everyone else had rubbish in theirs. "There's nothing wrong with our horses," she retorted, huffily. "Joe McHugh bought two really good prospects from a point-to-point yard down south."

"Uhhuhh," Derry replied, disinterestedly. "Hardly in the same class as my horses, though." Before she had time to reply he rolled over, taking the cup out of her hand and dumping it on the bedside table and pulling her back down into the bed. "Come here, lover, and show me what a good wife you are going to make." He rolled on top of her, shoving her legs apart with his thighs and thrust himself into her, for a hasty and perfunctory coupling.

"OK, off you go to work," he said a few moments later, easing himself out of her and rolling away. "Bring me up the newspaper before you go, will you? Mrs McDonagh should have brought it with her, I heard her arrive a while ago."

Paris didn't reply. Had he always bossed her around like that? Had she just not noticed before? She went and showered. She felt sore where he had shoved himself inside her before she was ready. He was probably just over-keen, delighted that she was back. But at the back of her mind she knew that he had always been like that. Somehow though, she had never noticed. Maybe Kane's gentle lovemaking had made her more aware of it.

She dressed, pulling on a pair of jeans and a shirt that she had brought with her in a small overnight bag when she had arrived the previous afternoon. "I'll see you later, shall I?" Paris said, coming to sit on the bed and kiss him goodbye.

"Come around seven – we're having dinner with the Lydon's at La Bistrot."

Derry kissed her quickly on the lips, then turned away, reaching for his wallet which was on the bedside table. "Here," he said, peeling off a fistful of fifty-euro notes. "Get yourself a new dress, will you, and throw that thing you wore last night into the bin – it makes you look like a frump,"

She drove home, stinging. The dress she had worn the previous evening crumpled in a heap on the seat beside her. She had liked that dress. Kane had said that it brought out the colour of her eyes. She knew now that she would never wear it again.

To her utter horror, Kane's jeep was parked in the yard at Blackbird Stables. Her hear started to hammer at the thought of seeing him again.

"Kane wants to talk to you," Paddy said, getting to his feet. He nodded expectantly at Kane. "Come on, Elizabeth," He pulled at Elizabeth's chair, almost tipping her out of it in his haste to get out of the house.

Kane traced a circle of water on the table, dipping a long finger into a smear of tea and drawing it along the pine surface. The silence lengthened. Paris leant against the work surface and looked at the floor. She didn't want to look at Kane, terrified of the emotion that he might unleash in her.

"Paris!" His voice was barely above a whisper.

She raised her head and forced herself to look at him. Kane looked dreadful. He had lost weight, the shirt hung off his once solid frame. His face was grey, his cheeks pinched below the hollows of his eyes. Paris felt a sob choke at the back of her throat. How could she have hurt him so badly? Why had she led him on when she knew she was in love with Derry.

"Do you know why I bought the new farm?" Kane said.

She shook her head, turning abruptly away. It was too painful to look at him.

"Good business decision? Nice land?" Bleakly she shoved bread into the toaster. Anything to keep her trembling hands occupied. She heard the scraping noise as he pushed his chair back. She was aware that he had come to stand beside her.

"I bought it for you," he said, quietly, gently taking the toast out from the toaster and shoving it on a plate. "I had hoped that we might have something good between us. That you could fall in love with me. Move in together, see how things worked out." Paris took the plate from him, staring at him, unaware that the plate was tipping up and the toast sliding downwards until it hit her foot. "Shit," she sobbed, crouching down to retrieve the toast, scraping the worst of the dog-hairs off it. She stood up slowly, looking at Kane. The angry colour had vanished from his cheeks; he was pale now; his eyes the only colour, blazing with an unspoken emotion. His lips were pressed tightly together as if he were afraid of what he might say.

"But you knew that I only wanted Derry," she whispered, shaking her head – it was as if it was stuffed with cotton wool that was dulling her senses. There had been a time when she was with him that she had forgotten Derry, but Derry's charisma had dragged her back to him, she couldn't walk away from him. She belonged with Derry, she had always known that. She had taken him off Merrianne, fought for what was rightfully hers. Now, she was the victor and she was claiming the spoils of her war. Kane sighed. Gently he reached up and touched her face.

Paris flinched and then was still, letting him gently glide his fingers over her face, her eyes narrowing with annoyance as he touched the hated scar.

"I loved you for who you are. Not as some accessory to make my life easier," he said, gently lowering his hand. "I hoped that you would see that."

Paris could feel his touch gentling her, like she was a restive horse.

"I came to beg you not to marry Derry." Kane said. "Please, you deserve better than him. He will never make you happy." He took the dirty toast out of her hand, threw it in the bin and shoved more bread into the toaster.

"It's too late, Kane," Paris said wearily, sinking down on a chair and burying her face in her hands. "Everything's arranged. This was what I wanted....Derry and I...." she stopped. She had fought so hard to get Derry back. She couldn't give it all up, not now. She had to make Kane leave her alone. She couldn't risk changing her mind and flinging herself into the safety of Kane's arms. She had made her choice. It was Derry that she had to have.

"Go away, Kane," Paris said slowly. "Don't come back. I want Derry."

Kane walked slowly towards the door, shuffling as if he had become an old man, carrying the weight of the world on his shoulders. He pulled it open and then turned, looking at her for the longest while until he finally said, "It might be what you want. But it's not what you need."

CHAPTER SIXTY

The wedding dress was glorious. Elizabeth fastened the last of the tiny buttons at the back and stood back so that they could both admire Paris's reflection in the mirror. "You look beautiful," she whispered, turning to wipe a tear away.

Paris turned slowly, looking at her reflection from different angles. Elizabeth was right, for once. The dress, cream silk, highlighted her skin tone, making her look as if she glowed with life. It flattered her from every angle; the neckline, scooping low gave the impression of a decent bust, instead of her usual boyish body. It clung to her waist and over her hips, making her look tall and slender, then flared out into a wide train that when spread out would trail behind her for ten feet. The dressmaker had spent hours, working long into the night, sewing tiny seed pearls and glittering cream sequins into an intricate pattern on the bodice and train making it sparkle in the light. "I still believe that you are making the biggest mistake of your life," Elizabeth told her, taking Paris by the shoulders and glaring at her in the mirror, "but you look beautiful making it."

Paris forced herself to smile. This was what she wanted. To marry Derry. Once they were married she would forget about Kane. He would forget about her, find some nice girl to marry. She would live her life with Derry as she had planned for so long. Eventually she would stop comparing Derry to Kane, would stop missing his tender lovemaking and his gentle kindness.

Paddy was waiting downstairs, surly in his disapproval. "Right then," he said, getting out of the armchair. "Lamb to the slaughter. Ready are you?"

Paris clamped her lips tightly together. She had promised herself that she wouldn't row with them again, whatever they said. And they had said plenty, cajoling, pleading with her not to marry Derry. "He won't make you happy" should have been tattooed on her mother's forehead.

"Come on then," Paddy sighed, leading the way outside.

In the yard stood a brand new burgundy-coloured Bentley. Derry had bought it especially for the occasion. He had come home in a furious temper as they hadn't been able to get him the dark navy blue that he had wanted to match the lorry. Con, who drove the lorry for Derry had been given the job of taking Paris and Paddy to the church. He sat, looking uncomfortable in an unfamiliar suit, waiting in the driver's seat, trying to pretend that driving such a flashy car was an everyday occurrence. Paddy slid into the back seat.

"See you at the church," Elizabeth called, getting into her own car to follow them.

Paris got in to the back seat beside Paddy and slammed the door. Con shoved the car into gear and it glided out of the yard, just squeezing through the narrow gateway.

Paris stared out of the window. She should have felt happy. This should have been the best day of her life. She wished everything would stop, that she could run away, have time to think, to put her churning thoughts into perspective. Everything was happening so fast. Derry had been true to his word; the wedding had been arranged immediately. It was as if he was determined to claim her as his own now that she was a winner again. As if he wanted to marry her while the glory of her famous win still surrounded her. As if he wanted everyone to know that he owned this famous rider.

But they were all right. Derry was never going to make her happy. She knew that at the back of her mind. She was like some trophy to him. A possession that he wanted because she was beautiful and talented. And now that she had proved that she was a brave fearless rider again. Someone that he could be proud of.

But that was what he was to her. A trophy. She had wanted him because Merrianne had him.

Now it was too late. She had been too stubborn to agree with her parents. Too stubborn to turn from the path she had decided on. She had hurt them. Hurt Kane. The pain in his eyes when she had said goodbye to him had haunted her ever since.

335

The car glided to a halt at the top of the drive, then pulled out onto the main road. That was where Daisy broke her leg, Paris thought, looking bleakly out of the window at the innocuous spot in the hedgerow. Kane had come to her aid, bringing her a new sheep, even though she had been so horrible to her. He had taken Daisy away when he had come to beg her not to marry Derry. Destiny, although she had Derry's sheep to keep her company, had still neighed palinteively when she saw Kane gently lifting Daisy into his Jeep.

Paris clutched her fingers around her bouquet, wishing that she could find the strength to open her mouth and scream at Con to stop the car, that couldn't marry Derry. But the words wouldn't come.

The road outside the church was crowded with the cars that hadn't been able to get into the carpark. They lined each side of the road, nosed up onto the grass bank. It was as if the whole of Ireland had descended onto the tiny church to watch. Con solicitously opened the door for her. Paris slid out, standing bleakly as Paddy fussed around her, straightening the train of the dress. Every fibre of her body seemed to quiver with nerves, as if her very soul recoiled from the wedding. Sorcha and Niamh, two young cousins, dragged in to serve as bridesmaids, hovered by the church door, pink with excitement.

Paddy held out his arm. "Let's get this over with," he muttered.

Paris managed a half smile, her stomach clamped into a tight knot of tension.

They walked slowly up the stone path to the church door. Sorcha was hopping from one foot to the other, unable to contain her excitement. The two girls, giggling, arranged the long train. Then as a blast of organ noise came from within the church to announce her arrival, someone swung open the double doors and Paddy dragged her forwards. Paris clung to him for support, feeling that if she let go of his arm she would slide to the ground.

They paused at the second doorway, as everyone in the packed church turned to stare. Every seat was filled, guests lined the church, leaning against the walls, a sea of enormous hats and pastel colours. Flowers crammed every space, their scent overpowering, making her feel nauseous. Black stars danced in front of her eyes, and a loud rushing noise filled her head. Hanging onto Paddy's arm, she took a stride forwards. At the far end of the aisle she could see the priest, resplendent in his robes, smiling at her. And beside him, to the right. Derry, handsome in a slate-grey morning suit.

His eyes raked over her and he smiled approvingly. He was happy with her appearance. She was going to look the part beside him. A suitable wife for one of Ireland's leading trainers. A suitable wife. Derry didn't care about her. He wasn't interested in her hopes and fears. All he wanted was someone to fill a role. A glamorous and successful woman. Someone who would make him look good. Paris just happened to fit the bill. For the moment. And then, as he had so brutally demonstrated before, if she failed to live up to his expectations he would dump her without a second's thought. What a fool she had been, to want him! To reject Kane, the nicest man who had ever existed, in her pursuit of Derry.

This wedding was a farce. She couldn't go through with it. She had to get to Kane. To beg his forgiveness, to try to put right the dreadful mistake she had made. And if he rejected her, then she would just have to live with that. She knew that she would regret losing him all of her life, but that was better than regretting marrying Derry. "I'm sorry," she said, to no one in particular. Then wrenching her arm from Paddy's, and turned and ran, scattering the bridesmaids and knocking over one of the flower arrangements as she did.

She ran out of the church, the leather soles of the cream satin shoes sliding on the uneven mossy stone path. Derry's new burgundy-coloured Bentley was parked on the road outside the gate, Con drumming his fingers on the leather steering wheel, listening to the reports of the hurling match.

"Paris!" Derry's voice rang in her ears, as she skidded around the bonnet of the car, her feet sliding as she desperately tried to get purchase on the gravelly surface of the road. "Paris! Stop!" Derry's voice was closer this time, the anger close to the surface. "Get out!" she shrieked, wrenching open the heavy door and hauling at Con's jacket. "What the fuck?" Con said as with almost superhuman strength she pulled him from the car and scrambled in to the seat that he had vacated.

She turned the key and the engine roared into life. Derry reached the car, cannoning off the bonnet as he hurtled around to the driver's door. Paris pressed the button on the central console that locked all of the doors. There was a loud clunk as all of the doors locked. "What the fuck do you think you are doing?" roared Derry, wrenching with all his strength on the door handle. Paris turned to look at him. His face was purple with rage above the pink cravat, his eyes glistening with anger looking like the diamonds in the pin that crossed his cravat. "Get out of the car," he roared, spittle flying from his mouth, splattering against the side window.

"Bye, Derry," Paris said, tearing her frightened gaze away from him. She shoved the gear-stick into the drive position and stuck her foot hard on the accelerator, sending Derry spinning out of the way. She glanced in the rear-view mirror to see him mouthing in anger in the middle of the road.

The powerful car surged down the lanes, the cow parsley in the hedgerows dancing in the slipstream as it passed. Paris shifted uncomfortably in the leather seat, her long skirt tight across her thighs, glancing down she saw that the cream silk train was trapped in the door, billowing behind the car like the standard of a medieval warrior. Ignoring it she drove on, laughing softly to herself at Derry's stunned face. He had never been dumped in his life. He would probably never get over the shock of being dumped from such a great height at his wedding. A horrific vision of the church swam into her imagination. All the guests assembled, waiting for the grand occasion, the bride walking in and then bolting like a scared rabbit. She pushed her foot further down on the accelerator, blotting out the vision. There was no going back now.

She roared through the village, giggling softly at the stunned looks of the people that stared at the car, the train of cream silk billowing out of the door. Past the turn-off for Westwood Park, its high walls foreboding – she would never go there again. Past Blackbird Stables, then on into the countryside, the powerful car sweeping around the corners as if it was on rails.

Derry would probably get the Guards to arrest her for theft, she mused, almost sweeping past the gate that she was searching for.

She got out of the car. The silk train was filthy, streaked with dust and tattered, where it had bounced along the road. Shoving open the gate she drove through, getting back out of the car to close it behind her. Finally she got back into the car and shoved the gear-stick forwards. The car bounded over the potholes like a ship, surging over mountainous seas. She reached the farm yard. Kane's Jeep was parked by the front door.

A sudden fear gripped her. What if he told her to clear off? What if he didn't want her after all that she had said to him? Her fingers tightened around the leather steering wheel. Slowly she shook her head: whatever happened she had done the right thing. He had been right all the time. They all had. Derry wasn't right for her. He would have never made her happy.

Her eyes scanned the windows of the cottage, looking to see him peering out to see who had arrived, but there was no sign of him. Slowly she got out. Where could he be?

"Kane?" she called his name, but the yard was silent, broken only by the sound of the lazy wind, playing in the trees, whistling through a gate and the squeak of a door rocking on rusty hinges. Her eyes raked over the derelict buildings for any sign of him.

And then she saw him, sitting on the hillside, where they had spent time when he had first shown her the farm. Hauling the long skirts up above her ankles she began to run along the track that led to the upper pastures. The long skirt dragged in the dried-up ruts of the track, the shoes slid on her feet as she tried to run as fast as she could.

She tore off the track at its fork with the path and turned onto the hillside, her breath escaping in loud gasps in her haste. Her thigh muscles burned as she hurtled upwards, her heart pounding with the effort. She kicked off the shoes that were hampering her, then ran on, the grass soft beneath the soles of her feet. Then she reached the top, the ferocious slope eased off. There less than a hundred yards away from her was Kane sitting on the low rock, his back to her, gazing out at the fabulous view.

She moved towards him. He didn't seem to hear her approach.

Then, when she was just behind him, he spoke.

"Nice wedding?" he said suddenly.

Paris jumped, startled. Then she grinned broadly. "Fabulous," she smiled, sitting down beside him, the acres of the wedding dress billowing out behind the rock in the breeze. "The bride ran away."

"Troublesome little madam."

"Very."

"Did they get her back?"

"No, they didn't. She's well and truly gone." She put her hand over his, feeling his fingers tighten around hers. "I hope that she won't do that at her next wedding," said Kane.

THE END

339

About Louise Broderick

Louise Broderick was born in Derbyshire, England, but now lives on the west coast of Ireland. She has been involved with horses all of her life as an owner and competitor. While working as the editor of an equestrian magazine Louise published her first book. She has published books in a number of genres, using different pen names, but all feature horses and the people who love them. If you would like to join Louise's VIP Reader Club and be the first to hear about new releases and special VIP book prices please vist www.louisebroderick.com

More books by Louise Broderick
Trainers
Millionaries are a girl's best friend

A plea from Louise

Thank you for taking the time to read this book. I hope you enjoyed it, I certainly enjoyed writing it. Each time I sit down to write – and that is every day – I realise just how lucky I am this is my job. I can only keep this job because people like you enjoy my books and buy them. No words can express how grateful I am for that.

If you would like to find out more about my other books please visit my web site.

www.louisebroderick.com

I love to hear from readers so please feel free to contact me on via my Facebook page or email. The details of these are all on my web site.

I hope you enjoyed this book and would like to help me carry on living the dream, writing for a living. If you would like to help please take the time to leave a book review on Amazon. Positive reviews really do help to sell a book, so if you would do that for me you are helping me to continue creating my books and continuing as a full time writer.

Can I just say a huge thank you in advance to anyone who takes the time to do this for me. I know very well how precious time is and am hugely grateful for anyone who cares enough to spend some of their valuable time helping me. Thank you

40295922R00204

Printed in Poland
by Amazon Fulfillment
Poland Sp. z o.o., Wrocław